Praise for the *Henrietta an

For *A Girl Like You*:

"Michelle Cox masterfully recreates 1930s Chicago, bringing to life its diverse neighborhoods and eclectic residents, as well as its seedy side. Henrietta and Inspector Howard are the best pair of sleuths I've come across in ages—Cox makes us care not just about the case but also about her characters. A fantastic start to what is sure to be a long-running series."

—**Tasha Alexander,** *New York Times* **best-selling author of** *The Lady Emily Mysteries*

"Fans of spunky, historical heroines will love Henrietta Von Harmon."

—*Booklist,* **starred review**

"Flavored with 1930s slang and fashion, this first volume in what one hopes will be a long series is absorbing. Henrietta and Clive are a sexy, endearing, and downright fun pair of sleuths. Readers will not see the final twist coming."

—*Library Journal,* **starred review**

For *A Ring of Truth*:

"An engaging and effective romp rich with historical details."

—*Kirkus Reviews*

"Set in the 1930s, this romantic mystery combines the teetering elegance of *Downton Abbey* and the staid traditions of *Pride and Prejudice* with a bit of spunk and determination that suggest Jacqueline Winspear's Maisie Dobbs."

—*Booklist*

"Henrietta and Inspector Howard make a charming odd couple in *A Ring of Truth*, mixing mystery and romance in a fizzy 1930s cocktail."

—**Hallie Ephron,** *New York Times* **best-selling author**

For *A Promise Given*:

"Cox's eye for historical detail remains sharp. . . . A pleasant, escapist diversion."

—*Kirkus Reviews*

"The mix of sleuthing and aristocratic life pairs well with Rhys Bowen's Royal Spyness series."

—*Booklist*

"Series fans will cheer the beginning of Clive and Henrietta's private investigation business in an entry with welcome echoes of *Pride and Prejudice.*"

—*Publishers Weekly*

For *A Veil Removed*:

"Entertaining . . . composed of large dollops of romance and a soup-çon of mystery, this confection will appeal!"

—*Publishers Weekly*

"This is a wonderfully written, engaging story with excellent character treatment and a thrilling mystery."

—**IBPA, Independent Book Publishers Association**

"Cox draws textured visuals of a 1930s Chicago mansion replete with cherrywood drink carts, embroidered goose down pillows, brand new wireless radios, Worth gowns, Rothschild coats, and the music of Artie Shaw, Benny Goodman and Tommy Dorsey. It puts us back in the romantically turbulent 1930s Chicago. This engaging story charms us."

—*BookTrib*

For *A Child Lost*:

". . . vivid, descriptive prose and historical accuracy."
—*Publishers Weekly*

"Michelle Cox's delightful storytelling has a bewitching charm that will keep readers glued to their seats with a perfect blend of absorbing historical facts, intriguing mystery, and thrilling romance."
—*Readers Favorite*

"Once again, Cox delivers the passion and intrigue of Henrietta and Clive with a story that leaps right off the page. *A Child Lost* is a true thrill . . ."
—*Paperback Paris*

For *A Spying Eye*:

"A fun and spunky heroine and a plot involving an old castle in Strasbourg make this a fast-paced, delightful read."
—**Rhys Bowen, *New York Times* best-selling author**

"An exciting mystery with engaging characters. It kept me guessing to the end!"
—**Clare Broyles, coauthor of *Wild Irish Rose***

"This book is an excellent read for historical romance and historical mystery fans. The author does a beautiful job transporting readers to another time and place."
—**Angela Thompson, *Vine Voice***

A Haunting
At Linley

A Haunting At Linley

A HENRIETTA AND INSPECTOR HOWARD NOVEL

BOOK 7

MICHELLE COX

SHE WRITES PRESS

Published 2023
Printed in the United States of America
Print ISBN: 978-1-64742-598-2
E-ISBN: 978-1-64742-599-9
Library of Congress Control Number: [LOCCN]

For information, address:
She Writes Press
1569 Solano Ave #546
Berkeley, CA 94707

Interior Design by Kiran Spees

She Writes Press is a division of SparkPoint Studio, LLC.

In memory of Benjamin Charles Gregory
6/11/1966 – 4/12/1999
Thank you for our short time together, for all
that you gave me.
I would not be me but for you.

Chapter 1

"It's a shame we couldn't have gotten here sooner," Henrietta murmured, a glass of cognac grasped tightly in her hands.

"Yes, it must have been a terrible few days for you." Clive leaned forward and looked directly at his cousin, Wallace.

"Days?" Wallace answered sharply. "It's been a terrible few *weeks*. No, make that months. A year. Oh, bloody hell. The whole thing has been miserable." He gestured absently around the darkened drawing room where he and his wife, Amelie, were seated on an old-fashioned horsehair sofa near the fireplace, the only source of light in the room save several small lamps emitting a soft glow at the other end of the room. Clive and Henrietta sat across from them on leather wingback chairs, their faces partly in shadow.

Sadly, despite an urgent telegram from Wallace informing them of a sudden, dangerous decline in his father's health, Clive and Henrietta had not arrived in time to say good-bye to Lord Linley, who had passed away in his sleep some two weeks ago, nor had they even made it to the funeral.

It had taken time for Edna, Henrietta's maid, to be well enough to be released from Lariboisière Hospital in Paris and in a fit enough condition to travel. And then there had been the whole awful business in Strasbourg to wrap up between the funerals for Claudette and

Valentin and the settling of the baron, who took the news of his adult children's deaths very hard indeed.

"Darling, there's nothing more we can do," Clive had responded to Henrietta's musings on the train back from Strasbourg to Paris. "And we must get on to Castle Linley. Already, I fear we're too late."

"Let's just hope they will release Edna."

"Well, if they don't, we're simply taking her."

Henrietta said nothing to this, knowing that the whole situation was a sore point with Clive. After a rather heated discussion, they had decided that while they traveled to Strasbourg to make the various necessary arrangements, they would leave Edna under the watchful eye of Pascal, the young French servant who had just weeks before helped them escape Château du Freudeneck and the Nazi contingent who had been guests there. Poor Edna had been accidentally shot in the shoulder during this misadventure and was still much too weak to travel, so Henrietta and Clive had finally elected to trust her to Pascal.

As it turned out, upon their return to Paris, they discovered that Pascal had indeed been faithful in his duty, according to Edna, anyway, and that, additionally, she was pronounced well enough to finally be released, her arm in a sling, with firm orders that she maintain complete rest, with no exertion under any circumstances. Given this rather severe prescription, the Howards felt obliged to share their first-class train carriage with the two servants, who sat opposite them, Edna resting her head on Pascal's shoulder as she slept.

Edna, poor thing, seemed to be not only overly grateful for the kind attentions showered upon her by the Howards, but, likewise, extremely embarrassed. She continued to apologize for her condition every couple of hours, which, Henrietta could tell, only served to further annoy Clive.

"Nonsense," Henrietta had said to the girl repeatedly. "It's *us* who should be apologizing to you, dearest. Think nothing of it. You're going to get better now. You'll see." She had tried to say such things confidently, though she had thrown Clive a worried glance more than once on the journey and prayed daily that the girl would indeed be eventually restored to her former self.

Clive, despite his annoyance, or maybe because of it, had so far said little about the incident, but Henrietta knew he was much disturbed by what had happened, realizing as much as Henrietta did that poor Edna could very easily have been killed. It was he, actually, who upon finally reaching Castle Linley, arranged with Mrs. Pennyworth, the housekeeper, and Mr. Stevens, the butler, that Edna be given the sick room, which was a pleasant room on the ground floor with its own fireplace and a big window looking out onto the grounds behind the estate. It was a room normally reserved for servants who took ill with some form of contagion so that they did not spread it to the rest of the house. Obviously, Edna was not contagious, but Clive did not approve of her having to traipse up to the third floor where the other servants were housed in some dim, probably cold attic room. Mr. Stevens and Mrs. Pennyworth were likewise given strict instructions to provide her with three generous meals a day and to keep her fire burning round the clock, despite the fact that it was August, lest she catch a chill and further worsen her condition. Edna was mortified when she discovered these elaborate arrangements made for her benefit, but her protestations fell on deaf ears, at least as far as Clive was concerned.

Pascal, on the other hand, presented a more difficult challenge in that there wasn't anything in particular for him to do. He offered to work in the stables, as had been his role at Château du Freudeneck, but Mr. Triggs, Linley's head groom, seemed oddly put out by this suggestion, nor did Stevens seem very enthused about having him join the household staff, as it would take far too long to train him, especially considering that none of the servants apparently had even a sliver of extra time with which to do so. But neither could Pascal just be allowed to lounge about, eating and drinking at his leisure while the other servants worked, so Clive, to avoid any further disquietude, appointed him his valet. But only for the time being. He would certainly, Clive warned, pointing a finger in the young man's face, *not* be assuming this role back at Highbury, the Howards' palatial home back in Winnetka, Illinois.

Poor Pascal had readily agreed to this new assignment, though he was quick to remind his new master that he had absolutely no notion regarding which jacket was which, or shoes, for that matter, or grooming, or the tying of ties, or the adjusting of button studs or cufflinks, or really any such thing. Clive had merely sighed and said that he would teach him.

"Honestly, Clive," Henrietta had scolded once Pascal had scurried from the room assigned to the Howards for their duration at Castle Linley. It was the Peacock Room, designated as such presumably because of the intense aquamarine of the papered walls and the very large vase of peacock feathers dominating the desk in the corner. The last time they had visited, they had been given the Rose Room, which, Henrietta had quickly decided after a brief perusal of the Peacock Room, she slightly preferred. But this was no time to be particular. "You're forever declaring you have no need of a valet in this modern age, and yet all you've done to Pascal is berate him."

"Darling, I wouldn't say *berate*. I merely pointed out to him that a top hat is not required for a dinner at home. That should be rather obvious, at any rate, from the Hollywood films he claims to so admire."

"You *did* live through the war, remember?" She folded her arms. "I'm sure you had some young lieutenant or someone or other who served as your valet of sorts. Pretend that someone is Pascal and have a little mercy. He'll learn if you give him a chance."

"The term would be 'batman.' And, yes, I see your point," Clive had said, pulling at his chin. "All right, I'll try. Would that make you happy?" His face relaxed into a grin as he folded his arms loosely about her waist.

"Yes, it would." She kissed his nose, and he leaned his forehead against hers.

"I'm sorry about your uncle," she said softly.

"Poor old Montague. Sad that he never recovered after Father died."

"Yes, what a shame. Two brothers in the space of a year. Heartbreaking, really. First Valentin and Claudette," she murmured, referring to her newly discovered distant relatives, "and now the two Howard brothers. So much death."

Clive pulled away and reached into his pocket, his fingers deftly finding his pipe.

"And speaking of death," Henrietta said, stepping away and looking around the room, "why does this room resemble a mausoleum?" Thick black crepe covered all of the mirrors and paintings in the room. "It's rather ghastly, don't you think? I mean, I know we're all in mourning, but this seems a bit extreme."

"It's an old Victorian custom," Clive said through gritted teeth that held his pipe. He struck a match and lit it. He puffed deeply as he tossed the match into a nearby ashtray. "One is supposed to cover all the mirrors in the house and draw the curtains or the spirit of the deceased may find himself trapped inside the glass." He exhaled a perfect ring of smoke. "There's another one, I think, that says that if you see yourself in a mirror in the house of a recently deceased person, it is thought that you will be the next to die. Thus, the drapery serves a double purpose, you could say."

"That's ridiculous! I feel sorry for Lady Linley, of course, but this is all so unnecessarily morbid. And how am I to dress?" Henrietta gestured at the covered mirror of the ornately carved cherrywood vanity in the corner, two cherubs on the legs poking out from beneath the cloth. Clive merely grinned and annoyingly shrugged his shoulders.

In truth, Henrietta was a bit disturbed by these superstitions. It was clear, however, that Clive didn't believe in them, so why should she? She marched over to the vanity and gripped the black crepe. She looked over her shoulder at Clive, who was leaning against the bedpost now, his arms crossed with his pipe in one hand.

"Aren't you worried about what might happen?" she teased, the edge of the cloth balled into her fist now. "Normally, you're overly keen."

"Not in the slightest." He took another puff of his pipe, his eyes amused.

A flicker of her old rebelliousness coursed through her then, and she yanked the cloth from the mirror and bent to stare into the glass. "There, I've done it!" She gave her auburn hair a toss.

"I see that." Clive shifted slightly. He looked so handsome in his brown tweed suit. "Now, come here and lie down." He gestured toward the big four-poster bed. "I'll examine you for any ill effects."

"Don't be silly, Clive," she said, holding back a laugh. "We haven't time for that, you naughty thing."

"That's what you always say, and then we do. And anyway, isn't this supposed to be our romantic second honeymoon? Though I think the Nazi chase back in Strasbourg may have irrevocably put an end to that notion."

Henrietta tossed the black crepe gathered in her arms onto the end of the bed and went to him, lacing her fingers behind his neck. "Nonsense. We can still have a romantic honeymoon here. Don't you think?"

"That entirely depends on you, darling." He slyly raised an eyebrow.

"Well, you did promise to someday return me to the fairy bower. Remember?" she asked coyly. She was referring, of course, to a place somewhere on the grounds near a little creek where Clive and Julia had played as children during their summers at Linley. Clive had shown it to her on their original honeymoon trip and had proceeded to begin shamelessly undressing her there—in the open air!—only to be interrupted by none other than Wallace, sneaking through the woods on what they had suspected at the time to be some sort of nefarious outing.

"Minx," Clive whispered, kissing her lips. "Don't tempt me, or I really will throw you onto this bed and have my way with you."

"We haven't time, Inspector." She pulled away from his embrace but traced his lips with her finger. "Wallace is expecting us below."

"Very well." Clive sighed. "If anything can put a damper on romance, it's Wallace. I can only imagine his mood, as he is rarely what one would call pleasant, even under the best circumstances."

"Clive," Henrietta reprimanded. "He's suffered a great loss. We'll need to be patient."

"I suppose." He held his arm out to her. "Shall we?"

Henrietta looked across the darkened drawing room now at Wallace. "Well, at least he's at peace," she offered hopefully.

"Who? Father?" Wallace shook himself from staring at the fire. "Yes, I suppose so," he said begrudgingly, "but what about the rest of us? A terrible mess is what we're left with."

"Is it really so bad as that?" Clive asked.

"I'm afraid it is. I've spent these last weeks trying to sort through Father's rubbish pile of papers. He was horribly disorganized, which is rather a surprise given his military disposition. Churchwood has been of little help."

"Who's Churchwood?"

"His solicitor. Or secretary, or something like that. Little beetle of a man. Always creeping about, simpering this and simpering that."

"Wallace!" Amelie scolded in a heavy French accent. "You are most ungenerous. Monsieur Churchwood has been very helpful."

"Yes, helpful in explaining that the estate is horribly shipwrecked. No hope at all of salvaging it, old boy." He glanced over at Clive, one eye squinted shut. "It's the end of Castle Linley, I'm afraid."

"So, Uncle Montague was correct in his dire predictions, then."

"What is that supposed to mean?" Wallace snapped. "Some sort of backhanded jab at me?"

Amelie took his hand and squeezed it, but Wallace pulled it away.

"Of course not, Wallace. Don't be such a twit. You married for love, as did I," Clive said, glancing at Henrietta, "and that's the end of it. Can't be helped."

"God, why did Linley have to die?" Wallace groaned and braced his head in his hands. "He would have been so much better at this than I."

As Wallace's older brother, Linley Howard was supposed to have been the future Lord Linley and heir of Castle Linley, but he had tragically perished on the Somme. Wallace, on the other hand, had survived the Great War, but not without cost. He had come away with not only a bum leg but a bitter, sarcastic disposition that so far had not softened over time, as everyone had hoped it might.

"Don't say that, Wallace. That's not true," Clive put in. "The estate was in trouble long before you came along. Has the will been read?"

"Last week, in fact."

"And?"

"Well, as usual, Father, with his damned pigheadedness, has routed us. He's left the whole of the estate to Mother for her lifetime, which is admirable, to be sure, but not very forward-thinking."

"Wallace," Amelie said softly.

"I know, I know. I'm sure he thought he was being kind, but leaving the estate to Mother only furthers its ruin. Churchwood claims he advised otherwise but that Father wouldn't listen."

"I'm afraid I don't understand," Henrietta said, looking quizzically from Wallace to Clive.

"He's referring to the death duties; am I right?" Clive directed his question at Wallace, who nodded grimly.

"Death duties?"

"It's an inheritance tax." Wallace took a long drink of his cognac. "The new owner of the estate must pay a sizable portion of the estate's value in tax, which is bad enough. But then when Mother dies, the whole thing will be taxed yet again. Father could have willed it directly to me, thereby avoiding at least one taxation. Even if we had been able to scrape together the money to pay one duty, we'll never be able to pay two. No, I'm afraid we're utterly ruined."

"Well, there must be something that can be done, surely?" Henrietta looked pointedly at Clive.

Clive cleared his throat. "Yes, of course. I can telephone my assistant, Bennett. But I do warn you, our cash flow is likewise a little light these days, especially after Father's dealings with what turned out to essentially be the mob. But perhaps we can sell something off. Julia's been writing to us about some Texan who wishes to purchase one of Father's paintings for an exorbitant sum. I'm sure I could convince Mother, given a little time."

"Yes!" Henrietta perked up. "What a good idea."

Wallace shook his head. "No, Clive, Linley can't keep ciphering money off of Highbury, or your mother's private fortune, if we're being brutally blunt. And anyway, selling a painting, unless it's the *Mona Lisa*, won't even begin to scratch the surface of what's needed. We're talking about thousands of pounds!"

"Goodness," Henrietta exclaimed.

"Well, we don't possess the *Mona Lisa*, of course, but we do have some rather valuable works," Clive said stiffly.

"I'm not trying to insult your precious art collection, Clive; I'm just saying, what's the point of shoring up a sinking ship? It's just putting off the inevitable."

"What about selling the London house?" Clive suggested.

Henrietta opened her mouth to protest this idea, having fallen in love with the beautiful row house in St. James during their recent time in London, but she quelled it, sensing that this was not the time to voice her opinion.

"Yes, I've already made some inquiries. It might be enough to at least pay the death duty for now, allowing Mother to stay here until she passes, but that's it."

"Then what?"

"Then I either sell bits of this place off, such as the Upper Forty, maybe, or the Dowager's House—it's empty at the moment, though technically Mother should have moved there once Amelie and I came back, but it seemed a waste. What need have we of all this space? Plus, as you know, I don't give a fig about tradition." Wallace stared into his now-empty glass. "Alternately, I could sell the estate in its entirety or donate the whole bloody thing and avoid the tax altogether."

"What about your idea of turning it into a home for shell-shocked soldiers?" Clive asked.

Wallace let out a deep sigh. "I obviously don't have the money to start it myself, and, turns out, there's not so many such soldiers about anymore. Most of them have shot themselves."

"Wallace!" Amelie exclaimed.

"Apologies," he said bitterly, glancing briefly at Henrietta, whose own father had tragically met his end this way. "No, my new idea is to donate the whole thing to the Fabians or the Democratic Socialists. Both are in need of a headquarters, and this monstrosity is perfectly situated. Unfortunately, though, I've mentioned this one too many times in front of Mother, and she's horrified at the prospect. And worried that she'll have to leave her beloved Linley."

"But surely you plan to wait until she . . . until she passes?" Henrietta suggested.

"If I can manage it."

"When is the tax due?" Clive asked.

"Three months."

"Hmmm. Not long."

"Mother doesn't know of course, but I have an estate agent coming round tomorrow. A Mr. Arnold. A bit of a pest, really. Damned pushy, but I suppose they have to be that way. Says the best thing would be to knock the whole thing down and build a council of smaller houses. That or put up a factory."

"Surely you're not entertaining that, are you, Wallace?" Henrietta exclaimed.

"I wish I weren't. But who else is going to buy this thing? All of the old estates are coming down these days. No one can afford to keep them up, much less pay the death duties every generation. Arnold is of the opinion I should sell the whole rather than slice off bits. I don't know what to think, honestly. It's either this or donate it now and have Mother move— possibly into the Dowager's House if I can exclude that from the sale."

"Or sell the London house."

"Or sell the London house," Wallace agreed, "though that's unlikely to happen that fast."

"I'm afraid I'm horribly confused." Henrietta looked pointedly from Wallace to Clive. "And it all seems so sudden," she added.

"Well, it *is* sudden, but I don't have a choice. I have to do something.

There's apparently no money in the coffers at all." Wallace stood up, limped to the sideboard, and poured out another cognac. "God knows when the servants have last been paid. What's left of them anyway. Most have run off. Gotten better jobs in factories. Can't say I blame them, really. It's a good thing you've brought your own." His voice was grim. He hobbled over to where Clive was seated and topped up his glass.

"Yes, I'm sorry they're not more help, Edna being laid up as she is." Clive shifted uncomfortably.

"What the bloody hell happened, anyway?" Wallace asked. "Servants being shot? You being chased by Nazis? Is this all true?"

"Yes, we'll explain it all later."

Wallace tilted his head. "As you wish. The other guests will surely love to hear all about it. God knows they must be bored out of their minds. Why they're hanging on here, I don't know."

"Wallace," Amelie said gently, "zey stay out of consideration for your mother after your father's death."

"If they were really all that concerned, they'd bugger off."

"Other guests? Who else is here?" Clive asked. "I wasn't aware."

"Well," Wallace said with a sigh as he sat back down on the sofa, "there's Mother's brother, Uncle Rufus. He's only recently back from India. Between stationings, so he says, and therefore a bit homeless at the moment. I think he's trying to use the situation, meaning Father's death, to his advantage. Seems damned unwilling to leave. Brought his irritating son, Phineas, along. Remember him?"

"Cousin Phineas?" Clive's brow furrowed. "I think the last time we saw him, he was just a baby."

"Well, he's not a baby now. He's all of eighteen, and he's nothing but a rotter. Thinks it's immensely funny to play practical jokes on the staff. That might pass in India, but it's damned reprehensible here, especially now, with Father barely cold in his grave. I've had words with him *and* Uncle Rufus, but neither of them seemed to take a blind bit of notice. And if they weren't enough, there's Miss Simms, also a nuisance."

"Who's Miss Simms?" Henrietta asked.

Wallace took a long drink. "She's Mother's latest interest. A pet project. She appeared a couple of weeks before Father died and has since managed, even in that short space of time, to wrap Mother around her little finger. A perfect vulture."

"For what purpose?"

Wallace gave her a withering look. "The usual reason. Money."

"But I didn't think there was any money." Henrietta blinked rapidly.

"There isn't. But Miss Simms doesn't know that. Or maybe she does. My guess is that she wants Mother to will her the estate."

"What?" Clive asked incredulously as he eased himself back in his chair and crossed his legs.

"She's the head of some ludicrous charity in London. The Ladies Association of something or other. She'll no doubt tell you all about it; though I warn you, don't give her a chance. You'll never stop her once she starts. Oh, Miss Evie Simms comes off as pleasant enough, but she doesn't fool me. Why else would she be hanging around these past months instead of slaving away for her cause in the hovels of London, or wherever it is they do what they do? It's bloody obvious. To everyone but Mother, that is. Miss Simms has quite attached herself to her, like a veritable lamprey."

"That seems a bit farfetched, Wallace."

"Which part? That she's a lamprey?" He grinned.

Clive shot him a look of irritation. "No, that your mother would will the estate to her. It's an absurd notion."

Wallace shrugged. "You never know. As I've said, I'm afraid I've made the mistake of mentioning perhaps one too many times my plan to donate the whole thing to the Socialist cause, which throws her into a right state. It's my own bloody fault."

Clive cleared his throat. "How is Aunt Margaret? How is she holding up?"

"She is not well," Amelie answered. "Lord Linley's death was a great shock to her."

"Yes, she's quite frail these days, not to mention confused." Wallace exhaled deeply. "One day she seems quite lucid, and the next she thinks it's 1912 and that Father's up in his study. She even sometimes asks where Linley has gotten himself to. It's terrible."

"Is there anything we can do?" Henrietta asked, thinking about how similar Lady Linley's mental state seemed to Baron Von Harmon's, and in some ways her own mother's. *Is this what it meant to grow old?* "We certainly don't want to add to your burden," she said sincerely.

"Don't be ridiculous. I asked you to come. I very much want your advice about the estate. I—"

He broke off, then, at a noise at the other end of the room. It sounded distinctly like a little cry or maybe a moan. The group turned almost in unison to locate the source, which turned out to be Lady Linley herself, her old-fashioned long white nightgown and flowing robe making her resemble a sort of ghostly figure.

"Mother!" Wallace exclaimed, standing up. "What's wrong? What are you doing down here?" He hurried over to her.

Clive stood as well, buttoning his suit coat, and followed at a reserved distance. Having arrived late, he and Henrietta had yet to greet Lady Linley.

The old woman reached out a paper-thin hand and gripped Wallace's coat sleeve. "Did you not hear that?" she asked timorously.

Wallace let out a little sigh and closed his eyes for just a moment, as if gathering strength. "No, Mother, I did not. Why did you not ring for a servant? You shouldn't be down here. You'll catch your death."

"I did ring, but no one came," she said absently and then looked over at Clive. She stared at him for several seconds, as if trying to place him.

"Hello, Aunt," Clive said gently, drawing nearer. "I'm terribly sorry about Uncle Montague."

"Is that you, Clive?" she warbled, taking his face in her hands. Tears were in her eyes. "You've come, have you? Oh, maybe you can help us."

"I'll do my best, Aunt Margaret," he said, kissing the folds of her wrinkled cheek.

"Did Wallace tell you?"

"Yes, yes, he did, Aunt. Terrible business, this, but we'll come up with a solution, I'm sure. Nothing to worry about."

"But it *is* worrying. No one is safe here anymore."

Clive threw Wallace a quick glance and then looked back at Lady Linley. "What do you mean?"

"Why, the ghost, of course," she said softly, as if afraid some supernatural entity might hear. "Did Wallace not write to you?" She scowled at Wallace. "I specifically asked him to write to you about it." Her voice was one of irritation now. "It's most troubling, Clive. Surely, you can get to the bottom of it, can't you?" She gripped his hands tightly.

Clive glanced again at Wallace, who merely shrugged with an I-told-you-so look.

"I'll certainly do my best, Aunt Margaret. Not to worry."

Henrietta, who had remained seated with Amelie by the fireplace, rose now and silently joined the little group. She was shocked to see how old Lady Linley looked, her frizzled white hair peeking out from underneath her Victorian nightcap.

"You remember my wife, Henrietta?" Clive asked, gesturing toward her.

Lady Linley's watery blue eyes lit up. "Yes! Yes, of course I do!" She pulled her hand from Clive's and took Henrietta's. "You look lovely, my dear. Montague was so very fond of you. But where is your baby?" She looked confusedly around the room. "Did you not bring him?"

Henrietta drew in a quick breath but then felt the comforting pressure of Clive's hand on her lower back. She bit the inside of her cheek. "No, Lady Linley. I . . . it didn't take."

"But I'm sure your mother wrote to me about the baby, Clive," she said, looking at him now for confirmation.

"Mother!" Wallace scolded. "Enough! It's late. It's time we were all in bed."

Amelie approached and put her arm around the old woman's shoulders. "Come, Lady Linley. I will help you," she said gently and pulled her toward the door.

The old woman shrunk a little in defeat, her shoulders rounded all the more now as she allowed herself to be led away. She paused at the door, however, and turned back. "You might ask Amelie, here, for advice," she called out. "She's expecting yet again; are you not, dear?"

Amelie did not respond and instead shepherded Lady Linley into the hallway.

Wallace pinched the bridge of his nose. "I'm terribly sorry."

"It seems congratulations are in order," Clive said tightly, followed by a rough clap on the shoulder. "A third. That's marvelous."

"Yes, thank you. We weren't going to announce it just yet, not with Father and all of that." His face was uncharacteristically red as he looked nervously from one to the other. "I'm sorry, Henrietta. I told you she was changed. She wasn't always the best with tact, and now she sadly has none at all."

Henrietta swallowed hard and made herself smile. "Not to worry, Wallace. I'm perfectly fine. Where are the boys, anyway? Upstairs asleep, I imagine?"

"Yes, you'll see them tomorrow, no doubt. Shall we call it a night?"

"Yes, perhaps we should," Clive answered. "But what was all this business about a ghost?"

Wallace exhaled loudly. "As if I don't have enough to worry about, Mother has now gotten it into her head that the house is haunted."

"Haunted?"

"Yes, remember the stories when we were little?"

"A few of them, I suppose." Clive frowned.

"Well, someone has resurrected these tales, and now Mother is obsessed, which is horribly ironic, considering she never believed any of them in the first place. Thinks that Father is standing by her bed at night, whispering things to her."

"What sort of things?" Henrietta asked, suddenly chilled. She rubbed her arms and then wrapped them about herself.

Wallace looked at her. "Rubbish mostly. Who knows? It's nothing that makes sense to me. Come, let's call it a night. I'm shattered."

"Yes, as are we," Clive agreed.

"Well, get some sleep. You'll need your strength for breakfast. The guests are eager to meet you, and now that you have a Nazi chase scene to add, you'll be quite hounded, especially, I'm guessing, by Phineas. Might keep him entertained for two bloody seconds. Between him and Uncle Rufus and Miss Evie Simms, you'll be in for it."

"I'm sure we'll manage, won't we, darling?" Clive said, holding out his hand to her, a forced smile about his lips.

"Yes, of course." Henrietta took Clive's hand and squeezed it. "Good night, Wallace," she said over her shoulder and then followed Clive through the darkened foyer and up the grand staircase, past the larger-than-life portraits of long-dead family members. Henrietta glanced at them, mostly in shadow save for the uneven swaths illuminated by the sconces that flickered every few feet. The pictures looked somber and old, hairline cracks rippling across their paint. Henrietta shuddered. There was a heaviness about Castle Linley now that she hadn't felt the last time they had visited, when she had been an innocent new bride.

Something had changed.

There was a feeling in the air now that was difficult to describe, and she felt peevish and out of sorts. She shook her head, trying to dispel it. Perhaps it was simply Lady Linley's tactless reference to her recent miscarriage that was unsettling her, but it seemed more than that. Something was off, but she couldn't quite put her finger on what. Well, she thought wearily as she ran her fingers along the mahogany banister, hopefully things would look brighter in the morning.

Chapter 2

"I say, how very extraordinary!" Colonel Rufus Beaufort exclaimed, his fork gripped tightly in his thick fingers as he speared—with what seemed excessive force—a rather large kipper lying prominently on his plate next to a pile of runny eggs. "How I would have loved to be there, giving those Nazis what for! Must have been damned exciting, Clive."

"Rufus! Must you use such language at the breakfast table?" Lady Linley snapped, her voice quavering a little. She turned toward Miss Evie Simms, who sat near her left elbow, and with an altogether more cheerful voice asked, "Would you mind passing the jam, dear?" Miss Evie Simms obliged with a very charming smile.

Henrietta, sitting on Lady Linley's right, took a large drink of tea. She had slept poorly, having tossed and turned all night, unable to shake her feelings of dread, which had only increased as the night had gone on with the sound of various odd noises that seemed to be coming from either the hallway or the floor above them. She had lain awake for what seemed like hours until she finally drifted off into sleep in the wee hours of the morning, the result of which was that Clive had had to positively shake her awake to dress. Besides this annoyance, he had furthered it by claiming, when asked, not to have heard any such noises at all, insisting that whatever she *might* have heard was merely the creakings and groanings of an old house.

Henrietta glanced at Lady Linley now, happily munching her toast, and marveled at the fact that her hostess now seemed perfectly sane, reminding her, again, of Baron Von Harmon in the way that his fits of confusion came and went with no apparent rhyme or reason. She considered asking her about the "noises" she claimed to hear nightly, but thought better of it, as this was clearly not the time.

"Was there really a shootout, Mr. Howard?" a rail-thin young man asked eagerly from the other end of the table. "I say!"

As Wallace had predicted, young Phineas Beaufort's curiosity was proving to be insatiable.

"Yes, there was, unfortunately. We were lucky to have escaped," Clive said firmly. Henrietta could tell he was already tired of repeating the details of their last adventure, guessing that it was probably because, in many ways, it had been a failed case.

"Reminds me of the time we were in Manipur," Colonel Beaufort boomed, his thick face flushed, which seemed, if the last forty-five minutes were any proof, to be a permanent condition. "We were outnumbered by the Manipuri ten to one, and yet we managed to take the Kangla Palace anyway." He stabbed a sausage. "Received the East Frontier Clasp for that battle. Our commanding officer, Colonel Bittersby, received the Victoria Cross. Now that was a man!" he declared, brandishing the sausage a little before biting it roughly. "Lived in fear of that man, we did. But it was an honor to serve under him."

"Yes, Father," Phineas interrupted in a bored tone. "But we want to hear about the Nazis!" Phineas pushed back a lock of dark brown hair that kept falling over one eye.

"Balderdash!" Colonel Beaufort exclaimed. "Clive's told the story and that's that. Went over the side of a cliff. Well done! A superior shot," he said, nodding at Clive appreciatively. "What regiment did you say you were in in the war?"

"Second cavalry." Clive wiped the corner of his mouth with his napkin.

"Ah! Might have guessed. That's the way to go into battle, is it not? Mounted on a steed, dashing into the fray! Not like poor Wallace, here, who got stuck trudging through the trenches, eh? Knee deep in mud. No, by Jove. Not the thing at all." He let out a little chuckle.

Seated as she was next to Wallace, Henrietta could almost hear him gnashing his teeth. He tossed his napkin onto the table and stood, leaning heavily on his cane.

"Excuse me," he said brusquely. "Clive and I have an appointment." He looked pointedly at Clive and inclined his head toward the door.

"An appointment?" Lady Linley chimed in. "At this hour? With whom, Wallace dear?"

"I'll explain later, Mother. It's nothing to signify." He quickly limped across the room despite his handicap.

"Excuse me, Aunt Margaret," Clive said, standing now, too. "Henrietta?" he asked expectantly, clearly inviting her.

"No, I'll stay. You go on." She tilted her head slightly toward Lady Linley. Clive paused for a moment, as if assessing her sincerity, and then shot her a wink before turning and following Wallace out of the room.

Henrietta was grateful that he wanted to include her, a previous sticking point between the two of them, but in fact, she had little desire to sit with an estate agent to discuss the potential sale or, worse, demolition of this beautiful old house. Besides, she wanted a chance to speak to Lady Linley alone, should the opportunity arise, *and*, despite Wallace's warning the night before, she was eager to learn more about Miss Simms, to whom she had as yet barely said two words.

Miss Evelyn "Evie" Simms was nothing like what Henrietta had imagined a woman from a London charity would be. Henrietta had unkindly envisioned her as a middle-aged woman, dressed in black, and having a sort of pinched, sour expression and grasping hands. On the contrary, Evie Simms was quite a beautiful young woman, barely older than herself, Henrietta guessed, with her glossy black hair cut in the latest style and the most immense violet eyes

Henrietta had ever seen. They were the type that bulged slightly, but which were at the same time both mesmerizing and shocking. Miss Simms was dressed this morning in a bright-green dress with tiny white polka dots and a white collar and cuffs, which, if Henrietta was not mistaken, was a Chanel, her cherry lipstick and painted nails complementing it in the most satisfactory way. Miss Simms had a perfect figure, a fact she seemed to be aware of by the way she managed to twist her body advantageously when speaking, which was often. Indeed, as Wallace had mentioned the night before, she was a bit of a chatterbox, and there seemed to be an undeclared contest between Colonel Beaufort and Miss Simms as to who would control the morning's conversation. Never in a million years would Henrietta have guessed that the young woman across from her was a charity worker. In fact, she seemed more like a movie starlet than a representative of the London poor.

True to Wallace's previous description, Miss Simms was indeed excessively attentive to Lady Linley, who seemed to take great delight, or maybe just comfort, in treating Miss Simms as a favored child or even as a pet, though, Henrietta quickly concluded, the reality of the situation seemed to be that it was Miss Simms who exercised control over Lady Linley and not the other way around.

"What exactly did you say was the name of your charity?" Henrietta asked the young woman, pouring a bit more milk into her Royal Copenhagen teacup. Lady Linley's china collection was really quite extraordinary.

"I don't believe I *did* say," Miss Simms answered pleasantly. "But I don't mind telling you now. It's called Mrs. Christiansen's Ladies Association for the Promotion of Female Education among the Heathen."

"My, that's quite a title!"

"It is a most excellent cause," Lady Linley chimed in. "Mrs. Christiansen does much good in the world, does she not, my dear?"

"We like to think so." Miss Simms offered her hostess a sweet smile as she dropped a lump of sugar into her tea. "However, Mrs.

Christiansen is no longer with us, remember, having died in her work in Ethiopia. That was some time ago now, of course, but we carry on where she left off."

"Yes, of course," Lady Linley acquiesced, nodding her head vigorously. "Their work is most impressive," she said to Henrietta.

"What exactly *is* your work? Educating women in poor countries? Is that it?"

"Oh, yes! But it's *so* much more. We give them a new skill, a new life, you see. So much better than what they have."

"A waste of money!" boomed Colonel Beaufort from the other end of the table. "Poppycock!"

"I beg your pardon, Rufus!" Lady Linley snapped.

"I am merely stating the facts, Margaret. Educating these women does little good. It only makes them overwrought and distressed. They're taught a skill, maybe how to read. And for what? They are still made to marry and breed. Scads of children they have. Why, there was one woman I saw in the hills of Anantagiri who had twenty-one children. *Twen-ty-one*," he emphasized. "Now, that's a fact. Saw it with my own eyes. All of them huddled in a hut, diseased and starving. What say you to that, Miss Simms? How does teaching that poor woman to read do anything at all except to make her painfully aware of what she doesn't have?"

"We must trust to Providence, Colonel Beaufort," Miss Simms responded rigidly. "We do what we can. Perhaps some education will not help certain women, such as the one you met, but it might help her daughters."

"Poppycock! It just stirs up the masses. Best to let things be as they are. Don't upset the natural order of things."

"Have you been to Ethiopia?" Henrietta asked Miss Simms, genuinely intrigued and deciding to ignore Colonel Beaufort's boorish comments.

"Me? Goodness, no!" Miss Simms sipped her tea. "Not my department at all."

"What do you do, then?" Henrietta gave her a quizzical look.

"My job is to raise sensibility for our cause and to attempt to secure, well, certain private donations."

Henrietta was about to ask a somewhat delicate question, but she was beaten to it by Colonel Beaufort, who was by no means delicate.

"And so you've parked yourself here," he said, finishing off the last of the bacon and swishing it down with a large gulp of tea. "We all know what you're up to, miss." He tapped the side of his bulbous nose.

Miss Simms shot him a venomous dagger. "You will excuse me, Lady Linley," she said politely and rose. "I have some correspondence."

"Oh, must you go?" Lady Linley twittered. "I thought you might read to me a little after breakfast." Her voice was almost pleading.

"No, not just now." Miss Simms threw Colonel Beaufort another dagger. "I'm a bit indisposed." She gave Lady Linley an obsequious little tilt of her head and then elegantly retreated.

"Rufus! Must you always be a beast!" Lady Linley scolded.

"Don't be a fool, Margaret! She's certainly playing you for one. The reason she's here is as plain as a turban on a Punjabi."

"If you are referring to the estate, you needn't worry. I have Wallace constantly hounding me on that score. I'm not completely out of my mind, you know!" She set her napkin on the table. "I *am* sure of one thing, though," she said regally, "you would never have spoken to me this way in Montague's presence!"

"Now, now, Margaret, you needn't work yourself up into a state. All I'm saying is that I don't believe in all of these money-grubbing charities. A new one pops up every day, it seems. Not like when I was a young man. People worked for what they got."

"You're hardly one to talk, Rufus! You haven't worked a day in your life."

"I beg your pardon! I most certainly have. Been in the King's Own Royal Regiment, Lancaster, second battalion, most of my life," he said, looking around the table as if to gauge everyone's impression. "And that was certainly no walk in the park, I'll tell you. Not my fault that I was born the third son. My duty was laid out for me, and I did it. With gusto, too, I might add. None of this mamby-pamby feeling sorry for myself. I got on with it. You're too soft on Wallace, Margaret. All he does is mope about and whine. Grumbling about selling the place or giving it away to some infantile idiots, waving placards about and demanding equality for all. Balderdash!" He stabbed the last kipper lying feebly on the plate in front of him. "We must be very careful, Margaret," he went on, "or the ordered world will crumble down around us." He waved his fork around the room.

"Don't be absurd, Rufus!" Lady Linley exclaimed.

"And now you have Miss Simms creeping about," he went on, ignoring her. "You'd better keep your eye on that one, or before you know it, the whole place will be in her hands. What do these people think they're to do with a place like this? Create choice suites of rooms for themselves and then what? Fill up the rest with the unfortunate poor? I rather think not. And even if they did, what bloody good would it do? Get maybe twenty people out of the poorhouse. So what? Doesn't solve the problem of poverty. As our good Lord said, the poor will always be with us. I'm not a vicar, but I do believe that means that there really is nothing we can do. It's just a fact of life."

"That's enough, Rufus! I won't hear any more of this at my own table. You forget yourself. This is not a regimental dinner. It is simply breakfast in what used to be a respectable home!" She rang a little silver bell by her place, and Stevens appeared. He hurried over to pull out Lady Linley's chair. "Poor Montague would be turning in his grave if he could hear you," she said sorrowfully as she rose.

Henrietta thought she saw tears in the old woman's eyes as she hobbled from the room, and she felt a surge of sympathy for the poor woman, knowing as she did that Wallace was in fact at this moment discussing the estate's possible demolition just one room over. Having completely lost her appetite at this point, she pushed her plate away. "And how long do you plan to stay, Colonel Beaufort?" she asked briskly, hoping he would catch her disapproval.

Colonel Beaufort leaned back in his chair and began picking his teeth with a toothpick. "Don't rightly know, do we, Phineas? I'm between stationings, you see. Waiting for my next orders to come through."

"I would have thought you'd be retired from service by now," Henrietta probed.

"Well, it's hard to teach an old dog new tricks. Wouldn't know what to do with myself. No, the army life is for me. It's what I want for young Phineas, here, but he is dead set on going to Oxford. Waste of time, to my mind. Don't know why you wouldn't want to be out in the action!" he exclaimed, surveying Phineas now with a stern gaze.

The young man seemed completely unfazed by his father's criticism and surprisingly returned it with his own.

"I say, Father, you were a bit harsh just now with poor Aunt Margaret and even poor Miss Simms. I'm sure she's perfectly harmless. And anyway, who would want this place? It's horribly haunted."

"Haunted? Nonsense! No such thing as ghosts," Colonel Beaufort chortled.

"There are according to the servants." Phineas leaned back and linked his hands behind his head. "Apparently, there's a mysterious beast that roams the grounds at night." His eyes darted between Henrietta and Amelie, the only two left at the table besides Colonel Beaufort, as if to gauge their level of fear.

"I rather think you're thinking of *The Hound of the Baskervilles*," Henrietta said dismissively.

Phineas grinned and then leaned forward eagerly, his arms on the table now. "Ha, ha! Just so, Mrs. Howard. You've found me out. Ha, ha," he said, gleefully. "Just so." He leaned back again. "But there *is* a ghost," he said with all seriousness this time.

"Phineas!" Colonel Beaufort warned.

"But, Father, it's true! Honestly. Apparently, the ghost of a maid wanders the hall at night. She hung herself years and years ago, so the story goes, over some unrequited love. Fell in love with a fellow servant or something like that, and when he didn't show up at the altar, she despaired and hung herself in her bridal gown." He again looked eagerly around the table.

"Monsieur Beaufort!" Amelie exclaimed. "Please."

"I *do* apologize," he said brightly, looking unabashedly from Amelie to Henrietta, "but isn't it fascinating?"

"It is most certainly not," the colonel scolded. "Bosh!"

"But, Father, I *heard* her. The ghost that is. Did you not?" He looked questioningly at the ladies. Amelie shook her head. Henrietta did not answer, but goosebumps broke out down her neck.

"Phineas," Amelie said, clearing her throat a little, "zese are old stories. Zey mean nothing. Surely every old castle or manor house in Europe has the story of a ghost. It is a story. Nothing more." She rose abruptly. "Excuse me now. I must see to the children." She gave the two men, who had likewise risen, the briefest of nods and Henrietta a quick smile before exiting the room.

Not wishing to be left alone with the two Beauforts, Henrietta stood, too. "You'll excuse me, as well," she said to the colonel and Phineas before they resumed their seats.

"Don't leave on our account, Mrs. Howard," the colonel blustered. "Don't mind Phineas. He's an utter boob, aren't you, Phineas?"

"If you say so, Father," the young man said with a sigh as he slumped back into his chair, a mischievous smile about his lips. *Was everything a joke to him?*

"Not at all, Colonel, but, like Miss Simms, I have some correspondence. Good morning," she said with affected politeness and left the room, trying to tell herself all over again that the noises she had heard were easily explained away. She hurried from the room. Once in the hallway, however, she leaned against the wall and tried to catch her breath, convinced, despite her quick attempts at rationalization, that there was definitely something wrong in this house.

Chapter 3

Elsie looked out the window at the billowing clouds and knew that something was definitely wrong. A storm was brewing for sure.

"Come, Anna, bring me the bucket."

The girl did not answer but dutifully moved to where the chipped wooden bucket sat near the dry sink. Carefully, she lifted it, her little muscles straining, and waddled with it between her skinny legs, some of its water sloshing over the edge, to where Elsie stood by the windows. "That's it," Elsie said, smiling encouragingly. "Now go get some more rags. They're out on the line."

Anna stared at her for a moment with her big blue eyes and then retreated to seek out the haphazard clothesline that was stretched between the wall of the sod house and an old dead sapling. Elsie looked out the front window again.

Since their arrival in Nebraska, she had learned to read the sky with some degree of accuracy. And if she hadn't been able to tell that it was about to rain by the way the clouds were collecting on the vast horizon, she could tell by the way the flies were biting. She swatted one away and let fall the thick, dirty piece of burlap that hung stiffly in front of the window. It served as a rudimentary curtain, presumably tacked up by the previous occupants, and though it disgusted Elsie, she had not yet had the time nor the material to replace it. She dropped her rag in the bucket of dirty water Anna had set before her and, wringing it out partially, proceeded to try to wedge the cloth as best she could between the sill and the glass in a feeble attempt to keep out the dust.

The thick sod that made up the walls of their little house kept out most of the dust that covered nearly all of Nebraska, but the windows and doors were the weak spots. At least three times a day, Elsie had to wipe the dust from the sill and the floor beneath. Even with this vigilance during the day and the wet rags placed like sandbags in a flood, fresh dust would make its way in while they slept each night, covering them and everything else in a fine layer of dirt.

Still, it was better than the flophouse they had found upon stepping off the train in Omaha. Not knowing where to go first, they had taken refuge there for the first two weeks while Gunther tried to locate the friend who had urged him to come to this God-forsaken place to begin with. Elsie suggested that perhaps Gunther should abandon the search for his friend and instead look for a job in town, but Gunther didn't think this wise, considering that there were long lines of other jobless men collecting at the factory gates each morning before the sun even came up.

Eventually, Gunther did finally manage to trace his friend to a sugar beet farm in a small town outside of Omaha called Millard, but by then, the little makeshift family had unfortunately almost burned through their feeble resources. Gunther's friend, he bitterly discovered, had long since abandoned the sugar beet farm, but the owner, one Mr. Wilkins, agreed to take Gunther on anyway at the rate of $1.50 a day, or $1.30 if he wanted to room in one of the sod houses lining the west side of the property.

Gunther took the sod house rate and brought Elsie and Anna from the boarding house. At first Elsie had been excited about the prospect of setting up their first home, but she nearly despaired at the sight of the piles of dust, like snow drifts, inside the house. Despite her shock, she did not murmur one word of complaint and instead had quickly begun to shovel out the dust with an old tin pot that Gunther had brought with him. Eventually, she had borrowed a broom from their neighbor, a Mrs. Muñoz, who didn't speak a word of English, to finish the job and had then thrown herself into the task of wiping down the walls, which took several days to get to a point of cleanliness that was perhaps not perfect, but at least acceptable.

Several times in this process, she had contemplated whether or not it would have been better for her and Anna to stay in the boarding house, but she quickly dismissed this idea. For one thing, there had been cockroaches the size of a grown man's thumb scurrying across the walls and rats as big as cats in the alley out back. And for another, the long low room in which all the inhabitants were forced to sleep, with its rows of beds lined up against the wall, was mostly filled with men. More than once, especially when Gunther was out searching for his friend, she had felt them staring at not only her but at little Anna as well.

No, it was better, she told herself as she scrubbed, for them all to be together out here in the country. Wasn't this one of the reasons Gunther had wanted to flee Chicago in the first place? To provide fresh country air for Anna as a way of possibly calming her epileptic condition? She had already had two fits, poor thing, but luckily neither of them had happened on the train, as they would have then perhaps been forced to disembark. Instead, the fits had taken hold of the girl while in the flophouse, an appropriate name, Elsie had grimly realized later, leaving the poor thing pale and lifeless on the dirty floor. And while several people had witnessed Anna's convulsions, no one seemed to care besides one old crone in the corner who labeled Anna a "devil child" from that moment on.

The few doctors who had examined Anna in the past, including one in Germany before Gunther had fled that country, had all said the same thing: that there was no cure for such a malady, besides possibly bromide salts, and that the girl would best be served in an epileptic colony. Short of that, fresh air, good food, and mild exercise might help.

But Millard, Nebraska, despite being far from a city, seemed disappointingly not in possession of any of the things that might be conducive to better health. In fact, it seemed not a very healthy place at all. Elsie had envisioned them living in a green sort of paradise, growing their own food and harvesting it, canning it, maybe having a few chickens. But there was nothing particularly green about this place at all. Instead, it was a brown wasteland where barely anything grew, except, it seemed, sugar beets and sorghum. To make matters worse, dust storms frequently came up out of nowhere, choking everything and causing anyone caught in their wake to huddle inside any available shelter and to walk with a damp cloth tied around their noses and mouths in order to be able to breathe.

Once a week, the little family walked into town to buy supplies, though sometimes Mrs. Wilkins, the farmer's wife, would sell them eggs or bread and then deduct an exorbitant sum from their wages. It made Elsie determined, then, to bake her own bread, as she had done often enough during her childhood in the Von Harmons' shabby apartment on Armitage, but it was difficult to do on a woodstove, and often her efforts came out flat or else horribly scorched.

It was the neighbor women, eventually, who had come to her rescue and showed her the best way to do it. Most of the families in the long row of sod houses were Mexican, though there were a few Swedes down at the end. None of them knew any English, so Elsie tried to teach them a few words, the least she could do, she felt, for all that they were teaching her, which included how to wash clothes on the antiquated laundry press in the undercroft of the barn, how to stop some of the dust with wet rags, and how to make a type of griddle cake out of sorghum, which wasn't half bad, actually, and which filled them up more than bread. In exchange, Elsie tried extending her English lessons to some of the children, the ones still too little to be out in the fields, that is, which meant that they were two, three, four, and five years old. It was a gift for which the other women seemed grateful.

To her delight, some of the children learned very quickly, and she found she loved being called *profesora* by them. Their rapid advancement had one misgiving, however, which was that it drew a stark contrast to little Anna, who remained, even now, strangely mute. Elsie despaired that the little girl had lost her voice. It had occurred after she had been inappropriately admitted to Dunning, Chicago's notorious insane asylum, as a result of suffering an epileptic fit at the orphanage in which Gunther had temporarily placed her. The poor girl had only been in Dunning for a few days before Elsie and Gunther, with the help of her sister Henrietta, and her husband, Clive, had rescued her, but even so, Anna seemed oddly changed by it. She still had her sweet disposition and could clearly still hear, but she had not spoken a word since, causing Elsie to feel positively nauseous when she tried to imagine the things that the poor little girl must have witnessed there, even in such a short space of time. Something had clearly frightened her into speechlessness.

Immediately after they had rescued her, they had brought Anna to stay with Elsie's mother and young twin siblings in Palmer Square under the watchful care of Nurse Flanagan, whom Henrietta and Clive had generously hired specifically for this purpose. Elsie had hoped that this new environment would at least restore the girl to her former self, if not advance her beyond, and while she did make some progress in that she eventually began to run about with the twins, she still, sadly, did not speak. In fact, she didn't make a noise at all, not even a giggle, and when she cried, she was silent then, too, which was somehow the most pitiable of all, watching the girl sob with absolutely no sound escaping.

Likewise, Nurse Flanagan had once related to Elsie in her thick Irish brogue that "the lass seems right terrified when Doris and Donny want to play hide and seek. Runs for her bed, then, and won't come out fer dear life." This and other strange phobias, such as that of spiders and flickering lights, worried Elsie immensely. The girl had also become oddly attached to Elsie, so much so that she rarely left her side. She positively clung to her whenever the neighbor women stopped by or when she was trying to teach the other children, and only once in a while, with great urging, would she go outside to play with them. If she did, Elsie noticed that she would never stray far from the house and was, indeed, always looking back at it, as if making sure it was still there.

Anna ran into the house now, carrying a little bundle of rags, stiff from hanging in the hot sun.

"Here, you get them wet for me," Elsie said, nodding at the bucket. Anna quickly obeyed and dropped them into the water. In the beginning, Elsie had used clean water from the well to block the windows, but she had quickly realized it was a waste and now simply used the old dish water. "How many are there?" Elsie asked, always trying to think of ways to both teach her and to get her to speak, though she never forced her.

Anna held up four fingers.

"Very good!" Elsie said.

The girl smiled.

"How many windows?"

Anna gave her a look as if the answer was obvious and held up two small fingers. She pulled a sopping rag from the bucket.

"Wring it a little first," Elsie suggested and when the girl had done it, she took it from her and again looked out the window. The sky was growing darker. Elsie prayed it would rain. Sometimes, the clouds gathered but then refused to release their precious water and were blown further east across the plains by an angry wind. She could see flashes of lightning now, far in the distance, which was not a good sign. The neighbor women had told her of terrible *tornados* that ripped across the plains

"Dump this out back now for Mama," she said to Anna. The girl stared at her for several moments before eventually obeying. It made Elsie's stomach clench just a little. She wasn't sure Anna liked her referring to herself as her mother, but she had no way of reading exactly what was behind those soft blue eyes. Gunther had insisted on it, however, telling Anna that "this is Mama now."

The only mother the girl had ever known had been Gunther's mother, whom she had called Oma, and who had sadly died on the voyage to America from Germany. It was one of the reasons, though, that Elsie so loved Gunther, the fact that he acted as the father of this child, protecting and loving her, when he had, in reality, simply been an innocent bystander in the tragic drama of Anna's parents. Her mother, Liesel Klinkhammer, had died in Dunning, and her real father, Heinrich Meyer, had only recently appeared out of nowhere, after all these years, demanding to take Anna or to be paid off, hoping that Gunther would avail himself of Elsie's rich relatives and produce the cash. That was the other reason Gunther had decided to flee Chicago: to get away from Heinrich and to separate himself from Elsie and her family, once and for all. It was a sacrifice, he had insisted to a tearful Elsie, that he was willing to make.

But it was *not* a sacrifice that Elsie had been willing to make, and she had therefore followed him to Union Station and escaped with him, leaving her mentor, Sr. Bernard, to believe she had gone to the motherhouse of the Sisters of the Blessed Virgin Mary in Dubuque, Iowa, in order to begin the process of becoming a nun. It was a spur-of-the-moment decision, and thus she had brought nothing with her but herself. But she was willing to give *all* of herself to Gunther and Anna. She had felt terrified when she stepped onto the train with them, knowing that there was no going back, but she felt oddly euphoric as well.

Gunther, too, seemed to have at least initially shared her euphoria, but he grew more agitated as the journey continued, causing Elsie to worry that perhaps she *had* made a mistake—that, rather than helping him, she was merely adding to his burden. Finally, when Anna had succumbed to the gentle rocking of the train and darkness without and fallen asleep, stretched out on the seat across from them, did Gunther take Elsie's hand, turning slightly toward her.

"You are sure, Elsie?" he whispered.

Elsie made a point of staring into his blue eyes for several moments before answering to solidify her words. "Yes," she said evenly. "I'm sure."

"Then we must marry as soon as we get to Omaha."

Elsie blinked. She had not expected this. True, Gunther had once before asked her to marry him, but he had then rescinded it when her grandfather threatened to cut off not only her from his financial support, but the whole Von Harmon brood, if she proceeded. Elsie had spent the last month attempting to change Gunther's mind, to no avail, and now here he was, insisting upon it.

Gunther obviously took her silence to be apprehension. "Elsie, I will not . . . dishonor you." He took her hand. "I have ask before, but I ask again, with nothing to give you," he said, gesturing with his free hand at the empty train car around them. "Will you have me as husband? Will you marry me?"

Elsie looked again at his deep blue eyes. It was not for lack of love that she paused. It was just that it was so soon—they would be in Omaha in a matter of hours—and, she worried, it would obviously not be in a church. But a church wedding, Elsie knew, was impossible anyway. She was Catholic, and he professed to be Lutheran. It was a fact that had initially given her pause when she first met him, but on the other hand, she hadn't thought about him romantically way back then and, anyway, it was currently the least of their problems.

"Yes, I will," she murmured, swallowing her fear. He leaned toward her then and softly kissed her, which had filled her with a deep longing.

True to his word, Gunther led both Anna and Elsie, not three days after they had arrived in Omaha, to a tiny office in the grand courthouse on Farnham Street. There it was, with only little Anna looking on, that Elsie Martha Von Harmon was joined in marriage to Gunther Alphonsus Stockel. Gunther had managed to pick some wildflowers for his bride in the scrub behind the flour mill—some black-eyed Susans and wild senna, and even a stalk of gayfeather, its purple spikes offsetting the gold of the other flowers nicely.

As soon as the simple vows had been exchanged, the officiating clerk, himself sweating profusely where he sat on a wooden stool behind the counter, the little electric fan propped up on a stack of outdated log books offering little comfort, shoved the license across the counter at them and offered a quick congratulations before he shouted, "Next," causing Elsie and Gunther to quickly step aside to make way for the next couple.

Gunther held Elsie's hand and, after staring at her for several moments as if trying to etch this memory into his mind, kissed her. "Hello, Mrs. Stockel."

"Hello," Elsie answered, a little laugh escaping.

"Come, we celebrate," he said, grasping Anna's hand.

"Celebrate? Where?" Elsie asked, hoping he didn't mean the flophouse.

"You will see."

Gunther proceeded to lead them to the trolley stop on Sixteenth, where they rode to Cuming and then changed for a bus that took them west. Elsie delighted in the ride, as it allowed her to see much of the city. It was the farthest they had yet ventured. Before very long, however, Gunther reached up and pulled the cord, signaling a stop. The bus ground to a halt at Maple, and Gunther quickly alighted, Anna on his hip and his hand held out to help Elsie down the steps.

"What are we doing here?" Elsie asked, tenting her hand over her eyes and looking around.

"Come. This way," he said with a smile and led the two of them up a little hill to where Krug Park stood in all its glory. As they walked closer, Elsie peeked at Anna's face and was delighted to see it lit up with a big smile, her eyes wide. Gunther set her down and paid the thirty cents for them to get in.

"Gunther, we don't have the money for this," Elsie fretted.

"I have little bit. I can spend it on *mein kleines Mädchen*—my little girl. And my wife," he said with a big smile, taking Anna's hand and simultaneously kissing Elsie on the cheek. He led them first to the carousel, which stood majestically in the center of the park, and paid for them all to ride. Anna clung to Gunther, who had mounted a tiger, and Elsie chose the elephant next to him. As the ride jerked into motion, Elsie let out a little gasp and then a laugh as the merry-go-round began to spin faster.

Afterward, they wandered the grounds, marveling at the roller coaster and the other rides until they came to the monkey house, which Anna adored. It was difficult, in fact, to peel her away, but Gunther managed to do so with the lure of having a genuine ice cream cone in the beer garden.

The beer garden was a tented construction with a sort of dance pavilion attached, and after procuring an ice cream cone for Anna and two glasses of beer for himself and Elsie, Gunther joined them at a little table and sat down. The band was playing an old-fashioned polka and after staring at her for several minutes, the freckles on his face very prominent in the sun, Gunther stood formally in front of Elsie, clicked his heels together and bowed before her. "May I have this dance, Fraulein? Or, I should say, Frau Stockel?" His smile was infectious.

Elsie blushed as she took his hand, and he led her to the dance floor, Anna looking on as she licked. Gunther skillfully swirled Elsie around the floor as if he were used to dancing to polkas every day of his life. It made her despair for the life he had given up in Germany as a prominent professor, but she forced the thought from her mind. Today was her wedding day, and she didn't want anything to spoil it.

"Elsie, I love you," he said as he looked into her eyes. "I promise to make you happy."

"I already am." She was unable to keep from smiling.

They danced to several numbers before returning to their table, Anna waiting patiently and slowly swinging her legs back and forth under her chair. Gunther then bought them each a hot dog, and when they finished, they continued walking through the whole of the park until the sun began to set. Finally, they made their way out through the tall wrought-iron gates and caught the trolley back toward the center of town. Elsie dreaded having to go back to the flophouse, a feeling Gunther seemed to share, and instead they walked down toward the river and watched the boats, all lit up, travel up and down the Missouri.

Finally, they had nothing left to do but return to the boarding house, Gunther carrying a tired Anna in his arms. Eventually, she rested her head on his shoulder and went to sleep. They made their way as quietly as they could to the far end of the sleeping room, even having to step over some snoring bodies on the ground who weren't lucky enough to have secured a bed. When they reached the last two beds in the row, under which were stored their few things, Gunther laid Anna on one of them and then sat down heavily on the other, the thin springs bending almost to the ground. He held his hand out to Elsie.

Elsie took it hesitantly, hoping that Gunther did not mean to consummate their marriage here in this crowded, dirty place. He pulled her down to him and laced his fingers through hers. Elsie swallowed hard and tried to relax, but her heart betrayed her and began to race.

Gunther leaned his forehead against hers for several moments and then kissed her, softly, tenderly. He rubbed her cheek with the back of his hand. "You have nothing to fear, *Liebling*. I will not ask what you are not ready to give."

"Gunther, I . . . I want to," she lied, "but . . . but . . ." she looked down the dark row of huddled bodies.

"No, not here. This is not *würdig*—worthy of you, of my bride. I promise, Elsie, to give you life you deserve."

Elsie could think of nothing to say to this, so she closed her eyes and kissed him. She could sense by his sharp intake of breath that he was fighting his own arousal, but he pulled out of the kiss and laid down on the edge of the bed, making room for her. Slowly, she laid beside him, trying not to make too much noise, though the springs squeaked horribly. He wrapped his arms around her, and she could feel the beating of his heart on her back until she finally fell asleep.

They spent each night this way, huddled together on the stinking, squeaking bed until they finally moved to the sod house, which contained only two rooms. The main room held a dry sink and a woodstove and a small table and chairs, while the second room contained only a thick, wood-framed bed supported by strong ropes beneath. The mattress, as far as Elsie could tell, was made of down and cornhusks. It was immensely heavy, but with the help of Mr. Muñoz, Gunther was able to get it outside so that Elsie could at least attempt to beat some of the dust out of it. While it aired for several days, Elsie and Gunther slept on the floor on a quilt lent to them by one of the Swedish women, Mrs. Larsson, at the end of the row, and Anna slept on the little trundle they found lodged under the bed. Finally, after airing for three days, Elsie determined that the mattress was clean enough to bring in, and after Gunther had left for the fields, she made it up with sheets and a quilt borrowed from Mrs. Muñoz.

"*¡Señora!*" Mrs. Muñoz suddenly called to her now from the yard next door. Elsie had stepped outside to look for Anna when she hadn't returned with the bucket. "*¡Entra, rápido!*" Mrs. Muñoz shouted, pointing at the sky. "Storm!"

Elsie looked up and saw that the sky was indeed growing blacker by the minute and loud cracks of thunder could be heard. Instinctively, she glanced at the fields, but Gunther and several of the other men, she knew, weren't there. It was Friday, the day Mr. Wilkins sent them to take a wagonload of beets into town. She prayed he wouldn't be caught on the road when the storm hit. Elsie hurried around to the back of the house.

"Anna!" she called, but there was no sign of the girl, just a wet mark on the grass where she had presumably dumped the bucket. "Anna!" she shouted again, holding her hand up to her forehead as she searched the horizon. About a hundred yards away was a thick hedgerow demarking one field from the next, but Elsie couldn't imagine that Anna had wandered there. The girl was terrified of thunder and lightning and usually crawled into Gunther's lap whenever a storm came up. Elsie quickly pulled the laundry from the line and hurried back into the house.

"Anna?" She tossed the washing on the table and after quickly checking the bedroom, ran back outside. *Where could she be?* Elsie's heart began to race as big drops of rain began exploding into the dust. She looked in every direction and then scurried toward the

Muñoz house, her hand over her head in an attempt to block the rain that was pouring down now. She pounded on the door, and Mrs. Muñoz quickly opened it, her face confused and worried. "*¿Si?*"

"Is Anna here?" she said pointing to the interior of the house. "Anna?" she repeated.

"No!" the woman said, understanding her meaning. She pulled the shawl from around her shoulders and, wrapping it over her head, stepped out into the rain. Bending against the wind that had suddenly whipped up, the woman marched to the next house, Elsie following. Mrs. Muñoz banged on the door, and a child answered.

"*¿Ana está aquí?*" she asked. The little boy shook his head. Mrs. Muñoz looked back at Elsie and shrugged. Elsie felt her heart constrict. Mrs. Muñoz pointed at herself and then to the rest of the houses in the row. Then she pointed at Elsie and gestured back toward where they had come. "*Seguiré buscando aquí, y tú vuelves a casa y compruebas.*"

Elsie did not understand her words but took them to mean that she would proceed down the row while Elsie was to hurry back to her own house to look again. Quickly, she ran back to the house, the interior of which was now almost as dark as night despite the fact that it was still only the afternoon.

"Anna?" she cried as a bolt of lightning briefly illuminated the room, followed by a thunderclap that hit so close the very glass in the windows rattled.

A thump was heard then, which nearly stopped Elsie's heart. She followed the noise and flew into the bedroom, hoping Anna wasn't having a fit and looked desperately around as another clap of thunder shook the house. Anna was nowhere to be seen. She was about to run out, thinking she must have heard wrong, when she thought to get down on her hands and knees. She peered under the bed and saw Anna, huddled into a ball and shaking.

"Anna! I'm here. It's all right," Elsie said, trying to keep her voice calm and measured. She inched herself a little ways under the bed and reached her hand toward the girl, who remained in a ball like some sort of wild animal. Elsie could see her eyes, though, bright and wide with terror. Another thunderclap struck, and Elsie could hear the wind roaring now. She desperately needed to get up and try to secure the door at least. "I'll be right back," she grunted and began to inch herself backwards.

"No!" Anna cried, causing Elsie to freeze. It was the first time the child had spoken in almost five months.

"What did you say?" Elsie asked hoarsely.

Anna stared at her for several moments, and Elsie began to wonder if she had imagined it. She began moving backward again, at which point Anna stretched out her hand, her little fingers shaking. "No," she said in a tiny squeak. "Don't leave me, Mama."

Chapter 4

"We can't possibly leave now," Lady Linley quibbled from where she stood by the nearly floor-to-ceiling windows in the drawing room of Castle Linley. "It looks like rain."

"It's not going to rain, Mother," Wallace responded from the other side of the room. "There's not a cloud in the sky."

"Even so, I feel it in my bones. My rheumatism is acting up. And it would be unseemly to picnic so soon after your father's death."

Wallace sighed loudly in what was obvious frustration, and for once Henrietta could see his side of things. Besides the heavy black crepe that covered all of the mirrors and paintings, Henrietta had also observed that all of the clocks in the house had been stopped at exactly 2:57, the time, apparently, that Lord Linley had drawn his last breath. Yet another Victorian custom, Clive had explained. Poor Lady Linley, stuck in time herself, Henrietta observed as she watched the woman stare out the window at the sky.

"If you'd really rather not go, then so be it, Mother," Wallace continued now. "But the rest of us are. We can't sit around this house moping eternally for Father. It's not what he would have wished."

Lady Linley turned rapidly upon her son, her eyes wide. "And how would you know what he wished?" she snapped. "You, who spent such precious little time with him!"

Wallace bristled and opened his mouth to retort when Miss Simms, who was standing very near Lady Linley, broke in. "I think it would do you good, Lady Linley," the young woman said encouragingly, wrapping her arm through the elderly lady's. "A picnic on an English summer day would cheer anyone. Please say you'll come. We won't stay out long, and if you want to come back before the others, I'll escort you. I promise." Miss Simms flashed her most charming smile.

"Well . . ." Lady Linley murmured, her shoulders crumpling a bit. "Perhaps for just a short time."

"The children will certainly enjoy your company," Wallace added with only a trace of bitterness.

"The children?" Lady Linley seemed surprised. "The children are coming along?"

"Yes, Mother, it's a picnic."

"Children never attended picnics with adults in my day! How absurd. And Alcott is just a baby. Too much fresh air will give him colic."

Henrietta saw Wallace bite his lip. "Mother, it's a picnic here on the grounds. It's not Ascot. No one will mind. And if they do," he looked purposefully around the room at thus-far assembled guests, "they can abstain."

Lady Linley let out a loud sigh. "Very well," she said, limply waving her hand. "Do as you wish. You will anyway. No one ever listens to me."

"I'll go and get your shawl, shall I?" Miss Simms suggested.

"Yes, dear, thank you," Lady Linley answered, laying a hand briefly on the young woman's arm.

Miss Simms's silent exit was overshadowed by the somewhat loud entrance of Amelie and the two young Howards. Henrietta and Clive had been at the castle for nearly forty-eight hours now, and yet this was the first they had seen of their little nephews. Linley, all of three years old, broke free of his Mama's grasp and ran to where Wallace stood next to Clive.

"Hello, Nipper," Wallace said with a rare smile. "Look who's here. It's Uncle Clive. What do you say?"

Linley grasped his papa's leg and stared up uneasily at Clive. "Hello, Uncle," he warbled, his voice high.

"My, you're a big lad, aren't you," Clive said with a smile that melted Henrietta's heart.

"Nearly grown." Clive ruffled the boy's hair, and Linley stared back up at him with the biggest blue eyes Henrietta thought she had ever seen. "Here we go," Clive said, putting both hands behind his back. "Pick one and see which has a sovereign." The little boy stared up at Clive, a tiny grin on his face now as he put his finger in his mouth.

"Go on," Clive urged. "Which one?"

Linley's little brow crinkled as he studied both of Clive's arms in turn and then finally pointed to the right. Clive brought his right hand forward and opened it to reveal the coin. "First try! Well done. Here you are."

Linley looked up at Wallace for permission to take the coin, and when he nodded, the boy took it. Clive ruffled his hair again. "Shall we try another?"

"Clive, you'll spoil him," Wallace said with a laugh.

Amelie sidled up to Henrietta, startling her, so absorbed was she in watching Clive interact with a child. The only other time she had seen him do so was when he had interacted with her young siblings one Christmas Eve, and she had been surprised and delighted with his manner then, too.

"Would you like to take him?" Amelie asked, laying little Alcott, the second son of the house, in her arms before she could even respond.

Henrietta drew in her breath as she grasped the baby and immediately tried to arrange him into a comfortable position. With seven younger brothers and sisters, she was certainly experienced with children, but it had been ages since she had held a tiny baby in her arms. She had begged to hold her miscarried child in her arms at least once before it was whisked away, but the midwife would have none of it. "Bloody mess is all it is," she had said sharply, quickly rolling up the stained sheets from under Henrietta. "Don't do no good to look at it."

Henrietta stared at the baby in her arms now. He was so light! And perfectly lovely, with cheeks that were already chubby and big blue eyes that matched his brother's. She pulled back the satin blue blanket in which he was wrapped and marveled at his tiny features. Without thinking about it, she kissed his little head, inhaling the intoxicating still-newborn smell of him. She pushed down a lump in her throat.

Alcott gurgled then, and she couldn't help but smile. She looked across at Clive, who had somehow noticed the transaction and was watching her now with anxious concern. She smiled at him, and his face relaxed into a grin.

"He's beautiful, Amelie," Henrietta murmured.

"*Oui, merci*. He is a good baby. Not like Linley, who fussed constantly." Absently, she rubbed her still-small belly as she looked on. "Let us hope zis one is a girl."

"It must be difficult with them so close in age. Do you not have a nanny?" Henrietta asked, though as soon as she did, it struck her as incredible that only a very short time ago, she would not have even thought of asking about a nanny, her own family having grown up in abject poverty.

Amelie surreptitiously glanced over at Wallace and then back to Henrietta, a rare rueful look on her face. "No, as Wallace said the other night, we cannot seem to keep one. Zey begin and zen leave for better prospects. But zat suits Wallace, to be honest," she said in a low voice, a smile about her lips. "He rails against zis life, as you know," she said, looking around the elegant morning room. "He detests having servants."

"Well, easy for him to say," Henrietta said, rubbing Alcott's downy cheek with her finger.

"*Oui, c'est ça*," Amelie said with a little laugh.

"But what about the servants that *are* here? Can they not assist you?"

"Zey could, *oui*, but zey say zey are too busy. But I think the real reason is zat I am a foreigner, and they resent me. Like Lord Linley, zey prefer zat the son of the house should have married someone English."

"But that's ridiculous."

"Yes, well, it is not just the aristocracy zat can be . . . what is the word? Snobs."

Henrietta laughed, and as if on cue, Stevens entered the room. "The wagons are ready, sir," he announced to Wallace.

"Yes, all right, Stevens." Wallace surveyed the room. "Where's the colonel? And Phineas, for that matter? Are they coming?"

"They are already without, sir," Stevens answered when no one else did.

"All right; let's go. Where's Miss Simms?"

"Here I am!" called the young woman, blustering into the room with a black shawl draped across her arm. "I found it, Lady Linley!"

"Well, come along, child. You can sit next to me and help me."

In all, two carriages, or rather wagons, were needed to carry the assembled party and all the provisions to the Upper Forty, a term that had evolved to describe the roughly forty acres of the estate that overlooked the Derwent River and the Vale of Matlock below. It was a very picturesque spot, Henrietta observed once they arrived, and she could see why it would be desirable as a parcel of land for sale, and likewise, for the very same reason, why Lady Linley would be loath to agree to such a sale, if she were even cognizant, that is, that such a proposal was on the table.

Jeremiah, the footman, and Dick, one of the grooms, had been charged with driving the carriages, and once at the grounds, Dick took charge of leading the horses to a nearby grove of trees, while Jeremiah hurried to set up the picnic. Thick tartan blankets were laid upon the long grass, and hampers unloaded and arranged. Several cushions had been brought along for Lady Linley's benefit, and she very carefully now tried to find a comfortable position on top of them while also balancing her black parasol. Henrietta sat down near Amelie and watched Linley run about in the long grass, his white sailor suit bright against the lush green.

Jeremiah soon had the picnic neatly arranged to everyone's satisfaction—cucumber sandwiches, egg salad, cheese, potted shrimp, biscuits, a lemon cake, tea, and of course some champagne, which Jeremiah kept cool with the aid of several blocks of chipped ice.

"I say, this is the life, is it not?" blustered Colonel Beaufort, munching now on a wedge of cheese.

"Quite," Clive agreed languidly, his eyes resting on Henrietta.

"I think if I lived here, I'd walk back here every day," Henrietta said, shooting him a grin before closing her eyes and lifting her face to the sun.

"Henrietta, dear, do put your hat back on," Lady Linley advised. "You don't want your skin to darken."

Henrietta laughed to herself, knowing as she did that there had been little time for such ladylike considerations when she was growing up in their shabby apartment on Armitage. If Lady Linley only knew the number of hours she had spent in the sun, working. But she obeyed and set her white straw sunhat back on her head. She looked again at Clive, who winked at her.

"You should have brought a parasol. Why don't young ladies carry parasols anymore? I find it most distressing."

"Perhaps because it's an antiquated accessory, Mother," Wallace said as he stretched out on his back amidst the grass, his hands behind his head.

"Well, I don't see why!" Lady Linley countered. "And why do you always have to disagree with me, Wallace?"

"*I* find them most charming," Miss Simms put in from where she sat next to Lady Linley. "I wish they would come back in style. They're rather pretty, don't you think?"

"Pretty and *useful*," Lady Linley replied. "I don't know why young ladies these days seem to have no regard for their skin. It's positively shocking to see how they run about now. I blame the war."

"You should see the heathen in Namibia. Practically naked they are. No shame at all. Dark as chocolate."

"Really, Rufus! Must you dredge up these awful subjects?"

"My apologies." He raised his glass to no one in particular and took a large drink of his champagne.

"Linley!" Amelie suddenly called out. "Not so close to the bluff. Come here!"

"I'll go fetch him!" Miss Simms stood up quickly. She was wearing a flowing sort of dress with a cream crocheted lace overlay, which Henrietta could only describe as Bohemian, accompanied by a crocheted scarf that very prettily held her dark bobbed hair in place. It was certainly not the attire typically expected on an English afternoon picnic, but a concoction that perhaps a starlet might don. Regardless, Miss Simms pulled it off nicely.

"I'll come, too," Phineas added, eagerly following her.

In only the short time they had been here, Henrietta had observed a certain mild attraction perhaps between the two, despite the fact that Miss Simms was several years senior to the young Beaufort. She watched as Phineas caught up to Miss Simms and the two of them began to play a little game of chase with Linley, who squealed with delight.

"Will you be needing anything more, sir?" Jeremiah asked of Wallace, who lay now with his eyes closed.

"No, that will be all for now, Jeremiah. Thank you."

"Very good, sir." The servant made his way across to the grove where the carriages were parked and sat down heavily on a stump next to Dick.

"I say, Wallace," Uncle Rufus said, reaching for another slice of lemon cake, "I wouldn't stand for that impertinence if I were you. Shows weakness."

"What impertinence would that be, Uncle?" Wallace asked wearily from where he lay, his eyes still closed.

"Why, the servants addressing you as 'sir.' You are Lord Linley now, and they should address you as such."

"This is true," Lady Linley said querulously. "I hadn't thought. He's right, you know, Wallace."

"I don't care two figs what they call me. And anyway, I'm not Lord Linley. That was my father's title. Or Linley's. Not mine."

"Wallace!" Lady Linley scolded. "Why must you always be so cross. It does tire one so."

"Well, I'm very sorry, Mother, but I'm simply being true to my beliefs."

"Well, sometimes beliefs can be wrong—" she broke off, then, when a little cry was heard coming from the direction of the bluff.

Everyone quickly turned to see Miss Simms sitting upright in the tall grass, her face flushed as she held her ankle.

"Dear Evie!" cried Lady Linley, stretching to see better. "Are you hurt?"

Clive rose immediately from the blanket and went over to where Phineas was trying to help her stand. Little Linley stood a few paces off, watching the drama, a finger in his mouth. Wallace, meanwhile, did not move at all, except to put his hat over his face, apparently having had enough of the sun himself.

"Wallace!" Lady Linley scolded. "Go see if she's all right! How can you just lay there like some sort of cad?"

"I'm sure she's fine, Mother. She's always doing this sort of thing," he said through his hat. "She loves melodrama. Surely you have perceived that by now. And anyway, I'm sure that between the two of them, Clive and Phineas are more than capable of sorting her out."

"My word!" Lady Linley blustered. "The phrases you come up with! 'Sorting her out'? I'm glad your father is not alive to witness such vulgarity!" Lady Linley quarreled. "Evie, dear!" she called. "Are you hurt? What happened? Henrietta, help me up."

"No, Lady Linley," Evie called. She was standing now, supported by Clive and Phineas, though when she attempted to walk, her leg buckled. "I'm afraid I've been rather stupid. I think I've sprained my ankle!"

"Oh, dear!" Lady Linley exclaimed. "Are you sure it isn't broken? We'll need to fetch Dr. Graham right away."

"It isn't broken," Clive called. "It's just a sprain. But she should go back to the house."

Wallace rose up on his elbows, suddenly interested. "Surely that's not necessary, is it? We've only just arrived."

"I'm sorry to be such a nuisance," Miss Simms said prettily. "I wouldn't worry." She tried to take a step on her own, which resulted in a little cry of pain.

Clive then bent and scooped Miss Simms up in his arms, which caused her to let out another charming little scream, after which she very snugly wrapped her arms around Clive's neck. Something inside of Henrietta niggled. "I'll take her back," Clive grunted, carrying her toward the wagons.

"No, let me! I insist," Phineas exclaimed, his face beet red as he tried to dart in front of Clive like an annoying puppy. Wallace slowly got to his feet with the aid of his walking stick and stood watching, his hands on his hips, as Clive deposited the young woman into the front seat of the wagon.

Jeremiah appeared now from somewhere deeper in the woods, flicking what looked to be a cigarette. "What's happened, sir?" he asked Clive worriedly as he hurried toward the wagon.

"Miss Simms has injured her ankle and must return to the house."

"Certainly, sir." Jeremiah went to retrieve his jacket, which he had hung on a low branch. Dick accordingly scrambled to retrieve one of the horses, both of which were leisurely ripping up large tufts of grass and methodically chewing them. With effort, Dick pulled the large gray from his feast and led him back to the wagon and began to hurriedly hitch him.

Before either Jeremiah or Clive could climb up into the driver's seat, however, Phineas beat them to it and snatched the reins. "I'll take her," he announced, beaming at his victory.

"Perhaps we should all go?" Lady Linley called out. "Haven't we had enough of sitting on the damp ground?"

"No, Mother, we were to make a morning of it," Wallace snapped, angrily running his hand through his thin hair.

"I'm dreadfully sorry," Miss Simms apologized, though her tone had a certain level of gaiety to it, Henrietta thought, considering she was apparently in pain. "I've ruined it for everyone."

"Nonsense," Lady Linley declared. "You haven't ruined a thing, my dear. Of course, you should return. We all should, before it rains. It's only Wallace's pigheadedness that keeps us out of doors. We'll all catch our deaths."

Wallace pinched the bridge of his nose.

"And how are we all going to fit into one wagon?" Lady Linley continued. "Some of us should go now. Poor Evie shouldn't be unchaperoned anyway, riding along alone with Mr. Beaufort."

"Mother, it's 1936," Wallace said disgustedly. "Evie doesn't need a chaperone. Besides, it's only Phineas."

"As soon as I deliver Miss Simms to the house, I'll return with the wagon," Phineas offered, ignoring Wallace's snide comment. "It won't take long; I promise."

"Go on, then," Wallace said, giving the horse a bit of a slap on the rump and jerking him into motion.

As the wagon began to roll forward, Miss Simms turned and waved at the group, most of whom were still sitting on the blankets. Henrietta followed the young woman's gaze and perceived that the last person she made eye contact with was Clive, who was still standing in the grove, his hands in his pockets as he watched them go.

Once the wagon rounded the bend, he and Wallace sauntered back to the picnic.

"Wallace, what's gotten into you?" Lady Linley scolded as Wallace flopped back down onto the blankets, which were exceedingly rumpled at this point. Jeremiah, having followed the two men, obsequiously tried to straighten them and then began repouring the champagne.

"I don't know what you mean, Mother," Wallace answered as he opened his arms to Linley, who was sitting close to Amelie now, a large strawberry clenched in his little hand. The boy popped it into his mouth and crawled across the blanket to his father.

"Yes, you do. There's something going on. You're acting very strangely," Lady Linley quipped, drawing herself up as best she could, considering the fact that she was propped up with cushions.

"Yes, Wallace, what are you up to?" Colonel Beaufort asked as he surveyed the remains of the picnic, looking, it would seem, for anything worth salvaging.

Wallace sighed. "All right. If you must know, there is an estate agent looking at the grounds this morning." He shot a knowing glance at Amelie.

"An estate agent?" Lady Linley twittered. "Whatever for?"

"He's showing the property to a prospective buyer, a Burmese man, as I understand," Wallace answered, depositing a kiss on Linley's head.

"A prospective buyer!" Lady Linley put her hand to her chest. "Of what?"

"The estate, of course, Mother. Or maybe part of it. I've explained this all before."

"You can't sell Castle Linley!" she declared, apparently forgetting any part of what Wallace might have previously related to her. "It's been in the family for generations. What would your father think? Oh, poor Montague," Lady Linley whimpered, putting a lacy gloved hand over her eyes. "If only you were here."

"Mother, I'm the last to cast blame, but it is exactly because of Father's mismanagement of the estate that we're in this predicament."

"How dare you!" Lady Linley's head shot back up instantly.

"I do dare, Mother," Wallace continued, apparently unphased by his mother's sudden show of wrath. "But as it happens, Mr. Arnold is merely showing the grounds, not the house."

"Aunt Margaret," Clive said gently, "I wouldn't worry. Nothing has been set in stone. But as you know, the taxes must be paid, and unfortunately, that means that some part of the estate will more than likely have to be sold. Or donated. Mr. Arnold is simply helping to weigh up the options."

"But didn't you just say he was bringing round a buyer? A Burmese man?"

"What, what?" Colonel Beaufort chortled from his corner of the blanket where he had, up until this moment, been studiously attacking a block of Wensleydale cheese. "Selling the estate to a Burmese, did you say? Bloody monstrous, that is. What is this country coming to? This is what we fought for in the trenches, in India, in Burma. For king and country! Not to come home and see it all being sold to the lowest bidder, and a dirty foreigner at that. What were we fighting for, then? We thought the enemy was out there somewhere in the Bushveld or the Rajasthan steppes, but they've found a different way to infiltrate us—by coming along, buying up our noble estates, and chopping them into bits! Does no one else see the insidiousness of this?"

"Uncle!" Wallace snarled. "Kindly hold your tongue. You forget that my wife is a 'foreigner,' as you say."

Colonel Beaufort looked abashed. "France is hardly a foreign land, is it? Of course, I didn't mean you, my dear," he said, lifting his hat to Amelie. "One has only to reference the Plantagenets."

"Do you really hate foreigners so very much?" Amelie asked quietly, though Henrietta heard a rare iciness in her voice.

"I suppose there are always exceptions, such as yourself, my dear," the colonel capitulated. "But as a rule, no, they are not to be trusted. Especially the Burmese. Very sneaky, they are."

"Rufus, really! You go too far!"

"I simply speak the truth, Margaret. You forget that I have seen much of the world and have had many experiences upon which to call. Experiences you, or any of the ladies present, I daresay, would naturally have no idea about." He munched another piece of cheese. "You forget your sheltered state," he said, looking at each of the ladies in turn. Henrietta bit back a smile at the sheer outrageousness of the old man's comment, but Amelie's face, she quickly noticed, was flushed a deep red.

Wallace, too, seemed to have noticed it. "Women of Mother's generation may have been sheltered, Uncle, but you forget that Amelie was a nurse in the Great War. She, too, has seen her share of bloodshed and misery. Atrocities committed by both sides. She is far from sheltered. Nor is Henrietta. I'm sure—"

"Are we going to fly my kite, Papa?" Linley asked now in his little voice as he looked up at Wallace. Wallace stared at him for a moment as if he had forgotten he was holding the child.

"Now, there's an idea, Nipper. Why not?" Wallace's angry expression melted into a weary smile as he lifted Linley out of his lap, propping him up on his little legs, and got to his feet as well, again with the aid of his stick. "Where is the kite?" he asked, looking around at the ground and then at Amelie.

"It's in the wagon," she answered vaguely, looking toward the far grove. "Oh, no! It was in the other wagon. Linley, dear, I'm afraid it might be gone."

The little boy's face instantly fell. "But, Papa, you promised!" Linley whined, his lower lip quivering.

"I'm sorry, Linley," Wallace said, rubbing the boy's head. "We'll fly it another day."

"But, Papa!"

"Linley," Amelie urged gently, "we will do it later. Zere is nothing we can do. The wagon will be back shortly."

Linley did not answer back, but little tears were welling in his eyes. Henrietta's heart broke for the little boy, and she was about to rise and offer to entertain him, when Colonel Beaufort got heavily to his feet. "I'll go fetch it."

"No, Colonel," Amelie exclaimed, tenting her hand over her eyes as she looked up at him. "It is not necessary. Phineas will be back soon. There is no need."

Colonel Beaufort patted his stomach roughly. "I don't mind walking. All that cheese, you see. Do me good. Anyway, I fancy a walk.

Phineas hasn't the foggiest notion of how to drive a wagon. I daresay he'll have run aground somewhere along the way, or he'll be going so slowly that I'll catch up to them."

"Rufus!" Lady Linley exclaimed. "Don't go. It's going to rain soon!"

Colonel Beaufort looked at the sky, which did seem to be clouding over. "Well, Margaret, it's not the first time I've been rained on. Reminds me of the time we were in Jabalpur. Hit by the monsoons, we were. Now *that* was rain." The colonel raised his hat to them and then turned down the path while Linley sank into the tall grass, his legs crossed under him, as if to wait.

Lady Linley let out a deep breath. "He never listens, you know. Never did when we were children. Father was always displeased. He'll catch his death," she said, nodding toward the direction he had disappeared. "We should have all simply gone back. Look; there are clouds on the horizon. I said it was going to rain, but I'm never listened to."

"That isn't true," Wallace said, lowering himself unto the blankets again, this time next to Amelie, who had picked Alcott up out of his basket and was holding him now. "Daily you insist on any number of things, which we oblige you."

"Honestly, Wallace. You are most unkind today," she sniffed. "I thought things might be different after Clive and Henrietta arrived, but they are not. You are still boorish, and Clive has not helped at all."

Clive, who had been gazing at Henrietta, abruptly turned his head toward the old lady. "I'm sorry, Aunt, if I've been remiss," he said with sincere puzzlement.

Before Lady Linley could respond, however, big drops began to fall on the little party, and the elderly lady uttered a little cry of dismay.

"You see?" She was desperately trying to huddle under her parasol. "I was right!"

Clive jumped up and immediately helped the older woman to her feet, while Jeremiah came running over in an attempt to pack up the picnic. Against proper form, Henrietta helped him, while Wallace quickly took Linley's hand and led him to the wagon, Amelie following with Alcott. One by one, the party climbed into the wagon while Dick hurried to hitch the horse and Jeremiah loaded the provisions, after which he slung himself up onto the seat beside Dick. Only Clive and Henrietta were left without.

"Here, Henrietta," Wallace said, standing awkwardly without his cane. "You take my seat. I'll walk back with Clive."

"Oh, no, Wallace! You stay with Amelie and the boys. I want to walk. Honestly. Besides, it's letting up a little now." Indeed, the rain had stopped as suddenly as it had started, the sun having broken free from the cloud it was hovering behind and shining brightly now. Fat droplets glistened on each blade of grass.

"Are you sure?" Wallace asked, looking at Clive now, who gave him a nod.

"Right." Wallace sat back down with a grunt.

"Wallace! You can't leave a lady behind!" Lady Linley quipped.

"That's what she wants, Mother. Or do you think she doesn't know her own mind? Walk on," he called to Dick. The servant gave a quick stray look back and then flicked the reins against the horse's behind, lurching the cart and its passengers abruptly forward.

Chapter 5

"Are you sure you want to walk?" Clive asked, glancing at the sky. Despite the fact that sun was shining, more dark clouds threatened on the horizon.

"Goodness, yes. I need a respite. I don't know what is worse, listening to Colonel Beaufort's boorish retellings of foreign wars or Wallace and Lady Linley's squabbling."

"Yes, Aunt Margaret seems unusually antagonistic toward him lately. Perhaps it is her grief."

Henrietta remained silent and pulled the head off a pretty yellow wildflower as they began to walk along the track of flattened grass left by the wagon wheels. "I'm not sure what we're doing here, Clive. I mean, it's lovely and all," she gestured back toward the bluff, "but I'm not sure why Wallace was so eager for us to come."

"I think he wants my blessing or some such thing," Clive mused.

"About the estate, you mean?'

"Yes."

Henrietta reflected for a few moments. "I don't mean to be old-fashioned," she said finally, sticking the wildflower in her hair just above her ear, "but I can't help but be on Lady Linley's side in all of this. I would hate for the house to be torn down and all of this poured over with concrete." She gestured at the field they were walking through. "It seems a sin somehow. Don't you think?"

Clive pursed his lips. "Now you sound like Colonel Beaufort or Lady Linley herself, hearkening back to the way things used to be. I suppose I agree to a certain extent, but on the other hand, there are those who think that one family owning all of this while the poor starve is a sin. An obscene one."

"Now *you* sound like Wallace." She brushed the top of the tall grass, which rose nearly to her waist, dispensing the tiny droplets that had collected to the ground below.

Clive gave a little laugh. "I don't mean to. But you know that even *I* struggled with taking over Highbury for the very same reason. You could say that I'm more of a coward than Wallace in having agreed to shoulder the responsibility, propagate the status quo, instead of standing up for my ideals as Wallace is doing. I admire him in many ways. I think Linley would have approved. Come, this way," he said, leading her off the main track into a small copse to the left of the road.

"From what I know about Linley, he would *not* have approved." Henrietta carefully stepped over the root of a tree, a part of it bulging out of the ground. "He would have done his duty, whatever his private feelings were. And you're not to compare yourself to Wallace. It's a different situation altogether."

"I'm not sure it is." He pulled a thin branch out of her way and held it as she passed through.

"Where are we going?" Henrietta asked, looking around now at the place Clive was leading. "This isn't the way, is it?"

"It's a shortcut."

Henrietta tromped along after Clive. Now that they were deeper into the woods, the ground was still dry. She knew she should probably let the topic drop, but she just couldn't. "Wallace likes to pride himself on his high ideals," she called out to Clive, "and yet he never stops to consider who suffers for them."

"What do you mean?"

"He insisted on marrying Amelie, a penniless French nurse, when he knew very well that the estate's existence depended on him marrying money. Who suffers for that decision? Not him! But some, including Lady Linley, perhaps in her heart of hearts, might say it drove Lord Linley to his grave. And now that the estate is indeed bankrupt, or very nearly will be, and he's forced to sell something or donate it, he is angry that Lady Linley, or anyone else, is upset by it. He's like a spoiled child that wants his way and then gets angry when the adults around him aren't pleased."

"My!" Clive said, turning and looking at her appreciatively. "You've pegged Wallace well enough. He was that way even as a child. Always complaining of being the victim. Can't say I entirely blame him. Linley was Uncle's favorite, and nothing Wallace did ever measured up. I could see that early on. Aunt Margaret spoiled him as a way to make up for it perhaps, which didn't serve him well." Clive continued walking. "I feel sorry for him, actually. The shipwreck of Linley is really not his doing. As Wallace mentioned, rather crassly, I'll admit, it was Uncle Montague's mismanagement of the estate, or probably *his* father's before him, that has brought it to its present state of insolvency. Wallace has been gifted a dying horse, and it's not entirely fair to blame him."

"I'm not blaming him for the estate's bankruptcy. I'm blaming him for his childish way of handling it. And him railing against having servants and all of that . . . that's fine for him, but what about poor Amelie?"

"Well, darling, I agree, but most women manage to have children without the aid of servants."

"Yes, but not when they are expected to exist within this realm. For the children to be perfectly dressed and perfectly mannered and perfectly schooled? It would be different if they were on a farm, running about and getting dirty and helping with the chores."

"Darling, you sound like a socialist yourself now. Very idealistic."

"All I'm saying is that Wallace needs to choose the world he wishes to live in and then agree to live by whatever rules exist in that world.

By living in luxury but constantly railing against it, he only makes things worse for those he portends to love. It's a cheap way to deal with his own guilt. *He's* the coward." Henrietta paused, looking around. "Where are we? I think we've lost the trail. I'm sure we didn't pass this on the way."

"Do you not recognize it?" he asked, nodding toward the little brook that ran off to the right.

Suddenly it dawned on her that they were indeed in the fairy bower. "Clive!"

He took her hands in his and, shifting his weight onto one foot on the uneven ground, kissed her. She thought it was to be one kiss, but he continued, his arousal evident. He wrapped his arms around her, pulling her closer.

"Clive!" she exclaimed, breaking their kiss. "You can't possibly be serious."

"But, darling, I am. I made a promise." He bent to kiss her neck.

"I release you from it," she said, trying to push him away.

"We might never get this chance again," he mumbled, kissing her hair, her cheek, her ear. "And weren't you just talking about breaking the rules? It's something you've done a time or two."

"Inspector, really!" She let out a little laugh at the absurdity of the situation.

Ignoring it, he kissed her lips again, deeply this time, until she began to respond despite herself. She was wildly attracted to him and ran her hands down his back, feeling his muscles stiffen under her touch. He began kissing her neck, then, and she took the opportunity to look nervously around. *Did he really mean to make love to her here in the woods?* Despite the extreme impropriety, she felt unexpectedly aroused. As if in answer to her thoughts, he began roughly unbuckling his belt.

"Clive!" She let out another laugh and stepped away from him, inadvertently backing herself up against a tree. She looked at him coyly.

"Ah, just where I want you," he said with a grin, moving toward her and bracing himself against the broad tree trunk with an arm on either side of her.

"You naughty thing!" She ran a finger along his jawline.

He stared intently at her, his eyes seductive and knowing, as he reached down and began lifting her skirt. She let out a little cry of surprise.

He gently took her face in his hands, then, and kissed her again, pressing her up against the tree as he did so. The tip of his tongue found hers, electrifying her, and the touch of his hands softly tracing the side of her breasts resulted in a corresponding pull in her groin.

"Pretend I'm a woodsman, and I've come upon you, a fair maiden, and now I mean to have my way with you," he said huskily between kisses.

She found his proposal strangely attractive. "All right, squire," she whispered into his ear and then kissed his stubbled cheek and then his Adam's apple, loosening his tie as she did so. "If you must." She ran her hands along his buttocks.

Clive groaned and sank to his knees, pulling her with him.

"This will positively ruin my dress." She looked around at the ground. She had chosen a lavender chiffon with a tiny floral print for today, thinking it would be perfect for an English picnic.

"I'll buy you a new one," he said breathlessly between kisses, but then shrugged out of his jacket and spread it awkwardly behind her.

"You always say that, and then you never do."

Henrietta gave one more furtive look around and then locked eyes with Clive and slowly laid down on his jacket, her heart racing. Clive knelt in front of her, his trousers undone and his eyes fraught with longing. His face shifted slightly, then, as he stared at her. "God, Henrietta, you are so lovely. So beautiful."

Henrietta returned his look of love and slowly she pulled up her skirt, exposing her stockinged legs and just a bit of her underthings. "Come on, then, squire, don't keep this maiden waiting. Or I'll have to call upon the river god to strike you down."

Her invitation was apparently all he needed. He bent and kissed her then, easing himself down upon her. He continued kissing her and ran a hand up her inner thigh, which caused her to moan. His hands moved to her breasts then, and knowing from past experience that he would probably rip her dress if she didn't assist him, she quickly undid her buttons. As soon as she finished, he pulled her dress off her shoulders and kissed each of them and then her chest. His hands found their way back to her breasts, now bare, and he began to again finger them until she let out a little moan. He kissed her, his tongue fully exploring hers as he pulled her underthings down to her knees and began caressing her until she began to pant and mew, at which point he yanked them off completely. Freed of any constriction, she opened fully to him, enjoying his resultant look of excitement.

Without waiting any longer, he entered her, his forearms balanced on the ground near her head, his fingers entwined in her hair as he began to thrust, slowly at first, then with less control. She could feel herself losing control as well, and at the verge of her climax, she suddenly opened her eyes and drank in the beauty of the dappled sun in the green canopy above her, and her mind exploded in an ecstasy of color and light as her body shuddered. Clive arched his back and, with one final thrust, exploded inside of her with a loud guttural cry. He remained on top of her, breathing heavily for several moments before finally rolling off.

"Oh, Henrietta," Clive said breathlessly. "I love you. God, I love you. I can die happy now."

"Clive!" Her tone was one of amusement. "Don't say that. Rescind it!"

"Oh, all right, darling," he said raggedly. "I rescind it, but it's true."

They lay there in silence, then, side by side. Clive took her hand and laced his fingers through hers.

"Isn't there something wrong with wanting to pervert what was a place of innocence for you?" she said, coyly looking over at him now.

"I'd hardly call making love to my wife a perversion." He lifted her hand to his lips and kissed it. "And it's more than a place of magic than innocence, if you believe in all that sort of thing."

"Inspector Howard! Surely not!"

Clive turned to her and, raising himself up on his elbow, traced the side of her face with his finger. "All right, perhaps not magic, but I believe in *you*," he said seriously. "And that's all I need."

Henrietta stared at him, allowing herself to soak up the love she saw in his lovely hazel eyes, so warm and inviting for her alone. To everyone else, he came across as cold and almost hardened. In that way, he was more like Wallace than he knew.

"I'm pretty sure that's sacrilegious," she said with a mischievous grin. A drop of rain fell directly between her eyes then, and she blinked. It was followed by another and then another. She sat up. "See? This is proof. God's punishing you for your sacrilege."

"I will endure any punishment as long as I'm with you."

"Come on." She got to her feet and began to dress. "We should hurry."

Clive slowly stood up beside her and began languidly stuffing his shirt back into his trousers. "Let's just wait here until the rain stops. We're relatively protected." He picked up his jacket off the ground and tried to hold it over her as a form of shelter.

Henrietta stepped out from under it. She felt restless and weirdly invigorated. "No! Let's run. I feel like running; don't you?" She knew that the last thing he would want to do would be to run in the rain, but she couldn't help herself. It came out before she could think.

He looked at her intently now, his eyes bright with love. "Did I mention that I love you?" he asked with a broad grin as he took her hand and slung his jacket over his shoulder with the other.

"Yes, I think you have. Once or twice."

"Come on, then; let's run!"

Chapter 6

Having run out of people and things to pray for, Melody Merriweather let out a sad little sigh. The prayers for the dead—and for the living, for that matter—seemed to go on forever, and, already bored of them, she tried to instead pass the time by counting the tiny alcoves carved into the far wall, which supposedly contained ancient relics of the saints: a small fingerbone of St. Cuthbert, a hair of St. Dymphna, even a tiny piece of the true Cross. She had already examined them all, both horrified and fascinated by the macabre display of human remains (whether they were really from the saints or not), but like everything else in life, it seemed, she quickly tired of it and gave up counting.

The light where she knelt in the back of the chapel of Mt. Carmel in Dubuque, Iowa, was dim, the only illumination being whatever light filtered in through the stained-glass windows that ran all the way around the top of the circular structure and the candles, which seemed paltry by comparison, flickering on the altar. Melody, still masquerading as Elsie Von Harmon, was unsure any longer if it was night or morning and simply hoped that by this time, Elsie was no longer Elsie *Von Harmon*, but was in fact Elsie *Stockel*.

Melody had no way of knowing, of course, if Elsie's elopement had really come off, as Elsie wasn't even aware that her friend was here. Melody wondered if Elsie had perhaps since sent her a letter, but if she had, she would have mailed it to Mundelein or perhaps to her parents' home in Wisconsin. Melody hoped that when Elsie *did* eventually discover what she had done that she wouldn't be angry. *But why would she be?* Melody considered. After all, she had done it to *help* Elsie, to buy her some time to get away. But, if she were being perfectly truthful, she had also done it for the adventure, having been just a trifle jealous of her friend's daring deed. If nothing else, it would be good for a laugh, as at any rate, the whole thing was simply too funny for words!

Melody had spontaneously come up with the idea of taking Elsie's place at Mt. Carmel—since no one there yet knew what Elsie looked like—and had suggested it to Elsie as they said a hurried good-bye at Union Station before Elsie boarded the train bound for Omaha with Gunther and Anna. Elsie had been resistant to the idea, saying that she couldn't possibly deceive Sr. Bernard, who had taken her under her wing from the very beginning and had made all the arrangements for Elsie to begin studies to become a nun at the motherhouse in Dubuque. It was bad enough, Elsie had said, that she was thwarting Sr. Bernard's efforts by running away with Gunther without adding a further deception into the mix. Instead, Elsie had insisted on quickly writing a note for Sr. Bernard in an attempt to explain that she had changed her mind about becoming a nun and begged her forgiveness. Elsie had given the note to Melody and charged her with delivering it to Sr. Bernard, but Melody, deciding in the spur of the moment to take matters into her own hands, had shockingly crumpled the confession and thrown it away as soon as Elsie was out of sight.

Melody had then hurried back to Mundelein and had promptly written her *own* letter, addressed not to Sr. Bernard, but to her parents in Merriweather, Wisconsin, telling them that she had failed her summer classes (a lie—they were, in fact, still in session, and she was averaging a B+ in both) and that she was therefore required to stay in Chicago longer than she had originally intended. Then, having quickly mailed it, she went to Sr. Bernard's office on the second floor of Mundelein's Skyscraper and had informed the school's principal that she needed to withdraw from her summer classes and urgently return home for the funeral of a great aunt. That was the easy part. The harder part had been to explain why Elsie had also needed to suddenly leave campus, which Elsie's last-minute note would have explained. Melody had to think quickly.

"She had to go home to Palmer Square," Melody blurted. "She asked me to tell you."

"Oh?" Sr. Bernard seemed genuinely concerned. "Is something wrong?"

"She . . . it's her mother. She has the influenza. And so does her little brother and sister," she quickly added. "She went to help them."

"Was that wise?" Sr. Bernard murmured almost to herself. "Considering she is to leave soon?"

"Yes! I did tell her that," Melody lied further, surprised by how easy it was. "But she insisted. You know how she is."

"Well, how will she get her things?"

Melody squirmed for a moment, then had a sudden burst of inspiration. "I said I'd pack for her! And then one of her servants is coming to pick everything up."

"I see." Sr. Bernard folded her arms neatly under her habit, a sign which Melody knew was not a good one.

"She . . . she said to tell you good-bye and thanks for everything and that she'll write to you when she gets to Dubuque."

"That's unfortunate," Sr. Bernard said slowly. "I would have liked to give her my blessing. And I had several instructions for her. Perhaps I should go and visit her and her mother." One eyebrow was raised now.

"Oh, no, Sister! They are all quite . . . quite contagious," Melody said hurriedly.

Sr. Bernard did not say anything but simply stared at her in such a way that Melody was sure she could see through the ruse. Finally, she spoke. "Well, safe travels back to Wisconsin, then, Melody. Please give my condolences to your family. We will see you for the autumn semester."

Flooded with relief, Melody had practically flown back to Philomena Hall to the room she had up until that very morning shared with Elsie and had hurriedly begun to pack her things. She would have loved to confide the whole of the prank to her very best friend (besides Elsie, of course), but Cynthia Forsythe had already returned home for the summer. Well, Melody thought as she gathered up the last of her things and surveyed their little room, she would have to tell her later. It would be a scream, and Cynthia would laugh for days! Melody hailed a cab on Sheridan and arrived at Union Station in plenty of time to collect the ticket waiting for Elsie at will call and to jump on board the train bound for Galena, Illinois, which was the end of that particular line and likewise the closest stop to Dubuque.

She was on pins and needles for the entire trip, expecting to be found out at any moment, and was almost, truth be told, a little disappointed when she was not. The clerk behind the counter at the station had not suspected anything, if the sleepy way he had pushed the ticket across the counter to her was any indication, nor had the train conductor, who methodically punched her ticket with barely a second glance. Even the other passengers seemed unaware of how hard her heart was beating, sedate as they all were, reading newspapers or sleepily looking out the window at the cornfields rolling by.

Finally, after almost an hour of sitting pertly on the rocking train, looking anxiously around her, Melody finally began to relax herself, her racing adrenaline eventually dying down enough for her to doze off. It immediately picked back up again, though, once the train arrived at Galena. As her fellow passengers began to gather their things against the screeching of the train whistle, Melody took a deep breath and tried to remember what a brilliant actress she was, convincing herself that she could easily play this part. Gingerly, she stepped off the train and, after looking up and down the platform, eventually spotted a youngish-looking nun at the far end. Sr. Jerome, as she discovered the nun was called, greeted her politely as "Miss Von Harmon" and had then helped her to carry her things to the waiting car. Her heart pounding in her chest, Melody wasn't sure whether to laugh or scream.

Sr. Jerome, while seemingly friendly, was not overly talkative as she drove Melody across the Mississippi to Mt. Carmel. Melody took her cue and tried to amuse herself by looking out the window instead of chatting, which she normally spent an inordinate amount of time doing, even more so when she was nervous. Alternately, she gripped her hands in her lap and made herself focus on the old river town of Dubuque, through which they were passing, and the hilly terrain surrounding it. It was not so unlike her hometown of Merriweather, she observed, though Merriweather was certainly much smaller. She was not prepared, however, for the beauty of the motherhouse of the Sisters of the Blessed Virgin Mary when it came into view, perched as it was atop the bluffs overlooking the Mississippi glistening below.

Sr. Jerome pulled the car into a circular drive and came to a stop in front of an old redbrick building with "A.D. 1889" chiseled into the lintel above the main doors. An older nun was standing there, her hands folded neatly under her habit, apparently waiting for her, her black-and-white veil billowing out behind her. As she gingerly stepped out of the car, Melody again half expected to be found out then and there, so much so that she had her witty excuse waiting on the tip of her tongue. The nun surprised her, however, by instead greeting her with an embrace and warm smile.

"Hello, Elsie, my child," the woman said kindly. Her face was a sea of wrinkles held at bay by the tightness of her wimple. "I'm Sister Mary Magdalen."

Melody managed an uncomfortable smile.

"Sister Bernard wrote and told us all about you." Sr. Magdalen looked her over carefully. "I was somehow expecting something different," she mused.

Melody bit her lip. "I hope I'm not a disappointment, Sister."

"Not at all, my child. You're here now. That's all that matters. How was your journey?" she asked, gently putting her arm around Melody's shoulder.

"Fine, Sister." Melody swallowed hard. This was going to be harder than she thought.

Sr. Magdalen led her inside and proceeded to give her a brief tour of the convent, promising a more extensive one later, and eventually deposited her in a little bedroom in the dormitory wing. It was very sparsely furnished with just a bed, a tiny dresser, and a small chair—hard and straight like those in a schoolroom. The only ornamentation, besides a crucifix, of course, was a small vase of daisies on the dresser.

"Those are from Sister Cecelia," Sr. Magdalen said, nodding at them. "She's in charge of all the new recruits. You will meet her later. This room is only for sleeping," she explained, gesturing toward the bed. "You will spend the majority of your time studying in class or the library, or praying in the chapel, or working at whatever daily chores you're assigned. You'll find your novitiate's habit in the closet, there." Sr. Magdalen tilted her head. "Put it on and come down to the refectory for dinner at five sharp." Melody looked around the room forlornly. It certainly lacked the charm of the room she had shared with Elsie back in Philomena Hall, the whole of which had once upon a time been one of the glittering mansions that lined Lake Michigan.

Almost as if she could read her mind, Sr. Magdalen spoke, "Doubtless everything is strange and new now, Elsie, but you will find a home here amongst us. We sincerely hope that you will be happy in this life you have chosen." She gave her a final encouraging smile and left.

Melody felt a tug of guilt. She hadn't expected everyone to be so kind. She walked the few steps from the bed to the window and was disappointed that her view was of the circular drive and not of the Mississippi, but she supposed that made sense. Those rooms with the nicer views were probably for the higher-up nuns, or whatever they were called. She let out a little sigh and decided she needed to make the best of it. It would certainly make the most delicious story when she got back to Mundelein, and for a few moments she allowed herself to imagine telling the tale back in the cozy front parlor of Philomena Hall where she frequently held court, her throne being the cushioned window seat facing Lake Michigan and her subjects being the usual motley assortment, namely Cynthia, Charlie McAllister, and, of course, Douglas Novak, whom she suspected she might be a little bit in love with and whom, she felt certain, just might be equally smitten.

Melody pulled open the tiny closet to reveal the novitiate's habit she was supposed to wear and laughed out loud as she held it up. It was an absolute scream! Quickly, she undressed and slipped on the simple black dress and, not knowing what to do with the white rope that was draped over the hanger, tied it around her waist. Then she pinned the tiny veil on her head. She twirled slightly, wishing the gang could see her! She looked around for a mirror and was shocked to find none at all! Well, that made sense, she supposed—vanity, and all that—but how on earth was she supposed to get dressed each morning without a mirror?

Melody quickly unpacked, which didn't take long, and decided to while away the time before dinner by flipping through the *Vogue* and *Look* magazines she had fortunately brought with her. Finally, when she could no longer stand the boredom, not to mention her hunger pains, she emerged from her room and happily found several other young women in the hallway, apparently enroute to dinner. They said hello to her and welcomed her, but beyond that they did not say much more as they all filed silently down the long hallway toward the refectory. Once there, Melody observed that they were not allowed to choose their seats but were expected to fill in the rows of tables as they arrived.

The meal placed before Melody was very simple but hearty. It was a type of beef stew, she discerned, with a slice of bread, a very small pat of butter, a square of gelatin, and water. Melody was normally not overly fond of beef stew, but she ate it anyway, as she was absolutely famished, though the beef, she observed, was laced with rather too much gristle for her liking.

After dinner, the novitiates filed into the chapel, where they spent an hour saying the Divine Office, after which they were released to their rooms, presumably to sleep. Melody was shocked by this, as it was only nine o'clock and practically still light out, but she went back to her room anyway, her few stray efforts to engage some of the girls in conversation failing outright. No one took her up on her suggestion that they walk the grounds or perhaps sit up and chat. They all looked at her curiously and slightly disapprovingly, causing Melody to fear that she may have blown her cover.

Thus, she sadly had no choice but to slowly return to her room, the only advantage of which was that she could shake off her ludicrous costume and instead put on her pajamas, which consisted of a pink silk nightgown, complete with matching sleep mask and fluffy slippers. She had discovered a white cotton nightgown neatly folded in the top drawer of the dresser, but after holding it up, she tossed it back into the drawer with a snort of disgust. She wouldn't be caught dead in such a horribly old-fashioned thing, though it *did* remind her of what Elsie usually wore to bed. She was such a fuddy-duddy! But not anymore, Melody thought thrillingly. By now, shy old Elsie must have indeed done "the business," and surely she no longer wore long cotton nightgowns to bed!

Arrayed in her pink silk, Melody slipped between the stiff cotton sheets. For a moment she worried about what would happen if there was a fire, for example—that she would be discovered . . . But, she reasoned as she tried to fluff her very flat pillow, she would take her chances. If there *was* a fire, she concluded, what one novitiate was wearing to bed would hardly be anyone's main concern. She closed her eyes, trying to imagine Elsie and Gunther's romantic escapade, and finally fell asleep.

Fire must have been on her mind, however, because when she heard a loud knock on her door at midnight, she let out a little scream and tried to determine if she indeed smelled smoke as she pulled off her sleep mask and stumbled to the door.

Upon opening it, she did not see the random pandemonium she half expected, but instead simply saw the girl from next door, whose name she was pretty sure was Millicent. The girl stood, fully dressed in her habit, and looked Melody up and down with a vague expression of horror while several other girls sleepily filed down the hallway behind her.

"What is it?" Melody asked, wishing she had put on her silk robe.

"What are you doing still in your night things?" Millicent exclaimed.

Melody was confused. *Was it morning already? But why was it so dark?* "What time is it?"

"It's midnight. We're expected in the chapel. You have to get dressed, quickly!" she hissed.

"For what? Did something happen?" Melody asked, looking up and down the hallway for some other sign of disaster.

"No, it's the Liturgy of Hours. We pray through the night. Did the sisters at Mundelein not do this?" Her brow was furrowed in disapproval. "Hurry," she said and bustled down the already deserted hall.

Melody shut the door with a groan and pulled off her nightgown and dressed as quickly as she could. By the time she reached the chapel, prayers had already begun. She glanced nervously at Sr. Mary Magdalen, who frowned at her as she slipped into a pew at the back, disheveled and bleary. The prayers seemed to drone on and on, and Melody was barely able to stay awake. All she could do was wonder why anyone thought this was conducive to closeness to God. She had never felt further from Him. She couldn't help dozing off, though the girl next to her perpetually nudged her, which was irritating. Didn't she realize she was *trying* to go to sleep? She tried to give the girl what she hoped was a meaningful scowl, but the girl did not look at her.

Finally, God be praised, the service was over, and the girls were allowed to file back to their rooms. Melody decided not to waste time changing back into her nightgown, a decision she was grateful to have made when another loud knock was heard on the door not two hours later.

It was Millicent again, who this time seemed at least a little impressed that Melody was already dressed, though she reached out and adjusted Melody's veil, which had slid nearly off her head from her sleeping on it.

"Elsie, this will never do," the girl said, trying to hurriedly re-pin it. "It will have to be ironed in the morning. "Don't you know you're supposed to set the alarm clock? We can't be banging on your door every two hours."

"Every two hours?" Melody mumbled, suddenly horrified.

"Yes, come on. Are you sure the nuns at Mundelein did not do this? How long were you in the novitiate there? Come on; hurry!"

Millicent disappeared down the hallway, then, and Melody followed, wondering how she would ever survive this and hoping bitterly that Elsie would someday realize the great lengths she had gone to help her.

Melody squeezed her hands together now in yet another attempt to stay awake, but it was no use. She was so very tired! She resorted to pinching herself on the hand, trying to dig deep with her fingernails, but even that didn't seem to have an effect. Finally, she decided to simply give in, to allow herself to fall asleep as she knelt. What did it matter if anyone noticed? Just as she closed her eyes, however, the girls around her all rose. As disappointed as she was that her proposed little nap was over before it had begun, she was buoyed up by the prospect of a proper sleep, or even a sliver of sleep, in her bed in her little cell, as she was calling it now.

Blearily, she filed out of her pew, but before she even passed through the main chapel doors, Sr. Magdalen stopped her by touching her on the arm.

"Elsie, you are on kitchen duty this morning," she said gently.

"Kitchen duty?" Melody thought she might cry.

"Yes, did Sister Cecelia not tell you?"

Melody felt tears well up in her eyes. A protest rose to her lips, but she found she couldn't speak at all for the aching in her throat. She couldn't possibly endure this any longer. The joke had gone on long enough, she decided, and she would simply have to confess.

Chapter 7

When Henrietta and Clive arrived back at Castle Linley, dripping wet and breathless, they were surprised when no servant greeted them at the door.

"Hello?" Henrietta called to no one in particular as Clive helped her out of his jacket, which he had insisted she wear when the sky had opened up and unleashed a sudden downpour. They had already reached the estate lawns by that point, but still they had carried on running, Henrietta shrieking as she sloshed through puddles, and Clive trying—not very hard, she could tell—to catch her, succumbing to a rare fit of laughter as he ran.

"Hello?" Clive called, holding the drenched coat away from his body. His wet shirt stuck to his skin in the most delicious way, revealing his muscled body beneath, though the little puddle forming under him was somewhat comical. "Where is everyone?"

A noise was finally heard from somewhere deeper down the hall, and Phineas suddenly appeared. Spotting them, he hurried over, a wide grin across his face. "I say, you've missed it all!"

"Missed what?" Clive said, finally tossing the wet jacket on the tiled floor.

"The ghost, that's what! Apparently, he—if it is a *he*—has struck again. The house is in an uproar! Never seen the likes."

"What do you mean by 'the ghost'?" Clive ran a hand through his wet hair, delightfully curling now. "Speak plainly, man."

"It's written in blood across Lady Linley's mirror up in her room. *Beware the dead!*" His eyes were bright with merriment.

"Blood?"

"Yes! Blood!"

"Look, Phineas. Is this another one of your pranks? I'll not have it."

"Of course, it's not a prank!" Phineas exclaimed with false indignity.

"Where's Wallace?"

"He's up with Lady Linley, I believe. She fainted dead away, you know."

"Fainted?" Henrietta asked through her suddenly chattering teeth. "Has a doctor been called?"

"On his way," Phineas rocked on his heels, his thumbs stuck in his waistcoat pockets.

"I should go to her," Henrietta said to Clive.

"You'll do no such thing. You're shivering. You need a hot bath. Blast Edna for not being able to run you one. Ring for someone," Clive urged.

"Don't be absurd, Clive. I'm perfectly capable of running a bath if I need to," she said, heading toward the main staircase. "But I won't take the time just now. I'll put on something dry and meet you in Lady Linley's room. I want to see this ghostly writing for myself."

When Henrietta, dressed in a warm wool skirt and a fresh blouse, made her way into Lady Linley's room not twenty minutes later, she was glad to see that Lady Linley had apparently recovered consciousness and was now lying on top of the bed, her head propped up by various pillows. Miss Simms, herself still attired in her picnic garb, was perched on the edge of Lady Linley's bed. She held one of the elderly woman's wrinkled hands and was methodically rubbing it. The odd tinkling of a music box could be heard from somewhere nearby. Neither Clive nor Wallace was anywhere in sight.

"Oh, there you are, dear!" Lady Linley called at the sight of her. "Do come in."

Henrietta approached the bed. "How are you, Lady Linley?"

"Very bad indeed! Oh, very bad." She held a lace handkerchief to the corner of her eye. "This is wretched business, this. But now perhaps someone will believe me!"

Henrietta looked eagerly around the room, but saw no ghostly writing nor, in fact, any mirrors at all, as they were all still covered with black crepe.

"Where is this . . . this writing?"

"It's in my dressing room." Lady Linley gestured awkwardly. "But you can't mean to examine it. It's too terrible, Henrietta. You'll take a turn if you do. Clive's already in there." Lady Linley let out a little moan and put an arm across her forehead. "I've asked Addie to clean it," she went on, "but she refuses. Says she's afraid of evil spirits attaching themselves to her or some such thing. Can't say I blame her, but the absolute cheek!"

"I'll do it for you, Lady Linley," Miss Simms said sweetly.

"Oh, would you?" Lady Linley exclaimed, grasping their already-clasped hands with her other. "I don't know what I'd do without you, Evie."

"I'll just check on Clive," Henrietta said, letting go of the bedpost she had been holding.

"Oh, Henrietta, would you wind my music box first? It brings me such comfort."

Henrietta looked around the room and, following Lady Linley's pointing finger, finally spotted the music box on a little side table by her chaise lounge.

"Oh, I'll get it!" Miss Simms said, jumping up.

"But what about your ankle?" Henrietta asked, suddenly remembering Miss Simms's injury.

"It's . . . why, it's ever so much better," Miss Simms declared as she walked, albeit with a slight limp, across the room. "It hardly hurts anymore. It was never all that bad in the first place, but you know men. Always thinking we are the weaker sex." She quickly wound the music box and then hurried back to Lady Linley's bedside, as if afraid that Henrietta might take her place there. "Clair de lune" tinkled out.

"Well, we are!" Lady Linley butted in. "Don't you agree, Henrietta?"

Henrietta wasn't sure what to say to this but was spared having to answer when Stevens suddenly entered the room, followed by a man she assumed was Dr. Graham by the black medical bag he carried.

"Hello, Lady Linley," he said, his voice deep but kindly as he approached the bed. "Had a fright, have you?"

Stevens bowed himself out of the room, and Henrietta, too, seeing as how the doctor's attention was now completely on the sick woman, took the opportunity to avoid introductions and to instead retreat to the dressing room.

She was relieved to see Clive within, still damp, however, standing in front of the vanity and staring at the bright-red letters written there.

Beware the dead!

Henrietta shivered despite her dry clothes and slipped her arm through Clive's.

"What do you think?" she asked, not looking at him. She couldn't take her eyes off the cryptic message.

"That it's someone's idea of a bad joke. To quote Mr. Dickens, 'There's more of gravy than of the grave about this.' It's not even really blood. It's lipstick."

"Lipstick?" Henrietta looked closer. She reached out and smeared a bit of it onto her pinky finger and examined the cherry-red material. It *was* lipstick. "But, that's odd. Lady Linley doesn't wear lipstick."

Clive's brow wrinkled. He slipped out of Henrietta's grasp and hurriedly began opening all of the drawers in the vanity. "You're right. There are no lipsticks. It must be someone else's."

"Well, it isn't mine," Henrietta murmured. "I don't have this particular shade. And I don't think Amelie wears any, either." She looked at the color on her finger again. "Miss Simms?"

Clive tilted his head toward Lady Linley's bedroom.

Henrietta followed him, stepping silently back into the room where the doctor was now standing over Lady Linley, her wrist in his hand, taking the old woman's pulse. Miss Simms hovered nearby.

"Oh, Clive!" cried Lady Linley upon spotting them. "What have you discovered? What's to be done? Where did Wallace run off to? He was just here a moment ago, but now he's disappeared! How typical!" She was quickly becoming almost hysterical.

"Lady Linley!" the doctor commanded. "You must lie still for just a moment." He looked at Clive, then, both bushy white eyebrows raised so that he oddly resembled an old owl, in what seemed a plea for assistance.

"Right," Clive said, giving the doctor a nod. "We'll leave you to it, Doctor. Miss Simms, perhaps you'd be so good as to step out. I'd like a word with you."

"Can it not wait? I don't think I should leave her," Miss Simms said hesitantly.

"I'm quite sure the doctor has everything in hand   "

"Oh, no, don't leave me!" Lady Linley exclaimed, looking as if she were about to cry.

"Lady Linley, please!" the doctor said irritably.

"Aunt," Clive said gently. "We must let the doctor do his work, and then we will be back. Not to worry."

"I'll just be outside," Miss Simms said to Lady Linley, patting the lady's free hand as she passed.

"All this fuss," Lady Linley groaned, closing her eyes briefly in disgust. "I'm perfectly fine. It's the mirror you should be examining. Not me!"

"Well?" Miss Simms asked sharply, once the little group was assembled in the hallway. Henrietta was surprised by this new tone.

"You seem upset, Miss Simms," Clive began, his eyes narrowed.

"Well, of course I'm upset." Miss Simms crossed her arms. "Aren't you? I confess, I didn't really think much of this haunting business, but this is really quite frightening."

Clive observed her for several seconds. "Miss Simms, this is hardly the work of a spirit."

"What makes you so sure?"

"Well, for one thing, this 'ghostly' message is written in lipstick."

"Lipstick!"

"Yes, and since Lady Linley doesn't seem to possess any modern-day 'paint,' as she might refer to it, I'm wondering if the lipstick in question might be one of yours."

"Mine?" Miss Simms looked from one to the other. "Mr. Howard, you don't half say mad things. What exactly do you mean? Surely you don't think *I'm* responsible?"

"I didn't say that, Miss Simms. All I *am* saying is that . . . *someone* . . . may have used one of your lipsticks to write that message."

"Well, it could have just as easily been yours," Miss Simms declared, looking at Henrietta with a little pout.

"Perhaps, but I don't think I have that shade."

"Shall we all go and take a look in your room to see if this lipstick is there?" Clive suggested.

"I think not!"

"We're not accusing you of anything, Miss Simms," Henrietta put in in a softer tone. "But we must discover any little clue to get to the bottom of this. Ultimately, it will help Lady Linley; do you not see that?"

Miss Simms gave another little pout. "Well, I suppose. But I don't think you'll find anything."

"Did you notice if any of them were missing?" Clive asked.

"Well, no. I . . . I didn't look."

"Which room is yours?" Clive glanced down the hallway.

"It's this one right here," Miss Simms said, pointing to the door nearest Lady Linley's room.

"So close? That's convenient."

"Yes, it is," Miss Simms chirped, either not catching or simply choosing to ignore Clive's insinuation. "Lady Linley insisted I move to this room about a week after I arrived." Miss Simms went to open the door. "She said it would be a comfort to have me close by in case she needed something." She gestured for them to enter.

"Why not simply ring for a servant?" Clive asked as he and Henrietta stepped into the room.

"Well, in case you haven't noticed, they are rather scarce these days."

Clive looked around the room, his hands on his hips. "Where does that lead?" he asked, pointing to a door on the far wall.

"To Lady Linley's room, of course."

"They're connected?"

"Yes, that was the whole point."

"Where do you keep your lipsticks?" Henrietta asked.

"In here," she said with an irritated sigh and then moved to the vanity. She pulled open the top right drawer and after a quick perusal, set four lipsticks on the top of the vanity. She continued ruffling through the drawer, then, apparently looking for more. "That's strange," she muttered.

"Is one missing?" Henrietta asked hopefully.

"Yes, I believe so." Miss Simms opened all the rest of the drawers, frantically searching through each.

"You're sure?" Clive asked.

"Yes, perfectly sure. There should be five here. Where could the other one be?" She looked worriedly from one to the other. "You can't possibly think that I would do such a thing, do you?"

"Why don't we start from the beginning," Henrietta suggested calmly, shooting Clive a quick glance. "Why don't you tell us what happened from the time you arrived."

"All right," Miss Simms agreed wearily. "But might I sit down? My ankle is beginning to throb again." She made a show of hobbling to the armchair in the corner, while Henrietta proceeded to take a seat on the lilac tufted bench at the end of the bed. Clive leaned against the wall, his arms folded loosely across his chest.

"So you came back to the house with Phineas about an hour or two ago. Is that right?" he asked casually.

"Yes, I think so. I'm not sure what time it was."

"Then what?"

"I . . . I went to my room. To rest my foot."

"How did you get upstairs?"

"Mrs. Pennyworth and Addie helped me."

"Not Stevens?"

"Well, no. He was busy, I believe."

"Busy? With what?"

Miss Simms thought for a moment. "How should I know? What does it matter? Oh!" she said then suddenly. "Something about a fire in the stables."

"A fire!" Clive stood up straight.

"Yes," Miss Simms languidly waved her hand. "A small one, apparently. Easily put out. An accident, I'm told."

Clive rubbed the back of his neck. "Well, what about Phineas? Didn't he help you?"

"No, he did not." Miss Simms frowned. "He disappeared, too."

"Disappeared? Where to?"

"I really couldn't say, Mr. Howard."

"I find that damned odd."

"Why is that?" she asked with mock innocence.

Henrietta could swear she was batting her eyes at him. She knew a flirtation when she saw one. "Because he went through such great lengths to escort you home," she interjected. "Why would he not escort you up the stairs?"

"How should I know? You know men," she looked back at Clive. "Always so fickle."

Henrietta studied her carefully. She was sure she was hiding something.

"Then what happened?" Clive went back to leaning against the wall. If he *was* affected by Miss Simms's charms, Henrietta could not tell. He seemed aloof.

"What do you mean, 'then what happened?' " Miss Simms said with a little scowl.

"After you came upstairs." Clive let out a sigh. "What did you do then?"

"Why, nothing, really. Addie eventually appeared with some ice for my ankle."

"Was there anyone else about?"

"I'm not sure." Miss Simms paused to rub her temples in an aggravatingly pretty sort of way. "I don't recall."

"You don't recall?"

"Well, I was in quite a bit of pain at that point; I can hardly remember."

"Did you hear anything? Anyone creeping about the hallways?"

"No! Nothing like that."

"And then what?"

"Well, I . . ." She paused again, thinking. "I must have dozed off, because the next thing I remember was hearing Lady Linley scream."

"From next door?" Clive nodded at the connecting door.

"Yes, I jumped up and ran to her, of course."

"Though your ankle was sprained?" Henrietta pointed out.

"Well, yes. I guess the ice had helped it. That or I just forgot the pain in the moment."

"Ah." Clive shot Henrietta a fleeting glance with eyebrows raised. She wanted to laugh.

"And then I ran in and saw the ghostly message and Lady Linley lying in a heap," Miss Simms rushed on with dramatic flourish. "I called for help, and then . . . well, that's when everyone came rushing up."

"You saw the message?"

"Yes . . . it was terribly frightening. I suppose I didn't realize it was simply lipstick." She gave a dismissive little shrug.

"How did you know to look in the dressing room? Wouldn't you have first run to Lady Linley, collapsed as she was on the floor?"

Miss Simms's eyes grew wide and her lips formed a perfect "O" of surprise. Her cheeks grew pink. "Well, yes, I . . . I did see Lady Linley on the floor, but I . . . I ran to get her smelling salts. I'd fetched them from her vanity before, you see." Her lips curled into the tiniest smile.

"Quite." Clive shifted his gaze from her to the floor and put his hands in his trousers. "So, everyone came rushing up after you cried out for help. Who exactly?" He looked up at her now.

"Well, everyone," she answered, seeming confused by the question. "Wallace and Phineas, Mrs. Pennyworth. Amelie was there for a moment, but then she left. Said she was going to settle the children, I think."

"Not Colonel Beaufort?"

Miss Simms thought for a moment. "I don't recall seeing him, no." Clive ran his hand through his hair. "Listen, Miss Simms. Are you quite sure that this wasn't some silly scheme devised by Phineas, or perhaps the two of you together? Now would be the time to confess it." He stared at her intensely.

"How dare you suggest such a thing, Mr. Howard! Why would I want to do anything that might upset Lady Linley? It's illogical. Not to mention ruin a perfectly good lipstick. It was really rather expensive."

"Indeed. And isn't it a wonder that you, a charity woman, own five?"

"Really, Mr. Howard! I've had all I can take of your questions. And yours, too, Mrs. Howard. I thought you might be a friend, but I can see I was wrong. Well, I'm used to false friends in this business." She stood up.

"And what business would that be?" Clive asked, perplexed.

"Charity work, of course. You can't imagine how people turn on you. It's deplorable, really. Now, if you don't mind, I'm going back in to Lady Linley. She needs me, and this is just silly. You can stay or leave, just as you like," she said, gesturing about the room, and then walked to the connecting door, opened it easily, and disappeared through it.

Henrietta let out a little sigh and looked at Clive. "What do you think?"

"I don't know what to think, except that we need to find Phineas again."

"Agreed, but you can't go like that, Clive. You're still soaking wet. You've got to change. I'm going to check on Edna. Perhaps she heard something."

"I doubt it, being all the way at the other end of the house and two levels down. But, yes, I'll meet you below."

"Actually, on second thought, I'll come with you and get my cardigan. I'm still cold."

"Perhaps you should take a warm bath, as I suggested," Clive said as they traversed the long hallway.

"I will later, darling. There's no time right now."

"I don't want you catching cold," he said sternly as they climbed a short set of curved steps that led to yet another little hallway.

"You're the one walking around in wet clothes."

"I've had worse, darling," he said and promptly sneezed.

"See?" Henrietta asked as she opened the door of the Peacock Room. "Perhaps the doctor should examine *you* before he goes."

"Don't be ridiculous," Clive said as he began untying his tie. "I won't be a moment." He passed into his dressing room. "No surprise," he called from within. "Pascal's nowhere to be found."

"Well, he can't be expected to just sit in the dark in your dressing room on the off chance you might randomly need a change of clothes in the middle of the day, Clive."

"Darling, that's the job of a valet. To always know where his master is and to anticipate his needs before they even arise."

Henrietta did not respond, as her attention had already been caught by a rather fat letter lying on her writing desk in the corner. She picked it up and saw that it was from Julia! It was the first she had gotten from her since they had left Chicago. She held it for a few moments, trying to decide if she should open it or wait until later. Finally, she decided to tear it open to at least skim the contents. As she did so, however, her heart sank.

"Did you hear me?" Clive asked now, poking his head out of the dressing room. "What's wrong?" he asked, stepping into the room in just his undershirt. "Now *you* look like you've seen a ghost."

"Oh, Clive," Henrietta said, holding up the letter half-heartedly. "It's a letter from Julia."

Chapter 8

Julia set down her pen and perused the letter in front of her one more time before crumpling and tossing it into the little basket beside her desk. Yesterday, she had somehow managed to compose a letter to Henrietta, though that one, too, had been extremely difficult. There had simply been no good way to relate to her and Clive that Elsie had run off with Gunther and gotten married, a situation about which Julia still felt horribly guilty.

She realized now that she should have kept a closer eye on Elsie, but to be fair, Elsie had not responded to Julia's various overtures at communication. She supposed she could have had herself driven to Mundelein to speak to the girl in person, but Randolph did not like her to be gone for long periods of time except to visit her mother at Highbury, and even then he complained about it, saying that whenever she frequented the palatial Winnetka estate, she returned peevish and sullen. She didn't think that was true, but if it was, what of it? These days, Randolph was barely around long enough to witness her "moods," as he disdainfully called them, which was fine with her. The whole house, not just her, labored under a cloak of fear and dread whenever he was at home.

She nervously tapped her pen against her monogrammed stationery and looked out the window. It was a beautiful August day, but the large pines near the house blocked out the sun. Perhaps being at Highbury did make her peevish, she mused. How could it not? Her father was gone, and though he had never had much to say and had kept to himself most days, pottering about in his study, she found she missed him terribly. Antonia, too, had changed since Alcott's death. Grief had not been kind to her; her temper was shorter now, and she frequently snapped at the servants about insignificant things. There was a different feel to the house these days, which, while not exactly terrible, was certainly unsettling.

Julia turned her attention back to the paper in front of her and took a deep breath. If yesterday's letter had been painful, this one was nearly impossible. Glenn Forbes had written to her weeks ago now, and she had yet to reply. But what could she possibly say to him; how could she possibly answer?

For what seemed the hundredth time, she let herself remember the last time she had seen him. It had been on the terrace at Highbury under the cover of darkness. He had begged her to come to Texas with him, but she had turned him down, saying that she couldn't leave her two small boys, nor could she give up her place in society, the thing she had already sacrificed so much for. He had begged her to allow him to protect her, wrapping his strong arms around her as he spoke.

She should have pulled away in that instant, but she hadn't. Instead, she had allowed herself a few moments to lean against his broad chest, trying to commit the smell of him and the resultant feeling of safety to memory. Softly, he dared to kiss her on the side of her head, and when she pulled back in surprise to look at him, he kissed her again, this time on her lips. Stunned at first, she had then suddenly returned his kiss with a passion that frightened her, even now.

"I'm not going to force you to do anything, Julia," Glenn had said, the velvet timbre of his voice connecting with something deep within her chest as he traced her jaw with his thumb. "I'll wait for you. I promise. You just say the word, and I'll be here."

Julia had not responded and instead had merely stared at him, fearing that the despair welling up within her might in truth kill her. No words would come. Every fiber of her being longed to do what poor Elsie had done, to flee, and she suspected that in her heart of hearts it was the real reason she had been so upset by Elsie's news. But she just couldn't allow herself to imitate Elsie; she didn't have the courage. Instead, she simply took Glenn's large hand in her tiny one and kissed it before letting go and practically running back into the house. Almost immediately, she had regretted her decision.

She had not seen him again. He left promptly the next morning, a grateful Antonia had reported cheerfully. Her mother seemed glad to be rid of him and his continued "gauche" attempts to buy *El Rio de Luz*, a famous Frederic Church painting in Alcott's massive collection, which had been Glenn's original purpose in making the trip to Chicago. "I daresay he overstayed his welcome with poor Sidney," she said to Julia as she sipped her coffee. Julia found she could not eat and excused herself from the table.

A part of her hated herself now for not having the strength to have gone with him. Once upon a time, she would have. She would have thought it a lark and jaunted off for the adventure. But she was not that person anymore, no matter how merry she still tried to appear in public. In fact, she hardly recognized herself anymore, her true self, that is. She was utterly useless now, and afraid. But that's what having children did to you. Made you constantly afraid. Not for yourself, but for them. She hadn't understood the meaning of the word *fear* before she became a mother. Not really. Randolph had been brutal with her before the boys were born, but after they arrived, he discovered a new way to terrorize her.

More than once, outraged about some imagined indiscretion on her part, Randolph had punished her by locking the boys in their rooms. The first time it had happened, she pleaded with him, as loud as she dared lest the servants hear, and begged him to punish her instead. He had obliged by punching her in the stomach, so hard that she had sunk to her knees, but he ordered the boys to be kept in their rooms anyway, leaving Julia lying on the floor in a miasma of misery.

In addition to these occasional outbursts, Randolph had recently begun to persecute her with threats of sending the boys away to boarding school. Part of her thought this might be good for them, to be away from this sad house and their sad little lives, locked up in the nursery all summer with a governess and a nanny, but part of her didn't think she could bear being separated from them, especially little Howard. They were the only bright spots in her life, her only source of joy, even though she was not allowed to see them for very long each day, as Randolph had arranged a very strict schedule for them. Besides their school lessons, they had riding, violin, fencing, elocution, deportment, and sailing lessons. In short, everything they would need to make them perfect gentlemen, on *either* side of the Atlantic.

She had tried to explain Randolph's threats to Glenn that night on the terrace, but while he hadn't exactly scoffed, he seemed unphased by them, saying that they would simply take the boys with them before Randolph even knew about it. But Glenn didn't know Randolph as she did. His ruthlessness and cruelty, his cunning. She knew that Randolph would eventually find them and take the boys, if not by force, then by legal means. He would accuse her of adultery and probably of being an unfit mother. And a judge would more than likely side with him. After all, any average lawyer would only have to point to how she had taken her children and left her husband to take up with another man. Who would side with her?

Certainly not a court of law, and certainly not her mother nor any of the socialites in the very narrow society in which she lived and breathed. She knew she shouldn't care what society thought of her, but the sad truth was that she did. She was losing her ability to think independently, so worn down was she by Randolph's relentless abuse. Where once she had been confident and bubbly and dismissive of societal rules, she was now complacent, depressed, and full of self-loathing. She doubted herself constantly. She had tried in the beginning to fight against Randolph's denigrating comments, but as the years passed, a little part of her had begun to believe them. Perhaps she *was* stupid and small and incompetent, as Randolph always said she was.

And if all of that were not enough to paralyze her, there was still another fear—that of Glenn himself. Perhaps he was not the knight in shining armor that he appeared to be, she worried. He had asked her to trust him, but did she? Could she? After all, she barely knew him. What if she were to leave one brute only to take up with another? And Texas? Could she really live in a wilderness? He was apparently a millionaire living on a huge piece of property, but, like her mother, she had a hard time envisioning him as a part of high society. Though, Julia had mused more than once, on the nights he had been invited to Highbury during his visit to Chicago, he had appeared appropriately each night in a tuxedo and white tie. In fact, he had cut a very handsome picture. And anyway, what did it matter if he knew which tie to wear when? Didn't Randolph equally know these things? Or any good valet? It didn't prove he was a gentleman, nor a gentle man.

And yet, she felt safe with Glenn in a way she never had with Randolph. It was as if she had known Glenn for years instead of weeks. There was a quiet strength in him that she was drawn to. The way he spoke to her, the deference he showed her, the look in his eye of respect and, dare she say, love? He was unlike any man she had ever met. He was obviously well regarded by society, and yet he stood outside of it somehow, the way Julia had always wanted to do herself but had never quite achieved. He handled every situation with calm grace and even humor. In fact, it thrilled her heart when he laughed or even smiled. They had been thrown together on various occasions during his extended visit to Chicago, and each time, she had felt her insides twist and her pulse quicken whenever he entered the room, no matter how many glasses of champagne she downed or how she tried to quell it.

Still, she reminded herself, she had been fooled before and tried to school her emotions before they got out of hand, though, she realized bitterly, it was now of no real consequence either way. She had refused his offer, and that was that. She needed to get on with her life, forget about him, though the ensuing depression since he had left was unusually oppressive. She had tried to rally herself by going to the club more, which certainly pleased Antonia, and had even taken on more meaningless committee work in an attempt to distract herself. If her mind did stray to thoughts of Glenn and their night on the terrace, she quickly dismissed them by telling herself that he hadn't really been in earnest. That it had been a silly dalliance, similar to any number of flirtations that occurred during the typical ballroom season. It meant nothing and was just a bit of fun on the part of Mr. Forbes.

But when she one day received a letter from him out of the blue, the fragile house of cards that she had been so carefully constructing fell instantly.

It was a rainy afternoon when it had arrived. She was in the library, attempting to pass the time by reading, when Woodward had knocked and silently entered the room. He was carrying the silver mail salver and politely held it out to her. Julia sat up eagerly, her novel, *The House of Mirth*, sliding down the side of the leather chair in which she was ensconced. She supposed the letter to be from Henrietta and Clive, confirming that they had safely arrived in England from Paris. But when she saw that the return was Austin, Texas, her heart betrayed her, and she flushed. She looked guiltily at the butler, whose angular facial features remained expressionless.

"That will be all, Woodward," she tried to say sternly and waited for him to bow and then remove himself. Once he was out of sight, she looked back at the letter, staring at it and trying to drink it in and even sniffed it, hoping that it might smell of him—a delightful mix of tobacco and cologne and something else, maybe pine?—but it did not. It smelled simply of damp paper. The moist envelope tore easily, and she pulled out the letter inside. It consisted of just one sheet, though it was of good quality—thick, ecru in color, and with a gold embossed monogram at the top:

GFL

Quickly she began to read:

Dear Mrs. Cunningham,
I pray this letter finds you well and safe. Not a day—nay,
barely a moment—passes in which I do not think of you.

Julia put her fist to her mouth.

Before you judge me to be weak, which would in actuality
be not so very far from the truth in this, I trust, one and only
instance, I can assure you that I have endeavored to put you
aside, to honor your refutation of the question I so indelicately
put to you at Highbury and for which I beg your forgiveness a
thousand times over. I realize now that I put you in an impos-
sible situation, and one for which I, again, beg your forgive-
ness. It was a rash suggestion, and I will not make that mistake
again. Indeed, I would not have burdened you with even this
brief missive except that I find it impossible to rest, to close
this sad chapter, until I am perfectly sure of your conviction,
especially now that you have had some little time to consider.
Julia—might I call you Julia one last time?—I beg you to
accept my offer of protection. You needn't fear any obligation,
as I no longer selfishly attach my heart and my hand to this
proposal. I see now that was a grave error. I took advantage
of your vulnerability in a moment of great personal tribula-
tion, for which I am sorry. But, please, do not let my previous
behavior be an obstacle in your consideration of my current
plea. Please allow me to help you and your sons escape the
cruel situation in which you find yourselves. Allow me to offer
you shelter and protection under the law.
I have taken the very great liberty of discussing the situa-
tion, in extreme confidence, with my uncle, and he is ready at

the slightest word from you to set legal wheels in motion that would allow you to divorce your tyrant of a husband. We are both in agreement that it would not be a difficult case to win, considering Mr. Cunningham's various vices, on which I will not here elaborate lest they cause you pain. But I urge you, Julia, to accept my ministrations, which cost me nothing and by which you would gain much. Think of your sons, if nothing else, and not of the societal reaction you might face. If you are treated unkindly by various family or friends, know that you will always have a friend in me. And should you find yourself in need of an abode, I am happy to offer you the use of a large home, albeit small by Texas standards, on a neighboring ranch to mine, of which I own the deed. You would be quite alone there, save the servants—if you want them—unencumbered by any societal or personal obligations, including, and most especially, from me. I promise I would not pursue you or grossly force myself upon you. In fact, might I go so far as to suggest we never see each other or communicate in any way once you are here, as proof of my sincerity.

Dearest Julia, my only wish is to offer you safety and what I hope might someday be happiness—not with me, of course, but in the general course of life. Please consider my invitation in the spirit with which it is offered, most sincerely. It is an offer that is not bound by time—it will remain open as long as there is life within me—yet I do urge you to act before some serious injury befalls you or your sweet sons.

I remain forever, madam, your servant.
Yours,
Glenn Longfellow Forbes

Julia read the letter several times before finally lowering it. Her heart was beating hard in her chest, and she didn't quite know what to think. It was short enough, but there was so much to take in. His style of writing was very formal, almost old-fashioned—perhaps the result of his law school education? It was so different, though, from his almost jocular speech that for a moment she wondered if he had really written it. But of course he had; he wouldn't have dictated such a thing to a secretary or assigned it to a junior member, would he?

She read it through again, her cheeks flushed. Part of her was angry and humiliated that he had gone so far as to actually discuss her marital woes with Sidney Bennett—Clive's right-hand man at Linley Standard, her deceased father's best friend, and now her mother's close companion. It was monstrous! Glenn wrote that the discussion had been in extreme confidence, but would Bennett really keep such news from her mother, who had a way of prying things out of the most unwilling victim, especially when it came to gossip? But then again, Bennett, she knew, had kept many of her father's secrets through the years and had been faithful. Besides, anyone could probably see that there was no love lost between her and Randolph.

But this was not the worst of the letter. The worst part was the reversal of all that he had said to her on the terrace that night, his regret in having offered his heart. She read it through again, this time her stomach knotting as she carefully picked out the most damaging phrases. *It was a rash suggestion, and I will not make that mistake again.*

She bit the inside of her cheek.

I no longer selfishly attach my heart and my hand to this offer. I see now that was a grave error.

Oh, God! So she had been right. He hadn't been serious. She must have imagined the love in his eyes, the tenderness of his kiss.

Might I go so far as to suggest we never see each other or communicate in any way once you are here?

Tears blurred her eyes.

Oh, what had she done? She had chosen to stay with a brute instead of escaping with this good man, another proof of her stupidity. But no, she told herself, fighting to keep from falling into a yawning chasm of self-blame and despair, she had done it for her boys. Leaving Randolph would have ripped them from her. She took several deep breaths. Neither Glenn nor Sidney Bennett would be able to thwart him, she rationalized. He had proven, many times over, that he was the master of not only this house but of her as well. There was no escaping him.

She stood up and began to pace the room. All of this she could oddly bear, she realized bitterly, but she could not bear the fact that Glenn did not think she reciprocated his feelings, that he felt himself in error for revealing the emotion of his heart. She couldn't abide it! She longed to tell him that she thought of him every moment of every day as well, that she desired to be held and kissed and loved by him above all else . . .

She would write to him, she decided quickly and hurried toward the library door. But once she reached the thick mahogany panels, she paused and leaned against them instead, another thought occurring to her. *Should* she write to him? Would it not be unfair? Would it not be best for him to believe she didn't care? Yes, she slowly realized, a pain rippling across her chest. It *would* be for the best. Let him believe she didn't love him. The pain increased. He would be free then, free to pursue someone more eminently suited to him than she. Yes . . . she decided, wiping away the tears that were rolling down her cheeks now. Yes, she would leave it.

But it had been hard to leave it. She should have thrown the letter away or even burned it, but she had not. Instead, she had kept it, hiding it under the tray of rings in her jewelry armoire and taking it out only when Randolph wasn't at home. Over and over she read it, glossing over the parts about the divorce and the damaging phrases and focusing only on the brightest bits, rearranging them in her mind to form a secret message:

Dearest Julia, Not a day—nay, barely a moment—passes in which I do not think of you. My only wish is to offer you safety and what I hope might someday be happiness for you and your sweet sons. I remain forever, madam, your servant. Yours, Glenn

Eventually, she no longer needed to pull it out from beneath her jewels. She knew it by heart and repeated it almost constantly. She convinced herself that she could live on his words alone, but as each day passed, she felt increasingly anxious and panicked at the thought that he did not know the truth. That he had misunderstood her silence and her retreat into the house that night. Already this week, she had suffered several nervous attacks that had left her struggling for breath and shaking, the latest one being just this morning. Her maid, Robbins, having come up to do the room after breakfast, had found her mistress curled up in bed and tightly gripping the bed-clothes as if her life depended on it.

"Oh, madam," Robbins had exclaimed. "I'll run and telephone Dr. Morgan, shall I? You've taken a funny turn again."

"No, Robbins. No, I'm all right," Julia insisted, forcing herself to sit up. The very mention of Dr. Morgan, with his horrible tonics or leeches, filled her with fear. He had wanted to use the leeches on her the last time. She had protested so loudly, however, that he had finally acquiesced and irritatedly put the jar of the horrid creatures back into his bag, promising that the next time he was called out for a case of the nerves, he would have no choice but to use them. "It's the only way," he said gruffly as he snapped his scuffed leather bag shut. But Julia did not agree. Surely the use of leeches was horribly outdated? It was outrageous.

"The master won't like it," Robbins sniffed unfeelingly. Julia glanced at the young woman as she tried to tuck up the loose tendrils of hair hanging down about her face. Though she was probably very near to her in age, Julia had never quite got on with Robbins. She didn't trust her. Like all the rest of the servants in the house, she knew her to be blindly faithful to Randolph. She suspected that the girl reported her every move to him.

Julia forced herself to stand. "I don't need a doctor, Robbins. I need to write a letter. Help me, will you?"

"A letter?" Robbins's voice was disdainful. "I don't think that's a good idea, madam. You should stay in bed."

Julia ignored her and sat down at the little desk by the window. "You may go, Robbins," she called to her without looking over her shoulder.

"As you wish, madam," Robbins said with little or no deference and exited silently.

Julia opened the top drawer and pulled out her stationery and then her ink pen. How should she begin? What could she say to him? The problem was that she didn't know what she really wanted. She felt nervous and distracted and unfocused.

Dear Mr. Forbes—she began and then crumpled it.

Dear Glenn—she crumpled it again.

Dearest Glenn,
I received your letter with not a small amount of surprise. She paused to think. *I am indebted to you for your kind offer of support, but*—

"There you are!" Randolph said bitterly from somewhere behind her.

Julia jumped and gave a little cry. She spun around to see him standing in the doorway of her room. There was a time—a very brief time—when her husband had observed polite convention and would knock before entering her sanctuary, but those days were long gone, traded as they had been for ones of suspicion and mistrust. Instinctively, she moved her left arm ever so slightly to cover the beginnings of the letter to Glenn.

"What are you doing up here?" he demanded.

Julia wanted to ask him the same thing. He was never home at this time of day. "Would you kindly knock?" she asked, her chin daring to jut just a little.

Randolph's eyes glanced around the room suspiciously as if she were hiding someone or something up here, his gaze briefly resting on her jewelry armoire before flicking his eyes back to her.

Julia's heart began to race. Had he somehow discovered the letter? Had Robbins?

"I asked you a question." Even from this distance, she could smell the alcohol on him. He was almost always drunk now, even in the morning.

Julia stared at him for several moments, hoping that her fear and disgust did not show, and then answered, determined to keep her voice steady. "I'm writing to Henrietta, if you must know."

"Shall I check your early copies?" he asked evenly, his eyes darting to the trash can as he stepped closer.

"If you'd like." She gave a little toss of her head. "You will anyway, or you'll get the servants to do it."

"Don't you dare talk to me that way!" He reached out and gave a lock of her hair a hard yank. Stinging tears formed in the corners of her eyes, but she did not wipe them lest she reveal the damning words beneath her arm. Mercifully, he turned from her for a moment, and she swiftly covered the letter with a blank sheet of stationery.

"I've only come to tell you that I'll be out tonight," he growled. "And very possibly tomorrow as well."

Julia blinked rapidly, trying to understand what this new information meant. "But Randolph," she faltered. "We're expected at the Adlers' tonight. We *have* to go."

"Well, I'm not. Make some excuse. I'm in no mood to listen to Max Adler drone on all night about his latest charity or his golf game. It bores me to tears."

Julia did not immediately respond. Normally, Randolph never missed an opportunity to mingle with the North Shore elite, but of late he was becoming more and more antisocial. It was most unusual. "It will be horribly awkward, Randolph," she faltered. "What will I say?"

"Say what you like. Say I'm ill."

"Well, where are you going?" she asked, though she could probably guess his destination. Glenn had mentioned Randolph's "vices" in his letter, obviously believing that she was somehow not aware of them, but she was. Or at least some of them, anyway.

"It's none of your concern," he snapped.

"You're going to the track again, aren't you?" she dared to ask with a trace of defiance.

His eyes flashed. "That's my business. You'll do as you're told." He pointed a finger at her.

Julia bit the inside of her cheek, knowing she shouldn't respond, but she couldn't help it. "Randolph, please," she blurted. "You can't keep on this way—going to the track every night. You'll ruin us."

His face erupted in fury. "How dare you question me!" He stepped quickly toward her and grabbed her lace collar, violently pulling her up to within an inch of his face. "You don't fool me. You'd love it if I lost everything, wouldn't you?" His breath reeked of whiskey. "It'd be your excuse to take up with someone else. Dennis Braithewaite maybe? Or the cowboy?" At the reference to Glenn, Julia's stomach clenched. "I know your type. You wouldn't be able to live for a day without money. You and your mother always looking for the best handout, isn't that right? That's the Howard way, isn't it?" He gave her a final shake and then released her.

Julia knew she should simply remain silent, but she burned with indignation. "Handout? My mother brought the money to her marriage, as you very well know," she said bitterly. "As did I."

Randolph promptly slapped her across the face. "Let me remind you, you trollop," he said, "if you even dare to step one foot outside of this marriage, you'll never see the boys again. Don't think I won't!"

Julia cradled her stinging cheek as she looked at him with pure venom.

"And just to prove it," he continued, adjusting his tie, "I'm sending them to Phillips in the fall."

Julia lowered her hand, forgetting her pain for the moment. "In the fall?" she murmured. "Randolph, no! They're still too young to go to boarding school. We agreed!"

Randolph gave her a grin, as if pleased that he had finally upset her. "Yes, and if there is further indiscretion on your part," he snarled, glancing again at the crumpled sheets of paper in the basket, "I'll take a step further and arrange for them to be schooled in Switzerland, followed immediately by a commission in the Navy."

"You wouldn't dare!"

"Try me. You'll find me quite in earnest. So, I would be very, very careful if I were you, my dear."

Julia felt an attack coming on. Pain ripped across her chest, and she found it difficult to breathe. She braced herself, arms outstretched and knuckles down, on her writing desk.

"My dear, you seem ill. Now you have your excuse for this evening. See? Easily handled," he said lightly and walked out of the room.

Desperately, Julia fought for air, convinced that she would pass out at any moment. She sat down and tried to control her breathing, tried to move it in and out, which was difficult with her mind reeling. Finally, she managed to get some air into her lungs, enough to burst into tears. "Oh, Glenn," she murmured, as she put her hands to her face and sobbed.

Chapter 9

"How are you holding up, dearest?" Henrietta asked anxiously from where she stood just inside the door of Edna's room behind the kitchens. She knew she should not really call her personal maid *dearest*, but she couldn't help it. Yesterday's letter from Julia informing her of Elsie's marriage had produced various reactions within her, one of them being a rather odd increased attentiveness to Edna, as if she were somehow a surrogate Elsie.

Upon first reading the letter, Henrietta was tempted to again blame herself for what seemed Elsie's . . . if not exactly waywardness, then certainly rashness. But, then again, what really could she have done? At eighteen, Elsie was a grown woman, and if she chose to run away with Gunther to Nebraska—of all places—what was she to do? Her sister obviously knew her own mind. It was not the life Henrietta would have chosen for Elsie, which left her feeling not only a little despondent, but, if she were honest, irritated that Elsie had chosen not to finish her studies at Mundelein College after all Henrietta had done to get her there. But, Henrietta also knew, love was a difficult force to counter.

Which was another thing. Gunther, while seemingly both intelligent and kind, from the little Henrietta knew of him, was again not the choice she would have made for Elsie. While Henrietta was of course not in collusion with Aunt Agatha and Grandfather, who wanted to basically sell Elsie to the highest North Shore bidder, neither was she in favor of a penniless, foreign custodian (and now farm worker, apparently) as Elsie's betrothed. All she could do was to hope that Elsie really did love Gunther and was not confusing love with pity, as she had done more than once in the past. And, Henrietta realized with a certain uncomfortable flush, Elsie was not only a wife now but a mother, too, and Henrietta wasn't sure how she felt about that, given her own childless state.

"Oh, I'm fine, miss!" Edna exclaimed. "You needn't have come all the way down here, like."

"How is your shoulder?" Henrietta had asked Dr. Graham if he might examine Edna's wound before he left yesterday, having finally calmed Lady Linley with a sedative, a request he seemed happy to oblige. His observation was that Edna's wound was healing cleanly, and he recommended removing the sling for several hours a day to permit movement. "Furthermore," he had added in his deep voice, "I am prescribing fresh air and sunshine. Mild strolls about the garden or time in a chair on one of the terraces. That sort of thing."

"Oh, miss, it's fine." Edna gingerly bent her arm as proof. "It's almost good as new."

"Are they treating you well?" Henrietta looked around the room. A vase of white lilies intertwined with pink and purple sweet peas sat on the low dresser. "That was kind of Mrs. Pennyworth," she said, nodding at them.

Edna blushed. "They aren't from Mrs. Pennyworth, miss. I mean, madam."

Henrietta's brow furrowed. "Pascal?"

Edna nodded shyly.

Henrietta bit back a smile. "I see."

"But they're *all* very good to me, miss," Edna added eagerly. "In fact, I feel so silly having them wait on me. I can't bear it, really. Can I not help out? I could lay out your gowns," she suggested eagerly.

"Definitely not. You heard the doctor. I don't want you risking your arm. I'm perfectly fine."

"Well, to be honest, miss, I'm right bored. I always thought I'd like to be a lady, lounging about . . . Oh, no offense, miss! You're not like that. Not at all! But I find that a lady's life is not all it's cracked up to be."

Henrietta let out a little laugh. "Why don't you read?"

"I'm not much of a reader, miss," the young woman answered, picking at a stray thread on the quilt.

"I see. Well, why don't you stroll about the gardens, as Dr. Graham suggested? But not alone," Henrietta cautioned. "In case you grow weak."

"I'm hardly weak, miss. I feel stronger than ever. I've been asking Mrs. Pennyworth for little chores. Just little things!" she added hurriedly before Henrietta could protest. "And she's ever so grateful. Especially after yesterday's events." Her eyes were wide now. "You should have seen it down here. Pandemonium, it was."

"I can imagine."

Between Miss Simms's accident and Lady Linley fainting, much less the "ghostly" message and the fire in the stables, yesterday had indeed been tumultuous. In addition to all of that, poor Amelie seemed to have taken a chill from being caught in the rain on the way home and had accordingly taken to her bed. As it was, only Wallace, Henrietta, and Clive had come down to dinner, Miss Simms and the colonel both claiming a terrible headache, and Phineas oddly announcing that he was dining out, a fact that frustrated Clive, as he had yet to pin him down to question him further regarding his movements upon returning from the picnic. Somehow, Phineas had managed to elude him.

"You should have seen Mrs. Pennyworth," Edna went on. "She was in a right state. First, it was the hustle and bustle of getting all the hampers for the picnic packed, and then Mr. Arnold turned up. She certainly had a few choice words regarding him, she did. Mrs. Caldwell would have been scandalized," Edna added, referring to Highbury's prim housekeeper. "You should have heard Mrs. Pennyworth when they rang for tea! Swore like a sailor, she did!"

"What do you mean they rang for tea?" Something struck Henrietta as odd about this detail. "Mr. Arnold and his client took tea?"

"Oh, yes, miss. Went all round the house they did. Well, Mr. Arnold did, anyway."

"That's strange. I thought they were just surveying the outside."

"That's what Mrs. Pennyworth said. Reckon that's why she was so upset. She doesn't like surprises, you see."

"Where did they go?"

"Well, I'm not sure about the little foreign man, but I saw Mr. Arnold upstairs."

"Upstairs? Why on earth was he upstairs?"

Edna shrugged again. "I'm sure I don't know, miss."

Henrietta's eyes narrowed. "Why were *you* upstairs?"

"Well, with all the commotion, I offered to take all the mail upstairs for Mrs. Pennyworth. It was the least I could do to help out, like. There was a letter for Miss Simms, though when I knocked at her door, there was no answer, so I slipped it under the door. There was another for Colonel Beaufort, which I set on his desk, and then that one for you."

"And you saw Mr. Arnold? You're sure it was him?"

"Yes . . . I think it was him. No, I'm *sure* it was. I was coming out of your room, and I saw him coming out of Lady Linley's."

"Lady Linley's?" Something was definitely amiss here. Could *he* have written the cryptic message? Surely not.

"Well," Henrietta said, crossing the room from where she had drifted by the window. "I should go now." She was eager to relay this new detail to Clive. At Wallace's request this morning at breakfast, Clive had gone to the stables to investigate the mysterious fire, as Wallace himself tended to Lady Linley and now Amelie, not to mention the children.

Henrietta paused at the door, the flowers catching her eye again. "I'll stop back a little later if I can. Perhaps we could take a stroll about the garden together."

"Oh, no, miss! That would never do. A lady walking with a servant?

Mrs. Pennyworth would really have it in for me then. She already seems to dislike me."

"Edna," Henrietta said, laying a hand on her good arm. "I don't see you as a servant. You're my friend."

Edna gave her a sad little smile. "If you say so, miss. But that can't be the way back at home. We both know that. And I don't mind. I like being your maid. You're kind."

Henrietta let out a sigh.

"And if you must know," Edna added, blushing again, "Pascal said he would take me walking."

Henrietta sighed, wondering if she should address Pascal's increasing attentions. Unlike Clive, she liked Pascal, but she had no desire to lose control of Edna the way she had with Elsie. She would have to think of what to do about them.

"We'll have to have a talk about Pascal, Edna. I don't have time at the moment. But, remember, don't be too familiar."

Edna blushed again. "But, miss. He likes me. And I like him."

"Yes," Henrietta said impatiently. "But you also claimed to have liked Virgil. *And* James, and look what happened there."

Edna's eyes widened. "That was different, miss. Me and Pascal have been through a lot together. That means something, you know." She gave an uncharacteristic pout.

Henrietta sighed again. "True enough. But I must hurry. We'll discuss it further later."

As Henrietta wound her way up from the kitchens to the front of the large Georgian house, she poked her head into various rooms, hoping that Clive might have returned. Upon reaching the front hall and still not coming across anyone, however, she considered going out to the stables herself, but before she could decide, Clive himself slipped through the main doors. He was wearing riding breeches and a white shirt open at the collar, a look Henrietta was surprised by, as he rarely presented himself in anything less than a full suit. She found it very attractive, however, but worried when she noticed that his face was flushed. Likewise, he looked to be perspiring.

"Darling, you look a state. Are you ill?" she asked, quickly pulling out her handkerchief from her dress pocket and dabbing a streak of what appeared to be dirt from his temple.

"Of course, I'm not ill," he said, taking the handkerchief from her and wiping the rest of his face.

"You look feverish."

"Well, I'm not." He handed her back the handkerchief.

Henrietta studied him and felt his brow. He *did* seem to be a normal temperature.

Clive grinned. "Come, Mother Hen, I need a drink."

"Mother Hen!"

"Isn't that what your brothers call you? Hen?" He let out a little laugh, presumably from the look of shock on her face.

"You've never called me that before!" she said, following him into his uncle's former study. She wasn't sure she liked it. After all, she wasn't a mother, and might never be.

"Well, there's a first time for everything, isn't there?"

"Yes, I suppose so," she said, still surprised by his sudden blitheness. Maybe being in the country was good for him, she mused, thinking back to him chasing her in the rain. He seemed more relaxed, more at ease. "Why are we in here?" She looked around the masculine study with its thick leather chairs and the heads of various wild game mounted on the walls.

"Because this is where the best brandy is kept. Well, the stuff that isn't locked up, anyway." Clive made his way to a sideboard where several decanters sat. "Want one?" He looked over his shoulder at her.

Henrietta hesitated. It was still relatively early. "A sherry," she answered.

Deftly, he poured it and carried the glass to where she was standing in front of one of the bookcases, absently reading the titles of the books stored behind the glass. They were mostly old Greek works and some military biographies. Nothing of interest to her.

"How is Edna?" he asked, clinking his glass to hers before taking a drink.

"She's much better, actually," she said eagerly, taking a sip herself. "The doctor says she can remove the sling for a few hours a day. She told me the most interesting tidbit, though."

"Oh?" Clive rolled his eyes. "Do tell," he said with a little sigh.

"You're very much a snob, you know." Henrietta rested one finger against her cheek as she chastised him. "You complain about your mother, but you grow more like her by the day."

Clive nearly choked on his drink. "A low blow," he said gruffly, though his eyes were bright as he returned her steely gaze. "Darling, I'm nothing of the sort. But I can hardly imagine what Edna might have said that was in the slightest bit . . . *interesting*, I think is the word you used."

"Well, I don't have to tell you, then," she said, turning away from him and making a show of reading the spines of the Greek texts in the case.

Clive laughed. "Darling, do tell. I'm only kidding."

She turned partially to look at him, a slight pout on her face.

"I promise, you have my complete attention." He folded his arms.

"Well," she began reproachfully, "Edna says that she saw Mr. Arnold upstairs, coming out of Lady Linley's bedroom."

"Arnold?" he asked, his brow creased now. "What the devil was he doing in the house, much less upstairs and in Lady Linley's bedroom?"

"Exactly!" Henrietta declared, pleased that he was taking her seriously now. "And what's more, he ordered tea for himself and his client to be served in the dining room. Mrs. Pennyworth was furious, apparently."

"I'll say." Clive pursed his lips. "But why didn't Edna mention this before? Or Mrs. Pennyworth, for that matter?"

"I suppose they haven't had the chance. Or perhaps they didn't think it was important."

Clive was thoughtful. "I suppose he could have been inspecting the house. Maybe his client was more enthused than expected and asked to see the interior? Is Edna sure it was Arnold?"

"She says it was and that he was alone. That his client wasn't with him when he came out of Lady Linley's room."

"Very unusual. I wonder if Wallace knows."

"You don't think he could be responsible for the cryptic writing, do you?"

"Mr. Arnold?" Clive looked incredulous. "I doubt it. For what purpose?"

Henrietta thought for a moment. "Maybe he was trying to frighten Lady Linley into selling?"

Clive frowned. "That seems ridiculously farfetched."

"Maybe he's a thief?"

Clive looked at her, intrigued. "A thief?"

Henrietta gave a little shrug. "Maybe he took advantage of the fact that no one was in the house so that he could pilfer Lady Linley's room, or *any* of the bedrooms, for that matter. No one would ever suspect him, an apparently respectable estate agent." She took a quick drink and then hurriedly went on as more of her theory began forming. "Maybe he and his client were even in league together. And maybe it was his client who started the stables fire while Mr. Arnold looked around the house," she suggested excitedly.

Clive laughed loudly, startling her.

"What? It's possible!" she said, slightly offended.

"Darling, it's *possible*, but it sounds rather like the plot of a cheap Victorian melodrama."

Henrietta put her free hand on her hip. "Well, what's your explanation then?"

Clive gave her an irritating smile. "I confess, I don't have one. But burning down the stables would perhaps not be wise, considering he's trying to sell the property."

"It would certainly devalue it, which would be advantageous to a potential buyer. Especially one who was planning on knocking the whole thing down anyway."

Clive tilted his head. "I suppose so."

She set down her sherry glass and crossed her arms in front of her.

"Well, since you were tasked with investigating said fire," she said, gesturing at one of the windows, "and since you've been so beastly as to dismiss all of my theories, what did you find? Any evidence of arson?"

"Hardly *beastly*, darling." He took a drink and shrugged. "There's not much to tell, actually. Seems a lantern was kicked over. Thank God they caught it before it grew into something unmanageable."

Henrietta considered for a moment. "Why are they still using lanterns, anyway? I mean, isn't the barn wired for electricity?"

"Apparently not. Uncle Montague probably thought it a waste of money, seeing as funds were scarce in the first place."

"So, you're sure it was just an accident, then?"

Clive shifted. "Well, it *seems* so, though it is a bit odd that the offending lantern had been set on the ground so near the animals where it might be easily kicked, which is apparently what happened. When I spoke to Mr. Triggs, the head groom, he insisted that this was most unusual. That all of the lanterns are normally kept on hooks on the barn posts."

"Maybe it fell?"

"Darling, whose side are you on? A moment ago, you were claiming it was arson."

"I'm simply trying to apply your methods of deduction, Inspector. Rule out the impossible, and what's left is the possible."

Clive laughed. "Come here, Minx."

"No, I will not. Just answer the question."

"What was it?" he asked with a grin. "I've already forgotten."

"Is it possible that the lantern could have simply fallen off the hook?"

"Ah, yes." He took another drink. "No, I did think of that. I examined the hook where this particular lantern should have been, and it was sturdy, so I ruled out that possibility."

"Well, then, someone had to set it on the ground. Either they set it down and got distracted, or it was put there for some more nefarious reason. Agreed?"

"Yes, agreed. I did suggest the former to Mr. Triggs, in case that is your next question, and he swears that none of his grooms would have done something like that."

"Did he see anyone in the stables at all? Someone that didn't belong?"

"He did mention seeing Pascal pass through." Clive stared at her over the rim of his glass, a mischievous smile hovering about his lips.

Henrietta raised an eyebrow.

"Before you scold me, no, I don't think it was him," he said finally, breaking the tension.

"Perhaps it really was Mr. Arnold's client, or should I say, accomplice?"

"I think that's a bit of a stretch, don't you?"

"Well, someone had to do it. And I don't think we can keep blaming Phineas for everything, do you?"

"What's this about Phineas?" Wallace asked, stepping into the room. Henrietta startled. "I'm sorry," he said, looking at them both. "Am I interrupting? I keep forgetting you're on your honeymoon. Blasted trip that it's been for the two of you. I do apologize for my part in its demise."

"Not at all," Henrietta said with a smile and took a seat in one of the leather armchairs. "How is Lady Linley today?" she asked, trying to shift her mental focus.

Wallace sighed. "She's calm. Graham gave her an additional tonic to help her sleep last night." Wallace ran his hand through his thinning hair, suddenly seeming much older than his thirty years. "It's not the first time she's fainted, you know. The doctor thinks she's still exhausted from Father's illness. Not really recovered. A deficiency of iron, I think he said." He went to the sideboard and poured himself a drink. "And possibly a disorder of the nervous system. Which Phineas's silly prank did not help. I've half a mind to thrash him. He's not too old, you know. It's what Father would have done to me. I don't understand why Uncle is so lenient with him. You would think it would be the opposite, wouldn't you, as a military man?" He took a long drink of his whiskey.

"Wallace, I'm not so sure it *was* Phineas," Clive suggested, despite the fact that he had yet to question him.

"Not Phineas? Well, of course it was Phineas. Who else would have done such a thing?"

"More than likely, you're right, but it seems that Mr. Arnold was—"

He was interrupted by the appearance of Stevens, who quietly entered the room. "Excuse me, sir," he said to Wallace.

"Yes?" Wallace answered, irritated.

"There's an Inspector Tobias Yarwood at the door, sir. He'd like a word, if you're at home."

Wallace looked at Clive curiously, as if he might know who it was. "What else can possibly go wrong?" he asked with a deep sigh. "Fine, fine. I'll see him."

"Will you attend him in the drawing room, sir?"

"No, show him in here."

"Very good, sir," Stevens replied and silently exited.

"Would you like us to step out?" Clive asked.

Wallace gave a little laugh. "No luck there, old boy. Why do you think I asked him to come to this room? Saves us all tramping to the drawing room. No, as the resident detective, you're stuck listening to whatever this is going to be. Hopefully, it's nothing serious."

Stevens reentered the room then, and announced, "Inspector Yarwood."

A short, stout man dressed all in tweed and sporting a very thin moustache that curled up at the ends stepped into the room. Henrietta was instantly reminded of Hercule Poirot, Mrs. Christie's wonderful character, but as soon as the inspector spoke, any resemblance to M. Poirot sadly evaporated.

"Lord Linley, I presume?" the inspector asked, not in Poirot's elegant Belgian accent, but in a thick Derbyshire one instead, as he held his hand out to Clive. Clive shook the man's hand, but before he could correct him, Wallace spoke.

"*I'm* Lord Linley. Though I prefer to be called Mr. Howard."

Inspector Yarwood turned his attention from Clive to Wallace and slowly looked him up and down, as if judging the truth of his statement, before holding his hand out to Wallace. "Ah. Forgive me, *Mr.* Howard." He turned his gaze back to Clive. "You resemble each other, I think."

"No, we don't," Wallace said impatiently. "But he *is* my cousin. Allow me to introduce you to Mr. Clive Howard and his wife, Mrs. Howard. They are visiting from Chicago."

"I see," the inspector said, his eyes widening a bit. "Pleasure," he said briefly and then looked back at Wallace. "How may I be of service, sir?"

Wallace threw Clive a quick look of confusion. "*You've* come to *us.*"

"Ah, yes! Indeed." The inspector cleared his throat. "Might I have a private word, sir?"

"Look here. We don't have time for this at the moment. Just out with it. You can speak freely." He waved weakly at Clive and Henrietta.

Inspector Yarwood again looked from Wallace to Clive and back again before speaking. "Very well. I believe you are acquainted with a Mr. Edmund Arnold?" he asked briskly.

"Yes, the estate agent," Wallace said matter-of-factly. "He was here yesterday, as it was. What of it?"

The inspector gave his round stomach two swift pats. "I'm afraid, sir, that Mr. Arnold has been found dead."

Chapter 10

Oldrich Exley gave his cane two swift taps and reached inside his jacket for his pocket watch. The woman was late, confound it! *Did she not know who he was?* He was sitting in a rather dull hallway outside of Sr. Bernard's office on the second floor of the Mundelein Skyscraper, his wrinkled hands resting lightly on his silver-topped cane while balancing it perfectly between his legs.

He had telephoned Sr. Bernard this past week, demanding information about his granddaughter Elsie, but the damned nun had strongly suggested discussing the matter in person! Oldrich had countered this audacity by informing her that he would send his man of business, Mr. Bernstein, to speak with her, but Sr. Bernard had infuriatingly insisted that she speak with him, and him only. The nerve! In the end, however, Oldrich realized he couldn't fight the church, not in this instance anyway, and had therefore reluctantly driven to the city from Lake Forest.

Though he was a Catholic, he had no great love of the church, or nuns in particular. Not after his own experience at Catholic school. And he certainly had no great respect for an institution of higher learning for women. Who ever heard of such a thing? A tragic waste of money was all it was. He conceded that a certain number of women, of course, had to be trained as teachers and nurses, but those were easily plucked from the dregs of society. What need had women, especially society women, to learn chemistry and Latin and physics, for God's sake? It was outrageous in the extreme.

Angrily, he tapped his cane again on the tiny-hexagon-tiled floor. He didn't understand how the world was changing in such a horrible way. The old order thrown out, as if it meant nothing. Well, he assured himself, money would always have a place in the world. No one could change that. He looked down the hallway at two girls scurrying along, giggling.

He should never have let Elsie come here. Agatha had advised him to wait it out, that this desire of Elsie's to go to school would soon fizzle out. But it had not! And worse, now she appeared to be tangled up in some sort of romantic affair with a dirty immigrant. Granted, the man had held himself with dignity when he had turned up asking for Elsie's hand, but he was poor as a mouse and a foreigner to boot. *His* granddaughter marry a German custodian? It was unthinkable.

He rapped his cane again and stood up. He had had enough of this waiting! At that moment, however, the door to the office opposite him opened, and a nun filled the space.

"Mr. Exley?" she asked firmly. "I'm Sister Bernard. Do come in."

Oldrich followed the nun into her tiny office, which smelled irritatingly of candle wax.

"Do sit down," she said, gesturing toward a plain cane-backed chair. Oldrich obliged, and Sr. Bernard gracefully took her own seat behind her desk. The looming crucifix behind her, added to the candle wax, made him feel immediately small and vulnerable. It was as if he were a boy again sitting in church beside his austere father and mother.

"Well?" Oldrich demanded.

"It was *you* who wished to see *me*, Mr. Exley," she reminded him calmly.

"Yes," he said, clearing his throat. "I'm here regarding my granddaughter, Elsie Von Harmon."

"In what regard?"

"She wrote to me with some ludicrous suggestion that she was to take Holy Orders. Whose idea was that? Yours, I'm assuming. Well, you won't get her so easily. Whatever promise she's made, she'll just have to undo." Oldrich rapped his cane.

Sr. Bernard folded her hands. "I'm afraid that's not possible. I've just this morning had a letter from Elsie herself."

"A letter?" Oldrich blustered. "She's not here? Where is she? Where did you send her?"

"Where she is now, I did not send her, Mr. Exley. She left of her own volition."

"Don't give me that. And don't tell me that it's too late, that she's taken your silly vows. That means nothing to me. It can be undone. I'll write to the bishop. The cardinal if I have to. I'm well-connected."

"As it happens, Elsie *has* taken a vow," Sr. Bernard went on calmly. "She has taken a vow of matrimony."

"Matrimony?" Oldrich felt a pain shoot across his chest. "What devilment is this? I . . . I don't believe you," he stammered. *God be damned if it was true!* He gripped his cane tightly. Would Elsie really have defied him after his threat to cut off her entire family's allowance if she proceeded to marry the Kraut? *How could she?* He never dreamt she would call his bluff!

"Well, it is true," Sr. Bernard said quietly. "Here, you may read her letter, if you wish." She passed a thin envelope across the desk to him. He stared at it for a moment and then picked it up, noting that the return was Millard, Nebraska. He felt another pain shoot across his chest. He pulled out the thin sheet of paper and quickly read it.

August 12, 1936

Dearest Sr. Bernard,

By now you will have surely received my hurried note via Melody. Please do not blame her for the small part she played in my elopement. She merely accompanied me to the train station and then carried my message back to you. Please give her my kind regards and tell her that I will send a letter soon.

I can hardly write what follows, but I promised in my note that I would write a longer letter of explanation to you, and I would keep this promise, if my only one. I am writing to tell you that Gunther and I have married. It occurred shortly after we arrived in Omaha and was conducted at a registrar's office. I did hesitate at not having a church wedding, Sister, but with Gunther being Lutheran, I know we would not have been able to marry in the Catholic church anyway, so I agreed to a civil ceremony. It seemed the best thing. I know it may have been wrong, but was this not better than living in sin?

Dearest Sister Bernard, I am so very sorry for having deceived you. I would have perhaps told you the truth and sought your advice had I had the time. As it was, I made a hurried decision, one that I hope you might someday understand and forgive. The lure of a life of Holy Orders was certainly strong for me, serving God and His people, but in the end, I found that the love I have for this man and this child was stronger. Surely God will not blame me, will He, Sister? Can I not serve God in this way, too?

I do wish I could have continued my studies and become a teacher, but I have found a way to do that here, in a small way—I teach the children of the other migrant families. And, of course, I try to teach Anna, who, I am afraid, is quite damaged by all she has seen and heard in her little life thus far. Pray for her, Sister. I am making some little progress with her, I think, and for this I thank God. Is He not wonderful? I praise Him daily for all that He has given me. My chosen life is not without trials, but I am happy and content, for whatever that is worth.

I will miss Mundelein and the girls, especially Melody, and the happy life I had there, but most of all, I will miss you, Sister. Thank you for taking me in and for trying to educate me. But more than that, I am grateful for your loving kindness. Dare I say that I have grown to think of you as a surrogate mother? Is that wrong? I would not for the world disparage my own mother, but the warmth and kind attention I have felt at your hand has been more than any I have ever received at home. I fear I have always been a great disappointment there, which is another reason that leaving seemed the best option. With everyone but Doris and Donny gone, I seemed a peg that didn't quite fit, and doubtless they are better off without me. I will at some point, of course, write to Henrietta, though I'm sure she will be glad to be rid of the extra burden I surely have been to her and Clive.

I do not expect anyone from home to inquire after my whereabouts, but if they do, simply inform them of where I went. Tell them I am happy and that they needn't worry about me anymore and that I love them, unequivocally. I do imagine that my grandfather, Mr. Oldrich Exley, will eventually inquire, and for that I am sorry. He can be quite forceful and abrasive, but please forgive that of him. He is merely lonely and has made many mistakes in his life for which I believe, deep down, he harbors regret. I did write him a letter, telling him that I was taking Holy Orders, but that was before I decided to elope with Gunther. Please tell him that I did not willfully deceive him, that I am sorry to have dashed his plans, that I forgive him. No doubt, he will be exceedingly angry. Tell him that he must do as he thinks best, but I hope and pray that he does not disown the family because of my disobedience. He will eventually see that he is better off to be rid of me, for I would never have been able to live up to his expectation of me. Assure him of my love and prayers.

I will close this letter now, Sister, with an appeal for your blessing. I will understand if you cannot bring yourself to forgive me, but I beg you to pray for me, as I surely do for all of you each day. Do not feel sad for me, for I am happy. Truly.

Your loving daughter in Christ,
Elsie Stockel

Oldrich crumpled the letter and tossed it onto the desk in front of him. He was seething. It was the second time this type of betrayal had fallen upon him, like a dead tree or a curse. First his own daughter, Martha, and now *her* daughter, Elsie. It had almost been expected with Martha. She had ever been a willful, stubborn child, but Elsie he had thought to be perfectly compliant and amenable. Her disobedience was unthinkable. What had happened?

"This is your fault," he growled at Sr. Bernard. "Putting ideas into her head! I won't stand for this, I'll have you know! I'll have it annulled and drag her back here myself if I have to!" With every passing second, he grew more enraged at the thought of Elsie's defiance, and, to be honest, that she pitied him! *She* pitying *him*; it was egregious in the extreme!

"For what purpose?" Sr. Bernard asked calmly, though he could see the fierce disapproval in her eyes. Typical of a nun, but a small part of him relished the fact that he had managed to finally ruffle her smooth exterior.

"To marry the man of my choice! She's a witless girl. She doesn't know what she wants. As her grandfather, I know what is best for her. And this is certainly not it. Married to a farmhand? And do you know that this . . . this child they care for is mentally deranged? No, this is not the life my granddaughter should be leading."

"And yet your own daughter lived most of her life in squalor not thirty miles from you."

"That was her choice."

"As this is Elsie's."

"This is different!" He slammed his fist on the desk. "Martha was a lost cause from the beginning. Elsie had—no, *has*—so much potential."

"To do your bidding? To marry a man she does not love because it will increase your bank account and social standing in the world?"

"Yes! It will benefit her in the long run, her children, too. This is her part to play in the bigger scheme."

"And who will marry her now? She will be a divorced woman if you have your way."

Oldrich paused. Unfortunately, the nun was right. "I'll send her to Europe," he said quickly. "She can marry some Italian count or duke. He won't understand her tarnished reputation, and we'll increase our own nobility."

Sr. Bernard stared at him for several hard moments. "Do you hear yourself?" She stood up. "Elsie is not a piece of property for you to dispense of as you like. She is a living, breathing woman with her own thoughts and feelings and soul. How dare you try to possess her! And if you will not release her for her own happiness, will you not do it for yourself? Have you no fear for your soul? You are speaking as one possessed by the devil himself."

Oldrich waved his hand at her dismissively. "You can spare me your sanctimonious lecture. I'm not interested."

"Not interested in your eternal salvation? You are in grave danger, Mr. Exley. Learn from Elsie herself, who has been forced to flee to a farm in Nebraska to escape your machinations, and even then forgives you. It is not too late to turn from your sins. To repent." She gestured lovingly at the crucifix behind her. "Even now, you can be forgiven. To make amends for the many wrongs you have committed."

"How dare you correct me as if I'm a recalcitrant child!"

"Mr. Exley, an idol of gold has taken hold of your heart and has blinded you. I beg you to shake it off. Be the man God is calling you to be."

"You believe what you want, and I'll believe what I want," he snapped. "There is no sin in accumulating wealth. Look at the church itself. The Vatican is filled with half the gold and treasures in the world. Our bishop lives in a palace, for God's sake! No, you can spare me your bleeding-heart speeches. I'm doing this to preserve my family."

"Are you? This is your way of preserving them, is it? To send your grandsons to a boarding school hundreds of miles away, to rip your granddaughter from the man she loves and from her desire to teach and serve the poor? You would do well to examine your conscience, Mr. Exley."

"This is for their own good. They'll thank me one day."

"Will they? I sincerely hope so. Let us pray that the opposite is not true—that they will not curse you, as you have clearly already done to yourself."

"Enough of this!" Oldrich rose. He was, in fact, feeling a bit weak. He needed his pills, but the chauffeur had them. "I *will* find Elsie, and nothing or no one will stop me." He grabbed the envelope off the desk and hobbled from the office, leaning heavily on his cane.

Chapter 11

"What do you mean Mr. Arnold is dead?" Wallace snapped, leaning heavily on one of the leather armchairs. "He was here just this morning!"

"So he was." Inspector Yarwood looked carefully at each person gathered in the study. "Which begs several questions. May I?"

"Yes, yes, of course. But I don't see how *we* can help." Wallace gestured toward a chair.

"Thank you; I'll stand." The inspector removed a small, worn notebook from the inside pocket of his tweed jacket and carefully opened it to a clean page. "What time yesterday did you see Mr. Arnold?" he asked Wallace.

"I didn't. I saw him two days ago. He came here to discuss the potential sale of the house. We went over a lot of the financials. Then he rang later in the afternoon, saying that he had an interested party and could he bring him round to see the property."

"And that was yesterday?"

"Yes."

"I see." The inspector gave the tip of the pencil he had likewise unearthed from his pocket a quick lick and then carefully wrote something. "And you saw neither him nor his client, a Mr. Maung, I believe? How was that?" he asked, perplexed.

Wallace let out a sigh. "I arranged for us all to be out of the house on a picnic while they were here."

The inspector's eyebrows raised. "Why was that?"

"Because I didn't want to upset my mother, or anyone else, for that matter."

The inspector's eyebrows immediately toppled into a crease. "Why would Mr. Arnold's presence be upsetting to Lady Linley? Or did you fear it would be Mr. Maung who would disturb her?"

Wallace rolled his eyes. "Because I'm thinking about listing the estate for sale, and she's rather resistant to the idea, as I'm sure you can imagine."

The inspector continued to write. "So, there was some animosity between them, you'd say?"

"No! Oh, for heaven's sake. They've never met!"

"I see." The inspector began to aimlessly pace, looking at the pictures on the walls, as if he wasn't sure what to ask next. "And what time did Mr. Arnold and company arrive?" he asked, turning back toward Wallace now.

"I'm not sure. We'd have to ask the servants."

"Yes, I'd like a word with them, if I may. Presently, that is. Who else was in the house, besides the servants? No one? They all went on the picnic?"

"No! I mean, yes. They were all at the picnic."

"Well, that's not exactly true, Wallace," Clive put in quietly.

Inspector Yarwood abruptly turned toward him.

"Don't forget that Miss Simms and Phineas returned early," Clive said, ignoring Yarwood and speaking directly to Wallace. "Perhaps *they* saw one of them. Also the colonel, though I'm not sure he would have made it back in time to have caught sight of Mr. Arnold and Mr. Maung." He wasn't about to offer the fact that Edna had seen Mr. Arnold wandering around upstairs, but he was so far not impressed with Inspector Yarwood and decided he would keep his cards close to his chest. He couldn't help but think how differently he or even Hartle would have handled it. The thought of Hartle, however, caused a surge of anger to course through him. He still couldn't believe Hartle's treachery, double-crossing him by working with the Nazis . . . or some other foreign entity.

"Ah!" The inspector poised his pencil just above the notebook, ready to record his first suspects. "A Miss Simms, did I hear you say? And a Mister . . . ?"

"Beaufort. Phineas Beaufort."

"I should like to speak with this Miss Simms and this Mr. Beaufort. And a Colonel Beaufort, did you say? Any relation to Mr. Beaufort?"

"Yes, of course there is. They're father and son."

"Which is which?"

Wallace let out a little groan. "Look, Inspector, is all of this necessary? You've established that Arnold was indeed here. What more do you want to know?"

"Do you suspect foul play?" Clive casually crossed his arms, guessing that this had to be the reason for the inspector's extended questioning.

The inspector looked at him curiously. "As a matter of fact, we do. Mr. Arnold, it seems," he gave his pencil another little lick, "was unfortunately poisoned."

"Poisoned?" Henrietta exclaimed. "Are you sure?"

"Quite. We'll have the coroner's report eventually, but all the signs are there."

"Such as?" Clive asked.

"Froth about the mouth, locked jaw, stiff as a board. As I say, all the signs."

"How awful!" Henrietta muttered.

"No previous illness?" Clive pursued.

"Not that we know of. His missus reports he returned home midday, which is not his usual, she says, complaining of stomach cramps. Didn't take anything to eat but laid down in his bed. Never got up, poor bugger."

"That's odd. Strychnine usually produces quite violent spasms. Did his wife not hear anything? Any thrashing about?"

Inspector Yarwood's eyes narrowed. "How did you know it was strychnine?"

Clive rubbed his brow. "Because those are the symptoms of strychnine poisoning, as opposed to something else, like arsenic, for example."

"I see," Inspector Yarwood said suspiciously and continued to eye him carefully.

"So, did his wife report any fits?"

Inspector Yarwood stared at him for several seconds, as if deciding how much information to share and, seeming to finally come to a decision, looked down at his notes. "As a matter of fact, she did not. Says she stepped out to borrow an egg from a neighbor, a Missus," the inspector held the notebook close to his eyes, "Thompson. Not gone fifteen minutes she claims, but when she went in to check on him, he was stone-cold dead."

Clive put a finger to his lips. "What about this Mr. Maung? Have you talked to him? Perhaps he could shed some light on the situation."

"Of course, I've talked to him. He was the first one we hauled off to the station."

Clive's face grew dark, his sense of injustice inflamed. "Hauled off to the station? Why was that? Do you have reason to suspect him?"

"Not yet, but you know these little foreigners. Wouldn't put it past him."

"What motive would he have to kill the man who was helping him buy a property?" Clive asked indignantly.

Inspector Yarwood shrugged. "Never know with these types. Can't be too careful."

"This is disgraceful!" Wallace nearly shouted. "Are you holding him?"

"Couldn't, in fact. Had to let him go. But we're watching." The inspector raised a finger to his temple and then pointed toward one of the windows.

"Well, what did he say?"

"That is more or less confidential, but I *will* say that it wasn't much.

His English is atrocious, as you'd expect. He says they came here, stopped at the White Hart in Cromford on the way home for a quick dinner and a pint and then split ways. They were to see two more properties the next day, which would have been today, of course."

"Well, there you go!" Wallace exclaimed. "It could have happened at the pub. Go interrogate the landlord."

"All in good time, Mr. Howard." The inspector observed him carefully.

"Could it have been self-induced?" Clive asked, still trying to control his irritation with the man.

"A suicide, you mean? Not likely. Left behind three children."

Clive knew from experience that children left behind was rarely a reason to prevent a suicide, but he did not say as much.

"Perhaps it was accidental?" Henrietta suggested.

"Perhaps, but not likely. How would he accidentally ingest strychnine?"

"Does it have a taste?" Henrietta looked at Clive for the answer, but it was Inspector Yarwood who answered.

"No, it does not."

"So, your conclusion is that it was definitely a deliberate murder?" Clive asked.

"More or less." The inspector pursed his lips. "Which is why I'll have to interview various members of this household."

"Are you suggesting that he was poisoned *here*?" Wallace snapped. "That's absurd!"

"Nothing is absurd when it comes to murder, Mr. Howard." He gave his stomach two swift pats. "You'd be surprised. The fact is, I already deduced that it was strychnine even before this Mr. Howard here's clever guess. Suspected it all along, I did." He tapped the side of his nose again. "And if that's the case, we can trace back with a fair amount of certainty just when the poisoning might have occurred. Strychnine has a somewhat predictable reaction time; death usually occurring about three hours after the time of ingestion. But we'll know more once we have the coroner's report and the official time of death, though if I put two and two together, I'd say that it was more than likely the poisoning occurred here."

"But that's madness!" Wallace exclaimed. "No one was here!"

"But you've just told me that one Miss Simms and one Mr. Beaufort and possibly one Colonel Beaufort were here." Inspector Yarwood twirled one end of his moustache.

"Yes, but it wouldn't have been them! For one thing, what would their motive be?"

"Perhaps a prank that went too far?" Henrietta suggested.

"Yes, perhaps a prank," Inspector Yarwood said, eyeing her now.

Wallace shot Henrietta an irritated look. "Phineas is a little rotter, I'll grant you that, but this is beyond him. I'm sure." He turned his gaze back to the inspector. "And where would either of them have gotten strychnine in the first place?"

"Oh, you've no idea how many poisons can be found in plain sight," Inspector Yarwood answered, almost cheerfully. "Strychnine, for example, is a common ingredient in rat poison, which could be found in almost every stable in Derbyshire."

Wallace began to pace a little. "Look, you can question us all you want, but you won't find the murderer here. More than likely, it was the publican, or someone else—Arnold's wife, maybe. Carrying on with some other bloke or something like that. They're the ones you should be questioning!" Wallace sputtered.

"You seem much disturbed, Mr. Howard," the inspector said, eyeing him coolly, an observation that Clive, in truth, shared. *Why was Wallace reacting so strongly?*

"Look, my mother is already not well," Wallace went on. "This will be very upsetting to her."

"Are you resisting cooperation with the authorities, Mr. Howard? Something you seem to have, might I remind you, a certain penchant for, not to mention an official record of? And might I further remind you that this is the second murder investigation you've been linked to."

Wallace looked as if he were about to strike the man. "I had nothing to do with Ernest Jacobs's death, as you bloody well know."

"It's not a bad idea, Wallace, to let him question everyone," Clive said calmly. "We can at least establish the time Arnold was here, and also rule certain suspects out."

Wallace looked at him as if he had betrayed him. "Fine," he finally mumbled and walked to the servants' cord hanging beside the fireplace, pulling it with extra force.

"Did any of Mr. Arnold's neighbors see or hear anything out of the ordinary?" Clive asked the inspector. "Any strange people in or out?"

Inspector Yarwood's eyes narrowed again. "You seem more than curious, my friend. But, I'll kindly remind you, *I* am the one in charge of this investigation. You needn't worry yourself over it. I have it quite in hand."

Clive felt another surge of irritation, but before he could retort, Wallace beat him to it. "You'd do well to involve him, Inspector," Wallace snapped. "He's a former detective with the Chicago Police. He just might be able to help."

"What did you say your name was?" The inspector eyed Clive suspiciously.

"Howard. Clive Howard."

"Ah!" The inspector let out a low whistle. "But, of course. Read all about you, I have."

"In what capacity?" Clive fought to keep his voice level.

"Seems my predecessor was very admiring of you. Kept a whole file on you. Read it all, I have."

Clive was shocked by this reveal. Clearly the man was referring to Hartle. Desperately, Clive wanted to know what was in this mysterious file, to delve further into Hartle's background, his time on the force, his possible connections, any indication as to why he had double-crossed him. But he had promised MI5 that he would let the case lie. He had given his word. But that was before he had been called back to England by a weird twist of fate . . .

"Well, go on, then," he said, crossing his arms. "Enlighten us."

"Confidential, I'm afraid," Yarwood said with a twirl of his moustache.

"Where the bloody hell is Stevens?" Wallace said in a half-shout and roughly pulled the cord again.

Almost immediately, a frazzled-looking Stevens entered the room. "You rang, sir?"

"Where have you been, Stevens? Did you not hear the first bell?"

"I . . . I'm very sorry, sir, but . . . but the staff are rather at sixes and sevens. It's been a very trying day yet again. I'm very sorry, sir."

Wallace waved his hand dismissively. "Fine. Fine. Inspector Yarwood would like to speak to Miss Simms and Phineas."

"Separately," Inspector Yarwood inserted.

"And then various members of the staff," Wallace added wearily.

Stevens paused, as if uneasy or simply unsure what to do. "Very good, sir. I will endeavor to locate Miss Simms and Mr. Beaufort."

Inspector Yarwood turned to Clive then, gave his stomach another two swift pats, rubbed his hands together in a very pleased manner, and looked about to speak, but Clive interjected first.

"Well, you'll excuse us, Inspector." He looked at Henrietta and nodded toward the door.

"Clive!" Wallace said incredulously. "You can't leave! You must stay!"

"Inspector Yarwood seems to have the case in hand, as he has most expressly stated."

"Quite right," the inspector agreed, a smug smile about his face.

"Don't be awkward, Clive!"

Clive ignored Wallace's piercing, pleading eyes. He would try to explain it to him later. "No, we mustn't interfere," he said modestly. "Coming, darling?" He gazed across at an equally befuddled-looking Henrietta.

"Yes, of course," she said haltingly, rising slowly and following him to the door.

"Just one question." Clive suddenly turned back toward the inspector and a clearly fuming Wallace. "Was Mr. Arnold found with anything of value on his person? Or perhaps a tube of lipstick?"

"Lipstick? Anything of value?" Inspector Yarwood's eyebrows

raised again. "What singular questions. Not that I'm aware. I suppose the coroner will reveal what the contents of his pockets were along with the contents of his stomach." He smiled at his own attempt at a joke, but seeing that no one else shared in his humor, his face resumed its serious demeanor. "Why?"

"Just curious," Clive said. "Anyway, we'll leave you to it."

Clive slipped out of the room, Henrietta following close behind. He walked quickly through to the next room, which appeared to be a small library, or perhaps a reading room. It was very dim. The afternoon light was beginning to wane, and none of the lights had yet been switched on by the overtaxed staff. Clive's plan was to cut through to a doorway on the opposite wall, which, he knew, led to the main foyer, but Henrietta stopped him.

"Clive!" she hissed, pulling at his arm. "Was that wise? Why did you insist we leave? Don't you want to hear what is said?"

"Not particularly." He put his hands in his trouser pockets. "He'll only bumble it. Ask all the wrong questions. We've already spoken to Miss Simms, and I don't think he's going to get too much more out of her. I do have a few choice questions for Phineas, but I don't want to do it in front of that clod."

"He does seem to be a bit out of his depth," Henrietta mused. "Is that why you didn't mention the fact that Edna saw Mr. Arnold creeping about upstairs?"

"Exactly." Clive gave her a wink.

"But he might find out anyway."

"Yes, well, if he does, so be it. But I'd like to keep it quiet as long as I can until we've had a chance to investigate on our own. Which," he said, tilting his head toward the main foyer, "is another reason why I wanted to make a quick exit from the room. I'd like to speak to Mrs. Pennyworth and Stevens before Yarwood gets his hands on them."

"What's this?" came a voice from what seemed to be an armchair at the other end of the room.

Henrietta gave a little cry of fright.

"Who's laying his hands on someone?" asked the voice, which they now recognized as belonging to Colonel Beaufort. Indeed, Colonel Beaufort rose in front of them, like a ghost materializing from the darkness.

"Oh, it's you!" Henrietta exclaimed.

"What's going on?" he rasped, coughing horribly as he walked toward them. "Some sort of trouble, is it?" His cloudy eyes were eager.

"You should have announced yourself, Colonel," Clive said, irritated. "This was meant to be a private conversation."

Colonel Beaufort coughed again and cleared his throat. "I apologize," he wheezed. "But not to worry if it was a tête-à-tête of a romantic nature." He gave Clive a sly smile. "As it was, I was asleep. What time is it, anyway?" He fished around in his vest pocket for his watch. "Must be nearly teatime." He looked out the window. "Have I missed it?"

"Have you been here this whole time, Colonel?" Clive asked suspiciously.

"Why, yes, if you must know," he said with a wry grin as he examined his watch and then snapped it shut. "Nothing wrong with an old man having a nap."

"In here?"

"Well, why not, my boy? Didn't plan it out that way. Just happened."

"When did you arrive back from the picnic yesterday?" Clive observed him coolly.

Colonel Beaufort stared at him blankly. "Back from the picnic? How should I know? Didn't notice the time."

"So, you didn't catch up with Phineas and Miss Simms in the end. Or did you?"

Colonel Beaufort looked confused.

"Remember? You went after them to retrieve Linley's kite?"

"Ah, yes!" The colonel gave a forced little chuckle. "No, afraid I didn't. Seems Phineas was able to commandeer the wagon better than I judged he would. Didn't catch them. Phineas would be of great service if he would only put those skills to use in the infantry. Reminds me of the time—"

"Colonel, please," Clive interrupted. "What did you do when you returned from your walk? Did you see Phineas or Miss Simms?"

"Did I see them? No."

"Well, what did you do? Did you go into the house?"

The colonel considered for a moment. "Well, of course I did. No!" he said forcefully, holding up a finger. "I'm telling lies. I went to the stables first. Wanted to see if the wagon was there, and if I could find the kite after all."

"Did you see anyone about? Anyone that didn't belong, perhaps?" Clive asked eagerly.

"In the stables?" The colonel thought for a moment. "Not that I can recall. Found it damned odd, now that I think about it. No one about but the head groom."

"Mr. Triggs?"

"I suppose so. Don't know his name. Don't like the man. I can always tell the character of a man by his eyes, and I daresay his are hiding something."

"Colonel, did you happen to see Mr. Arnold at all or Mr. Maung, his client? Even after you went into the house?"

"The estate agent? No. Don't recall." The colonel looked at him suspiciously. "Why do you want to know, anyway?"

"I'm asking because Mr. Arnold has, in fact, been murdered. The police are here even now, investigating," Clive said nodding toward the room they had just come from.

"Murdered! You don't say. How?"

"He was poisoned, apparently."

"Ah, then you'll be looking for a woman," the colonel said matter-of-factly.

"Why is that?" Clive's eyes narrowed.

"Why, my boy! You call yourself a detective. Everyone knows that poison is a woman's weapon."

"Or the old."

Now it was the colonel's turn to narrow his eyes. "I say! Just what are you suggesting?"

"I'm not suggesting anything, Colonel, but I must account for everyone's whereabouts at the time of the murder."

"Balderdash! Why would *I* want to kill this Mr. Arnold? Doesn't make any sense! More than likely, it was the Burmese. I warned you they were sneaky."

Clive pinched the bridge of his nose.

"Where did you go after the stables, Colonel?" Henrietta asked in a calmer voice than Clive's.

Colonel Beaufort turned to her and blinked several times. "Why, I suppose I came in here. Helped myself to a drink, if you must know, and then went upstairs to my room."

"Did you hear or see anyone upstairs?" Henrietta asked.

"Not that I can recall. I must have dozed off up there."

"Did you not awaken when Lady Linley cried out upon her arrival back and the discovery of the . . . of the violation of her room?"

"I suppose I did not."

"Though your room was just down the hall?" Clive asked, observing him carefully.

Colonel Beaufort's face grew red. "Well, seeing as how I'm an *old* man," he said stiffly, "one cannot entirely account for one's actions. But if my opinion is worth anything, I'd look to this Burmese man. He's the ticket to this dastardly business. Now, if you'll excuse me. Good day, Mrs. Howard," he said with the slightest of nods and then hobbled out of the room.

"Oh, dear," Henrietta said with a sigh. "I think you've offended him, Clive."

"Well, so be it. I've certainly had worse slung at me." He looked at her wryly. "But he is right about one thing. We need to talk to Mr. Maung."

"You don't really think he did it, do you?"

"No, but we can't rule it out. I'm sure he has some choice information. If he hasn't left the country already. But first we need to get to Mrs. Pennyworth and Stevens before Yarwood befuddles them with his extreme incompetence."

"Clive! Don't be so hard on the man."

"I wouldn't be if he had one ounce of sense."

"You don't like him because he's Hartle's replacement," she said, patting his cheek. "Am I correct? Which makes you more than eager to solve this case."

He attempted to frown at her, but he couldn't hold a straight face and broke into a grin. *How did she always know?* "All right, then. Yes. I'm more than intrigued. I'm invested now. And if we're going to get ahead of Yarwood, we need to hurry."

Chapter 12

Melody hurried into the cemetery, trying her best not to step on any graves. Normally, she had an aversion to cemeteries. Even on Remembrance Day every year, when Pops made them all go and lay a wreath of poppies on Uncle Bert's grave, she always tried to get out of it, claiming one thing or another, but Pops would have none of it. "Died on the Somme, he did, for you! Least you can do is lay a wreath." But it was so horribly morbid. Didn't anyone see that? She was all for remembering the dead, of course, but standing on a sea of dead bodies, with only a few feet of earth between you and them, whilst crying and laying flowers that represented the blood of the fallen—this was surely *not* the way to honor anyone, was it?

But her current situation called for extreme measures. She desperately needed a place to rest and to think, and the cemetery, she had discovered after over a week in this prison, was the only place where she could truly be alone. There was always her room, of course, but it was horribly claustrophobic. She needed air.

She stepped carefully, walking along the fence to what had already become her favorite spot within the cemetery—the far eastern side, propped precariously as it was on the edge of a bluff, which overlooked the powerful Mississippi below.

Melody wasn't sure how much longer she could keep up this

impersonation. Why on earth had Elsie ever thought that this life was for her? Did she even know what it really consisted of? Daily chores, classes, and what seemed to be endless prayers. During the school year, the girls apparently attended nearby Clark College, but since it was summer, they took lessons at the convent. At first, Melody didn't mind the idea of this, thinking it would at least take away from the time they were required to be on their knees in the dark chapel, but when she discovered that all of the classes were *religion* classes, she nearly despaired, yet again.

The Merriweathers possessed a Bible, of course, but it sat preserved in a bookcase in the front parlor and was rarely touched, an unfortunate fact that was becoming more and more clear to Melody after only a few days in her new classes. Sitting amongst her fellow novitiates, she was beginning to realize how shockingly little she actually knew about the Bible or her faith in general. Twice now she had been assigned extra dish duty for asking inappropriate questions. But, she had persisted, she really *did* want to know who Cain and Abel had married. Their sisters? It seemed horribly obscene or perhaps a flaw in the story. She had always wondered about this passage and assumed that this might be the place to finally ask her question, but, alas, it was not.

Melody gripped the fence at the end of the long narrow graveyard now, having finally arrived at the end, and looked out at the Mississippi below. It looked calm and peaceful, but already she had heard stories amongst a few of the girls of people being pulled under by hidden currents and catfish as big as men living at the bottom.

What was she to do? Her delicious plan had somehow gone awry, and now she didn't know how to get out of it. She had squelched her earlier decision to confess, as surely Elsie needed more time than this, didn't she? Who knew if she had even reached Nebraska yet, much less have had the chance to have gotten married. Melody sighed. But how much longer could she endure this miserable existence? Who would willingly sign up for this drudgery and torture for the rest of their lives? It was horrible! Even Elsie, Melody was sure, would have found this difficult. Well, maybe not, Melody considered. Elsie was awfully studious and quiet. Eager to obey and please.

Melody gazed out at the barges traveling slowly downstream and let out a deep sigh. What had started as a jolly lark now seemed so much more serious. What would Sr. Bernard say when she found out? Would she expel her from Mundelein? What would her parents say? Her father, she knew, if he found out, would be furious, as he already thought that sending a girl to college was a waste of money. Now he would be proven right. Oh! Why hadn't she thought this through better?

She looked down at the town of Dubuque sprawled out along the edge of the river and, for a fleeting moment, considered simply running away. She could hitch a ride to Galena and then take the train back to Chicago and then another to Wisconsin, she reasoned excitedly. No one would be the wiser. But surely, the sisters here would raise the alarm for the missing Elsie Von Harmon. Would the police be called in? Elsie's family would probably be contacted, including her perfectly awful grandfather. Would he hunt her down? But by then, Elsie would surely be married, and there would be nothing he could do! Or was there? Would he have the power to have Gunther deported, or Anna sent to an asylum?

Oh, what should she do? The summer would soon be over, at which point, she would absolutely need to make a decision. She would either have to confess and be in a heap of trouble and possibly jeopardize Elsie's elopement, or simply flee and escape back home and hope that she had bought Elsie enough time to land on her feet.

Her eyes traveled to the little patch of grass on the other side of the fence. Perhaps there was a path that ran down to the town below? A shortcut, as it were. *Not* that she had necessarily decided to flee, but if she did, it would be good to know what the possibilities were . . .

But how could she get over the fence? She looked to her right and her left and noted with a bit of excitement that the fence corner to the north seemed a little shorter. It could be an optical illusion, she suspected, but decided to inspect it. Tenting her eyes from the afternoon sun, she made her way over and discovered that yes, it *was* a bit sunken. She considered it for a moment and decided that, though it would take some maneuvering in this silly habit, she thought she could scale it. Despite what the gang back at Mundelein thought of her, she had, in fact, been a bit of a tomboy growing up.

Glancing around one last time, she lifted her habit and perched her right foot on the thin crossbar near the bottom of the fence and heaved herself up. She lifted her left leg over and managed to grip the bar on the other side with her foot. Then, giving herself a lift, she pulled her right leg over and neatly hopped to the ground.

Pleased with herself, she decided to explore the thin ledge running along this side of the fence line. She gripped one of the iron spikes and gingerly took a few steps.

"Be careful there, Sister!"

Melody spun around and saw a man standing at the edge of the cemetery on the other side of the fence. Startled, she nearly lost her balance and let out a little scream. *Where on earth had he come from?*

"You'll fall to yer death, ya will." She had never seen this man around the convent before. To her eyes, he looked old, maybe sixty? But she was very bad at guessing ages.

"Who . . . who are you?" Melody called nervously, still gripping the fence.

"Name's Junior. I'm the caretaker of these here graves." He gestured behind him. "And those," he said nodding in her direction. "Though they don't need no carin' for, not really."

Melody nervously looked around but saw no other tombstones. "What graves?"

"Them there," he said, pointing at several mounds of earth just beyond her. They were covered with tall grass. She looked closer and could see that river rocks had been placed in a large circle all around them. She hadn't noticed before. Melody stepped closer, still holding onto the edge of the fence.

"Wouldn't go any closer if I was you," Junior said, aimlessly scratching his head.

"Why not?" She wondered if they were contaminated somehow. Maybe cholera victims? Or suicides? She could imagine this place had known several suicides . . .

"'Cause that there beyond them rocks is sacred ground. Well, not sacred for you and me, but sacred to the Indians."

Melody peered back at him, wondering now if he was teasing her. Or maybe touched in the head. She grew nervous again.

"Them's Indian graves. Can't walk on 'em, or you'll be cursed."

Melody stared at the mounds of earth, instantly fascinated. "Indian graves! Are you sure?"

"Well, course I am. I's the one who had to dig 'em up." He pulled out a red bandana from a pocket in his overalls and wiped his large brow.

"*You* dug them up?" Shivers ran down Melody's back as she hiked up her habit and climbed back over the fence into the proper cemetery. "Isn't that a sin or something? Weren't you afraid?"

"Well, no. Well, a little, I guess. Father Byrne was here and blessed everything, so I guess that made it all right. But the authorities said they had to call in a gen-u-ine Indian medicine man." He gestured toward the graves. "Had to get him in here all the way from some place in Nebraska where they still have a reservation. Chantin' and shoutin' up a storm, he was. Dressed all in feathers. You wouldn't a believed it. Burned something terrible; sage, I think someone said. Even had a local newspaper man up here takin' pictures. You go look it up if you want. In the *Telegraph Herald* it was, if you don't believe me. Oh, yeah, they documented it for sure."

Intrigued, Melody instinctively looked around for some kind of marker or plaque but saw nothing. "Shouldn't there be some sort of sign or something? I mean, anyone could just wander on them."

"That's what those rocks are for, I'm guessin'. Also, the medicine man put a curse on that land. Anyone who dishonors it, see, will be cursed."

Melody shivered again at how close she had come to stepping on them. She wasn't quite sure she believed all this, but if it was true, she didn't think it was quite fair to curse a piece of land and not have a way to announce it besides a circle of rocks, which were barely visible, by the way—they were practically buried themselves.

"Well, if you dug them up, what was in them?" She was morbidly curious.

"You dumb, or somethin'?" He scratched his head. "Why, skeletons, a course. 'Bout four of 'em. And a baby. Some pottery and stuff. Nice arrowheads. Reckon they were on a spear, but the wood musta rotted. There was a fight about it all. The city authorities or whoever thought all that stuff shoulda been sent off to Chicago to that big museum they got there, but the medicine man said no, that they had to be reburied or the spirits wouldn't be able to rest. He won in the end. Father Byrne wanted to bless them before they were put in the graves, but the medicine man wouldn't let him."

Melody pondered this for a few moments. "How were they discovered in the first place? The graves, that is?"

"Diggin' a grave I was, here in the corner for Sister Luca—there's her grave, right there." He pointed, and Melody was surprised that it was an old stone. Shouldn't it have been new? Maybe he was mistaken. "I was digging away, and there they were. Didn't think it was a sister's bones, not with the arrowheads and such, so I reported it to Sister Francesca, and she reported it to Father Byrne, and then we had people crawlin' up here. It was a pretty big news story, like I said. Didn't you hear about it? Weren't that long ago."

"No, I'm . . . I'm not from around here," she answered, wondering who Sr. Francesca was.

Junior's right eye squeezed shut as he peered at her. "What you doin' out here, anyway? It's rosary time. Don't you know that? You lost? Or are you a bolter? Always one bolter in the mix. Reckon it's you, ain't it? Why else would you be on the other side a the fence? You weren't goin' a jump were you? Had a couple of those over the years. But you don't look like the jumpin' type. Nah. You got more the look of a bolter to you."

"I'm neither, thanks very much. I was . . . I was just taking a walk. I needed some air."

"That's what all the bolters say. Next thing you know, they're gone. Well, if you *are* goin' to bolt, I suggest you go by the road." He tilted his head backward. "Ain't no path down there. Fall to yer death, ya will. But you do as you like. I got to go now."

Melody turned and looked back toward the river, wondering if he was lying about the existence of a path, but when she turned back around, the man was gone. Her eyes quickly darted across the length of the whole cemetery, but he was nowhere to be seen. Where had he disappeared to? She blinked her eyes. Had she imagined him? She rubbed her eyes with her hands. Maybe she had dreamt him. Maybe she was so tired that she was dreaming standing up. She pinched her arm and shook her head, but nothing changed. She was still standing in the middle of a cemetery.

Maybe he was a ghost . . .

She wrapped her arms around herself, suddenly cold despite the hot August air. But why would a ghost, if there were such things, have appeared to her? To tell her which way to bolt? (Which *was* odd, considering the fact that she was actually thinking about it.) But no, she thought as she wound her way back through the cemetery, his purpose seemed to have been to warn her from stepping on the Indian graves . . .

Oh, this is silly! she scolded herself. *Of course, he wasn't a ghost!* She was simply overtired. She needed to get back before anyone discovered her. Careful not to step on any of *these* graves either, she hurried as fast as she could, which wasn't very, as she had to practically hop from space to space, and eventually made it back to the gate, closing it behind her with a loud screech. She lingered for a few moments, her eyes traveling back across the nuns' resting places to the Indian graves and, despite her own woes, she felt a moment of sadness for the poor souls who, even in death, had been forced to move. Had the medicine man really been able to appease the spirits, or did the dead continue to wander this land in search of peace?

Melody reluctantly turned back toward the convent, still unsure of how she was going to untangle the mess she had created, when she saw one of the novitiates hurrying toward her. She had been discovered! Instinctively, she looked around for a hiding place, but it was no use.

"Oh, Elsie! There you are!" the girl exclaimed as she came to a halt in front of her. "We've been looking everywhere for you." She paused to catch her breath. "You're to come at once. You have a visitor!"

Chapter 13

"There you are, Lizzie! Get a move on, girl! 'Them potatoes ain't gonna peel themselves!" Mrs. Godfrey shouted at the kitchen girl hurrying through with a basket of potatoes and then turned her attention back to Clive and Henrietta, who were standing in the midst of the Castle Linley kitchens, the staff bustling around them, hurrying to get dinner prepared.

"Is there anything else you can think of?" Clive asked. The smell of roasting chickens permeated the air, and he could feel his stomach rumbling. "Anything at all?"

"Can't say that there is, sir," Stevens said with a little shrug. "I've already told you all I know. Mr. Arnold turned up promptly, at about ten, just as Mr. Howard said he would. He and the little Burmese fellow."

"What did they do first?"

Stevens scratched the side of his head. "Well, they were outside mostly. Looked at the stables and the other buildings, the old dairy and such, and then even walked down a little toward the lower copse."

"What did they do there?"

"I don't rightly know, sir. I was busy with my other work. Didn't know I was supposed to escort them," Stevens said, his voice lightly laced with a rare irritation.

"No, of course not," Clive mused, ignoring the butler's impertinence. "And what time did they come back?"

"I'm not exactly sure, sir. Mrs. Pennyworth might know that," Stevens said, looking over at the housekeeper, who stood perfectly erect, her hands folded tightly, a grim look on her face.

"I'd say around eleven," the older woman said, her face pinched.

"You're sure?"

"I *am* sure. Because I was sitting here with Mrs. Godfrey," she paused to nod at the plump cook standing nervously by the stove, "going over the week's menu, which we do every Monday at eleven, don't we, Mrs. Godfrey?"

"Aye, we do."

"Then Addie comes through saying that the two of them were requesting tea in the drawing room! The absolute cheek!" she exclaimed, drawing herself up even more rigidly than before, if that were possible. "The day I serve the likes of Mr. Edmund Arnold and a little foreign sod in the Linley drawing room is the day I give my notice, I said. But Mr. Stevens, here, said that we had to, that Mr. Howard had instructed they be accommodated. Though I'm very sure Mr. Howard didn't have that in mind. Weren't even supposed to be in the house, they weren't." She sniffed.

"You were not fond of Mr. Arnold, then?" Clive asked carefully. Though it seemed unthinkable that one of the servants had poisoned Mr. Arnold, it at least bore some consideration. The supposed elapsed time between Mr. Arnold's visit and his death seemed to indeed point to the poisoning occurring here at Linley, just as Inspector Yarwood suspected. But why? Why would anyone, especially the servants, want to murder a local estate man? It didn't make sense.

"No, I was not," Mrs. Pennyworth put in. "Though that's hardly a crime."

"What reason did you have for not liking him?" Clive asked.

"No reason in particular. Just rubbed me the wrong way."

"I'll tell you why," Mrs. Godfrey suddenly put in. "Everyone in Cromford knows Mr. Arnold to be an ambitious pillock. Thinks he's better than the next. He'd step on anyone to get ahead, that one would. He'd a sold his own child if he thought he could get enough outta 'im."

"Mrs. Godfrey!" Stevens scolded.

"I ain't gonna apologize fer the truth, Mr. Stevens," the cook exclaimed, waving a wooden spoon at him. "Lizzie," she shouted, "don't you have those peeled yet? Stop yer gawkin' and get a move on, girl! God in heaven!"

"Yes, Mrs. Godfrey," the girl said meekly and began to peel faster.

"And you were the one to prepare the tea tray?" Clive asked Mrs. Godfrey, who turned

her attention back to him now.

"Aye, it were me, but don't go thinkin' I had anything to do with no poison, Mr. Clive," Mrs. Godfrey said, daring to point the spoon at him now. Somehow the servants were already aware that the dead man had been poisoned. One of them had probably been listening at the door of the study. Stevens, more than likely. "I made it up, like, and set it on the table there to be carried in."

"Who delivered the tray?" Henrietta asked, finally speaking. Clive shot her a tiny wink.

"Well, it should have been Mr. Stevens or Jeremiah," Mrs. Godfrey explained. "But just as Mr. Stevens picked up the tray, young Dick runs in and announces there's a fire in the stables. Well, you can imagine. We all ran out, then, and—"

"All of you?" Clive interrupted.

Mrs. Godfrey paused to think. "Well, I s'pose not everyone. Don't know where Addie or Lizzie were. And Mrs. Pennyworth stayed, too. And then there was *your* lass. She followed us out later, I think. Didn't do much to help." The cook sniffed.

"So, you stayed behind," Clive said to Mrs. Pennyworth, her face still pinched. "Why was that? Weren't you worried?"

"Of course, I was worried, but I assumed there was enough help out there. And someone had to attend to the *guests*," she answered bitterly.

"So, *you* served the tea?"

"Yes, I did. And very improper it was. A housekeeper serving tea? Never known such a thing."

"I see. So, you delivered it to the two men. Did they say anything unusual?"

"I wouldn't know," she said tightly. "As it was, I never did bring it in to them. I was on my way to, but just then Miss Simms and Mr. Beaufort burst in, crying out that Miss Simms was injured and required immediate assistance. As if we didn't have enough going on! In a hurry, I set the tea on the side table in the hallway and ran to help poor Miss Simms. I will say, she seemed in a tolerable amount of pain. Had to help her all the way up. I called to that ninny, Addie, but the girl never came. For the life of me, I don't know where she gets herself off to." She crossed her arms resolutely, as if that were the end of the tale.

"Then what?"

"Well, I left Miss Simms in her room and ran back down to see about some ice. Finally found Addie and sent her up with it."

"What about the tea? Did you go back and deliver it?"

Mrs. Pennyworth's eyes shifted a bit. "I tried to. I remembered that I had left it in the hall and ran back to get it, near exhausted I was by this point. But when I got to the little table, the tray was gone."

"Gone?"

"Seems the guests served themselves," she said, wringing her hands a little, the first thaw in her otherwise rigid exterior. "When I saw that the tea tray was gone, I hurried into the small drawing room to let them know I would have another tray prepared, but I was gobsmacked to see the tea tray sitting there before them and the two of them digging in." Her hands twisted severely now. "The shame of it!"

"Are you sure some other servant didn't come along and do it?" Clive asked.

"No, I'm sure because Mr. Arnold announced it himself. Said, 'Hope you don't mind, but we saw the tray there and decided to help ourselves, didn't we, Mr. Maung? After all, the Lord helps those who help themselves!' " Mrs. Pennyworth's face flushed. "Cheeky sod."

"I see." Clive rubbed a hand through his hair. It literally could have been almost anyone that dropped the poison into the tea.

"It ain't my fault!" Mrs. Pennyworth suddenly burst out. "I blame Mr. Howard, I do. Not nearly enough of us to do our jobs properly. Whoever heard of the housekeeper serving tea!"

"Mrs. Pennyworth!" Stevens scolded. "For shame! Kindly hold your tongue!"

"I'll do no such thing, Mr. Stevens!"

"Enough!" Clive held up his hands. "We need to get to the bottom of this." He let out a deep breath and looked at Stevens. "How long were you in the stables?"

Stevens's previously stern face dropped into one of unease. "Not long, sir. As you know, it was a small fire. Easily put out."

"Did you happen to notice if Mr. Arnold went upstairs?" he asked, looking from Mrs. Pennyworth to Stevens.

Stevens looked puzzled. "Went upstairs? I . . . I don't think so, sir, but I can't say for certain. We . . . it was a very trying day." Stevens wiped his brow with his handkerchief.

"Yes, I can only imagine," Clive answered, noting how old the butler suddenly looked. He positively sagged. "Perfectly understandable. You've all held up well, considering."

"Thank you, sir. You've always been fair, sir. Not like some."

Clive thought it was an odd comment, but he ignored it for the moment. "Do you know what time Mr. Arnold and Mr. Maung left?"

"I couldn't say exactly, sir. Maybe noon, or a little after?"

"Hmmm. Well, thank you for your help. If you remember anything else, you'll tell me?""What about the writing on Lady Linley's mirror?" Henrietta suggested quietly.

"Yes," Clive said, giving her a grateful nod for reminding him. "Can either of you explain that?"

Stevens looked uneasily at Mrs. Pennyworth. "No, sir. Can't say that we can. Can you, Mrs. Pennyworth?"

"No, indeed," she said stiffly.

"Who made up Lady Linley's room this morning?" Henrietta prompted.

"That would have been Addie," Mrs. Pennyworth answered.

"And she didn't notice anything written on the mirror?"

"No, madam. She wouldn't have done, would she, with everything draped in black, like."

"Do you have any idea who might be responsible?" Clive asked.

"Very likely the ghost, sir," Mrs. Godfrey put in, her eyes wide.

Clive let out a deep sigh. "Mrs. Godfrey, a God-fearing woman such as yourself surely doesn't believe in ghosts, do you?"

"It's *because* I am God-fearin' that I *do* believe in ghosts, Mr. Clive!"

"Well, if they were to exist, I'm fairly certain they wouldn't write a cryptic message in lipstick, aren't you?"

"Lipstick?" Mrs. Godfrey asked curiously, looking from Stevens to Mrs. Pennyworth for an explanation. "I heard it were blood. I don't know anything of it bein' written in lipstick, but it don't surprise me. You don't know half the goin's on in this house. This house is full of secrets, it is."

"Oh? Such as what?" Clive asked, one eyebrow raised.

"Don't mind her, sir. She's just upset," Stevens put in hurriedly. "Mind yourself, Mrs. Godfrey!"

"Well, there is some unnatural spirits in this house, mark my words. Surely you remember the tales from when you were a boy here, Mr. Clive? Remember when Miss Julia got locked in the attic that one summer? How we all searched the property for hours? Lord Linley even sent us out to look down by the creek?"

"I never heard that story," Henrietta said, looking curiously at Clive.

"Oh, aye, madam. Poor little thing. We found her asleep in the attic, sweating to death. Said she went up to hide during a game, but found the door locked behind her. Odd, it was, because there ain't no lock on that door, and it opened easily enough after she was found. Terrified, the poor thing was. Said she saw a lady in white standing in the corner, watching her."

Clive let out an impatient breath. "Yes, that's a tired old tale, Mrs. Godfrey. A childish accident. Tell me, where is Addie?" he asked, changing the subject. "I'd like to ask her a couple of questions."

"Well, all right, Mr. Clive, but we do need to get on." Mrs. Godfrey glanced up at the big black clock on the wall. "Dinner is in little over an hour, and I ain't even near close," she fretted. "Lizzie!" she commanded. "Go fetch, Addie."

Lizzie dropped her paring knife and retreated from the room. After only a few moments, she reentered, Addie trailing behind as she wiped her hands on her apron.

"You wanted to see me, Mrs. Godfrey?" The girl addressed her superior, but her gaze was on Clive and Henrietta.

"It's Mr. Howard as does." The cook nodded at Clive.

"I'm not in any trouble, am I?" Addie squeaked.

"No, Addie." Henrietta threw Clive a look, which he perceived to be one of caution. "Just a few questions," she said gently. "When you went into Lady Linley's dressing room this morning, did you see any writing on the mirror?"

"No, madam."

"You're sure?"

"Yes, madam, I am, because the black cloth was covering it. I would have noticed if it were off."

"Did you see anyone upstairs this afternoon?" Henrietta went on. "Anyone coming out of Lady Linley's room? Mr. Arnold, for example?"

Addie thought for a moment. "No, madam. But I did see Mr. Beaufort coming out of Miss Simms's room."

"Mr. Beaufort? You mean Phineas?" Clive asked.

"Yes, sir," Addie answered with a blush.

"You're sure?" Henrietta asked.

"Yes, madam. Miss Simms rang for ice, you see, and Mrs. Godfrey sent me up with it. I had just reached the landing when I saw Mr. Beaufort slip out of the room."

"I see," Henrietta said, shooting Clive a look of excitement. "Thank you, Addie. You've been most helpful."

The girl curtsied and looked to Mrs. Godfrey for instruction.

"You can get back to yer pots," Mrs. Godfrey barked with a tilt of her head toward the scullery, and the girl, after giving a brief curtsey, turned and scurried back across the room.

"Just one more question, Addie," Clive called out to her before she disappeared.

The girl stopped abruptly and turned around. "Yes, sir?" she squeaked.

"Did you happen to notice if any of Lady Linley's jewelry has gone missing?"

"Jewelry?" Mrs. Pennyworth exclaimed.

Addie's face paled. "I . . . I don't know, sir. I don't believe so, like. I can check, sir."

"Yes, you do that and report back to me as soon as you can."

"Yes, sir," she said and then fled.

"I hope you don't think Addie stole something," Mrs. Pennyworth said sharply. "She's a good girl, she is. She'd never—"

"No, no. It's not that at all," Clive said dismissively. "Just curious." Clive shot a glance at Henrietta and tilted his head toward the archway. "We'll leave you to it, then, Mrs. Pennyworth. Thank you all for your help. If any of you think of anything else, any small detail, please let us know."

"Certainly, sir." Stevens bowed slightly.

Clive exited the kitchen, Henrietta following, and proceeded down the servants' hallway toward the back stairs.

"Now what?" Henrietta whispered from behind him as they began to climb.

"We still need to find Phineas. Or perhaps Miss Simms again."

"Agreed. At least regarding Phineas. But why Miss Simms?"

"Because," Clive said in a low voice, pushing on the door at the top of the spiral staircase, "there is something they're not telling us. Either Miss Simms lied about Phineas not being in her room or Addie did." He stepped into the foyer and held the door for Henrietta. "And I'm pretty sure it wasn't Addie."

Chapter 14

Julia was sure she had put back the ruby ring she had worn the other night at the Adlers', and yet it wasn't here.

Of all of her rings, this one was perhaps her most precious, as it had been a gift from her father on her eighteenth birthday. It was for that reason that she rarely wore it. But she had decided it would look perfect with the crimson Vionnet gown she had chosen for the Adlers' dinner party and had opted to wear it. And now it was gone.

One more time, she hurriedly opened all of the drawers of her jewelry armoire. It simply wasn't there. Her heart began to race a little harder. She tried to think back to what had happened that night. She had come up to her room; Randolph was still out, and Robbins had helped her undress. But she felt sure that it was she herself who had put her jewelry back, hadn't she? Perhaps she was losing her mind . . .

Slowly, she pushed the last drawer shut. It wasn't the first piece that had gone missing. Over the past year, she had noticed that a pair of diamond earrings had disappeared, then a pearl brooch, followed by a gold signet ring, and now it was her ruby. At first, she had feared she had simply lost or misplaced the items, but then she began to wonder if perhaps Robbins, or one of the other servants, was responsible. But that seemed unthinkable. Or was it? Maybe they were growing over-brave, knowing that their mistress would not dare report any of them, especially Robbins, whom she was pretty sure was Randolph's number one spy. How else did he keep tabs on her every move?

Whatever the case, it was true that she dared not report the loss of her jewelry to Randolph. He would be furious and would no doubt take it out on her. She pulled open the top drawer of the little armoire again. She was *sure* she had put the ruby ring back. She was certain of it—

"Looking for something?"

Julia jumped, nearly letting out a little scream. She turned to see Randolph himself standing in the doorway. He was still dressed in last night's tuxedo, albeit rumpled, and his tie was undone. His face was one of cold fury. *He must know!*

Julia slowly pushed the drawer back in and shut the tiny doors of the case, swallowing hard. "As a matter of fact, yes," she managed to say. "I . . . I seem to have misplaced my ruby ring." She decided not to mention the other pieces.

"You didn't misplace it," he slurred. "I took it."

"*You* took it?" Her stomach dropped. "But why?"

"I sold it."

"You sold it?" Angry tears suddenly filled her eyes. "How dare you!" she cried, without thinking. "That was a gift from my father!"

"Yes, a good one, too. It fetched a pretty price."

Her mind raced, and it quickly dawned on her where all the other items had gone. She felt she might be sick. "It was you who took my other pieces, wasn't it? I was beginning to think it was the servants. Or that I was losing my mind!" she exclaimed.

"That you are losing your mind, feeble as it is, I do not doubt. But let me remind you, my dear, that as your husband, everything you own is mine. Everything." His eyes flicked to the armoire. "And if you suspected something was missing, why didn't you tell me?" he asked, his voice growing more cold and hard. She began to tremble slightly. This was usually the precursor to a violent episode.

"I . . . I wasn't sure," Julia faltered.

He took a step closer. "Anything else you're hiding from me?"

Julia suddenly thought of the letter, lying secretly in the hidden pocket under the ring tray. *Surely, he hadn't found that, had he?* Her heart began to pound with fear.

"No, Randolph, I . . . there's nothing."

"Really?" he asked coolly. "Then, how do you explain this?" He reached into his inner jacket pocket and pulled something out. It was Glenn's letter.

Julia stared at it, mortified, her whole body suddenly frozen in fear. Even if she had *wanted* to run, her legs wouldn't move. "I . . . I can explain—" she said faintly, her heart pounding in her chest.

Randolph crushed the letter, Julia feeling the pain of it as if Randolph were crushing something deep within her. He threw it to the ground. Julia knew what was coming next. She looked frantically around the room for an escape, but there was none.

"Randolph, please," Julia begged, helplessly stepping on strained tiptoes behind the vanity chair, as if that would protect her. "I . . . I can explain," she said, nearly vomiting from fear.

"Shut up, you bitch!"

With one swift move, he grabbed her by the upper arms and violently shook her. "I warned you to stay away from him!" he snarled as he struck the first blow. "And now you're going to get what's coming to you."

Over and over, he beat her, dealing one blow after another to her face, her stomach, her ribs, even her back. At one point she heard a sickening crack from her arm, and she felt herself fall, slowly, as if into a black void. A new burst of pain filled her when she hit her head on her bedside table as she fell. She let out a little cry of pain as her body collapsed into a heap beside the crumpled letter. Randolph gave her one final kick, and then she lost consciousness.

Julia lay there for hours until Robbins, entering the room to turn down her bedclothes, found her still unconscious on the floor.

"Oh, madam! Oh, you poor thing," Robbins said, rushing to her.

Julia came to, then, pain searing through every part of her body, as Robbins struggled to help her to her feet and into bed. One arm was hanging at an odd angle, and Julia actually screamed when Robbins attempted to lift her slip over her head. The pain was so intense, she thought she might pass out again.

"Oh, I'm sorry, madam!" Robbins exclaimed. "I'll go and ring the doctor!"

"No, Robbins! No," Julia groaned. "No. I'll be all right." She could barely see Robbins, as one eye was completely swollen shut. "No doctor."

"Oh, madam, but you can't stay like this. You need help."

Julia could feel that she was losing consciousness again. "Promise, no doctor, Robbins. "And don't let the boys see me this way. Promise," she begged, her voice hoarse, as she drifted back into blackness, the pounding in her head incessant.

Julia could hear someone banging on the front door now, but she couldn't move. She was in too much pain. Her eyes fluttered open. The banging was incessant. Why didn't anyone answer the door? An errant thought wandered into her mind that perhaps it wasn't the door. Maybe it was her ears. She vaguely remembered now that one of them had been bleeding. She turned onto her side, pain ripping through her ribs. Blessedly, the banging stopped, then, but it was disturbingly replaced by the sound of pounding footsteps on the staircase and a man's voice. Julia shrank under her blanket, bracing herself for what she hoped was not another beating from Randolph, though the voice, if she were not mistaken, was not his. It sounded more like—

"You can't go in there, sir!" she heard Robbins cry, but the door banged open anyway.

"Julia!" It was Sidney Bennett. "Julia, oh my dear, lord, what's happened to you?" He approached the bed tentatively.

"I'm sorry, madam. He just pushed right past me!" Robbins cried from where she remained in the doorway. "You'll have to leave, sir," she tried to say sternly to Bennett. "You can't be up here."

"My God, Julia," Bennett exclaimed. "What happened? Were you in an accident? Why were we not told?" He looked accusingly at Robbins and then back at Julia.

Julia's first reaction was to do what she normally did and lie, but she found she had not the energy to continue any more subterfuges. She released a deep breath, pain searing through her chest. "You may go, Robbins," she said thickly, her voice hoarse from lack of use. Her mouth was so dry.

Robbins wavered in the doorway, her face one of distress. "Mr. Cunningham won't like it, madam."

Julia responded with a slight wave of her left hand, and Robbins, after looking nervously from her mistress to Mr. Bennett, finally hurried out.

"Dearest Julia," Bennett said, stepping closer. "Please tell me what happened."

Julia did not meet his eyes. "I think you can guess," she said hoarsely.

Bennett did not say anything, and Julia, rather than look at him, turned her head to the wall.

"Oh, Julia. My poor dear."

"Please, Mr. Bennett—"

"Sidney."

"Please don't tell anyone," she said to the wall. "Don't tell Mother." She closed her eyes.

Bennett did not say anything and remained silent for so many moments that Julia wondered if he had possibly left the room. She turned slightly to look over her shoulder to check. He was still there, looking at her with pity.

"Has this happened before?"

Julia didn't answer.

"My God," Bennett said bitterly. "Does Clive know?"

"I think he suspects."

"How long has it been going on?"

Julia's throat suddenly ached with tears. "From the beginning," she finally croaked.

"Jesus Christ. That bastard! Why did you not tell Antonia?"

"I tried to after . . . after it first happened, but she said that was part of married life."

"What? I can't imagine your mother saying that."

"I don't think she realized how bad it was, and I was too ashamed to elaborate."

Bennett began to pace. "Well, you can't stay here."

Julia let out a tired little laugh that turned into a cough. "Well, I can't leave, either. You needn't worry, Mr. Bennett. Sidney. I'll soon be on my feet again."

"This is disgraceful!" Bennett continued to pace.

Julia felt her throat closing up. "Might I have some water?" she croaked.

Bennett looked at her in alarm. "Yes, yes, of course." He hurried to the bedside table and poured a glass of water from the pitcher sitting there. Julia tried to sit up, but the pain was intense, and she couldn't help but cry out. Bennett hurriedly set the glass down and tried to assist her. Finally, she managed to sit up enough to hold the glass and eagerly drink.

"Why are you here, anyway?" She peered at him with her good eye.

"Your mother hasn't heard from you in a week." He stepped away from the bed. "You did not return her calls, so she got worried."

A week! *Had she really been lying here for a whole week?* Then another thought occurred to her. "Why didn't she come, then? Why did she send you?"

Bennett shifted. "You know how she feels about Randolph. I suppose she was afraid. So, she asked me to investigate."

Julia wanted to scream, or perhaps just release the tears she was fiercely holding back. Her mother was afraid to come here and face her ogre of a husband, and yet she apparently felt no qualms about abandoning her daughter to the monster. The cruel irony of it crushed her. "I see," she said, a stray tear rolling down her cheek. "Well, here I am. You can report back to Mama that I'm quite well. Jolly old Julia. She'll persevere."

"I think you misunderstand her, Julia. She's very concerned."

"Oh, well, in that case." Julia turned her head to look at the wall again. The lump in her throat was so immense she thought she might suffocate. She knew she was being childish. What did it matter what her mother thought? About anything, really? She had much bigger things to worry about, but for some reason she was finding it hard to concentrate on them. What should she do?

"Julia, please. You must let me take you to Highbury. You must get well. We can worry about what to do later."

"I can't leave here!" she said with unexpected force. "Randolph would have a fit!"

"Well, let him, the bastard."

"Mr. Bennett, you are a man of business and the law," she tried to say calmly. "Surely you can see my predicament. If I leave to recuperate, especially to Highbury, I will eventually have to return and face his fury. Leaving now is tantamount to leaving permanently or returning to a death sentence."

"Fine. We will file for a bill of divorce."

Julia let out a bitter little laugh. "Mother would never approve."

"Julia, you do her a disservice, you know. She is . . . different since your father died."

Julia wondered how much of that had to do with the fact that her mother was in a . . . a relationship—for lack of a better word—with the man now standing before her, the man Antonia had loved before she had been forced to marry her father. Her mother's hypocrisy was almost too much to bear. But she couldn't think about that now. It made her head ache. In fact, her vision was starting to blur a little.

"I can't divorce Randolph," she said, closing her eyes briefly to see if her vision would clear. It did not. "He'll take the boys from me. He's already said."

"I don't think he can do that, Julia. Especially now, after this. It would be easy enough to prove him to be an unfit father."

"You don't know Randolph the way I do."

"Perhaps not, but I know his type."

Julia smiled briefly. "That sounds like something Glenn would say."

A ripple of something crossed Bennett's face. "Did you . . . did you receive his letter?"

She looked at him curiously, wondering how he knew. The pain in her eye was searing. "Yes, I did, but unfortunately Randolph found it." She gestured weakly at her bruised body.

Bennett began to pace again. "Glenn's terribly worried. He . . . he confided to me that he wrote to you, but that you didn't write back. He wondered if perhaps the letter had gone astray," he said grimly. "Which I suppose it did, in a way." Julia felt his warm hand on top of hers now, but she did not look at him. "He wanted me, if I should ever get the chance, to reiterate to you that his offer of help still stands."

Tears flowed freely now. She couldn't help it.

"I do not know what has passed between the two of you," Bennett said softly, "but surely this might be the time to turn to him. He is a most noble young man. You will not find one better."

Julia looked at him blearily and found she couldn't actually speak. Even if she could, what would she possibly say? Without realizing it, Bennett had come directly to the heart of the problem. She could never accept the help of such a man as Glenn Forbes. He was too good, and she, on the other hand, was too damaged.

Chapter 15

"He's very good at disappearing; I'll give him that," Henrietta said, putting her hands on her hips. "Where on earth could he be? Perhaps he has some secret hiding place. God knows, it would be easy enough to have one in this place." She and Clive had spent the last half hour searching the house for Phineas, and they had now arrived back basically where they had started, which was in the main foyer at the base of the grand staircase. The door to the servants' staircase through which they had originally come was closed now, blending into the wallpaper perfectly. Clive stood near the immense grandfather clock, still silent, and the large gong used to call guests to dinner, yet another carryover from the Victorian era.

"Maybe he's outside." Clive ran his hand irritably through his hair and then sneezed. He pulled out his handkerchief to blow his nose.

"Darling, I'm sure you're coming down with something. Why don't you rest before dinner. We can interrogate Phineas later."

"I'm perfectly fine," Clive said, stuffing his handkerchief back into his pocket. "Ah, there's Stevens!" The back side of the butler could just be seen entering the library down the hall. "Stevens!" Clive called.

The butler paused, hesitated for the briefest of seconds, and then retreated back toward them. "Yes, sir?"

"Do you happen to know where Phineas is?"

"Indeed, sir. I believe he's in the billiard room."

Clive's brow furrowed. "We've already checked there."

"He's only just entered, sir. Rang for some fresh soda water to be brought."

"I see. Thank you, Stevens."

"Very good, sir," he said with a slight bow and retreated.

"Don't be annoyed, darling," Henrietta said as she followed Clive down the long gallery, past the dining room, and toward the billiard room beyond. "But I'm not quite sure why we're concentrating on Phineas. You don't think he's responsible in some way for Mr. Arnold's death, do you? Shouldn't the murder take precedence over a silly prank?"

"Yes, but if Phineas was actually upstairs as Addie claims he was, perhaps he can tell us something of Mr. Arnold's movements."

"Ah. I suppose you're right."

"And I have a hunch there's something Phineas—*and* Miss Simms, for that matter—aren't telling us. Why else would she have lied about Phineas being in her room?" They had reached the billiard room now, and Clive paused just outside the door.

"I can think of one reason." Henrietta gave him a sly grin.

Clive stared at her for a moment, the corners of his eyes creased. "Are you suggesting that they are *romantically* involved?" he hissed. "That's ridiculous!"

"Why is that ridiculous? Have you not observed how he looks at her?"

"No, I have not," Clive said in a low voice. "For one thing, he's barely eighteen, and she must be several years his senior."

Henrietta let out a little laugh. "I hardly think that matters, Inspector," she said, taking hold of his lapels. "The two of us needn't look very far for an example." She smiled up at him.

"That's different!" Clive protested.

"Why? Because you're an older man? Why couldn't it be an older woman?"

"Because Phineas does not seem capable of such a thing," Clive insisted, removing her hands from his suit coat. "He's barely a man. And regardless of age, his behavior is still that of a mischievous schoolboy."

"Well, perhaps he merely went up to check on her ankle?"

"That's another thing." Clive rubbed the back of his neck. "I'm not so sure Miss Simms really did sprain her ankle."

Henrietta's lips twisted into another smile. "I've been thinking the same thing! But why would she fabricate an injury? Unless—" She tilted her head to the side. "Unless, of course, it was an excuse for the lovers to be alone together."

"Henrietta, I'm very sure they are not lovers."

Henrietta shrugged irritably. "Well, then, maybe she really was asleep, as she says she was, and he took advantage of the situation to steal a lipstick and pass through to Lady Linley's room through the connecting door?"

"Or were they in on the joke together?"

"I don't think Miss Evelyn Simms would participate in something so cruelly childish. She would be risking much in doing so, and to what end? It doesn't make sense."

"Maybe she wasn't a participant, but merely an unfortunate witness and not willing to rat Phineas out?"

"There would have to be a very strong reason," Henrietta mused. "Like love," she teased, one eyebrow raised.

"I give up. Come on," he said, pushing on the billiard room door with his good shoulder.

Phineas was indeed in the room, bent over the table and taking aim.

"I say! Here you are!" Phineas exclaimed, standing up straight. "Can't find anyone about. Everyone seems locked in their rooms. Care for a game?"

"We need to ask you some questions, Phineas."

"Not you, too. My word, this is tiresome. First that bloody inspector and now you, apparently. Anyone would think that *I* killed poor Mr. Arnold."

"Did you?" Clive asked.

"Of course, I didn't!" he said drolly as he bent down and shot a ball across the table.

"Why didn't you escort Miss Simms up to her room when you first arrived? According to her, Mrs. Pennyworth and Addie helped her up the stairs."

"Yes, that's right." His attention was still on the table.

"Well? Where were you?"

"If you must know, I did try to help, but Mrs. Pennyworth shooed me away. Told me to go find Stevens."

"And did you? Find Stevens, that is?"

"As a matter of fact, I didn't." He hit another ball and then stood up, facing them. "Couldn't find him in the end. Couldn't find any servants, actually. Never around when you need them, are they?"

"Did you see Mr. Arnold or Mr. Maung?" Henrietta asked.

"No, I did not. I went upstairs and changed." Phineas walked to the other side of the table, assessing his next shot.

"And then what?"

Phineas didn't answer but instead bent and aimed his cue at a ball, shifting it back and forth through his hands until he finally thrust it and it connected with a ball. "I don't know. Wandered about, I suppose."

"Did you go to Miss Simms's room?"

"Yes, I did, come to think of it."

"What for?"

"Well, obviously to check on her ankle. Couldn't get a bloody look in with Pennyworth bustling about, but as soon as she left, I popped in to see if I could be of any assistance."

"How long did you remain there?" Clive asked.

Phineas shrugged. "Don't know. Wasn't looking at the clock," he said, rolling his eyes.

"Phineas, you must realize how unseemly it was for you to enter and remain for any length of time in a lady's bedchamber," Henrietta said gently.

Phineas finally had the decency to at least appear offended. "I say! Just what are you suggesting?"

"Just admit it, Phineas," Clive demanded.

"Admit what?" The young man's face was suddenly flushed.

"Admit that you pinched one of Miss Simms's lipsticks on your way through her room to Lady Linley's and wrote that cruel message."

Phineas laughed. "Hello? Is that what you think?"

"Just answer the question."

"No, I did not."

"Who else would have done it?"

Phineas shrugged. "How should I know?" He leaned down to shoot another ball. "It was obviously meant to be a joke." He hit it with a loud crack. "I'm the one that told you about it in the first place. Why would I do that if I was the guilty party?"

Henrietta glanced at Clive's clouded face. She could tell that he was quickly tiring of Phineas.

Phineas stood up straight and brushed back his errant lock of hair. "Look, I know how you detective types like to have everything wrapped up neatly, but it wasn't me. Nor Miss Simms, in case that was your next thought. And what does it matter, anyway? Shouldn't you be more concerned with the death of that poor sod? What was his name? Arnold? I say!" he said suddenly. "Maybe it was the ghost! The hanged maid!" His tone was almost one of glee.

"Don't be asinine, Phineas," Clive scolded. "Now you're just acting the goat!"

"Stranger things have happened, you know," he said with a dismissive shrug. "There have been many cases where the hand of the grave crosses into our plane of existence." He wiggled his fingers beside his head.

"You seem quite knowledgeable about the macabre, Phineas." Henrietta shivered a little, her mind suddenly drifting back to Madame Pavlovsky, the spiritualist they had not long ago investigated back home.

"Yes, I am. I find the occult quite fascinating; do you not?" he asked eagerly.

"No, we don't!" Clive said harshly. "Come, Phineas, isn't there anything else you can tell us?"

Phineas tossed his cue onto the table. "For the last time, no." The gong was then heard waffling up from below. "Ah!" He flashed them a cocky grin and nodded toward the door. "You'll excuse me while I dress for dinner, won't you?" He gave them a final shrug and marched gaily from the room as if he hadn't a care in the world.

"What an annoying little rotter," Clive muttered.

"You take him too seriously, Clive. Don't let him get to you. Let's just assume he wrote the cryptic message as a joke and move on. I'm quite sure neither he nor Miss Simms murdered Mr. Arnold, and he apparently, if he can be believed, didn't see anyone else about upstairs. I think he's harmless. What we *should* do is—"

There was a faint knock at the door, then, from the other end of the room, and they both turned in unison to see Addie poke her head in and then enter fully.

"Forgive the intrusion, like, Mr. Howard." She curtsied and then stood hesitating, though she was clearly distraught.

"Come in, Addie," Henrietta said. "You're not intruding. What is it?"

Addie took a few steps closer. "It's about Lady Linley's jewelry case. You asked me to check, remember?"

"Yes?" Clive asked eagerly. "What did you find?"

Addie looked nervously from one to the other, twisting her hands. "Well, it's just as you suspected, Mr. Howard. There *is* something missing! One of Lady Linley's rings!"

"Are you sure, Addie?" Henrietta asked gently.

"Oh, yes, madam! It's the blue sapphire with two small diamonds on the side. Oh, she'll be so upset when she finds out!" She wrung her hands again.

"Are you sure it wasn't just put back in the wrong place?"

"No! I took a good look in all the drawers and saw that everything was in its place, but when I opened the ring drawer, I sees right away that it were gone. And since her ladyship only wears it on Christmas

Day, it ain't likely that it was used lately and put back in the wrong place. No, it's truly gone! I've looked everywhere." At this point, poor Addie began to cry, muttering that it wasn't her fault, that she wasn't really trained to be a lady's maid, and yet she had to wait on Lady Linley, plus do all of her own chores, and it's a wonder her head hadn't fallen off by now with all of the confusion.

"It's okay, Addie," Henrietta said, putting her arms around the girl. She was probably not much younger than Elsie. "You're not to blame. Leave it to us."

"But what will you tell Lady Linley or his lordship?"

"Nothing for now," Clive said sternly. "Don't tell anyone about this, Addie. Not even Mrs. Pennyworth or Stevens. You haven't already, have you?"

"Oh, no, sir. I came straight to you. But are you sure I shouldn't tell Mrs. Pennyworth? I could lose my place." She was back to twisting her hands.

"No, Addie. It's best kept a secret for a while yet. Just until we figure out who did it. You understand, don't you?"

The girl nodded unconvincingly. "If you say so," she said hesitantly.

"You won't be in trouble. I promise," Clive said in a gentler tone, after which the girl curtsied and hurried from the room.

"So," Henrietta said, folding her arms as she turned to Clive. "Your theory was correct."

"It was you that thought of it first, darling," he said with a smile. "But just like the poisoning, it could have been anyone that took that ring, and at any time. Who knows? A former servant could have snatched it the day after Christmas last and absconded with it and is far away with it at this point."

"True," Henrietta mused. "But it would seem to me that *someone* would have noticed it's absence by now."

"A lady's maid, perhaps. But since Lady Linley has been short a maid these many months, it makes sense. A frazzled Addie, filling in as she has been, may not have been paying as close attention."

"Yes, I see what you mean."

"I think a trip into town is in order, don't you? Fancy lunch at the White Hart?"

Henrietta brightened. "Oh, yes! Let's. It would be good to get away from here for a bit." She wrapped her arm around his. "And now, we need to dress as well. I think we've done enough for today."

Chapter 16

"That's enough for today, I think," Elsie said to Anna, shutting the book in front of her. She kissed the girl on the side of the head.

The book they had been reading from was a collection of Tennyson's poetry, the only book in English that Gunther had brought with him. The rest were in German. Elsie wished she could have brought some of her own books or had had the time to pack even a small valise before running off with Gunther, but as it was, she had eloped with only her handbag, which contained ten dollars and forty-seven cents, a handkerchief, a pencil, a small pad of paper, and a lipstick. They had already burned through the cash, of course, and the lipstick was utterly useless out here on the prairie. She didn't even wear any to church, which she attended only sporadically if they had the energy to walk into town—another sin to pile on top of her others, which she had surprisingly learned to live with quite easily. What did it matter at this point?

Even the pad of paper had gone quickly, as she had in the beginning stupidly used every inch of every page to try to teach Anna the alphabet. After that, she had begun tracing the letters in the dust with a stick and had Anna imitate her. Eventually, though, this grew tiresome, so Elsie had used the last of her money to purchase an old-fashioned slate and some chalk at the mercantile in town, which was infinitely better for Anna to practice with. She also bought a notebook, but she kept that to write out simple sentences for Anna to try to read, as teaching a child to read using Tennyson's poems was almost as useless as the lipstick had been. Still, she tried. And she continued to teach the neighbor children whenever they were free, but she gave Anna extra lessons at night.

They had been spared in the storm, though an old cottonwood had uprooted and fell onto the Wilkins's barn, crushing the back half. That meant extra work for the farmhands, and for several weeks, Elsie barely saw Gunther. The storm had been worth it, however, in a strange way, as it had been the inadvertent cause of Anna beginning to speak again. She was still abnormally quiet for a child of five, but Elsie thrilled that she was talking some, and, in particular, her heart melted when Anna timidly called her "Mama." It was almost as special as when Gunther whispered *"Liebling"* into her ear when they made love at night.

They had finally consummated their marriage, though it had not occurred for many weeks after their wedding day, Gunther being stoically patient, biding his time until the moment was right. While Elsie had adored him for this, she knew he could not wait forever and struggled with herself. In truth, a part of her longed to be intimate with Gunther—hadn't parts of her begun to tingle and hum with even just his kisses?—but the fact remained that she was terrified. Memories of being roughly handled by Lieutenant Harrison Barnes-Smith continued to haunt her, though that incident had happened over a year ago. She had never told Gunther all of the details surrounding Harrison's abuse, but he seemed to understand her reticence and respected it. And while Elsie was grateful for his consideration, it began to occur to her that the longer they waited to be fully man and wife, the more apprehensive she was becoming, until she could almost think of nothing else. Each night, as she lay chastely beside him, she wondered if he would choose *this* night to take her, but he never did. Eventually, then, a new thought entered her head, and she began to worry that perhaps he didn't mean to at all. Hadn't he said back in the flop house that he would wait for her to be ready? Was he really waiting for her to take the initiative? Surely not!

As it turned out, it happened not in the way Elsie had expected at all.

It was a Friday night, and when Gunther came back from his usual trip into town with the wagon of beets, he had entered the sod house with a smile on his face and a bottle of wine in hand.

"Look what I have," he had said, holding it up proudly.

Elsie looked up from where she was cooking at the stove. She frowned, worried. "Where did you get that?"

"I bought it in town," Gunther said, setting it down on the table.

"With what?"

"Never mind that," Gunther said, a small smile about his lips. "It is not every day that a man celebrates anniversary of two months."

Elsie's breath caught in her throat as she quickly calculated. Had it already been two months? Yes, it was, she realized, and bit her lip, guessing as to what the purchase of the wine implied. She said nothing more and instead tried to concentrate on getting supper on the table, but she ended up burning the biscuits, and the meat was tough. Indeed, her hands were practically trembling by the time she put the stew on the table. She ate little and said less as the evening passed, despite Gunther's attempts at conversation, and was grateful for the reprieve putting Anna to bed afforded.

Unfortunately, Anna drifted off to sleep quickly, and Elsie had no choice but to rise from the girl's trundle by the woodstove. Carefully, she removed her apron and hung it on the nail beside the sink. She smoothed her dress and pulled the curtain, which Gunther had previously hung in an attempt to create a separate front room, such as it was, from the kitchen.

She turned from the curtain and was surprised to see that he had already poured the wine and was sitting, waiting for her. He smiled gently and held out his hand. "Sit with me."

Elsie went to him and took his hand.

"I shall read to you?" His voice was low and gentle.

She had not expected him to say this, and she nodded eagerly.

Gunther released her hand and went to the little shelf he had crafted and fastened to the wall, which held the few books they owned. He selected Tennyson and sat back down and then began to read. He began with "The Princess" and then moved on to "The Lady of Shalott" and then to "Marriage Morning," the poem that had brought the two of them together. She was completely immersed in his words, which, between sips of wine, served to calm and relax her. She loved the sound of his voice and the poems that he had already read to her many times before. Indeed, his love of poetry had been what had drawn her to him in the first place. Finally, when the wine was gone and the candle burned quite low, he shut the book and set it on the table.

She studied his angular face, as she had done so many times before. The flickering flame illuminated his long blond lashes and blond stubble, and she felt a rush of love for him. He looked up at her and caught her staring at him, and she quickly lowered her gaze.

"I have something else for you," he said with a small smile and shifted to reach into the pocket of his trousers. He removed a small velvet bag. He tugged at the drawstring and dumped a small gold ring into the palm of his calloused hand and then held it up for her to see.

"Oh, Gunther!"

He stood and reached for her hand, pulling her up beside him. "I am sorry I did not have this on the day." Still holding her left hand loosely, he proceeded to slowly push the ring onto her fourth finger. "With this ring, I wed thee," he said, sliding it into place and then squeezing her hand. "*Ich verspreche dir mein Leben und meine Liebe, Elsie*—I pledge my life and my love to you, Elsie. You have made me happiest of men."

"Oh, Gunther!" Elsie exclaimed, rubbing the ring with her thumb. "First the wine and now this. Where are you getting this money?"

"That is not answer I was expecting," he said, the corners of his eyes creased playfully.

"Oh, Gunther, it's . . . it's beautiful," she said as she studied it again, "but I know we don't have money for this."

"I sold my father's watch." He said it matter-of-factly.

"Oh, Gunther, no! Not that! That's all you have left of his."

"It matters not, *Liebling*. Perhaps for this reason I was given it. To use when it is most needed."

Elsie's eyes filled with tears.

"*Liebling*, why do you cry?" He reached up and gently wiped a stray tear that tumbled down her cheek.

"I don't deserve you," she murmured.

Gunther grasped her hands. "Ach, no! Never say that, Elsie. You *do* deserve me. You deserve better than me—a prince. Look what I have brought you to."

"I don't want anything or anyone else. I want only you," she said through blurred eyes.

Gunther leaned forward then and brushed his lips against hers. It was the briefest of kisses. Elsie thought he would pull away then, as he usually did, but this time he did not. He kissed her again, deeper this time, and she felt the familiar stirring within her. For once, she didn't want him to stop. He seemed to sense this and continued kissing her, fully, exquisitely, until he was breathing quite raggedly, at which point he abruptly pulled away, as if to slow things down.

"Shall I tell you secret?"

Panting a little herself, she nodded.

"I have never done this before. Never lay with a woman." He looked at her furtively. "I am nervous, too. You will show me, yes? How to please you?"

Elsie blinked rapidly, stunned by this revelation, by his honesty, and felt an all-new waterfall of love for him erupt within her. Urgently, she wished to put him at ease, to put herself at ease, but she wasn't sure how. Tentatively, she put her hands on his torso, one on each side, and gripped his shirt.

He took her face in his hands. "You are sure?" he whispered.

She swallowed hard, mortified by how loud it was, and leaned forward and awkwardly kissed him. Gunther responded to her kiss with one of his own, wrapping his arms around her as he did so. He moved from her lips to her nose, her cheek, her neck, and then back to her lips, growing more urgent with each.

"Come," he said softly, finally breaking his kisses. "It is time."

He took her hand, then, and led her to their little bedroom, where night after night, they had lain together, not touching each other. He stopped when they were standing beside the bed and, turning to her, tucked a strand of her hair behind her ear. Elsie swallowed hard again and was sure that he must have heard it this time. Either way, he seemed to sense her nervousness and leaned in to kiss her again.

"Do not be afraid, *Liebling*," he said in a low voice. Softly, gently, he peppered her face and neck with kisses until she felt herself responding. This was nothing like her lovemaking with Harrison, if it could even be called that, who had barely kissed her at all when he had violently taken her virginity. This was something else altogether, and when she hesitantly touched her tongue to his, she felt him stiffen and pull her tighter to him so that she could feel his hardened state between them. His hands moved to her breasts, and though the rough fabric of her dress separated his fingers from her flesh, she felt inexplicably aroused. It must have aroused Gunther, too, because he began to quickly shrug out of his suspenders, even while kissing her. He struggled to free himself of his shirt, however, so he abruptly stopped his kisses to pull it off, followed by his undershirt. He stood before her, then, naked from the waist up, and, God help her, she could not look away.

Tentatively, she reached out and touched the blond curls on his heaving, muscled chest, and she felt him tremble beneath her fingers. He pulled her to him and kissed her while she furtively began to undo her own buttons. As soon as her dress hung partially open, he tugged the fabric off her shoulder and kissed the skin beneath. With shaking hands, Elsie undid the last of the buttons. The dress fell to her feet, and she gingerly stepped out of her shoes. She had given up wearing a girdle and stockings since she had begun working on the farm, and she stood before him now in just her silk slip, the only remaining vestige of her previous life of luxury.

"*Elsie, du bist so schön. Gott im Himmel, hilf mir*—Elsie, you are so lovely. God in heaven, help me." Roughly, he undid his belt, and while he quickly shed himself of his trousers, shoes, and socks, Elsie shyly looked away. When she looked back, he was standing only in his underthings, and Elsie could not help but see the bulge in them. He stepped closer and gently cupped her breasts in his hands through the silk, caressing them until her nipples hardened, and she felt a pull in her groin. He kissed her then, electrifying her when his tongue now found its own way to hers. He pulled her down to the bed without breaking his kiss and eased himself beside her. Elsie's heart was beating wildly as his calloused hands began to slowly travel over her, only the thin slip serving as a barrier between their trembling bodies. She felt positively on fire, humming like an electric wire across two poles. The desire inside of her was building to a point where she felt she might lose control, and she began to squirm. She had not felt anything with Harrison, and she wasn't sure what to do with her rising passion. Gunther seemed to sense her anxiety. "What is it? What is wrong?" he asked huskily.

"Nothing is wrong." Timidly, she ran a hand along his shoulder and felt it ripple.

"Show me," he nearly begged. "Show me how to please you."

Without pausing to consider propriety or modesty—or anything, really—Elsie took his hand and placed it between her legs. Gunther let out a deep groan and began to caress her, seeming to instinctively know what to do from there while he continued to kiss her neck and her lips. Elsie began to moan and pant, her head moving from side to side at the sheer pleasure of his touch. "Gunther, I . . . please," she mewed, fearing that her heart might suddenly explode in her chest. In response, Gunther eased himself on top of her, and she felt the tip of his stiff manhood enter her. He paused, breathing raggedly.

"Yes?" His voice was guttural.

She tightened the grip on his back. "Yes, oh, yes," she panted and groaned as he pushed all the way in. She felt him fill her, and when he began to rhythmically move on top of her, slowly at first and then with more fervor, her body uncontrollably contorted, her back arching and her breasts bouncing wildly as waves of pleasure washed over her. With a loud cry, Gunther simultaneously spilled himself inside of her, shuddering deeply.

He lay on top of her for several moments, panting and utterly spent as he kissed her cheeks, her forehead, her lips, her shoulder until he finally slipped off.

"Oh, Gunther," she whispered as she turned to him and traced the side of his jaw with her finger.

"Did I hurt you?" His voice was tender.

"No," she said, still breathing heavily. "No, it was lovely. I love you, Gunther."

"I love you, too," he said, reaching for her hand and bringing it to his lips. "For ever and ever, Elsie." He was still breathing heavily. "*Für immer*—Forever."

Their relationship changed from that moment on. Before, they had lived almost as a brother and a sister, respectful and helping each other, but now, their every action was filled with an added expression of love. A glance, a touch on the back, a quick kiss. Elsie felt fulfilled and delighted in a way she never had before, and more than once, she wondered if this was how Henrietta felt. She reveled in her new role of not just wife, but lover, too. For the first time in her life, she felt attractive and desired, truly loved. Likewise, she was caught up in an almost ecstasy of adoration for Gunther. Her heart had always been filled with utter love for him, but now that they were intimate, she found she adored him in a way she thought the saints in heaven must adore God. She was sure that was sacrilegious, but she didn't care.

And she loved Anna, as well, truly loved her as her own child. And she marveled at how strongly she could feel for a child that had not only not been born of her flesh, but who had only recently come into her life.

Thus, despite their utter poverty and the endless toil they all endured, Elsie could honestly say that she was the happiest she had ever been in her life. A quiet contentment had descended upon her, and no task seemed too daunting.

"Put the book back on the shelf and then come help me peel potatoes," Elsie instructed now, pushing up from the little table where they had been studying together. "We must get dinner started for Papa."

"Yes, Mama," Anna said obediently and hopped off her chair.

Elsie grabbed her apron off the nail near the sink and was tying it around herself when she was startled by a series of firm knocks on the front door. Her brow wrinkled, knowing that it wasn't one of the neighbors. They all knocked just once and then stuck their heads in with a friendly greeting. Elsie had learned to do the same at their homes, too. It must be Mrs. Wilkins, the farmer's wife, Elsie deduced, hurrying to the door. She was the only one that formally knocked. *But what could she want?* She hoped that Gunther had paid this month's rent . . .

Elsie smoothed down her apron and pulled open the door and was utterly horrified to see that it was *not* Mrs. Wilkins.

It was Oldrich Exley.

Chapter 17

"Well, it's no surprise," Inspector Yarwood said as he gave his stomach two swift pats and leaned so far back in his chair that Clive thought he might tip over, and wished, actually, that he would. "Looked everywhere for him, we have."

Clive's eyes darted to Henrietta and then around the dingy little police station office in Cromford, where he had once sat with Inspector Hartle, drinking brandy and discussing Wallace's possible involvement in a local murder. It seemed years ago. It was slightly obscene that this buffoon was now the one in charge, sitting in Hartle's old office, but why should he care? Hartle had since lost Clive's respect anyway.

"It's obvious it's this Maung character," Yarwood said, clearing his throat. "Warned him, we did. Told him he wasn't allowed to leave town. Here one minute, gone the next. Went back to Burma, I'd wager."

A wave of irritation passed over Clive. Was the man in front of him really this incompetent? "Maung? Why him?"

"Who else could it have been? It's obvious."

"It isn't obvious at all. It could have been any number of people." Clive gestured absently.

"Ruled them all out, we have. No, it was Maung, all right."

"What possible evidence do you have? And what was his motive?" Clive demanded, becoming more incensed by the moment.

"Some things is confidential, Mr. Howard, as you know from your own police work, though maybe they do things different in America, but don't you worry. We'll have all the missing pieces figured out all in good time. You needn't worry yerselves." He looked from one to the other, Clive noting, with fresh irritation, that his gaze lingered a few seconds too long on Henrietta's legs. A retort was on his lips, but before he could get it out, Henrietta spoke.

"Thank you, Inspector," she said sweetly. "I'm quite sure that you do have it in hand. I was wondering, though, if you might share with us what the coroner determined to be the exact time of death?" She batted her eyes at him and flashed him her brilliant smile, both of which made Clive's stomach clench. He turned his head away. He had learned that her flirtations were an extremely effective tool for extracting sensitive information, especially from men, but it still caused his insides to boil. "Just out of curiosity, you see."

"Well, guess it wouldn't hurt anything to tell you that," Yarwood said with a little cough as he snapped his chair forward. He reached inside his jacket and pulled out his little notebook. "Coroner ruled his death to be anywhere from one to two p.m.," Inspector Yarwood announced, squinting to read his own writing. "Makes it hard to pinpoint the exact time of the poisoning, but my guess is that Maung slipped it into his drink at the White Hart."

"And was it strychnine, as you suspected, Inspector?" Henrietta asked, batting her eyes at him again.

"Yes, yes. It was strychnine." The inspector said proudly, as if he had discovered it.

"And nothing was found on his person?" Clive finally spoke, unable to keep silent any longer.

"Nothing beyond his wallet, a handkerchief, a comb, and a little pocketbook. Why are you so interested in that?"

"Just a thought." He pulled at his chin. "May we see the pocketbook?"

"No, you may not."

Clive let out a disgusted sigh.

"Nothing of interest in it, I can tell you that. Now, if you don't mind," he said, standing up and gripping his lapels, "I'll bid you good afternoon. I do need to press on. This isn't my only case, you know."

"What will you do?" Clive stood, too. "Extradite Maung? If he did go back to Burma, that is."

"You have a very feverish mind, do you not, Mr. Howard? Inspector Hartle said as much." He looked Clive up and down as if he were to be pitied. "Well, you needn't have any more thoughts on the matter. We have it handled. I urge you to leave it to the officials." He gestured toward the door. "The sergeant will see you out."

Clive suppressed the insult on his tongue and instead glared at the man as they passed out of the office. They followed the sergeant, who had been standing at attention outside of Yarwood's door, through the office and out the main door without saying two words to him.

"I'm going to bloody well sock Yarwood in the mouth," Clive muttered to Henrietta as soon as they were out of earshot.

"Clive," Henrietta scolded gently as she descended the stone steps of the station. "You should see him for what he is."

"A self-righteous ass?" Clive roughly thrust his hat on his head.

"No," she laughed, putting her arm through his, "a comic boob. He's really quite entertaining."

"Well, I'm glad you're amused," he grumbled. "But if they do find Maung and arrest him for this, it will be a travesty of justice."

"Well, then, we'll just have to figure out the real culprit before that happens," she said, a charming optimism in her voice. "Come on, let's get to the White Hart. You promised me lunch, remember?"

Clive smiled. It was impossible to be angry in her presence for long. It was one of the things that had initially drawn him to her. "All right, then, Minx. Let's go."

He walked to the passenger side of the Bentley he had borrowed from the Linley garage and opened the door for her. He had had to fight Mr. Triggs for the use of the car, as the stubborn old gent was determined that he should drive them anywhere they wished to go, saying that it was most unnatural for a Howard to drive himself. Clive wondered how Wallace got away with driving, as he was sure his cousin, the socialist, wouldn't entertain being driven about. But, Clive further considered, now that Wallace was installed at Castle Linley as the heir, he rarely seemed to leave it. At any rate, Clive had had to be rather forceful in the end with poor Mr. Triggs, who was very determined to hang on to the old ways of doing things. Doubtless, if the older man had his choice, he would probably still prefer to drive about with a horse and buggy.

"No, let's walk, shall we?" Henrietta suggested. "It's a lovely day."

"It'll be a bit of a distance." Clive looked dubious. "It's all the way on the other side of the village on the way to Matlock Bath."

"Just what we need, I think," she said, patting his cheek. "I could do with some air after that moldy old place."

"All right, then," Clive acquiesced, shutting the car door and offering his arm.

"You know, it *could* have been this Mr. Maung," she suggested tentatively as they began to walk down the cobbled high street. "After all, he was the only one with Mr. Arnold for the better part of the day."

Clive sighed. "Yes, it *could* have been. But it's unlikely." Clive thought for a moment. "Although," he said slowly, "I suppose he *was* separated from him when Arnold snuck upstairs. I hadn't thought of that."

"And you seem quite fixated on Arnold having something of value on him. Do you actually think my theory that perhaps he was a thief has merit?"

Clive looked over at her and smiled. "As a matter of fact, I do. I can think of no other reason for him to have been in Lady Linley's bedroom."

"Except to write the ghostly message," she teased.

"Absurd."

"Agreed. But just to play devil's advocate for a moment, he could have been merely inspecting all the rooms for a potential sale, and Edna simply happened to see him come out of one."

"True, but why wouldn't he have Maung with him, then, if he was acting in an official capacity?"

"Good point." She paused in front of the shop window of what looked to be a milliner, and Clive prayed she didn't want to go in. Blessedly, she continued on, and he let out a little sigh of relief. "But I don't know how we're going to sort this all out," she continued as they passed a bakery now. "It's utterly confusing. There's a poisoning, a possible theft, *and* a haunting."

"I think we can cross 'haunting' off the list. More like a prank."

"Well, even so; it's a bit of a sphinx."

"A sphinx? Whatever do you mean?" Clive looked at her with amused curiosity.

She gave him one of her affronted looks that he always found so deliciously attractive. "Honestly, Clive. Do you not read? A sphinx is a puzzle or a mystery. Mrs. Christie sometimes uses the word in her novels."

"Ah. I see. Well, if Mrs. Christie uses it, then by all means." He led her across the street to what looked to be a very old wattle-and-daub building, the left half of which seemed to have sunken into the ground a bit. A wooden placard with a chiseled and painted white stag hung lazily from an iron rod, sticking out at a right angle to the door. Despite its shabby appearance, two flowerboxes overflowed with red and white geraniums in front of the large bay windows, thick and cloudy with age.

"Remember," he said as he held the door for Henrietta—

"Yes, yes, I know. Let you do the talking." She elbowed him lightly in the ribs as she passed by, and he embarrassingly let out a little "oomph" and bit back an unexpected laugh that threatened to escape.

Henrietta shot him a look but deferentially stepped to the side as he approached the bar. The interior was just as he remembered it— dim and smoky and trimmed in very dark wood. He had, of course, frequented this pub on several occasions on his summer holidays at

Linley and once as an officer in the war when he had been on leave. Being only late morning, it was still relatively empty, however, save a few of what were probably the regulars, talking softly at tables or perched on the well-worn stools.

"Good afternoon." Clive removed his hat and set it on the bar.

The barman nodded with a squint. He was lazily wiping glasses with a towel, the buttons of his white shirt stretched by his wide girth, which was held tightly in place by a green apron. A few strands of auburn hair were draped across his balding dome, which was in extreme contrast to his bushy muttonchops, auburn, too, but darker.

"A pint of bitter and a half shandy, please."

The man set down the glass he had been drying and tucked his towel into his apron. The small bit of his face that was not covered by his muttonchops was inflamed with acne. He reached for a pint glass. "Not from around here, are you?" he asked, pulling one of the taps. "Sound American."

"As a matter of fact, we are. I'm Clive Howard, and this is my wife."

"Howard, you say? Any relation to that lot up there?" He nodded in the direction of Castle Linley and set two drinks on the bar. "That'll be ten pence. Ladies' lounge is that way, missus." He nodded toward the front parlor, which looked, from this vantage point, to be empty.

Clive fished in his pocket for some change and avoided looking at Henrietta, who was more than likely frowning. "Yes, Lord Linley was my uncle."

The barkeep looked at him with narrowed eyes. "I know you!" he said finally, breaking into a smile. "You and Master Linley used to drink here sometimes. I remember now! You're young Clive."

Clive smiled. "Not so young anymore, I'm afraid." He picked up his pint and handed Henrietta her half.

"Sad about his lordship," the man said, warming a bit. "Though none of us saw him much these last years. Bit of a hermit, he was. Still. Sad."

"Yes, it was," Clive took a drink and wondered how to bring up Arnold when the barkeep suddenly did it for him.

"Now you got another death on yer hands." He leaned his outstretched arms on the bar. "Best be careful. Comes in threes, death does."

"You're referring to Mr. Arnold?" *Did the whole village already know?* Of course, they did, Clive chided himself.

"Aye, I am."

"I was told he ate here for lunch, or dinner, I mean, that day," Clive said, taking another drink.

"Aye, he did."

"Did anyone else get sick?"

The man's previously agreeable expression melted. "Just what are you suggestin'? He weren't poisoned here, if that's what yer thinkin'. It's *my* wife as makes all the food, and no one's ever died from her cookin'."

"That you know of," muttered an old man in a tweed cap seated further down the bar. His amused eyes were a very bright blue despite his face being a mass of wrinkles.

"Sod off, Jenks."

"I'm not suggesting he was poisoned *here*." Clive chose his words carefully. "I'm merely trying to trace his steps."

The barkeep looked unconvinced.

"Where did he sit that day?" Henrietta asked quietly.

The barkeep looked at her as if he had forgotten she was present. He nodded at a table in front of one of the bay windows. "Sat right there, he did. Had a mate with him. Little foreign fella. Hadn't seen him before."

"Mr. Maung?"

The barkeep shrugged. "Didn't catch his name."

"Was there anything unusual about them that you noticed? Anything at all?"

"Not that I can think," he answered slowly.

"Did he seem ill when he came in?" Henrietta asked.

"Matter of fact, he did look a little poorly." The barkeep scratched his head. "All white, he was."

"*Did* he have anything to eat?" Henrietta asked tentatively.

"Both him and his mate had steak-and-kidney pie, if I remember right."

"What did they drink?" Clive asked. "Do you remember?"

The barkeep scratched one of his sideburns. "I don't. No, wait; I'm tellin' lies. I do remember. Had two pints of Guinness. I remember 'cause I had to go down and change the barrel."

"So, they both had the same thing to eat and drink?" Henrietta confirmed.

"Aye, but Arnold didn't finish his. Nor his pint, come to think of it. The little foreign fella did, though. Almost licked the plate, he did."

Clive took a deep draft and tried to review the facts. "Was he a regular?"

"Arnold? Regular enough. Came in for his dinner most days. Gossipy type. He was all right, I suppose." The barkeep paused, thinking. "Bit of a braggart, though, if you know what I mean. Liked to bet on the horses now and again. And when he won, he let everyone know."

Clive's ears pricked. Finally, maybe a motive. "Had he lost recently?"

"Don't know. Coulda been. You know, Jenks?"

Jenks adjusted his cap, thinking. "Mighta. Seemed down in the mouth recently. That's usually how he was when he got himself in a losin' streak."

"Do you know of any reason that anyone would want to kill Mr. Arnold? Did he have any enemies?"

"Not that I know of. You know, Jenks?"

"Nah. Don't get much a that sorta thing in these parts, ya see," the old man colluded.

"Whole village has turned out for the family," the barkeep added. "Terrible distraught is Jenny. Mrs. Arnold, I should say."

Clive thought it odd that he had first used her Christian name, but let it pass. "What *about* Mrs. Arnold? What can you tell us?"

The barkeep shrugged, but his eyes shifted slightly. "Not much."

"Any trouble between them?" Clive suggested, thinking about Wallace's odd theory about the killer being the wife. "Maybe over this gambling?"

The barkeep's eyes opened wide. "Jenny?" His brow immediately creased. "You think Jenny mighta done this? Nah. You're wrong there. Dead wrong."

"How do you know?"

"I jist know. She ain't the type. And she loved him, she did. In her own way. And with three kids, why would she kill her husband and leave herself to raise three kids on her own? Daft, that would be. Nah, it weren't Jenny. And, anyway, she didn't know anything about his gambling. And it would be a shame if she found out now, if you take my meaning."

Clive eyed him carefully. "How do you know she wasn't aware of the gambling?"

"I just do," the barkeep snapped.

"Tell me, which house belongs to the Arnolds?"

"Why do you want to know? Don't you go botherin' Jenny. She's had enough to deal with between that pillock of an inspector and then the whole funeral to plan."

"We don't want to bother her," Henrietta put in. "We merely want to pay our respects and extend Lord Linley's help, if she should need it."

The barkeep looked unconvinced.

"Two streets down," Jenks said, his shoulders hunched over his pint. "Third house on the left."

The barkeep bunched up a towel and threw it at him.

Clive drank down his pint and put his hat back on. "Thank you. If you think of anything else, will you let me know?" He gave Henrietta a nod toward the door.

"Don't you go botherin' her," the barkeep warned as the two of them made a hasty exit.

Chapter 18

Not a half hour later, Clive knocked firmly on Mrs. Arnold's door and stepped back, waiting. No sound was heard within.

"I'm still not sure this is a good idea, Clive," Henrietta said quietly. "Mr. Arnold *has* only been dead a couple of days. Surely, Mrs. Arnold is still quite distraught. Maybe we should come back a different day."

"With everything going on back at Linley, who knows when we'll get this chance again?" Clive insisted. "No, we'll be quick."

"I don't think 'quick' is quite the right word."

"Okay, then, gentle," he said with a false delicacy, and knocked again, harder this time. Still, there was no answer.

"What did you make of the barkeep?" Henrietta asked, leaning against the little iron railing that ran up the two short steps.

"Jealous admirer who wanted to be more than just an admirer?" Clive tipped up the brim of his hat.

"Exactly my thoughts. But why—"

The door suddenly opened then, just a fraction, but enough to reveal a small, mousy sort of woman in a plain housedress. Her thin brown hair was tied up loosely in a bun, strands of which hung down about her gaunt face. She might have been pretty once upon a time, Clive decided, looking her over.

"Mrs. Arnold?"

"Yes?" The woman's sunken green eyes peered at Clive suspiciously.

"I'm Clive Howard, and this is my wife, Henrietta. We're guests of Lady Linley. She's my aunt."

"Yes?" The woman put one hand up to tent her eyes from the sun that had just poked through the clouds. "What of it?"

"We're very sorry to hear about your husband's death," Henrietta put in gently. "Might we ask you a couple of questions, Mrs. Arnold?"

"About what?"

"About . . . about the nature of your husband's death."

"The police is already been here. Told them all I know." She made a move to shut the door, but Clive put his hand out to stop it.

"Wait, Mrs. Arnold. I'm a private detective. I'd like to get to the bottom of this."

Mrs. Arnold squinted her eyes at them. "What for? I can't pay you. Now, please go."

"Mrs. Arnold," Henrietta said hurriedly, "do you know anyone that would have wanted to harm your husband? Did he have any enemies?"

Mrs. Arnold's face suddenly crumpled. "No," she said with a little cry of despair. "He wasn't that type of man. Was a friend to everyone, he was—"

"Who is it, Jenny?" a woman asked from behind Mrs. Arnold.

"A detective. Says he wants to know more about Ed."

"Well, you best show them in, then."

Mrs. Arnold hesitated. "This is my sister, Nell," she said, as if she couldn't think of anything else to say. "She come down from Durham to stay with me after, after—" She broke off here in a little sob, putting one hand over her eyes.

"Come on in," Nell boomed, opening the door wider. "Come on. Best get it over with, Jenny."

Mrs. Arnold didn't respond, but meekly stepped aside.

Clive gestured for Henrietta to go first and then entered the modest little cottage after her. He instinctively noted the interior, looking for any small clue. The décor, while not exactly modern, was not poor, either. It had a solid middle-class feel to it, indicating that Mr. and Mrs. Arnold, before his untimely death, that is, had maintained a certain standard of living. The walls were painted a light cream, and the furniture, while not new, was not worn either. There was even a painting on one wall that was tolerably good. Mr. Arnold, Clive concluded, must have made a decent income at his trade or was in the habit of winning at the track more often than losing. He remembered the barkeep's description of him being "a bit of a braggart" and also Mrs. Godfrey, the cook at Linley, who had called him an "ambitious pillock" who thought himself better than those around him.

"You go on in and make yerselves at home," Nell ordered, nodding at the front room to their left. "You go, too, Jenny, and I'll make a fresh pot."

As they stepped through to the parlor, Clive glanced into the kitchen, where three children sat mournfully around a little table.

"Janie," he heard Nell bark. "You take these out for a bit. Go on, now." The children dutifully rose, the tallest, apparently Janie, reaching for the baby in his little chair and simultaneously pulling the third, a toddler, out the back door.

Mrs. Arnold gestured for Clive and Henrietta to sit down on the sofa and perched herself on the edge of a petite armchair opposite. She gripped her hands tightly and looked as if she were about to cry at any moment.

"Well?" she finally asked.

Clive cleared his throat. "I apologize for our intrusion, Mrs. Arnold, but we are simply trying to find justice for your husband."

"Aren't the police doing that?"

Clive shifted. "Well, yes, but let's just say, we're trying to help. Her ladyship has asked us to do what we can," Clive fibbed.

"What did you say your name was?"

"Howard. Clive Howard."

"You sound American," she said suspiciously.

"I am. I'm from Chicago. We're visiting on holiday. My father, however, was Lord Linley's brother, the former Lord Linley, that is."

Mrs. Arnold seemed uninterested in any further explanation of Clive's lineage and looked away, staring at the curio cabinet in the corner. She ungripped and regripped her hands. "He couldn't have been murdered." She turned her gaze on Clive now. "I'm sure it was an accident. Who would want to kill Ed?" she cried, her voice suddenly desperate and fierce.

"So, your husband had no enemies, no rivals?" Henrietta asked gently.

"No!" Mrs. Arnold wailed. "Oh, there were those who were jealous of his success, a course, but none so much that they woulda murdered him!"

"What can you tell us about your husband's last day?" Clive leaned forward a bit, resting his forearms on his legs and folding his hands loosely.

Mrs. Arnold stared at him for a moment, as if thinking. "I already told this to the police," she said and then shivered. She let out a deep breath. "He had his breakfast, as usual," she recited, "and then he left for the day. Said he had several properties to show."

"When did you see him next?"

"'Round one o'clock, I'm thinking. It was just after the children's noon meal. I was cleaning up, and he came in unexpected. Said he wasn't feeling too good."

"Was it unusual for him to come home in the middle of the day?"

"Oh, very. Never came home for his dinner. Always ate at a pub."

"Always the White Hart?"

"Not always. Depends where he was. If he were in Matlock for the day, it'd be the Merry Bells. If it was Buxton, it'd most likely be the Fox and the Squire. Had a rotation, you see."

"His business would take him all the way to Buxton?" Clive asked, intrigued.

"Not usually. But sometimes."

"But if he were here in the village," Henrietta asked, "why not come home?"

"Oh, he wouldn't hear of it! Said that it was vital to his livelihood to hear all the gossip each day. That's how he drummed up so much business." Or betting tips, Clive thought privately.

"Did anyone accompany him that day? The day he came home ill? A Mr. Maung, perhaps?"

Mrs. Arnold shook her head.

"Did he ever mention Mr. Maung?"

"Not that I recall."

"Hmmm." Another dead end. "What happened then, Mrs. Arnold? After your husband came home feeling ill?"

Mrs. Arnold twisted her hands. "I told him to go lie down, that he was overworking himself. I was baking a fish pie for that night's tea, and I ran outta eggs. I called to Ed and told him I'd be right back, that I had to go next door. Mrs. Thompson gives me the egg all right, but then starts a tale about Mrs. Ryan down the street—her lad's in a bad way, you see. And by the time I got back . . . he . . . he were gone," she said, her voice trembling. "I poked my head round to check on him and there he was, all akimbo, froth about the mouth, eyes starin' straight up at the ceiling in terror. In terror!" she wailed.

"Now, now, Jenny," Nell said, coming in with a tea tray and setting it on a side table. Where Mrs. Arnold was rail-thin, her sister was as wide as the doorway, and had to turn slightly to the side to make it through. "Git hold of yerself. Won't do no good wailin."

"I'm sorry," Mrs. Arnold muttered and covered her face with her hands. Nell poured out a mug of steaming tea and handed it to her. Mrs. Arnold took it, but merely held it without taking a single sip.

"Now. How do you take yours?" she asked Henrietta.

"Milk and sugar, please."

"Aye," Nell said and poured some milk into a mug before covering it with tea. "You?" she asked Clive as she handed the mug to Henrietta.

"The same, please," Clive answered.

Nell accordingly poured out another mug. "There you be," she said, handing it to him with a grunt as she reached across to him. "Now, where were we?" she asked, folding her thick arms in front of her.

"Mrs. Arnold, was your husband given to gambling?" Clive asked, deciding to test the barkeep's insistence that she knew nothing about his vice.

Mrs. Arnold's face flushed. "Gambling? He would never do that! How can you even suggest such a thing?"

"The landlord at the White Hart suggested it." Clive studied her carefully.

"Amos?" Her face descended into a scowl. "What would he know? My husband worked constantly, he did. Wanted the best for us." Mrs. Arnold broke down here, and again covered her face with her hands. "He was the best of men!" she groaned.

Clive studied her. Perhaps she was simply a very good actress, but her grief over the loss of her husband, in his opinion, anyway, seemed genuine. And if the barkeep—this Amos—did have romantic designs on her, they were feelings clearly lost on Jenny Arnold. Still, it didn't rule out Amos's involvement in the poisoning . . .

"Now, Jenny. Get ahold of yerself," Nell scolded.

"I don't mean to be indelicate, Mrs. Arnold," Clive continued, "but can you tell us how he left you, financially, that is? I'm only asking because it might have some bearing on the case."

Mrs. Arnold looked at him blearily as she took the handkerchief Nell had silently offered.

"I hardly know. Haven't had a chance to sort through everything. There's some money in the bank, but not as much as . . . well, not as much as I'd hoped."

"Lucky you got that ring, though." Nell took a sip of her tea. "Might come in handy, Jenny."

Clive's pulse jumped a little. "What do you mean a ring?"

"Why, Jenny found a ring in Ed's vest pocket. Never seen anything like it. Go git it, Jenny."

"No, I couldn't! Wouldn't be proper," Mrs. Arnold hissed at Nell.

"Oh, please, Mrs. Arnold, I'd dearly love to see it," Henrietta urged.

"Yes," Clive insisted. "It might have a bearing on the case."

Mrs. Arnold eyed him warily. "Oh, all right." Slowly she made her way across the room and marched up the narrow staircase, the worn treads creaking despite her slight weight.

"Musta got it fer her birthday. It's comin' up, an' all," Nell said to Clive and Henrietta. "Beautiful, it is. He was always spoilin' her. Might not a made much money selling houses, but he did always buy her lovely things. Little did he know, she had to sell most of 'em, like, to pay the coal merchant and the butcher. But this one, now," she nodded her head toward the ceiling. "Now this one is different."

She stopped talking as Mrs. Arnold descended, gripping the banister with one hand and holding something in her other. "Here it is," she said, making her way back over to where the little group sat, and opened her hand. It was a sapphire with two diamonds, exactly as Addie had described Lady Linley's missing ring! Clive heard Henrietta gasp beside him.

"It's beautiful, isn't it?" Mrs. Arnold's face held the first smile Clive had seen on her.

"It's exquisite." Clive cleared his throat. "Do you by chance know where he got it? Or when?" Clive asked, throwing Henrietta a quick glance.

"Musta been someweer down in London, wouldn't ya say, Jenny? No shop round here would 'ave somethin' that fine. He was down that way 'bout a month ago, wasn't he, Jenny?"

Jenny merely nodded.

"And it was just in his pocket, no box?" Clive asked.

"Aye, that's strange, ain't it?" Nell said. "It was as if he was gonna give it to her right away, poor thing, and then he never got the chance."

Jenny broke down into sobs at this assessment, and Nell stood up, placing her hands on her sister's shoulders. "Not to be rude, like, but if you've got no more questions, I think she needs a bit of a rest."

"But—" Henrietta began, giving Clive an urgent look.

Clive raised his eyebrows at her, hoping she would understand his meaning. "Yes, of course. We were just leaving. Thank you, Mrs. Arnold. You've been most helpful. Please accept our deepest condolences."

Mrs. Arnold did not respond, nor did she even look up at them. It was Nell who saw them to the door.

"If you think of anything else, Mrs. . . . ?"

"Morgan." Nell folded her thick arms across her chest.

"Mrs. Morgan. You'll let us know?" Clive asked.

"Aye, I will."

Clive put his hat on his head and turned to go, but then, a sudden thought occurring to him, he stopped and turned back. "Just one more question, Mrs. Morgan. Does Mrs. Arnold keep any rat poison?"

Nell's eyes narrowed. "A course, she does. In the larder. Everyone does, so don't you go thinkin' what I think you're thinkin'." Nell's voice was elevated now.

"Of course not, Mrs. Morgan." Clive tipped the brim of his hat in deference. "You've been most helpful—" but before he could say anything more, Nell closed the door with a bang.

Chapter 19

A stray wind gently banged the door of the sod house against the rough siding, further intensifying the terror Elsie felt at the sight of Oldrich Exley standing before her. He was dressed in a full suit, complete with top hat, cane, and a gold fob hanging neatly across his black serge waistcoat, and, as such, looked as out of place on the doorstep of their dusty hut as if a dragon had suddenly appeared from out of a storybook. But he *was* a sort of dragon. Or more like an ogre. The scowl on his face was only partially covered by the fine linen handkerchief he held to his nose and mouth, presumably to keep out the dust.

Elsie's first instinct was to flee, which was a ludicrous thought, not only because there was nowhere to run, but because she was a married woman and a mother now, and she needed to stop running from her grandfather. She needed to face him. And even if she *had* been able to convince herself to run, she found she was oddly paralyzed at the sight of him, like a quivering mouse in the face of a snake about to eat her. She couldn't move, nor speak, apparently. She opened her mouth several times, but nothing came out.

"May I come in?" Oldrich's voice was hard and stiff.

Elsie bit her lip and swallowed. With great effort, she managed to step aside, gesturing weakly. He hobbled past her, and she slowly shut the door, leaning slightly against it and telling herself not to cower, not to be afraid. There was nothing, she reminded herself, that he could do to her. It was too late. She was a married woman.

She turned to face him. "What are you doing here?" she managed to ask, more rudely than she meant it.

"May I sit down?" Oldrich said with a slight cough, dipping his handkerchief back into his suit pocket.

Elsie did not answer but nodded at one of the chairs beside the kitchen table. The old man walked across the room and sat down heavily.

"How did you find me?" She tried to control the fear in her voice and took a few steps closer. Anna, she could see, was trying to hide behind the woodstove, so Elsie positioned herself in front of it to provide extra security for the frightened girl.

"I received your letter informing me that you had decided to become a nun," he said gruffly. "An absurdly childish notion. I wrote to you, even had my secretary attempt to telephone you, but to no avail. I would have sent Agatha, but she's in Connecticut visiting her son. In the end, I was forced to travel into the city. I met with the headmistress, or the principal, or whatever the head nun is called."

"Sister Bernard?"

"Yes. Her."

"What . . . what did she say?" Elsie's stomach clenched a little at the mention of her beloved mentor.

"She showed me your letter in which you confessed to running away here." He paused to look around the dingy interior. "It wasn't hard to find you."

"Was she . . . was she angry?" she asked, biting her lip a little.

"Angry?" Oldrich said indignantly. "What does it matter if *she* is angry? *I* am angry!"

Elsie twisted her hands.

"Just what did you think you could gain from this stunt? Is this what you wanted?" He gestured around the hut.

Elsie felt Anna's little hands grip the folds of her gray housedress.

She had obviously crept closer. "Yes, Grandfather. It is." Elsie tried to say it confidently, but it unfortunately came out warbled.

"I've always said that education is wasted on women. And this proves my point!" He rapped his cane twice.

Elsie spoke up despite her trepidation. "It hasn't been wasted, Grandfather. I've been . . . I've been teaching the children here."

Oldrich waved his hand dismissively. "Not for long. You're coming back with me."

"Coming back with you? What . . . what do you mean?"

"Just what I said. You're coming back."

Elsie felt her fear turning to anger. "Grandfather, I'm not a child any longer to be led about or commanded. I'm a married woman. I'm . . . I'm Mrs. Stockel now."

"Pshaw!"

"Grandfather, I'm not my mother," Elsie said with quiet determination.

His eyes narrowed. "What is that supposed to mean?"

Elsie hesitated to explain her theory but then plunged ahead, realizing in the quick space of a second that it didn't matter anymore what he thought. "Just that you must stop confusing me with her. You're still trying to get back at her for running away. But I'm not her!"

"Don't be stupid, girl. I know that!" he blustered.

"Do you? Then why this . . . this obsession with me? It is unnatural! I am nothing—a poor excuse for what you want me to be. You already have Henrietta mingling with the North Shore set, not to mention the English aristocracy; you have five grandsons and another granddaughter to mold into who you want them to be, God help them. Why can't you just let me alone!" she cried. "What difference does my tiny little life matter to you? I'm happy here. Why can't you just let me be?" Elsie's voice cracked.

"Mama?" squeaked Anna from behind her. Elsie could hear her fear. She knew she needed to calm down or the girl might have a fit.

"It's okay, Anna," she tried to say calmly, twisting to try to put her arms around the girl, but Anna squirmed and pushed herself deeper into her dress until Elsie could feel her pressed against the back of her legs.

"This is the child, I presume?"

"Yes, this is Anna," Elsie answered, brushing back a stray tear. "Anna, say hello; this is your great-grandpapa."

Anna did not answer and instead gripped Elsie's dress tighter.

"I am *not* her grandpapa," Oldrich said distastefully. "Send her outside. What I came here to say partially concerns her as well, and I wish to speak to you privately."

Elsie hesitated. "Anna, why don't you go outside and play for a moment. See if Luis is about." The little girl remained rigidly where she was.

"She's been ill," Elsie offered as a feeble excuse for what Grandfather would surely judge to be nothing short of defiance. "You'll just have to say what it is you've come here to say." She crossed her arms.

Oldrich let out a little cough. "All right. As I've said, you're coming back home with me. I will dissolve this poor excuse of a union, and you will accompany myself and Agatha on a cruise to Italy. There we will remain for the greater part of a year, and you will marry the man of my choosing."

"What?" Elsie exclaimed. She had expected something preposterous, but this was beyond the pale. "Marry the man of your choosing? I'm *already* married. To Gunther."

"That means nothing. Easily annulled."

"Annulled! You can't undo my marriage!"

"See if I can't." He peered at her. "Even now, I have my lawyers working on it."

"You can't possibly be serious! You can't annul a marriage without at least one of the parties desiring it. What do you plan to do? Drag me away?"

"Don't be vulgar," Oldrich chided. "Of course not. You will come of your own volition."

"No, I won't."

"I will not be defied!" he shouted. "And don't think I haven't forgotten my earlier threats, which you willfully ignored. I have no choice now but to carry them out. Because of your selfishness, the whole rest of your family will pay the price. I will rescind my financial support and throw them all back into poverty."

Elsie's legs began to tremble. "But why?" she murmured. "Why are you doing this? It has nothing to do with me and everything to do with Ma. Just admit it!"

"You will thank me one day, Elsie. Mark my words."

"No, I won't. I'll never give up Gunther and Anna. If you choose to make the whole rest of the family suffer, then so be it. Let it be on your conscience!"

Oldrich's face twisted in fury, but she saw him visibly repress it. "Let me put it another way," he said with forced calmness. "You don't care what happens to your mother and siblings, fair enough. But what if I told you that if you do agree to annul this marriage and come with me, I will provide a professorship for Gunther in the city, a house, an additional income besides what he makes at the college, and a private nurse for Anna." He paused and carefully observed her reaction.

She opened her mouth to reply, stunned by his deviousness, but he held up a hand.

"Before you answer, think. Think what it would mean for the two you claim to love so much that you would endure even this?" He gestured around the hut again. "Wouldn't it be better for them to live in a comfortable home, surrounded by good food, security a better life? Your stubbornness is keeping you all impoverished. They would be better off if you were gone. It is you that has caused this whole mess. Gunther would never have fled if it weren't for his damaging involvement with you and how that threatened little Anna. Oh, yes, I know about Heinrich, his attempts to bribe you," he said at the sudden look of surprise in her eyes. "Yes, you could say that this is actually all your fault."

Elsie's heart was pounding in her chest. She was so confused. A part of her brain wondered if her grandfather was possibly deranged, but she couldn't help but see some slight logic in his words. Maybe it *was* her fault . . .

"Grandfather, I—" She stopped abruptly, however, when she felt the little hands on her dress release. Elsie suddenly knew what was happening, and her heart accordingly filled with panic. She spun around, hoping to catch Anna as she fell, but the girl's little body jerked out beyond her grasp and she fell, hard, her head hitting the corner of the woodstove with a sickening smack.

"Anna!" Elsie cried, diving to her knees beside her, trying to contain the girl's convulsing body. She had never been alone during one of Anna's fits and tried to remember what Gunther usually did. She moved to cradle the girl's head in her lap and was horrified to see a pool of blood forming beneath it. "Oh, my God! She's hit her head." Anna continued to convulse uncontrollably, her eyes rolling back in her head. "Grandfather! Help me!"

Anna emitted a low gurgling sound now, as if she were choking. "She's going to bite her tongue! Oh, my God, there's so much blood!" *How had she hit her head that hard?*

Oldrich rose from his chair and hovered above them. "Shall I go for help?" he asked fearfully.

"No, hand me a spoon!" she cried, nodding toward the row of utensils hanging behind the stove.

Oldrich did not obey, however, and stood frozen in his spot, staring at the girl.

"Hurry!" Elsie cried.

Oldrich lurched into motion, then, and hobbled past them to grab the big wooden spoon. He handed it to Elsie, who pried it into the girl's mouth, holding it tight with one hand while she pulled off her apron. "Here!" She threw her apron at him. "Press this to her head while I hold her tongue!"

As if in a daze, Oldrich took the apron and slowly sank to his knees. He began to awkwardly dab the cloth against the gash on Anna's head, her blond hair quickly turning a sickening red. Elsie held her body as it violently convulsed. "Tighter!" she cried to Oldrich, who was staring at the girl's eyes, rolled back in her head, with absolute disgust and terror.

Mercifully, Anna's convulsions finally turned to mild twitches, and then she went limp. Elsie was sweating profusely as she released her hold on the wooden spoon. A pool of urine was gathering underneath the unconscious girl, and her head was still bleeding.

"Let me see," Elsie commanded, pushing her grandfather's hand away from the wound. "Oh, my God." The gash appeared to be very deep and very near Anna's little ear, which looked to somehow be partially ripped off. Elsie felt the urge to vomit, but she swallowed it. "She needs a doctor." She got unsteadily to her feet. "Keep that on it," she instructed, nodding at the bloody apron. "Keep the pressure on. I'll go run to the farmhouse."

"You can't leave me here alone with . . . with this," Oldrich stammered, looking fearfully at Anna. "I will go."

"No, I'll be faster. You stay here."

Elsie ran to the door, but before she hurried through, she took one look back, checking to make sure Oldrich was obeying her. Indeed, he was bent over Anna, his fine serge trousers soiled with the blood and urine and dust in which the girl lay while he held the apron to her damaged head, his fingers trembling.

Chapter 20

The smack of a croquet ball could be heard even from where Henrietta sat with Lady Linley under a little tent erected by the servants for the viewing pleasure of the guests.

The game had been proposed by Phineas this morning at breakfast, and Wallace had surprisingly agreed to it, thinking it might distract Lady Linley, who had not yet fully recovered from her fright. Indeed, poor Lady Linley seemed to have aged ten years almost overnight. While she could definitely have been described as elderly before all of this business began, she now seemed positively ancient, at least in Henrietta's eyes.

Henrietta glanced across the beautifully set table at Lady Linley, where she sat propped with cushions, which, their excessive number notwithstanding, did not quite succeed in keeping her from sagging a bit. But perhaps it was the heat. Her watery eyes observed the lawn in front of her, but she seemed not the slightest bit interested in the game.

"Good shot!" Phineas called now to Miss Simms, who had just hit her croquet ball clear across the lawn. Miss Simms, Henrietta observed, gave him a coy smile as she went to retrieve it, her ankle apparently fully restored. It was as if the accident had never occurred at all. To give her a small modicum of credit, Miss Simms had rarely left Lady Linley's side since her unfortunate collapse, though today she seemed to be making an exception by leaving the amusement of Lady Linley in the hands of the rest of the guests.

It was, to be sure, a very fine day. Almost too fine, if the intensity of the sun was anything to go by, though the lemonade that had just been delivered by Stevens went a long way in appeasing the heat. Poor Amelie seemed absolutely miserable. She sat next to Henrietta, fanning herself with an exquisite Chinese fan she had unearthed from somewhere in the house as she aimlessly rubbed her protruding stomach. Wallace, for his part, despite having both his wife and his mother out of bed and outdoors, was not in the slightest bit cheerful. In fact, he was in one of his moods, contradictory and short, which, among other things, thwarted any attempts at extended conversation. Only the colonel seemed his normal talkative self and continually tried to probe everyone for information regarding the murder, as it was now distastefully being referred to, a topic Wallace asked him, more than once, to politely refrain from.

"I say! I don't see why we can't discuss it. Most intriguing. I'm sure Clive, here, is most interested. Probably dealt with hundreds of cases of poisoning in Chicago, I daresay!"

"Well, I wouldn't say hundreds, Colonel. But a few, yes."

"Strychnine is a very straightforward, common sort of poison," the colonel said, taking a sip of his tea. "Now, the bushmen of Bechuanaland have a *real* poison. They make it by crushing the pupae of beetles found among the roots of infested marula trees, strangely enough. One drop is enough to kill a man. Seen it, I have." He set down his cup roughly so that it rattled in the saucer. "Worse is aconite. Used by the Malayan aborigines on the tip of their blowpipe darts. Easy to confuse, though. Derived from the buttercup family, it is." He reached for a piece of shortbread, arranged prettily on a plate and trimmed with sweetheart roses. "Isn't that strange? One so innocent, and one so deadly?" He took a bite of the sugary biscuit. "Brings on madness and then a horrible death. Knew a man, lost all feeling in his legs and then vomited blood—"

"Uncle Rufus!" Wallace bellowed. "You are upsetting the ladies!"

"Yes, Rufus, must you go on so? It's terribly tiring," Lady Linley said weakly.

Henrietta glanced at Amelie, who indeed looked as if she might retch. She was holding her handkerchief to her mouth.

"I do beg your pardon," the colonel said with mock deference. "You must forgive an old man." He glared at Clive. "Hard to teach an old dog new tricks." He reached for his teacup.

"Which brings up an interesting point," Wallace snapped as he tossed his napkin onto the lace tablecloth. "I wonder when—"

"I say," Phineas interrupted now, running up to the little group under the shade of the tent, "won't someone else play? We can't have a game with just two." He pushed back his lock of badly behaved hair. "Mr. and Mrs. Howard, you'll play, won't you?"

Henrietta folded her hands and looked over at Clive inquisitively.

"Not me," he said, "I'm content to watch."

"What about you, Wallace?"

"No," he said sourly.

Phineas frowned and turned his attention to Henrietta. "Oh, please say you'll play, then, Mrs. Howard. It's no fun with two," Phineas begged.

She glanced over at Clive, who returned the look with one of teasing amusement. "Yes, all right," she said to Phineas with a flirtatious little smile. "I'll play." She stood up, smoothing her white box-pleated skirt with navy ribboning.

"Oh, jolly good! What color do you want, Mrs. Howard?" Phineas asked, already jogging back to the field.

"Orange, if it isn't taken," she called and moved from behind the lace-covered table. She hesitated a moment, anticipating Lady Linley's disapproval, and then removed her navy bolero jacket, revealing her trim arms.

"Oh, Henrietta, do you think that wise?" Lady Linley chided. "You have such lovely skin."

"It's quite warm for sport, Aunt," Henrietta said deferentially.

Lady Linley sniffed. "Well, at least wear your hat!"

Clive picked up the hat from where Henrietta had set it near the large vase of roses and handed it to her, giving her a quick wink. Henrietta resisted the urge to stick her tongue out at him and instead dutifully put on the hat, while Clive shifted in his white wrought-iron chair and turned his attention back to his scowling cousin.

"What were you saying, Wallace?"

Before poor Wallace could answer, however, Stevens again appeared.

"There is a telephone call for you, Mr. Howard," he said to Clive as he stepped under the billowing white canopy. "From London. Will you take it, sir?"

"Yes, of course." Clive glanced briefly at Henrietta and then stood. "You'll excuse me," he said, giving Lady Linley and Amelie a slight bow, and followed Stevens back up to the house.

Henrietta watched him go, wondering who it could possibly be. Perhaps Inspector Yarwood?

"Are you coming, Mrs. Howard?" called Phineas.

"Yes!" she said, ducking under the tent. She selected the orange mallet from the little trolley at the side of the court and joined Miss Simms and Phineas on the lawn.

The first time she had ever played croquet was here at Linley on her honeymoon, and she found she was tolerably good. Miss Simms, she soon discovered, was also first rate and quickly took the lead. By the fifth wicket, Henrietta had pulled into second, though Phineas wasn't too far behind.

Henrietta took aim now and hit her ball, silently cursing when it missed the wicket. She looked back at the tent to see if anyone was paying attention and was surprised to see Clive striding quickly back across the lawn. She was so wrapped up in the game that she had almost forgotten all about the call.

"Excuse me a moment, won't you?" she said to Miss Simms and Phineas, and without waiting for an answer, walked quickly back to the tent. Phineas dropped his mallet and flopped onto the grass, while Miss Simms looked on, tenting a hand over her eyes against the afternoon sun.

"I'm afraid I must go to London," Clive said as Henrietta approached.

"Is something wrong?" she asked.

"Nothing too terribly serious. It was Mr. Bennett." He gave her a look, but she couldn't read his expression. "My man in Chicago," he explained to the rest of the table. "I need to go and meet with our London investors. Nothing to worry about."

"I'd offer to go with you, but I have another estate agent coming round, as it happens," Wallace said, glancing at Amelie. "He's got someone interested in buying the whole thing." He gestured languidly.

"What?" Lady Linley interjected, suddenly coming to life. "Not again, Wallace! I thought we were done with all that nonsense?"

Wallace audibly sighed. "Mother, we've been through this—"

"You'll excuse us," Clive interrupted and looked across at Henrietta, tilting his head toward the house.

"I hope you won't be long!" Lady Linley called.

"What's going on?" Henrietta asked, once they were a distance away. "Was that really Bennett on the telephone?"

"Yes, it was. He really does need me to meet with Mr. Osbourne, the head of our London group. Something about selling off some portion of the business and my signature is needed. Osbourne offered to send the documents via courier, but Bennett thinks I should go down."

"But, why? Now is not exactly a good time to go," she said, looking over her shoulder at the group behind them. From what she could tell, Phineas and Miss Simms had already resumed the game. "I'll come, too, of course."

Clive stopped. They had reached the stone steps leading up to the terrace behind the house. He put his hands on her upper arms. "No, darling. I need you to stay here."

"Stay here? Whatever for?"

"There will be nothing for you to do there. I'll only be gone a few days."

"A few days! I thought it would merely be overnight. And I should like to see the London house one last time before it's sold." Henrietta tried to read the conflicting emotions on his face. There was something he wasn't telling her. *Why would he want to go to London alone?* A niggling suspicion came into her mind that she instantly tried to squelch. It was unthinkable that Clive would be unfaithful to her.

"Darling, the truth is that I need you to stay here and keep an eye on things."

Henrietta laughed out loud. "Now I know you're teasing. You can't possibly be serious."

"Darling, I'm very serious. The case is nowhere near being solved, and there is still a murderer about."

"Isn't that all the more reason to whisk me away from here? Isn't that what you're always so worried about?"

Clive's face clouded, and she worried that she had gone too far in poking at what she knew were his very real fears. "Darling. I'm trying to trust. You know that. And, anyway, I'm leaving Pascal behind to watch over you."

"Ah! I see. I knew there had to be a catch. Well, even if you don't trust me to be able to take care of myself, it at least shows that you trust Pascal after all."

"Darling, must we have this squabble at the moment? You know I trust Pascal. He's just a very bad valet. And I do trust you to take care of yourself. Usually . . ." he said with a slight frown.

"Well, if I'm to be in charge of the case, then," she said, folding her arms, "what exactly am I supposed to be looking for?"

"I don't know. I suppose you simply need to keep tabs on our three suspects." Clive began to climb the stone steps but then stopped and turned to her. "Didn't you say that the colonel received an official-looking letter the other day? The one that Edna delivered to his room?"

"Yes, I think so," she answered, trying to recall.

"I'd give a pound to know its contents. Perhaps Edna could retrieve it. She could enter his room under the guise of dusting it, or some such thing."

"Clive! She's not supposed to work at all!"

"Well, I'm sure you'll think of something, knowing you." He shot her a wink, but she resolved not to be affected. "Also, Wallace tells me that Lady Linley has summoned her solicitor."

"Oh? Should that concern us?"

"Not us, but usually old ladies summon their solicitor when they want to change their will."

"And?"

"Well, seeing as how Miss Simms probably has a more-than-healthy interest in Lady Linley's will, I would keep an eye on her."

Henrietta's brow wrinkled, wondering how exactly she was to do that.

"And while I'm in London, I might just look up Miss Simms's charity," he mused. "Mrs. Christiansen's Ladies Association, or whatever it is."

"Yes, what a good idea!" She twisted a strand of her auburn hair around her finger. "That just leaves Phineas. What about him?"

Clive sighed. "Yes, what about him? Try to stay out of his path, lest you find a toad in your bed or some other boyish nonsense."

Henrietta laughed and wrapped her arm through his. "With five brothers, I think I can handle Phineas. But what about the ring? When are you going to tell Wallace? Surely, he should know that a family heirloom is missing and in the hands of Mrs. Arnold."

"In good time. I want to see how the rest of this plays out first. And I haven't ruled out Amos the barkeep in all of this. It seems unlikely that he was the poisoner, but it's certainly possible. Best not to raise the alarm just yet, though."

"But what if she sells it before then?"

"Unlikely. She believes it was a gift from her dead husband. The last one ever. She won't sell such a sentimental object unless she is absolutely destitute. Would you?" he asked coyly.

"Darling, don't joke about such things," she scolded. "I worry about you. What if this is some ruse to pull you away from me?" she asked, remembering the Jack Fletcher affair.

"Do I detect a smidgeon of concern? Dare I say fear?"

"Don't be silly," she said, though a shiver ran through her at the thought of the noises she heard almost nightly now.

"Well, regardless, I'm certain that Osbourne and Bennett are not luring me away for some nefarious purpose. You know how Bennett is. All business. Which reminds me," he said, turning to her now, his face suddenly serious. "I'm afraid there is some rather bad business at home."

"Oh, no," Henrietta murmured, her stomach clenching. "Is it Elsie? Or maybe Ma?"

"No," he said with a sad sigh. "I'm afraid it's Julia."

Chapter 21

Julia shivered despite the heat as she listlessly strolled past the bushes in one of Highbury's many formal gardens, thinking of the past weeks' events. She reached out with her good arm and brushed the phlox. She had lost track of how long she had been here, and while her body was beginning to heal—Dr. Ferrington had indeed been called out and had set her broken arm—her spirit was not. She had left her Lake Forest home with Sidney that day, the day he had found her so badly beaten, and she had not been back since. Though she was glad to finally be rid of Randolph, albeit temporarily, she lived in daily fear that he would turn up at any moment, as he had already once done.

Upon discovering his wife's defection, as he called it, Randolph had immediately driven—drunkenly—to Highbury, where he confronted first Billings and then a very stern Sidney. Randolph had demanded to see Julia, who was in fact at that moment pressed up against the wall of the upstairs landing, listening and barely daring to breathe. Sidney was blessedly firm.

"How dare you, sir! You will leave this instant!" he said in a surprisingly formidable voice. Normally, he was quite calm and even-tempered.

"Not without my wife! You have no right to keep her from me."

"Indeed," Sidney said in a more measured voice. "But I am not keeping her from you. She has chosen to recuperate here from the disgraceful injuries you have inflicted upon her. You should be ashamed! You're the absolute worst sort of man."

"That's a matter of opinion," he sneered. "Some would say that the worst sort of man is a spineless gold-digger."

Seemingly unabashed by this insult, Sidney responded calmly, "Then you *are* the absolute worst, as you encompass both."

"Julia!" Randolph bellowed. "I know you can hear me! Get down here!"

Julia began to tremble. Even if she had wanted to descend the grand staircase, she found she couldn't actually move.

"Julia, if you are not back home by midnight tonight, I will send the boys away in the morning, and you'll be lucky if you ever see them again."

A little cry escaped Julia, and she tried to will her legs to move, but they would not.

"That is an idle threat, and you know it," Sidney snapped. "To use such manipulations on a helpless woman is utterly disgraceful. Get out! You're little better than a ruffian. Go now, or I will be forced to telephone the police."

"I know you can hear me, Julia! Think carefully!" Randolph shouted.

"Out!" Sidney demanded.

Randolph swayed in place for several moments and had then surprisingly turned and stomped out, cursing loudly as he went, at which point Julia had finally collapsed, sinking to her knees. She was grateful to Sidney, of course, but even after she crawled her way to her room and to the comfort of her bed, she couldn't get his words— "helpless woman"—out of her head.

Indeed, it went through her mind now as she wandered through the garden. *Helpless, helpless, helpless.* She hated feeling this way. Hated being helpless. But she wasn't the only one. Sidney, as it turned out, had been helpless as well in preventing Randolph from actually packing up Randolph, Jr. and Howard, and having them delivered to Phillips Exeter, just as he had threatened. They were there now. They were not allowed to receive telephone calls in their first few weeks per school policy, and though Julia had written them each several letters, she had yet to receive one back. It was an utterly hopeless situation, though Sidney assured her that it was temporary only, and that he already had the legal wheels in motion to retrieve them, but that, unfortunately, it would take time.

She had been right! She had tried to warn them what a beast Randolph was, and they had not listened. It had made her angry at first, furious, especially with her mother. Not just regarding this situation, but for all the times she had not listened to her, not believed her. How could Antonia just ignore her? Was she so caught up in the expectations of society that she could so easily set her daughter aside? The idea was monstrous to Julia, and the little girl within her mourned. But she was not a child anymore, she tried telling herself, though she still felt hurt and betrayed, which in and of itself infuriated her. She hated feeling this way! She didn't want to feel anything anymore. She just wanted to be numb. In this way, she thought bitterly, perhaps her mother might be her mentor after all.

She and Antonia had had very little conversation about the extent of her abuse at the hands of Randolph. Antonia had dutifully stopped in her room each day when Julia was still confined to bed, but she had not discussed it. Indeed, she acted as though Julia really had been in a car accident, which had oddly also been Sidney's first guess as to what had happened when he had burst into her room that day. What was even more hurtful, however, was the conversation she once overheard between Sidney and her mother.

"What do you mean you've drawn up the divorce papers?" she heard Antonia say over the clink of her cocktail glass in the small drawing room where she and Sidney were having an aperitif before dinner. Julia had come down to join them, but upon hearing them argue, had stopped just outside the door.

"I just assumed . . ." Sidney answered. Julia could hear the confusion in his voice.

"Of course, she's not getting a divorce! What will everyone think? It'll be the scandal of the year at the club."

"Surely you don't expect her to go back to him, do you?"

"Heavens, no. He's a monster. I hate him." Julia heard the ice clink again as her mother took a drink. "I've always hated him. But that doesn't mean they need to divorce. They can separate. She can go to New York and stay with my sister for a while or stay at her place in the Hamptons. That or perhaps she should go to England. She could stay with Margaret and Wallace and Amelie once Clive and Henrietta return. It might be good for her. No, there's no need for a divorce."

"Antonia. It's the only way for her to gain custody of the boys. It shouldn't be too hard to prove cruelty. And adultery, if it comes to that." Julia bit her lip, thoroughly ashamed that Sidney, and now her mother, knew of the extramarital affairs she had long ago guessed at. Did everyone know? "Glenn's helping me to put a case together." At the mention of Glenn's name, Julia's stomach tightened. She had not heard his name spoken since Sidney had asked her about his letter, nor had she had the courage to ask about him. It was a subject best left alone, she told herself over and over, though, if she were honest, she thought about him constantly.

"Glenn? You mean your nephew? What has he to do with it?"

There was silence then between them, and Julia imagined them staring at each other. Finally, Sidney spoke, though his voice was lower now so that Julia had to strain to hear him.

"You must know he has feelings for her, Antonia."

"Feelings for her? That's absurd."

"Why is that absurd?"

"Why, because . . . because they hardly know each other."

"Even so, he has offered to help in any way he can."

"Help? We had a different word for that in my day."

"Don't be cheap, Antonia."

"What is he hoping? That she'll run off to Texas with him? It's obnoxious. It'll be the talk of the town. I can just see the society pages now: *Julia Cunningham Runs off with Texas Cowboy.* I think I'd prefer her to simply get divorced."

Julia heard the thunk of Sidney setting down his highball glass. "Sometimes I wonder about you, Antonia," he said, a trace of bitterness in his voice.

"Wonder? About what?"

"That you seem to care more about what the ladies at your club will say than those you love." Julia bit her lip again at how closely Sidney had hit the mark. "It makes me consider very carefully the two of us."

"That's different and you know it," she hissed.

"Is it? I'm not so sure."

Julia had slunk away then, not wanting to hear any more. She couldn't bear the hypocrisy. She had tiptoed back to her room and sat in the dark, trying desperately to think about what to do and raging against her inability to do anything at all.

Her very first instinct had been to flee to Massachusetts, where she was pretty sure Phillips was located, via train to see her boys. She considered it again now as she passed under the trellis, which led into the walled English garden. Perhaps she could even persuade the headmaster to release them to her, she thought eagerly. But that was doubtful. And it would no doubt upset the boys to see her but not be able to leave with her. And if he did release them, what was she to do with them? Where was she to go? She had no money of her own, no home. She briefly thought about Glenn's offer of a house, but how would she even get there? On the train? Then what?

She plucked a rosehead and anxiously began pulling off the petals as she listlessly wandered, remembering Antonia's words that perhaps the boys were better off at Phillips. "It's not a terrible idea, you know, Julia. It might be good for them. I believe Henrietta's brothers are at Phillips, are they not?"

Julia had not answered, but she knew she could not exist without her boys. Thoughts of them crying and frightened in a strange place haunted her. If she didn't have them near her, sustaining her, what had she to live for? She tossed the stripped rosehead to the ground as another thought occurred to her, which swept through her soul, freezing everything in its path within her. She was not the better for their absence, *but perhaps they might be better for hers.* Yes, she reasoned slowly, this new deadly thought occurring to her. Perhaps everyone would be better without her.

The thought terrified her but oddly brought her comfort, too, as she watched the sun's slow descent. The longer she stood there, the more it began to make sense. Yes, it made sense. It would be better if she were not alive, not a bother to anyone anymore. But how, she wondered, wrapping her arms around herself, suddenly chilled, would she do it?

Chapter 22

Henrietta paced back and forth in the Peacock Room, wondering what to do. She felt distinctly restless, but she couldn't put her finger on why. She supposed that it was because this was the first night of her marriage that she and Clive had spent apart, excepting the one night when they had quarreled and Clive had slept in another room. Strange that it had occurred in this very house, Henrietta mused, *and* while on their honeymoon—or what was supposed to have been their honeymoon. Maybe it's this house, she thought moodily. Something about it. She fingered her book, *Murder in Mesopotamia*, the latest Agatha Christie, but she was not in the mood to read.

She should have insisted on going with Clive to London! Even though it was decidedly smaller, she much preferred the London townhome to this behemoth. To her, Castle Linley, which wasn't a castle at all, merely a large Georgian estate house, had always had a sad, defeated air to it. It wouldn't surprise her a bit if it *was* haunted, and she tried to push away Phineas's story of the hanged maid, which had annoyingly just popped into her mind, and likewise the thought of the noises at night. She had hoped that they would go away, but unfortunately, they had not. In fact, they had intensified.

Clive, of course, did not believe in such things, but *she* did, remembering how the spiritualist they had encountered, Madame Pavlovsky, claimed to have channeled her father from beyond the grave, and how the old crone had described him as holding Henrietta's poor miscarried baby. Clive had proven the woman to be a fraud, but Henrietta knew she could not have been lying about her father and her baby. Somehow, Madame Pavlovsky had known. More than once, Henrietta had been tempted to return to her to find out more information, but Clive had forbidden it.

She glanced at the clock. Nearly ten. Why hadn't he telephoned, as he said he would? Was it possible he was dining out? But with whom? Mr. Osbourne? She tried not to think about Lady Alice, the Duke of Marlborough's daughter, with whom Clive had spent so much time during his summers here in England. Surely, Antonia would have been all for such a match, she fretted, unleashing her old insecurities.

Stop it! This was ridiculous. Of course, Clive had no interest in another woman. She knew that, felt it in her heart. And, yet, why did he not telephone? It was very unlike him . . .

To make matters even more depressing, almost as soon as Clive had left, the skies had opened up and delivered an absolute deluge for several hours. Eventually, the rain had stopped, but the grounds were absolutely saturated, dotted here and there with what looked almost like little ponds, having swelled into existence almost instantaneously from mere puddles. The result was that no one was the least bit interested in walking out of doors after dinner.

Henrietta had thus spent a rather tiresome evening playing whist, as there was little else to do and as it was the only card game Lady Linley would play, though Wallace claimed to have tried to teach her bridge many times. The players consisted mainly of herself, Lady Linley, the colonel, and Wallace, with Miss Simms and Phineas being left to entertain themselves, which had progressed into them banging out some rather silly tunes on the piano, popular numbers from films, Henrietta noted, and she was glad that Clive had not been here to witness it. He abhorred popular music, except the big bands she was fond of, and he probably would have been inclined to comment.

He could be so old-fashioned at times! Amelie, for her part, had retired early.

As it was, the card game was not particularly enjoyable; Lady Linley kept forgetting what was trump, and Wallace spent the majority of the game glaring across the room at poor Phineas. Only the colonel seemed intent on the game itself, as, in truth, Henrietta had herself been a bit distracted, a part of her brain continuously listening for the sound of the telephone.

No call had come through, though, so in the end, there was nothing more to do but to return to her room. Once there, however, she found she couldn't sleep and had taken to pacing, trying to distract her worry by attempting to unravel the case—or cases, depending on how one looked at the current situation—that were currently before them.

She was getting nowhere with this occupation, however, and suddenly felt rather exhausted, but she was convinced she wouldn't be able to sleep unless she spoke to Clive, if even for a few moments to say good night to him. She glanced at the clock again and wondered if perhaps she should try to telephone *him*. In order to do so, however, she would have to slip down to the study. She fingered the silk nightgown Edna had insisted on laying out for her and wondered if she should change. No, she decided, sure that everyone else was probably asleep by now. Besides, she would be quick.

She put on her silk robe and opened the door a crack and listened. The main hall was dark, with only a few table lamps still burning. She stepped out, looked both ways, and began to tiptoe down the hall. *Why was she sneaking around?* she scolded herself. She was doing nothing wrong! She stood up straight and proceeded down the dark stairs and made her way to the study, careful to close the door tightly behind her. Not only did she not want to wake anyone, but she likewise wanted their conversation to be private.

She looked around for the light switch, but after a halfhearted attempt to find it, gave up, as the whole room was already illuminated with a bluish-white glow from the moonlight shining in through the big bay window opposite. The curtains had not been drawn for the evening, another example of standards slipping for want of help, Henrietta judged. She crept toward the big mahogany desk positioned in the middle of the room and switched on the desk lamp, which bathed the desktop in a yellow glow and which was more than enough to see the numbers on the big black telephone. She picked up the receiver and rang the operator.

"St. James three-four-seven-two, please," she said, gazing around the room. With the glow of the desk lamp, the big window, previously illuminating the outside world, was now dark with the contrast. Henrietta wished she had pulled the curtains before she had initiated the call, as she became suddenly aware of the fact that anyone could look in, but that she could not see out. She felt as though she were suddenly in a fishbowl for anyone to observe. She tapped her foot impatiently. *What was taking so long?*

"That number is engaged, madam," the operator said now in a scratchy, nasally voice. "Do you wish to hold, or should I ring you back when it becomes free?"

Engaged? Who could Clive possibly be talking to at this hour?

"Madam?" came the nasally voice.

"No, thank you, I'll try—" she stopped midsentence, then, when the desk lamp suddenly went out and the line went dead.

"Hello?" she said into the receiver, but there was nothing but dead air.

She rapidly clicked the telephone's plunger, but there was nothing. No sound. Her heart began to beat a little harder as she tried repeatedly switching the desk lamp on and off, but to no avail. She instinctively looked to the window, which had reverted to the bluish glow now, and almost screamed when she detected what she thought was the shadow of a man withdraw, slowly, from the trellis against the wall leading up to Lady Linley's room. Her heart well and truly pounding now, she crept toward the velvet curtains. She sidled up to them in an attempt to hide herself and tried to observe the man's movements. His face was unfortunately in shadow, but she thought she recognized his shape—maybe Phineas?—though she couldn't be sure. He seemed to be watching for someone, looking up at the house, and waiting. Eventually, however, the man gave up on whatever his intent was and ran along the hedgerow toward the back of the house. Extraordinary!

Henrietta hesitated for a few moments, her heart still racing, before it occurred to her that she should probably raise the alarm that a strange man was on the grounds. Unless he was a servant, she considered, but she quickly dismissed this as being unlikely. Why would a servant be creeping around the property at night in such a way? No, she felt certain, as she hurried across the room, she needed to tell someone. Roughly, she pulled on the door, but it did not open. She pulled on it harder, guessing it to be stuck, but it did not budge. She twisted the knob both ways, her panic rising, but it remained impossibly shut. She was locked in!

"Hello!" she called through the door, placing her ear to the wood to hear if there was anyone about. "Hello?" She banged on the door. "Stevens?" she called, banging again, memories of being locked in Dunning Asylum suddenly flooding her mind and filling her with terror. She was finding it hard to breathe, her chest heaving as she tried frantically to pull on the door over and over.

She abruptly stopped in her efforts, however, the hair standing up on the back of her neck, when she perceived a deep chill in the room, as if someone had opened an icebox, and she was immediately filled with sickening dread. She had the distinct feeling that something or someone was behind her, and she frantically pulled on the door again. "Help!" she cried. But the door did not move, nor did she hear any sound without. Defeated and utterly terrified, she let her fist slide down the door and slowly turned around to face whatever lurked behind her.

At first, she could see nothing, but her eyes felt drawn to the corner of the room. She blinked rapidly, her eye movements matching the frantic heaving of her chest, and she thought she perceived the outline of what looked like a young girl. *The hanged maid?* Horrified,

Henrietta pressed herself as tightly as she could to the door, her heart pounding so hard now that she feared it might explode. The room was still terribly freezing. Henrietta stared at the figure, which remained in the corner, but when it raised an arm, Henrietta couldn't help but let out a piercing scream, which was oddly mirrored by another scream—Lady Linley's—coming from upstairs!

At that moment, the desk lamp came back on, the window faded to black again, and the ghostly presence disappeared. Henrietta stood, panting, before she came to her senses and turned quickly around to try the door again. This time it opened!

She raced out, looking back over her shoulder as she did so for any trace of the hanged maid . . . and collided squarely with Stevens. The old butler seemed equally surprised by her presence and struggled to right himself after her very near toppling of him.

"Stevens!" She wrapped her silk robe around her tighter. He, too, was dressed in his robe, red plaid, with black leather slippers.

"Madam, I heard you call. Is everything quite all right?"

"Yes, I was—" her voice trailed off. Suddenly, she wasn't so sure she wanted to explain what had just happened. "I . . . I saw a man outside on the lawn." She pointed behind her. "But, more importantly, I just heard Lady Linley scream."

"Yes, Mrs. Pennyworth is on her way to her ladyship's room now. More than likely, it was another nightmare. But if you're quite all right, madam, I'll leave you to investigate this other matter." He looked eager to escape.

"You'll alert Mr. Howard, won't you, Stevens?"

"Yes, of course, madam," he said, giving her the quickest of nods instead of his usual bow, and scurried away.

Henrietta stood, her back against the wall, and tried to catch her breath. A hundred thoughts ran through her mind at once about what had just happened in the study—had she *really* seen a ghost? But first priority, she decided, pushing all of that away for the time being, was to check on Lady Linley despite Stevens's report that Mrs. Pennyworth was on her way to attend her. Lady Linley's scream had not been one usually heard in nightmares, and Henrietta had a very bad feeling. Perhaps the intruder had reached her room!

Henrietta hurried up the staircase and then down the dim hallway toward Lady Linley's room. The closer she got, the faster she went, until she was practically running, her feelings of foreboding getting stronger with every step. When she finally reached Lady Linley's room, she briefly knocked, expecting Mrs. Pennyworth to answer, but she did not. Henrietta knocked again, this time louder.

"Lady Linley?" She waited. "Mrs. Pennyworth?"

No answer.

Henrietta quickly tried the handle, but the door was locked. "Lady Linley!" she called again, but there was still no response from anyone. Fresh panic erupting within her all over again, she ran to Miss Simms's room and pounded loudly, hoping to use the connecting door. "Miss Simms!"

She waited, but there was no answer here, either.

"Miss Simms!" she called again, leaning her ear to the door. She could hear a faint tune tinkling. Henrietta listened carefully. It was "Clair de lune"—Lady Linley's music box!

"Miss Simms!"

Giving up, Henrietta decided to try the door. It was thankfully not locked, and Henrietta opened it a crack and peered in. "Miss Simms?" she called gently, but when she saw that the bed was not only empty but still made up, she pushed the door open all the way. The window was likewise open, the lace curtains gently aloft on the damp night air, and on the sill was the music box, steadily churning out its metallic tune. Henrietta moved toward it to close it and then saw what looked like a heap of clothes on the floor in front of the window. Upon closer inspection, however, it looked to be a person! Henrietta crept closer. She reached out and touched the lump. Yes, it *was* a person! It was Lady Linley!

"Oh, Lady Linley," Henrietta cried, trying her best to turn the woman over, which was harder than she thought it would be. She was unable to tell if she was alive or dead. Tentatively, Henrietta felt the woman's neck for a pulse, and was relieved to feel at least a faint beating. She cradled the old woman's upper body in her arms as best she could. "Lady Linley!" she said loudly. "Can you hear me? Lady Linley!"

Miraculously, Lady Linley's eyes fluttered open briefly. "There was a man," she rasped.

"Yes, I . . . I saw him. Did he . . . did he hurt you?"

Lady Linley shook her head ever so slightly. "Wallace," she muttered.

"Wallace? It was Wallace?" Henrietta could hardly believe this.

Lady Linley gave her head a little shake again and closed her eyes.

"Oh! Do you mean that I should get Wallace?" Henrietta asked frantically, irritated with herself at having so easily jumped to the wrong conclusion. "Yes, I'm sure he's coming. Any moment now." She glanced over her shoulder, wondering where everyone was.

Lady Linley opened her eyes again, her gaze suddenly urgent. "No, I . . . I need to tell you something about Wallace," she croaked. "Before it's too late."

Henrietta's brow furrowed. "What do you mean, Lady—"

"What's happened?" Wallace interrupted from where he suddenly appeared in the doorway, startling Henrietta and almost causing her to scream again.

"Oh, Wallace! It's you!" she said, pressing a hand to her chest. "Your mother's had a terrible shock." She looked down at Lady Linley now, but the elderly woman had lost consciousness.

Wallace rushed to his mother's side and went down on his knees, feeling her forehead. "Good God!"

"I found her like this, collapsed on the floor. She said there was a man. And I *did* see someone out on the lawn."

"Someone on the lawn?"

Stevens entered, then, still dressed in his bathrobe.

"Help me, Stevens," Wallace barked. "We must get her to her bed."

Stevens hurried over and awkwardly took hold of Lady Linley's legs while Wallace lifted her upper body. Carefully, they inched her through the connecting door and into her own room.

"I'll ring for the doctor, shall I, sir?" Stevens asked, puffing slightly, once they had laid her on the canopied bed.

"Yes! Tell him to hurry!" Wallace ran his hand through his hair and cocked the other on his hip. "And wake Mr. Triggs and Dick. And Jeremiah. Check all the doors and windows. There may have been an intruder."

"Yes, sir. I've already taken the liberty. They are searching now."

"Good."

"I'll ring the doctor now, sir," he said, and bowed out of the room, managing to look elegant despite the situation.

Wallace felt Lady Linley's forehead again while Henrietta proceeded to begin unlacing the elderly woman's old-fashioned boots, noting that her breathing was extremely shallow.

"It'll be all right, Wallace," Henrietta said, prying them off. "She's strong."

"No, she's not," Wallace said, his voice thick. "She really isn't." He took his mother's hand and squeezed it. "I don't think she has long."

Chapter 23

Melody squeezed her hands together in a tight ball as she scurried back to the motherhouse, trying to guess who her mysterious visitor might be. The only person it *could* be, she decided, with an overwhelming sense of dread, was Sr. Bernard. She was the kingpin in this whole scheme, the only one who could have figured it all out.

Praying that it wasn't her, Melody nearly stumbled on a crack in the sidewalk. Righting herself, she considered the likelihood of Sr. Bernard traveling all this way simply to find her out and scold her. But what if she meant to do more than that? What if she expelled her? *Oh, God! She should never have come here!* Even if Sr. Bernard didn't expel her, she would surely inform her parents. What if Pops didn't let her come back? She had already tried his patience with several "shenanigans" (as he had called them) that she had been involved in back at Mundelein, the news of which had somehow reached his ears. The punishment for those infractions had been the stopping of her allowance for several months. But none of those had been her fault. They hadn't even really been her idea! Well, maybe a few of them. Still, it had been harmless fun. But *this*—this was something much more serious, and she dreaded what might happen if Pops ever found out.

Maybe, Melody hoped for a fleeting second as she rounded the corner of the main building, Sr. Bernard had not come in person. She was, after all, the president of the school; maybe she had sent an envoy instead, one of the lesser sisters. Melody prayed that it was Sr. Joseph, knowing as she did that she could quite easily twist Sr. Joseph around her finger without much effort at all. But, then again, Sr. Joseph was getting up in years. Would Sr. Bernard really have sent her all this way, simply to retrieve a naughty schoolgirl?

Which was another thing, she quickly considered. Why would Sr. Bernard waste the time of herself or one of her staff, not to mention the gasoline, to come get her? Why not simply telephone Sr. Magdalen to report that there was an imposter in their midst? If that were true, Melody concluded, suddenly slowing her pace as she passed the Stations of the Cross garden, then who was the mysterious visitor?

Perspiration was running down the back of her neck now, and she abandoned guessing who the visitor was and instead began to frantically invent apology speeches. She slowed her pace even more as she neared the front doors and stopped just outside of them to take a deep breath and to adjust her veil. Unfortunately, no imaginative excuse had formulated in her brain in the last few hurried moments, so she decided, with inner resolve, that she would simply have to tell the truth. That she had done it to help a friend who was mercilessly mistreated by her ogre of a grandfather. She gave a sharp little nod, as if convincing herself that this was indeed the best course of action and folded her hands reverently, trying very hard to look pious, and stepped as regally as she was able into the lobby.

Once inside, Melody quickly perused the area and was initially relieved to see that Sr. Bernard was nowhere in the vicinity. Her gaze then flitted to the far end of the lobby, and her stomach sank at the sight of a very stern Sr. Magdalen, who was normally so kind and encouraging, but who now wore an expression of extreme displeasure. Melody took a deep breath and proceeded over—not too fast and not too slow—her eyes lowered and her hands still folded in a half-hearted attempt at reverence. She stopped short in front of her superior and resisted the urge to curtsey. Instead, she gave a little bow.

Sr. Magdalen, apparently unmoved by Melody's sudden display of humility, simply folded her arms under her habit. She remained silent until Melody finally dared to look up at her, at which point the nun gave the slightest tilt of her head toward the little alcove to her left. Melody followed her gaze.

There, squeezed into a very narrow chair and nervously twisting his hat in his hands, was none other than Douglas Novak!

He immediately jumped to his feet. "Melody?" he squeaked.

"Douglas?" She could hardly believe it was him! "What . . . what on earth are you doing here?" She was tempted to throw her arms around him in relief, but she resisted and instead brushed away two little tears that had annoyingly sprung into her eyes. The sight of him, of anyone from home, was so very comforting. Perhaps she was more homesick than she realized.

"You are acquainted with this young man, Elsie?" Sr. Magdalen asked stiffly. "Or should I say Melody?"

"Yes, Sister, I . . . I *do* know him. He's my . . . my cousin. And Melody is my . . . my middle name. All of my cousins call me that."

"I see." Sr. Magdalen did not look convinced. "Well, it is unusual for novitiates to have visitors, even family, during their discernment period, but seeing as he has come all the way from . . . Chicago, is it?" she asked, turning to him briefly. "Then we will make an exception. Just this once." She unfolded her arms and gestured at the alcove from which Douglas had just sprung. "You may sit there," she instructed, pointing at two forlorn chairs separated by a pedestal table, upon which sat a very large statue of St. Joseph, "or you may walk in the garden. Either way, I will give you just thirty minutes." She pulled out a tiny watch on a thin gold fob from somewhere deep within her habit, noted the time, and then put it back.

"Oh, thank you, Sister. I'm sorry, Sister. We'll walk outside," Melody said hurriedly, her cheeks burning. She was, of course, utterly relieved that none of the sisters from Mundelein had turned up, but she knew she was still skating on thin ice. *Why was Douglas here?*

Melody gave him a questioning look and nodded toward the main doors. "Come along, Douglas," she said pertly and walked quickly across the lobby without looking back at him. Once outside, she made a beeline for the Stations of the Cross garden, not stopping until they reached the first station: *Jesus Is Condemned to Death*. Finally, she spun around to face the poor young man trailing behind her.

"What are you doing here?" she hissed.

"Oh, Mel, what are *you* doing here? Am I too late?"

"Too late for what?"

He gestured at her veil and her black habit. "Are you already a nun?"

"A nun? Of course, I'm not a nun!" At the sight of his befuddled face, she let out a loud laugh and was surprised at how good it felt. "I'm just disguising myself." She gave a little twirl. "Isn't it a scream?" she chirped, lapsing delightedly into her old self.

"Thank God for that," Douglas said, fanning himself with his hat.

"Why?" Melody's voice was teasing now. "Would it have mattered to you?"

Douglas looked at her abruptly, his blue eyes filled with hurt. "Of course, it would! You know I'm crazy about you, Mel. I just wish you'd let me show you," he said, his voice lower now, more serious as he averted his gaze to the ground.

Melody's momentary amusement faltered. She had told Elsie on numerous occasions that she was *in love* with Douglas Novak, but she had never really been sure. Now, as she stood observing him in this strange place, still not knowing how he had found her but admiring the effort it must have taken, she felt a stirring in her heart for him that had previously been lacking.

"You still haven't told me why you're here," she said, trying to squelch the feeling. She piously folded her hands, as if in prayer, as she wandered to the second station: *Jesus Takes up His Cross*. "Do you wish to repent of your sins?"

"Melody, for gosh sakes, be serious! You're in a mess of trouble. You can't even believe it."

Melody sighed, reality and her earlier fears suddenly returning. She knew she was going to have to face the consequences. Obviously, Sr. Bernard had found her out. "Did Sister Bernard send you?"

"Well," Douglas pulled at his polka-dot bow tie. "Not really. I volunteered."

Melody leaned against a walnut tree, waiting for him to go on. "Let's have it, then."

"Well, if you must know, I tried to telephone you. I . . . I thought maybe we could see a show or something."

Melody smiled internally. "I thought you were going to Ohio with your family."

Douglas shook his head. "The plans changed. My Aunt Millie got sick, and my mom didn't want to leave. So, I found myself stuck in Chicago for the summer. Charlie and Cynthia both went back home. So, I thought of you and hoped I could see you before you went home, too."

"That was sweet." She slightly batted her eyes.

He stared at her for a few moments, as if trying to judge her sincerity. "Anyway," he said, giving his head a little shake, "when I called Philomena, Sister Joseph told me that you had already returned home. That there was a sudden funeral you needed to attend." He looked at her, one eye squeezed shut. "So, I worked up the courage to telephone you in Merriweather. You gave me the number once, remember?"

"Oh, no! You didn't, did you?"

"I did. And they told me that you were still in Chicago, taking a summer tutorial."

"Oh, no," Melody groaned. "Did you say anything?"

"Not at that point. But I was extremely worried. I called Philomena again and asked to speak to Elsie, but I was told she was gone, too. At this point, I was nearly frantic. I took the bus up to Roger's Park and decided I needed to seek out Sister Bernard."

"Oh, Douglas! Why?"

"Why? Because I thought maybe you'd been kidnapped or some-thing. I was worried sick! When I told Sister Bernard the whole story, she just laughed. Laughed! Said she knew where you were but was very sorry that I had been put to so much worry."

"She knew I was here? But how?"

Douglas shrugged. "I think someone from here, the head nun, telephoned her." He gestured with his thumb over his shoulder. "I forget her name . . ."

"Sister Magdalen?"

"Yeah, that's the one."

Melody thrust her hands on her hips. "Well, why didn't they say something?" She wasn't sure what made her more upset—the fact that she had not gotten away with her prank after all or that both nuns were apparently willing to allow her to suffer here endlessly.

Douglas shrugged. "I asked Sister Bernard when you would return, and she told me that she didn't know. That you would have to decide that. Then I . . . well, I offered—sort of begged, if you must know—to come and get you. To escort you home safely."

"And she agreed to that?"

Douglas nodded. " 'I cannot stop you from traveling to Dubuque, Mr. Novak,' she said to me, 'but Miss Merriweather must decide her own fate. She has gotten herself into this mess, and now she must get herself out.' "

"Well, obviously, there's no point in continuing with this ruse," Melody said, tugging her veil from her head and running a hand through her hair. "I wonder if she told my parents," she mused. She looked back at him now and was pleased to see that he was staring at her blond tresses.

He gave his head a quick shake. "I almost forgot!" He reached into the breast pocket of his jacket. "Sister Bernard sent along these letters. Apparently, your mail has been piling up." He handed her a small stack.

Melody quickly flipped through them, noting that there was one from Cynthia, one from Elsie, and one from her mother. She sighed. She longed to open the ones from Cynthia and Elsie, but she would do that later when she was alone and could soak them up. Right now, she needed to face the music and see what her parents had to say about the whole mess. She hoped they wouldn't stop her allowance!

Melody tore open the letter and quickly skimmed it, her heart sinking as she read. "Oh, Douglas," she murmured, looking up at him.

"What? What is it? Are they angry?"

"It's much worse than that." She handed him the letter.

Dear Melody,

I'm not sure how to tell you this, my girl, but I need you to come home immediately. Your father has had a stroke, and I fear the worst. I cannot send a car to Chicago for you—I'll explain later. Perhaps you could take the train. Oh, Mel, please do hurry. We're all very worried.

Your loving Mums

"Oh, Douglas," Melody said, gripping the sleeve of his jacket as she brushed away the tears that had instantly formed. "Will you take me home?"

Chapter 24

"But when are you coming home?" Henrietta said into the telephone. She was again in the study, but this time, she had propped open the door with the heavy iron door stopper. Finally, she had been able to get through to Clive in London.

"I'm terribly sorry, darling, but there have been a few . . . developments, as it were, that I really must attend to."

"I find this very odd, Clive," Henrietta said, twisting the cloth telephone cord around her finger and repeatedly observing each corner of the room in turn as she spoke. "Why can't Osbourne deal with whatever it is?"

"It's . . . well, it's complicated. I'll explain it all when I return. I promise."

"Why are you being so secretive?" she persisted. "Should I be worried?"

"Worried? About what?"

"About a certain Lady Alice."

"Lady Alice?"

"The Duke of Marlborough's daughter you were once so fond of?"

Clive laughed out loud, which made Henrietta smile despite her suspicion. "Don't be silly."

"Well, what is it, then? I hope you're not trying to chase down

Hartle or mixed up with MI5 or some such thing. Remember, you promised."

"Darling, it's nothing like that. It's purely business, I assure you. Speaking of, how are you getting on with the case?"

As frustrated as she was with him at the moment, she felt a slight thrill that he seemed to be actually relying on her to work on the case, as if she were truly an equal partner in their fledgling detective agency, the source of so many past disagreements between them. She struggled to think of something to say, as, indeed, she had discovered little thus far. She had already related the story of the intruder and how no trace of him had yet been found.

"Well, there isn't much more to say, really. I did *try* to question everyone at breakfast about the intruder, but it seems that no one except me and Lady Linley saw anything out of the ordinary. Phineas denies that it was him, of course. Laughed, as usual, at my even suggesting it. But I'm not so sure. I have the distinct feeling that he's hiding something."

"Well, he's obviously not the only one. What about Miss Simms? What was her excuse for not being in her room last night?"

"She says she couldn't sleep and went for a walk."

"And she didn't see anyone?"

"She claims not."

"What about the music box?"

"She says she has no idea how it got there."

"Hmmm. This is all very odd."

"Yes, agreed." Her attention was diverted, then, by the sight of a tiny hummingbird hovering just outside the window. It was hardly bigger than her thumb, and its little wings were beating so fast she could barely see them. She made a move to get a closer look, but it flew away before she could. With a sigh, she turned her back on the window and resumed her nervous inspection of the corners. "Speaking of Miss Simms, have you had a chance to investigate her charity?"

"Not yet. I've been terribly busy. But, more importantly, how is Lady Linley today?"

"The same. She's very weak." She paused, then, wondering if now was the time to bring up her ghostly experience. She had not yet, as she was still trying to reason it out, and likewise, she was pretty sure he would dismiss it, anyway.

"What about Wallace?" he asked, interrupting her thoughts.

"He's his usual grumpy self," she answered, deciding she would wait until he came home to relate her strange experience. "But he did tell me that he might have some exciting news to share with you when you return. Something about a buyer for the London house, I think. He announced it this morning at breakfast, and everyone seems quite upset. The mood is dreadfully low."

"Ah. I see. Well, darling, I wouldn't worry. Things have a way of working out. But please be careful. In case there is an intruder still lurking around, try not to leave the house if you can help it. And if you must be outside, stay on the grounds."

"Fine." She let out a sigh. "I don't have anywhere to go, anyway."

"Promise me, Henrietta."

"Oh, all right. I promise."

"I need to ring off now, darling. I love you."

"I love you, too," she said softly and placed the heavy receiver in its cradle.

Luncheon was not a very joyful affair. Lady Linley was still in bed, and Amelie had likewise declared that she would remain in the nursery with the children while they had their meal. Everyone else was present but decidedly muted. Only Colonel Beaufort seemed undisturbed by last night's excitement, except to express regret that he had somehow slept through the whole thing. Brandishing his butter knife, he proceeded to tell a tale of a midnight intruder who had somehow made his way, knife between his teeth, apparently, across enemy lines while they were camped in Kuldana and had slit several men's throats before he was discovered and duly shot. Despite the gruesomeness of the tale, there was little reaction amongst the guests. Either they were lost in their own thoughts, or they had by this point become numb to the colonel's outlandish regalings. Only Phineas managed to mumble, "We've heard that one before, Father," as he sullenly picked at his potatoes. He seemed very down and out, and Henrietta could not help but wonder if he and Miss Simms had quarreled.

Oddly, then, as if she could read her mind, Miss Simms spoke. "I say, Mrs. Howard," the young woman said pertly. "How about a ride this afternoon? It's a perfect day for it."

"A ride?" Henrietta wiped her mouth with her napkin. She was not hungry in the slightest, and the little she had eaten was not sitting well. "Where to? Cromford?"

"No, I mean on horseback. You wouldn't mind, would you, dear Wallace?"

"No, by all means," Wallace said with a heavy sigh. "The horses need exercise. In fact, I might go with you, if you don't mind."

"Not at all. We'll make a party of it. Care to come along, Mr. Beaufort?" she asked, batting her eyes at him.

Phineas, however, seemed unwilling, for once, to take the bait. "No, thanks. I've some work to do."

"Very well," she said breezily, "what do you say, Mrs. Howard? Oh, do say yes. It's most frightfully dull without dear Lady Linley to attend."

Henrietta considered. She wasn't sure she really wanted to spend the afternoon in the company of Wallace and Miss Simms, but quickly decided that there was little else to do. She was tired of reading. "Well, I suppose," she said tentatively, but then remembered her promise to Clive to be careful and to not leave the grounds. Well, she considered, they wouldn't be leaving the grounds. And anyway, Wallace would be along.

Miss Simms clapped her hands together. "Oh, jolly good! I can hardly wait."

Not an hour later, Henrietta and Evie Simms, suitably dressed in riding habits, met Wallace at the stables. Dick held the white mare while Miss Simms mounted, and then held out the reins of a big black stallion to Wallace. The young groom returned to the barn, then, and eventually led out Daisy, the horse Henrietta had ridden once before on their previous trip.

"Afraid she's a bit lame today, sir," Dick said, addressing Wallace. "She'll be okay if you don't press her too hard," he said to Henrietta, holding the horse's reins under the chin so that Henrietta could step up on the wooden step stool to mount her. "Or we can saddle up Beauty, but she hasn't been ridden in a while. Bit ornery, she is."

"Lame? What do you mean 'lame'?" Wallace demanded.

"Just that she had a stone under one shoe and she's a bit sore," Dick explained quickly, his shoulders rounded with unease. "She'll be fine, like I said. Just go easy on her."

Wallace rubbed his brow for several moments. "No," he finally said. "Take Daisy back inside. I don't want to take the chance of her being injured further. Here, Henrietta, you take my horse," he said handing the reins to Henrietta.

"Shall I saddle Beauty for you, sir?" Dick asked.

"No, I was in two minds anyway. I'll return to the house. You don't mind, do you, ladies?" He squinted one eye against the sun as he looked at Henrietta and then Miss Simms, who was already sitting prettily atop her horse.

"Oh, no, Wallace, I wouldn't think of it! *I'll* stay back," Henrietta exclaimed. "I'm not really feeling up to a ride, to be honest, and I have some letters to write." She took a few steps back.

"I wouldn't hear of it. Come," he said encouragingly. "I really shouldn't leave Amelie. Or Mother." He gave the stallion a gentle pat. "And you needn't worry about Revolution, here. He's as gentle as a mouse. I wouldn't suggest it if I wasn't sure you'd be perfectly safe. Especially since I'd have to answer to Clive if something happened to you." He gave her a wry smile.

"Oh, do say you will, Mrs. Howard!" Miss Simms interjected. "I'll ride Revolution, if you'd rather. I quite like his name."

"No, I'll ride him," Henrietta reluctantly acquiesced, her face flushed. She wished she had never agreed to this ride, but it seemed impossible to get out of it now.

"Here, I'll hold him," Wallace grunted. Henrietta put her left foot in the stirrup and swung up. The horse was immense, and she was suddenly filled with trepidation, but tried to control it, remembering how Clive had once told her that horses could sense fear. She looked down at Wallace, who stood with his hands on his hips, a rare smile on his face. "A perfect picture, ladies. Two roses. No need of a thorn between you." He pointed toward the lane that ran behind the stables. "Just follow that. It's an easy ride. It leads you through that little woods and then eventually loops around. Just stay on the path. The horses know the way."

"Aye," said Dick, still holding Daisy. "It's only about a mile. Won't take you long."

"Come on, then," Miss Simms said gaily, gently kicking her horse into action. Revolution instinctively followed, and Henrietta gripped the reins tightly.

Before they had gone even a hundred feet, however, they heard a shout from Mr. Triggs. Henrietta slowed her horse and twisted around.

"What are you doing?" Mr. Triggs shouted at Dick. "Mrs. Howard should not have his lordship's horse!"

"But Daisy's a bit lame today, Mr. Triggs," Dick cowered.

"Then go get Beauty, you daft bugger."

"Don't blame Dick, Mr. Triggs," Wallace intervened. "It was my idea to give Mrs. Howard my horse. I've changed my mind about riding today. I have several things I need to attend to, anyway."

"But, sir!" the old groom fretted. "It's not right. His lordship, bless his soul," he said, quickly crossing himself, "would never have let anyone ride his horse. It's just not done."

"Mr. Triggs, you forget yourself," Wallace snapped, his previous good mood suddenly dissipating. "*I* am the master of Linley now, and I'll decide what's right and wrong. You must let go of the past, man, or you'll find yourself in want of a place. Walk on!" he called to

the ladies. Henrietta felt Revolution jerk into motion and turned to
see that Miss Simms was already pretty far down the lane.

"Wait!" Henrietta called and spurred her horse forward. She
quickly caught up to Miss Simms, and the two women rode in
silence for the better part of ten minutes. Despite the size of the
beast under her, Henrietta found he was actually quite gentle, and
she eventually began to relax a bit. She wished she was with Clive,
but, on the other hand, it was good to be with another woman her
age for a change. It made her realize how much she missed Lucy and
Gwen—and Rose, too—her friends from her days working in the
city, and hoped they were getting on. She wondered when Rose and
Stan, the neighborhood boy who had once professed to be in love
with Henrietta, would be married and hoped she and Clive might
be home in time to attend the wedding. If they were invited, that
is. She wondered if Elsie would be. Henrietta had tried numerous
times to foist Stan and his puppy dog affections onto Elsie, who, as
it happened, had had the most terrible crush on him. Stan had at
first gone along with the scheme, if only to please Henrietta, but it
hadn't gone to plan, of course, teaching Henrietta a valuable lesson,
which was that love could not be forced. Poor Elsie. She offered up
a silent prayer that her sister was happy in the life she had chosen
with Gunther. She had written Elsie a long letter, but she had not
yet received an answer. She wondered if Ma knew about Elsie's
elopement.

"How did you meet your husband?" Evie called over her shoulder.
The path had narrowed a bit, and she was only several paces ahead of
Henrietta now. They were nearly at the woods.

Henrietta smiled, wondering if she should tell the real story or
the false one that she and Clive had fabricated between them for the
more delicate ears of society.

"I was a taxi dancer in a club in Chicago, and my boss was murdered," she said, deciding on the spur of the moment to tell the real
story. "Clive was assigned to the case, and, well, one thing led to
another."

"Goodness!" Miss Simms exclaimed. "What a story! What's a taxi dancer, though? Never heard of it."

Henrietta laughed. "It's popular in America. In big cities, anyway. Taxi dancers are hired by a dance hall to dance with men for ten cents a dance."

"You don't say! How very risqué, Mrs. Howard. I'm most impressed," she said, turning in her saddle, as if to observe Henrietta in a new light.

"You needn't be. It's not as glamorous as it might sound."

"Still, what a life you've led. And a murder! How extraordinary. Just like the films."

"I guess you might say that." Henrietta smiled to herself.

"Did they ever catch him?"

"Who?"

"Why, the murderer, of course."

"Well, eventually. It's rather a long story."

"Oh, do tell! It's a shame Phineas isn't here. It's just the sort of story he goes for."

"Perhaps another time." Henrietta wrapped the thick reins around her hand, trying to think of how to turn the conversation on Miss Simms and to thus best use her time alone with her. After all, she *was* a suspect of sorts. "But speaking of Phineas," Henrietta tried to say casually, "you seem rather fond of him."

Miss Simms let out a little laugh. "Yes, I'm *fond* of him, but not overly so. He might have a quite different opinion of the matter, but that is not my concern."

Henrietta considered the truth of this statement, but before she could decide, Miss Simms clarified. "Phineas is a jolly sort. He's quite good fun, I'll give him that, but he's not at all a man. And anyway, I have my charity to think of."

"Ah, yes. Your charity." Henrietta bit her lip, wondering if she should gamble. "Do you mind me asking a terribly forward question, Miss Simms?"

"Not at all," she practically cooed. "But only if you agree to call me

Evie. 'Miss Simms' is so horribly formal. Don't you agree? And might I call you Henrietta?"

"Yes, all right."

"Well, what is the question, then?" she asked eagerly, as if they were playing a game.

"Are you hoping to inherit the estate from Lady Linley upon her death?" Henrietta braced herself for what she was sure would be Miss Simms's vehement denial, so she was surprised when she heard the young woman laugh.

"Yes," she said, turning in her saddle to look back at Henrietta again. "I am. Is that so terrible? It's no secret what state the estate is in. It's obvious it's going to have to be donated to charity, so why not mine? It's not as if I will personally benefit. And isn't ours a much more worthy endeavor than the Fabians? I mean, really! Whoever heard of such nonsense?"

Henrietta smiled, knowing that Wallace thought that the Ladies Association, or whatever it was, was equally ridiculous. They had entered the woods now, and the horses slowed, the path being somewhat overgrown in places.

"I've gone a step beyond hoping, though," Miss Simms continued cryptically. "I'll let you in on a little secret, Henrietta. But you must promise not to tell. Though I suppose you'll find out soon enough." She blinked her eyes several times and smiled coyly. "I have reason to believe she *has* willed it to me. She practically said so just the other day. That was the reason she had Mr. Churchwood come out.

"The solicitor?"

"Yes! Nothing has been said, of course. But I'm fairly sure. Lady Linley all but told me. Isn't that wonderful! Come on!" she called, suddenly spurring her horse into motion. "Let's race, shall we?"

The woods had opened up into a pleasant meadow now, and Miss Simms's horse broke into a gallop.

Startled not only by Miss Simms's revelation, but by her horse suddenly jolting into motion, too, Henrietta struggled to hold on. She did not encourage Revolution to run, but the beast, eager to catch his partner, bolted ahead. Henrietta gave a little cry and gripped the reins, holding on tight and trying to pull her horse to at least a quiet trot. "Whoa!" she cried over and over. "Miss Simms! Evie! Wait!" she called and tried to keep her seat. "Whoa!" she shouted again, pulling on the reins, but the horse had his own mind.

Terrified, Henrietta gave up trying to get Revolution to stop or to even slow down and instead concentrated on staying mounted. Suddenly, however, the horse did stop abruptly, for what reason it was never determined—perhaps a log in the path, a rut, or even a snake—the result of which was that Henrietta was thrust violently forward. She lost her grip on the reins, and before she could think, she was thrown. She felt herself falling, but before she could even fully comprehend the situation or hold out her hands to brace her fall, she hit the ground hard, her head connecting with a rather large boulder. The pain was dizzying. For just a moment she saw the blue of the sky, a lone bird floating above her, and then everything went black.

Chapter 25

"Careful, man!" Oldrich shouted to his driver as they bumped along the rutted road in the Rolls, the exterior of which, he worried, was surely now filthy. Elsie sat beside him, cradling Anna in her arms. She had wrapped her apron tightly around the girl's head, but the blood continued to seep through. Some of it had dripped onto the seat. He would have to sell this car, he thought disgustedly.

He looked out the window distractedly and then back at the girl again. She was so tiny. He didn't remember any of his own children or other grandchildren being this tiny. Both of her little hands could fit in one of his, wrinkled and creased though it was. But then again, he had not seen much of his children, especially when they had been small. With the exception of Martha, of course. He had had a soft spot for her when she was a toddler, enjoying the sweetness of a little girl after the three boys. Many times, unbeknownst to his wife, Charity, he had snuck up to the nursery to watch her play.

Oldrich delighted in Martha as a child, but as she grew older, he was disappointed that she was not the beauty he had hoped for. Her once lithe little body grew thick about the middle, and her previously perfect skin became riddled with acne. Her shy, demure personality underwent a change, too. By the time she was sixteen, she had become sullen and harsh, which annoyed him to no end. Both he and Charity admonished her, instructing her that no man wanted a sour wife, but it only seemed to make things worse. In desperation, they decided to send her to a finishing school in Switzerland, which had set him back thousands, only to have her return and betray him in the end by running off with the butcher's delivery boy, Leslie Von Harmon. It had been a crushing blow, and while Charity had seemed to easily be able to excommunicate her daughter with little or no emotion, he had had a harder time of it. On an almost regular basis, he would have Higgins, his chauffeur, drive him to the hovel in the city Von Harmon had taken her to, hoping for at least a glimpse of her, but then Charity had discovered these secret outings and put a stop to them. Likewise, she had been successful in stopping the boys from ever speaking of their sister again, which had further sounded the death knell for his wayward daughter.

And then, after all these years, he had finally been unexpectedly reunited with Martha through *her* daughter, the lovely Henrietta. The chances of such a thing happening were astounding, and yet it *had* happened, making him wonder if there really was a God. When he had finally met his granddaughter at her engagement party to the Howard heir, Oldrich had been exceedingly pleased with her exquisite looks and her unaffected grace. She was everything—and more—that he had once hoped for in Martha. To his utter delight, Henrietta more than made up for Martha's deficiencies, and he rejoiced that he could claim her as his descendant.

It was at that same party, however, that he had met Elsie, the younger sister, and she had also stirred something in his crusty heart, though it certainly wasn't pride. It was more akin to regret mixed with an odd, fleeting hope that perhaps things could be different. Elsie bore an uncanny resemblance to Martha at seventeen but without, blessedly, the acne and the acerbity.

No, Elsie, he saw right away, was quite a different creature from Martha in that regard. She was obedient, kind, and tender, and it gave him hope that she would be amenable to his will, as the recalcitrant Martha had never been. He would make up for lost time. He would see to it that Elsie's life turned out differently than Martha's. And what was the harm in increasing his coffers in the process? Was it really so evil, as that idiot nun had accused him? That was the way of business. After all, money didn't just grow on trees; it had to be cultivated.

He assumed that having grown up in poverty, Elsie would welcome his efforts at setting her up for a life of luxury and privilege by marrying up the social ladder, but she had shockingly not. She had proven to be as stubborn as Martha after all, resisting all his efforts and eloping, just as her mother had done. It utterly infuriated him! While it was true that he had yet another granddaughter, little Doris, and five grandsons to manipulate, as Elsie herself had reminded him, he could not help being obsessed with *her*, as if she were Martha all over again, and he didn't think his heart could bear to lose again. He had even called her Martha once, but she thankfully hadn't seemed to notice.

He looked at her now in her dirty, sack-like housedress, cradling a bleeding child that was not her own, and despaired. He examined the child again. Her gingham dress was thin, her knees scuffed, and her socks droopy. Worse was the fact that her shoes were literally falling apart, held together by bits of string, which, Oldrich guessed, was probably Elsie's handiwork. It was something Martha would have done as a child. She had forever collected strays or injured birds, insisting on trying to nurse them back to health. None of them had ever lived, though.

"How much farther?" Oldrich barked at Higgins.

"I'm not sure, sir," the chauffeur answered without turning around. "I'm not exactly certain of where I'm going."

"It's not too much further, I don't think," Elsie piped up, craning her neck to look out the windshield as best she could. "Mrs. Wilkins said it was on Woolworth." The farmer's wife, upon hurrying to the hut at Elsie's insistence to examine the girl's injury, advised that they skip Doc Fuller's in town and drive straight on to Omaha to a proper hospital. "That don't look good," Mrs. Wilkins opined. "Best get her to Douglas. That's the closest."

Higgins did as Elsie instructed and turned now onto Woolworth. Almost immediately, they spotted the old Victorian Douglas County Hospital looming ahead.

"This is it?" Oldrich exclaimed. "This looks like nothing more than a tuberculosis sanatorium. They won't be able to treat this type of wound. We need a surgeon!"

"Grandfather, we don't have a choice."

Higgins pulled around the center circle and stopped in front of the main doors, allowing the car to idle.

"Well, help us, Higgins!" Oldrich shouted.

Quickly, the driver hopped out from behind the wheel and hurried around to Elsie's side. He opened her door and, after several moments of hesitation, scooped up the girl. Elsie slid out and remained beside him, trying to hold the bloody apron in place, as Higgins jogged toward the front doors. Oldrich hobbled behind.

Once inside, they were immediately greeted by a nurse, who hurried from behind the massive front desk, her alacrity probably spurred on by the large amounts of blood splattered on both Anna and poor Elsie.

"What happened?" the nurse asked while carefully easing the bunched apron away from Anna's wound.

"She fell and hit her head," Elsie explained.

The nurse held the apron under her arm and gently examined the loose flap of skin hanging where Anna's ear should have been.

"We'll need to operate right away," she said, pressing the apron back into place. "Who's responsible for her?"

Oldrich was about to speak when Elsie spoke up. "I am," she said quietly. "I'm . . . I'm her mother. I'm Elsie Stockel." Oldrich gripped his cane tightly at hearing his granddaughter's name sullied with a German one.

The nurse looked her over. "How did it happen?"

"She . . . she was having a fit, and she fell—"

"A fit? What sort of fit?"

"She's an epileptic."

The nurse rolled her eyes slightly. "Surgery will be tough, then. It'll be up to the doctor. Bensen!" she called to an orderly standing nearby. "Take her back."

A young man hurried over and took the girl from Higgins, who seemed all too eager to give her up. Indeed, once he was released from holding Anna, the chauffeur produced a handkerchief from somewhere inside his uniform jacket and began wiping himself down.

"Will she . . . she'll be all right, won't she?" Elsie twisted her hands, hovering behind the orderly and the nurse.

"We'll try our best," the nurse responded with no hope whatsoever in her voice. "You can wait in there," she said, nodding toward what appeared to be a waiting room, and then followed the orderly through a set of double doors. Elsie stood staring at them, and for a moment Oldrich was afraid she was going to bolt through them.

Oldrich cleared his throat, hoping to get her attention. "Come, Elsie. Let's go."

Elsie turned and stared at him so forlornly that he felt his chest flutter a little. He gestured toward the lounge. "Shall we?"

Elsie did not respond, but marched, her shoulders slumped, toward the door marked "Visitors" in gold lettering on beveled glass. Oldrich held the door, and Elsie silently passed through and dropped into the first chair. Her face crumpled then, and she burst into tears. Oldrich sat down gingerly beside her, his insides twisting. He hated tears. It was one thing that Martha had never, ever done in front of him. She had refused to ever show him that vulnerability, and yet here was Elsie, sobbing her eyes out, her face in her hands. Oldrich was unsure what to do.

"There, there," he said, offering her his handkerchief. "Don't distress yourself. I'm sure the girl will be fine. It seems an adequate institution," he lied, looking around at the outdated Victorian furniture. He quickly contemplated whether or not the girl really would be fine. In some ways, he realized guiltily, if the girl died, the situation would be considerably easier.

Elsie sat up and looked at him. Her face was a mess, and it both appalled and intrigued him that she didn't seem to care.

"Do you really think so?" she asked hoarsely.

"Yes, yes of course I do," he lied.

"But she's lost so much blood," Elsie said, lifting a corner of her blood-soaked dress.

"Yes, well, head wounds tend to bleed profusely," he said, suddenly remembering a fight he had had at prep school. The only one he had ever been in, and it had resulted in him being hit squarely in the nose, which had produced a massive outpouring of blood. He hadn't thought of that in so very long. Perhaps ever. He had hated that school. "I wouldn't worry," he said gruffly.

"But you heard the nurse. The surgery will be difficult with her epilepsy," she said, wiping her eyes with his handkerchief. Another thing that would have to get thrown out. "And Gunther doesn't even know we're here. I should have left a note, but I didn't think. Maybe Mrs. Wilkins will tell him," she added mournfully.

Oldrich took a deep breath. It exasperated him when she spoke of this man, and he wondered, even now, how he could get rid of him. He would have to proceed carefully.

"Elsie, why are you so devoted to this man? Is it because you feel sorry for him, perhaps?" He tried to say it delicately, but it came off sounding harsh.

"No, it is because I . . . I love him, Grandfather," she answered, looking somewhat taken aback by the question.

"But, my . . . dear," he said awkwardly, as if the term of endearment caused him pain to utter, "do you not see what a bad situation this is?" He looked around the room for inspiration but found none. "Your tender heart does you justice, to be sure, but, Elsie, my dear," he added, the sentiment coming easier this time, "think of your poor family at home. Your mother. She will be brokenhearted."

He saw Elsie's face shift, and he allowed himself a moment of hope that he was perhaps getting through to her. Her response, however, crushed it.

"Grandfather, I don't wish to anger you, but Ma's heart has long since been broken, and dare I say, by the man sitting next to me."

Oldrich felt a spike of anger.

"My mother cares not what I do or don't do. She is lost to me and has been these many years."

Oldrich cleared his throat, not knowing what to say to this. So, he was not the only one to have lost Martha.

"I know I must remind you of her. I see it in your eyes. But, Grandfather, you cannot seek to undo the past with my mother by forcing me to do your will. Surely you can see that, can you not?"

Oldrich frowned. Blast the girl! How had she so easily found her way to the heart of the matter? Still, he could not allow her to get the better of him.

"Elsie, despite what you may think, I have only your best interest at heart."

"If that is true, then you will try to help me, not hinder me. Help me, Grandfather," she pleaded, laying her hands on his.

Oldrich felt the familiar pain in his chest and pulled his hands from under hers. He concentrated on keeping his voice calm. "Elsie, I would indeed help you. But . . . even if you do not set aside Gunther," he said delicately, realizing that this was the first time he had ever used the man's actual name, "you must consider, very carefully, sending the girl away. Now, now!" he said, raising a hand at the protest that was already on her lips, "You must think. Not to a colony. But to a good place. A place she will be adequately cared for, watched and aided in her disease. Look what has just occurred," he said, nodding toward the door. "Do you not think this will occur again? What if the injury is worse next time? What if it leads to her untimely demise? Would you have that on your conscience? You think by keeping her close you are doing the best for her, protecting her, but today's events have proven this to not be the case. Are you not being selfish in keeping her and not allowing her to grow and thrive in a place that is better suited to one such as her? Is it born of a desire to truly help the girl, or is it merely to prove something to Gunther . . . or anyone else, for that matter? Yourself? And what will happen when your own child comes along?" He stared intently at her and was pleased that she blushed. "How will you care for a baby, or two, or several, when you have to so closely attend this sickly child? No, you must think carefully, Elsie."

Elsie did not immediately respond, but sat staring at him as if he were a madman. It was unbearable! Finally, she spoke. "Grandfather, how . . . how can you suggest such a thing? She's only just recently started to speak again. She has been through much. She would never survive being sent away."

"Children are very resilient, Elsie. She will be the better for it, believe me. You will thank me in the end."

Elsie's face twisted in what he hoped was not anger.

"I might be willing to help you and Gunther," he said quickly before she could out-and-out refuse. "Help you to find a place to live back in Chicago. Find a professorship for Gunther. You could continue your studies," he offered carefully. "But you must set this child aside. It is for her own good, Elsie. And yours."

"Grandfather, I—"

The doorway swung open then, and the doctor, garbed in a long white apron that had its own pattern of blood splashes on it, stepped through. He approached Oldrich and Elsie. "Mrs. Stockel?"

"Yes?" Elsie said, standing and wringing her hands.

"You can come back now," he said heavily. "But there's something I should tell you."

Chapter 26

"She's going to be fine," the doctor said, snapping shut his black bag. Henrietta's eyes fluttered open. She was lying, as best she could tell, in bed in the Peacock Room. She lifted a hand to her head. It hurt terribly.

"What happened?" Henrietta asked, blinking rapidly.

"You had a fall," Amelie said from where she sat beside the bed.

Henrietta squinted in her direction. "Yes," she grimaced, "I remember now. It was the horse."

"You've suffered a mild concussion," the doctor said, standing up straight. "Not too serious. Rest for a few days. I've left some aspirin for the pain, should you need it," he said, nodding at a little brown glass jar on the bedside table. "The good news is that the baby is fine," he said pleasantly.

Henrietta felt her throat constrict. *Baby?*

The doctor, obviously noting the confusion on her face, paused in his efforts at gathering his things. "Did you not know?" he asked, a smile about his face. "You are with child, my dear. But all is well, from what I can tell."

"I . . ." Henrietta looked briefly at Amelie, as if she were in on some sort of joke, before looking back at the doctor. "Are you sure?"

"As sure as I can be. Have you not suspected?"

Henrietta gripped the silk coverlet. She *had* been late, but she hadn't wanted to get her hopes up. She had been late before. Tears filled the corners of her eyes. She nodded slowly.

"Well, as I said, nothing to worry about. I'll see myself out. I'll stop back later in the week to see how you're doing."

"Would you like something before you go?" Amelie asked, rising as well.

"No, I've best be going. I have more stops to make."

"Good-bye, zen, Doctor. Merci," Amelie called as he stepped into the hallway. Once he had gone, she sat back down beside Henrietta and took her hand. "Congratulations," she said, beaming.

"Oh, Amelie! I . . . I don't know what to think." Henrietta smiled weakly. "I'm happy, of course, but I'm worried. What if . . . what if I can't carry this one, either?"

"Tut tut!" Amelie said in her best English accent. "Do not fret. Zis one will take. I have a feeling," she said with a small wink. "But you must rest, as your *beau mari* is always saying."

"But *you* aren't resting!"

"But I do. Zat is why I remain upstairs sometimes. And besides, I have not had the worry you have recently endured."

"That isn't exactly true," Henrietta responded after a moment's consideration. "You might soon lose your home. Does that not worry you?"

"Not as much as you might think. It is more worrisome to Wallace. He does not like the place, *çest vrai*, but he does not want to go down in history as the lord who lost the castle."

"But it isn't his fault."

"Maybe, but maybe not. It was unwise, as you know, for us to marry."

"Do you regret it?"

Amelie laughed. "Do you mean because it ruined the estate, or because of Wallace's ill temper?"

Henrietta smiled, surprised by her candidness. "Either, I suppose."

"*Non*. I do not. *Que será será*, as the saying goes. I believe in fate. And I love Wallace, as strange as zat might seem to others."

"What will you do?"

"You mean when Lady Linley dies?" Amelie shrugged. "We could go and live in the London house, zough, as you know, Wallace is quite happy for someone to buy it. Zat would save us, for sure, at least for a little while. But if nothing else, we will return to France. All of my family is zere, and I miss zem."

"Oh. I didn't realize you still had family there," Henrietta said, inwardly chastising herself for actually knowing so little about Amelie. "What part?"

"Reims. In the northeast. It is quite beautiful part of the world."

Henrietta was silent, her mind absorbing the fact that she, too, was far from home and now carrying a child. "Amelie," she said suddenly, "you won't tell anyone, will you? About the baby, I mean? I . . . I don't want Clive to know just yet. I want to tell him myself."

"But, of course, *mon amie*. I will keep your secret. And now I must go. Shall I send you your maid? She has been hovering very near since you were brought in." She smiled gently.

"Yes, you may send her in," she said absently. "But what about Evie?"

"Miss Simms? What about her?"

"Is she okay? She wasn't thrown, too, was she?"

"No, she was here at your bedside for a short time, but zen the doctor arrived. I am not sure where she went. I will send Edna in now, *oui*?"

Henrietta gave a little nod, and Amelie left the room. Almost immediately, Edna scurried in.

"Oh, miss! I've been so worried!" she exclaimed.

"I'm fine, Edna. Just a bump on the head. A silly accident."

Edna stared at her as if she didn't know what to say. "Are you sure, miss?"

"Yes, I'm fine," she said, wondering suddenly if Edna could tell she was pregnant.

"No, I mean, are you sure it was an accident?"

"Of course, it was," she replied, wondering why Edna was acting so mysterious. Perhaps Edna had caught the detective bug and was trying to imitate her. The thought made her smile. "The horse stumbled, and I lost my balance and fell," she said, with a slight shrug that made her wince in pain.

"Well, it's just that . . . well, I don't know how to say this, miss, but Pascal doesn't think so."

"Pascal? How would he know? He was nowhere near the scene. We were quite far, as I recall . . ."

Edna shifted uncomfortably. "I think it best you should speak to him yerself, miss. He's most anxious." She gestured toward the hallway.

"He's outside?"

Edna nodded vigorously.

Henrietta grew slightly more concerned. "Oh, all right," she sighed. "Here, help me up. I don't want to lie in this bed." She peeled off the thin coverlet and was glad that she was still fully dressed. "Here, help me to that chair there," she said, moving to the side of the bed. She stood up and felt immediately dizzy. Quickly, she grasped Edna's good arm, which she held out to her. "Oh, Edna, how are you doing? How is your shoulder?"

"Almost good as new, miss, but that's not important now." Edna helped her into the chair and then tiptoed to the door and opened it a crack. Henrietta watched her step into the hallway and gesture at Pascal, who then crept quickly into the room behind Edna.

"*Pardonnez moi, madame,*" he said quietly, gripping his cap tightly in his hands. "I know you are ill, but I felt I should tell someone . . . and since Monsieur Howard is away . . ."

"This is sounding very serious, Pascal. What is it?"

"After your . . . mishap, I was helping in the stables. I know I should not, but I do not have anything else to do, especially with Mr. Howard being away. And he *did* instruct me to . . . *keep my eyes open*, I think was his phrase."

"Yes?"

"Well, it is a good thing I was, because Dick and Mr. Triggs were called away to help carry you to the house, so I saw to the horses."

Henrietta couldn't imagine what the young man was getting at and wondered if the horse she was riding, Revolution, had somehow been injured in the accident and was perhaps now lame. Perhaps this was the reason for Pascal's distress . . .

"Is he okay?" Henrietta asked, worried.

"Who?"

"Revolution. The horse."

"*Oui, madame*," Pascal answered, his face puzzled. "*Oui*, but it is not the horse zat concerns me. It is the saddle."

"The saddle?"

"*Oui, madame*." Pascal's face clouded. "It has been cut. I have a guess zat it is the reason you were thrown."

"Cut? Are you sure?"

"*Oui*, the girth was hanging by a thread."

"Maybe it was simply worn?"

"*Non, madame*, it was not frayed, but a clean, straight cut. Recent, by the look of it. Someone did it for a reason. To cause an accident, *peut-être*."

"But . . ." Henrietta fumbled. "But that doesn't make sense. Who would want to harm me?" She felt a rush of fear and instinctively wanted to put her hand to her stomach but resisted the urge.

"I do not know, *madame*, but the thought has occurred to me zat *peut-être* you were not the intended victim."

"Not the intended victim? What do you mean?" She tried to draw her attention back to what had unfolded at the stables. Wallace had given her his horse at the last minute. "Do you mean Wallace?" she asked, her brows deeply furrowed.

"*Oui, madame*. Once he returned from the house, it was Dick who mentioned that you had taken Monsieur Wallace's horse, and I began to wonder."

"Did you mention the cut saddle to anyone?"

"No, I thought I should not."

"Yes, that was probably wise," Henrietta mused, putting a finger to her lips. "But who could have done such a thing? And why? Who would want to harm Wallace—if that was truly the intent?"

Pascal shrugged.

"Did you notice anyone strange hanging around the stables this morning?"

"No one strange. Only Colonel Beaufort. But he's there most mornings. Very fond of the horses, he is."

"I see," Henrietta mused, thinking again about the poisoning and how the colonel was always in the vicinity of each crime.

"I will go now," Pascal said, giving Henrietta a quick nod and throwing a longer glance to Edna.

"Thank you, Pascal," Henrietta said again. "Please inform me if you discover anything else."

"*Oui, madame,*" he said with a slight bow and left.

"Oh, miss," Edna exclaimed as soon as he was gone. "What are we to do? Do you really think someone is trying to harm Mr. Howard? Or you?"

"It would seem so," she mused, trying to think back through it all again. But why? Obviously, whoever had cut the saddle could not have predicted the mix-up . . .

"Oh!" she gasped, sitting up straight. A sudden, random thought had come into her mind, and it startled her with its obviousness.

"What is it, miss?"

"The poison!"

"What about it, miss?" Edna asked, looking around the room fearfully.

"Maybe Mr. Arnold was also not the intended victim of the poisoning! What if the victim was supposed to be Mr. Maung?"

"Mr. Maung? Why would anyone want to kill *him*?"

Henrietta thought carefully. Why indeed? Her mind again floated to Colonel Beaufort, who had been very loud in his denunciation of foreigners buying up old English estates . . . But would that really push him to murder someone? It seemed unlikely, and yet, how difficult would it be for a man who had doubtless killed hundreds of men in battle? Still, this would have been in cold blood. Did his lack of scruples really extend that far?

"Miss?" Edna asked, breaking her reverie.

"I'm not sure," Henrietta answered finally, giving her head a little shake. "I need to look for something." She tried standing but collapsed again onto the chair. Her head ached, and she was still a bit woozy.

"Oh, miss, you can't get up. You should be in bed, even now. I'm sure I heard the doctor say so."

Henrietta bit her lip. "You might be right, Edna. Here, help me." She reached out an arm to the girl and hobbled back to the bed. She sat down on the edge. "I need you to do something for me then, Edna, since I don't think I can manage it just now."

"Anything, miss! I mean, madam."

"I need you to sneak into Colonel Beaufort's room and look for a letter."

"A letter?" she faltered. "What kind of letter?"

"Remember? You said there was an official-looking letter that you delivered to the colonel's room a few days ago. Do you think you could find it?"

"I suppose," Edna said reluctantly. "But what if I'm caught?" She twisted her hands.

"Take a dusting cloth. Pretend you're dusting," Henrietta suggested. "And while you're at it, you might check Phineas's room, too."

"For a letter?"

"No, for a lipstick."

"A lipstick?"

"Yes, I suspect he stole—or *borrowed*—one of Miss Simms's lipsticks to write that horrible message on Lady Linley's mirror."

"Mr. Beaufort? Why would he do that? I thought it was the ghost."

"Of course, it wasn't a ghost, Edna! I thought you had more sense than that," Henrietta chided, though she was acutely aware of her own hypocrisy, given her experience in the study last night. *Had it only been last night?*

"I suppose so, miss, but there's ever so many stories going round below stairs. Frightens the life out of me, it does!"

"Well, you shouldn't listen to them, then."

"I can't help it, miss. Me and Addie have taken to havin' a cup of cocoa in the kitchen by the servants' fire before we go up, and Dick always sneaks in and scares us with his stories. Did you know there was a maid who hanged herself here, miss?" Edna's eyes were bright.

"Yes, I've heard that one," Henrietta tried to say dismissively even as a shiver ran down her back.

"Dick was right in the middle of telling us the whole murderous story when Mr. Triggs comes down the back stairs and frightens the life out of us. Screamed, we did, and Mrs. Pennyworth came running in and scolded us something terrible. Told Mr. Triggs that his timing was terrible and to be careful next time. Tells him to take Dick out with him back to the stables where they belong. Then she turns her wrath on me and Addie, telling us not to be such stupid ninnies and to get to bed."

"Very wise, I daresay," Henrietta said briskly, not wanting to waste any more time. "You best get going, now, Edna, while the upstairs is fairly empty."

"Yes, miss. Do you want me to help you back into bed first?" she asked hopefully.

"No, Edna. I'll be all right."

Edna walked slowly to the door, as if she did not relish the task ahead. "Remember, miss," she said turning around. "You're to stay in bed. Mr. Howard will fire me on the spot if he knows I let you out of bed after what's happened."

"I'll be fine, Edna."

"You sure, miss?"

"Yes, go on."

Edna gave her one last look and then disappeared. As soon as she was gone, Henrietta stood, but had to grip one of the bedposts to steady herself. She was weaker than she thought, and for a moment, she wished she had accepted Edna's offer of help. So many thoughts fought for dominance in her mind. The first, of course, was of the baby, but she pushed her giddy nervousness on that score to the side for now, a part of her not really wanting to acknowledge it for fear that if she did, it would somehow put the whole thing in jeopardy. No, she needed to focus on the case. A man had been murdered and someone, possibly the same person, had just tried to take a second life—Wallace's.

But why Wallace? Someone who didn't want him to sell the estate? Someone who had a grudge against him, which seemed like many, unfortunately, Wallace being somewhat unpopular not only in his own house but in the countryside around. Henrietta sat back down on the edge of the bed. Her head throbbed, but something was niggling in her addled brain. Something about Wallace. She rubbed her temples, trying to think, and suddenly remembered that Lady Linley had wanted to tell her something about Wallace before the old woman had fallen back into unconsciousness. Henrietta had since forgotten about it, assuming it had been meaningless ramblings, but now, in light of the attempt on Wallace's life, she wondered if it was somehow connected. She rose again, gripping the bedpost with one hand to steady herself. She desperately needed to talk to Lady Linley before it was too late.

Chapter 27

Julia let out a long, slow breath. It was too late for any other course of action; she had made her decision. She sat in the dark in the room of her girlhood, waiting for the house to completely quiet. She had retired early and likewise had given Robbins the night off so that there would be no chance of her plan being foiled. Soon, she would finally be free of the pain. She would never again feel the back of Randolph's hand, nor his fist, and, better yet, she would never again feel the wrenching in her heart from being separated from her boys.

She would escape the black void she now found herself in, unable to see or climb her way out. She had tried many times in the past to escape this void and had always managed to somehow fend it off, but she was currently unable to do it, helpless. There was that word again—helpless. It circled her mind almost constantly, taunting her endlessly, until she had finally succumbed to it. Agreed with it. Was chained to it. Yes, she *was* helpless.

But then, like some sort of miracle, it had occurred to her how she might actually escape her helplessness, be victorious at perhaps just one thing. It made perfect sense, and she wasn't at all afraid of it.

She considered leaving a note—isn't that what people did?—and had accordingly sat at her desk for at least an hour, trying to think of something to say, but nothing came. Part of the problem was that she didn't know to whom to address such a missive. There seemed no one who cared enough about her who would benefit from her last words, her last blessing—if it were even possible for someone like her to bless anyone.

She knew that the boys of course loved her, but she imagined them forgetting her, absorbed in whatever new world they had been thrust into, a world of which she was not a part and never would be. They would eventually forget her. It was only natural. She had still to receive even one letter from them, so there was the proof.

Leaving a note for Randolph was out of the question. Whereas once she was filled with deep loathing—even hatred—for him, now she was numb to him. She had no feelings at all toward him, only ambivalence. Likewise, she saw no point of leaving a note for her mother, who would most probably crumple it in anger. Or maybe not. More than likely, her mother would be glad to be rid of her and her shameful self, she thought, not realizing that in taking her own life she would permanently shame her mother beyond all repair. But she wasn't thinking clearly. A whisper of Glenn filled her mind, then, but she let that go. Despite Sidney's assurances, she could not believe that he would still want her. *Might I go so far as to suggest we never see each other or communicate in any way,* he had said in his letter. And true to his word, he had not sent another letter beyond that single one, the one Randolph had disastrously found. She assumed Sidney had told him of her current shameful plight and that she was currently at Highbury, but still Glenn had not inquired. That was answer enough for her.

She set her pen down on the blank paper and wandered to her window, looking out one last time at the grounds that had held such delight for her and Clive when they were children. She would be sad to never see him again, but he had his own life now, too. Henrietta was perfect for him, and she could be the stunning, dutiful daughter that Antonia had always wanted. Not a renegade like her, and a failed one at that. She let the curtain fall and turned to study the clock. It was well past midnight. The time had come.

Noiselessly, she made her way down the grand staircase, her robe loosely tied around her, and tiptoed to the big Victorian kitchen. No servants were awake at this hour. Julia made her way into the dark room, illuminated only by the moonlight that streamed in through the tall casement windows. She placed one of the copper kettles, already filled with water for the morning, onto the cast-iron stove and reached into the cabinet for a cup.

While she waited for the water to boil, she made her way to the large walk-in pantry and switched on the light. Without fear or trepidation or hesitation, or any emotion at all, really, she rummaged on the higher shelves with the help of a step stool, looking for the rat poison. She knew it was up here somewhere; she had sought out its existence last week and had hidden it behind a jar of pickled beets. She slid the jar to the side now and grasped the worn box, a skull and crossbones printed warningly on one side, and climbed down. She poured hot water into the cup, dunked a tea ball she had stuffed loosely with tea from the canister, and methodically stirred in a scoop of the rat poison as if she were adding sugar. It dissolved almost instantly, proving, as if she needed a sign, that this was the right path.

There was nothing left to do now but to take a few sips, and it would all be over. She looked around the old kitchen and decided that she should probably not do it here. It would be a mess for the servants. She should do it in some other room, she decided. Some out-of-the-way room where her body, when found, wouldn't be a nuisance. Accordingly, she picked up the cup and proceeded back toward the front of the house. Silently, as if she were already a ghost, she made her way to the drawing room and stood in the dark, considering it. No, not here. Nor the morning room, she decided, passing through to it, as her mother spent the early hours of each day there.

She considered the upstairs gallery, where she had spent some happy moments with Glenn, showing him her father's collection, but she decided it would be too painful. She continued, then, along the downstairs corridor until it finally occurred to her that the library in the back of the house would be perfect. No one went there, and she would disturb no one.

Noiselessly, she practically floated along the remainder of the corridor, holding the cup tightly before her with both hands, as if she were in a procession to honor some god in a temple, as if in a trance, like some sacrificial victim.

As she passed her father's study, however, she paused when she saw a faint glow of light coming from it. For one quick second, her heart leapt in her chest when she thought that her father was still up, but in the next, it was crushed, as she remembered that he was, indeed, cold in his grave. *But who was in there, then?* She paused to listen, but not hearing anyone, gently pushed open the door with one hand, carefully holding the poisoned tea in the other. She assumed, as she stepped inside, that the occupant must be Sidney, which irritated her a little. Had he just assumed he could take over her father's study? Upon a quick perusal of the room, however, she found that it was empty. Maybe he had been working in here and had recently left to retrieve something? She went back to the doorway and looked up and down the corridor and stood listening, but she could hear nothing. Perhaps he had gone to bed and forgotten to turn off the light?

She stood there, wondering what to do next, when it occurred to her that this would be the perfect room in which to drink what would be her last cup of tea. An odd relief came over her that she had finally found a place, and she lowered herself into one of the worn leather armchairs. She set the teacup on the side table. She would take a moment and then do it. She looked around the room at all of her father's treasures and books, a deep longing coming over her. Her eyes alighted on his walking stick, which still stood in the corner, and tears erupted.

She missed her father so very much. She knew she had been his favorite, just as Clive was their mother's. It's not as if they had spoken much to each other, but they hadn't needed to. They had always known what the other was thinking, even when she had been a little girl. She sat thinking about all of the times he had taken her on walks with him about the property and beyond, tramping through wet grass and muddying her shoes, for which Nanny had mercilessly scolded her. It was worth it, however, for the time she was allowed to be with him. Willingly, she endured Nanny's punishments, never telling her father about them, afraid that if she said something, their precious jaunts would come to an end.

She wiped her tears, overcome now with a deep sense of shame. She was such a failure. Surely to him as well. He had been against her marriage to Randolph, but Antonia had gotten her way, which Julia tried, in these last moments, not to hold against her. In her heart, Julia knew that, ultimately, marrying Randolph was her own fault. A part of her had known that it would be a mistake, but she had done it anyway. She couldn't explain why. Surely, her father had been disappointed. He had tried to look happy on her wedding day, but his eyes had been sad. She had tried her best to ignore it, but look where it had gotten her.

"I'm sorry, Father," she murmured and looked at the teacup. She picked it up again and held it near her mouth. No need to blow on it, it was cool by now. But what did that matter? Nothing mattered anymore.

She tipped the cup toward her lips . . . but paused when she smelled a trace of cigar smoke. She lowered the cup and sniffed deeply, wondering if her senses were betraying her. Surely, she was imagining it? She sniffed again. No, it was definitely cigar smoke. Hurriedly, she set the teacup down and stood up, convinced that Sidney was approaching, though a part of her brain thought it odd, as Sidney did not usually indulge in cigars. A cigarette perhaps, but not a cigar. She took a step away from the incriminating teacup, innocent though it looked, and braced herself for his entrance, trying to think of what her excuse would be for sitting in her father's study in her nightgown at midnight. But after several minutes had ticked by and still no Sidney, she relaxed her shoulders. Still the smell remained, however.

She moved behind the desk, looking to see if perhaps Sidney had left a cigar smoldering in an ashtray, but there was none. In fact, the desk was devoid of any papers or ledgers at all, suggesting that perhaps Sidney had *not* been working in here. The hair on the back of her neck stood up, then, as she turned slowly around, the distinct feeling overwhelming her that there was someone here in the room with her. She did not see anyone, but she was suddenly overcome by a sensation of complete love, so much so that she could almost feel two arms go around her and hold her. She sensed immediately that it was her father, and she felt her dead heart begin to beat fast. "Father?" she said in her mind, and she heard these words back: "Not yet."

She felt the presence let go of her then, though she desperately begged in her mind for it to remain. "Father?" she murmured hopefully, but the presence was gone. All that remained was a feeling of warmth and love. Julia slumped into the leather armchair and began to cry. She knew she had been given a gift. A fleeting one. But though it had been brief, it was enough, and she buried her face in her hands and sobbed for a long, long time.

Chapter 28

Henrietta leaned for a long time against Lady Linley's door, trying to steady herself. Finally, when she had gathered her strength, she rapped lightly and then poked her head in. Addie was sitting vigil by the bedside and looked round as Henrietta entered.

"How is she?" Henrietta asked in a low voice.

"Oh, madam," Addie said, standing now and giving a little curtsey. "She's sleeping now, as you can see." She nodded at the old woman, dressed in her stiff Victorian nightgown, complete with lace night-cap, her hands folded neatly on her chest. But for the shallow rise and fall of her chest, she looked to be already dead. "She's been restless, though. Woke up once and asked for Lord Linley. The old Lord Linley, that is."

"I'll sit with her for a while if you'd like, Addie," Henrietta suggested.

"You sure, madam?"

"Yes, I'd like to. I need to rest myself."

"Well, if you're sure," Addie said, stepping away from her post. "But before I go, let me clear away this mud. If Mrs. Pennyworth sees it, she'll hide me." Addie then produced a miniature brush from somewhere deep in her dress pocket and proceeded to kneel on the rug beside the bed. "I've been starin' at this for the better part of an hour. Sorry, madam," she said, standing now, the dirt in her hand.

"Why is there mud on the floor?"

Addie shrugged. "Someone musta tracked it in on their shoes or their boots. I'd bet it was Dr. Graham. He's here, there, and everywhere. I'll be goin' now," she said, moving toward the door. "Mrs. Godfrey will be glad of my help with dinner."

Henrietta sat in the recently vacated chair, still pleasantly warm. "Thank you, Addie."

"Can I ask you something, madam?" Addie asked tentatively, pausing in her exit.

"Of course, you can. What is it?" She pulled her eyes away from Lady Linley and looked at the girl.

"I don't mean to be morbid, like, madam, but I'm just wondering what will happen to us when—*if!*—" she said hurriedly, "Lady Linley should, you know, pass on."

Henrietta's first thought was to scold the girl for asking something so disrespectful, especially with poor Lady Linley lying not three feet away, but she stopped herself, realizing that it was a fair question, the answer to which she herself would have appreciated had she been in Addie's same situation, which she very nearly had been, not so very long ago. "I'm not sure, Addie," she answered kindly. "More than likely, the estate, or a part of it, will be sold or donated. But maybe not for some time. I wouldn't worry."

"But I do, madam! Mrs. Pennyworth says we'll all be chucked out on our ears before too long. Says it's a terrible shame."

"Yes, I suppose it is," Henrietta agreed. "But you'll find another place, surely?"

"Aye, I suppose. I have a cousin in Brighton. She says there's work there, but I don't know what Mrs. Pennyworth will do. Or even Mr. Stevens. Mrs. Pennyworth has been at Castle Linley since she was all of eight years old. This is all she's ever known. Must be why she's so cross lately."

Henrietta considered this. "Well, I'll speak to Mr. Howard—Lord Linley, that is—about making sure the staff find places. But we really shouldn't get too far ahead of ourselves," she said with a slight nod toward Lady Linley. "Let's hope we don't have to worry about any of this for a very long time."

"Yes, madam." Addie gave a quick curtsey and departed silently.

Henrietta turned her attention back to Lady Linley and quickly became fixated on again watching the poor woman's chest rise and fall. Though she had been dismissive with Addie about Lady Linley's imminent death, it did, in fact, seem a quite real possibility. How much longer could Lady Linley's heart hold out? Her eyes began shifting rapidly beneath her paper-thin lids now. She must be dreaming, Henrietta guessed and wondered if she should wake her. She hated to disturb her rest, but she might never get this chance again to speak with her.

"Lady Linley?" Henrietta murmured finally, as gently as she could.

To her surprise, the woman's eyes fluttered open. She stared at Henrietta for several seconds as if trying to fathom out who she was. "Oh, it's you," she said, her voice hoarse. "I thought you might be the other one."

"You mean Miss Simms?"

"No, not her. The other one."

"Amelie?"

Lady Linley did not answer and instead closed her eyes again. Henrietta waited for her to open them again and when she didn't, she assumed the poor woman had fallen back asleep. In fact, Henrietta jumped a little when Lady Linley suddenly said, "No, Minerva," with her eyes still closed.

Minerva? Henrietta had not heard of a Minerva and wondered if it were a distant relative. Or maybe a friend.

"Lady Linley, I—"

Lady Linley's eyes fluttered open. "We were girls together, you know. We were like sisters in some ways, though I was older, of course."

"Who are you talking about, Lady Linley?"

"Minerva. As I said. She comes and goes. She'll be here soon," she said, her voice still raspy. "Montague sometimes comes, too. He whispers to me. I can never make out what he says, but I know he's angry. He knows my secret." She looked directly at Henrietta now, her eyes big and watery.

Henrietta blinked, not knowing what to say to this. She had come in here intending to ask about Wallace, but she wondered now if it had been such a good idea after all. Lady Linley seemed extremely confused, perhaps delusional. Could she really trust anything she might say in this state? But then again, what if Lady Linley really were to die soon and she had missed her opportunity?

Henrietta cleared her throat. "Lady Linley, you . . . you wanted to tell me something yesterday. Something about Wallace . . . ?" She looked eagerly at the old woman, praying she would remember.

Lady Linley's face was a blank.

"Remember? You said there was something you needed to tell someone before . . . before it's too late. Something about Wallace," she repeated.

Henrietta saw a ripple of something cross the old woman's face.

"Yes, there is something." Lady Linley's eyes traveled around the room. "Are we alone?" she croaked.

Henrietta felt a shiver. "Yes, we're quite alone, Aunt Margaret," she said, lapsing into a more familiar address, hoping it would elicit further trust. She placed her hand on Lady Linley's and braced herself for whatever was coming.

"Wallace is . . . Wallace is not Montague's child," Lady Linley whispered.

"What?" This was *not* what Henrietta thought she was going to say! The poor woman must be in fact delusional, just as she had suspected.

Lady Linley let out a tired breath and looked away. "Wallace was the child of my first love. Simon Gaskell was his name." She looked back at Henrietta now, her eyes filled with shame, or maybe it was fear.

Henrietta frowned and tried to ignore the goosebumps that had broken out down her arms. Logically, Lady Linley's revelation didn't make sense—Wallace was Lady Linley's second child, so how could he be a product of her first love? But it resonated with something inside her and a small part of her wondered if it could possibly be true.

"Simon was a friend of Rufus's," Lady Linley went on in a quivering, tinkling sort of voice, like a fairy on her deathbed. "They were in the same regiment. We were engaged to be married, but then he was shipped to India and killed. Or that's what the telegram said. It was a terrible blow, as you can imagine. I was heartbroken for months." She closed her eyes, then, and remained that way for several minutes.

"Then what?" Henrietta asked, fearing Lady Linley had fallen back asleep. Gently, she patted her shoulder, and the woman's eyes opened again. "Then what, Aunt Margaret?"

Lady Linley blinked rapidly, as if trying to remember where she had left off.

"You were heartbroken," Henrietta reminded her. "After Simon left. Then what?"

"Oh, yes. Why, then I met Montague," she said a little sadly. "We married quickly. I wanted to forget Simon, you see." She rubbed her hands together nervously as she looked up at Henrietta. "But then Simon returned! Like a ghost returning from the grave. Imagine my horror." She lifted a tiny arm and then dropped it. "I was now married to a different man, and there was nothing we could do. I had already had Linley by then, and I—"

She stopped abruptly, then, to cough, which unfortunately turned into a bit of a fit. Repeatedly, her frail upper body was thrust off the bed by the violence of the coughs and suspended this way for several moments before she finally collapsed back onto the pillows. It was horribly distressing to watch, and Henrietta wasn't sure what to do.

"Oh, Lady Linley! Shall I call for someone?" she asked, beginning to rise from her chair.

Lady Linley shook her head faintly and lay silent, trying to catch her breath.

"Perhaps I should come back later," Henrietta offered. "You need to rest." She contemplated whether she really should summon Mrs. Pennyworth, despite the elderly lady's refusal for help.

"No, I . . . I haven't finished," Lady Linley said breathlessly. "I just need a moment."

Henrietta hesitantly resumed her seat, her eye catching the stack of lace handkerchiefs on the bedside table. "Of course, Lady Linley," she said, reaching for one and handing it to the old woman. "Don't rush."

Lady Linley took the handkerchief in her wrinkled hand and balled it. "I couldn't leave Montague," she said finally. "It was unthinkable." She gave Henrietta a tired look, her exhaustion evident. "What made it worse was that Montague was a kind man," she rasped. "I loved him in a certain way, but not in the way I had loved—still loved—Simon. There was nothing I could do." Lady Linley held the handkerchief to her mouth as she let out another little cough.

Henrietta waited for her to go on, but Lady Linley remained silent, as if caught up in her own thoughts. Several moments ticked by before Henrietta finally ventured to speak. "I . . . I don't know what to say, Aunt Margaret. I'm so sorry."

"Yes," she said with a little nod. "It was a sorry state of affairs. It was torturous to see him at balls and galas," she added mournfully. "So much so that I used to pray that he would get shipped out. He eventually did, and then I regretted my prayers. On his last night in England, he came to me and I, well, we . . ." Her voice trailed off. She patted Henrietta's hand. "Doubtless you find it hard to believe that an old lady could have once felt such passion."

Henrietta wrapped her hand around the old woman's hand and gave it a squeeze. In truth, she did find it all hard to believe, but somehow it made sense.

"I never saw Simon again. Wallace is his child, though."

"Does . . . does Wallace know?"

"Heavens, no. Only Rufus knows."

"You mean the colonel?"

"Yes, it was obvious to him that Wallace looked exactly like Simon. I made him swear on our mother's soul never to tell."

"What about Lord Linley?" Henrietta asked tentatively. "Do you think he suspected?"

"Montague? Yes, I'm sure he did, though he never spoke of it. He tried his best, but I think that's why he and Wallace never got on."

Henrietta bit her lip and tried to figure out how this fit into the bigger picture. "Do you think anyone else suspects?" she asked, trying to keep her voice measured.

"I don't know." Lady Linley closed her eyes. "I suppose Minerva suspects," she eventually rasped. "She was always a clever one."

"Who *is* Minerva?" Henrietta asked impatiently.

Lady Linley, however, either did not hear her or simply chose to ignore her and remained silent, her eyes suddenly growing wide as she stared at the wall beyond her.

"Lady Linley?" The woman did not respond, however, and continued to stare, a look of terror on her face. Henrietta waved a hand in front of Lady Linley's eyes, and when she didn't react, turned slightly to see what the elderly lady was staring at . . . but there was nothing.

"Oh, Henrietta!" Lady Linley cried, finally drawing her eyes away from the wall and peering at her now. "Montague is so angry. Every night he whispers to me that he knows my secret. I have begged his forgiveness, but he does not give it. In death he is more unforgiving than he was in life. Do you not find that strange?" She gripped the coverlet and shrunk a little into the pillows. "He waits for me. Do you not see him?" she nodded at the wall behind Henrietta.

Despite having already looked into the corner behind her, Henrietta did suddenly fear what might have appeared and sat with her shoulders hunched forward, waiting for whatever it was to spring. After several seconds, however, she realized how silly this was and made herself again turn around, quickly twisting in her seat to face whatever was there. Again, she saw nothing. Nor did she *feel* anything—no cloud of chilly air, no sense of dread.

She turned back around, disgusted with herself. Clearly, Lady Linley was very ill and needed rest. She should never have bothered the poor woman. Clive had often said that there was a time and a place to question people, and this, she was sure, had not been it. Not only had she disturbed Lady Linley's rest, but probably nothing that had fallen from her lips was true. And yet. It had been very long and detailed to simply be a delusion. And it explained much. *But*, the mind was capable of elaborate tricks, she knew, remembering Mrs. Goodman, the insane woman she had encountered at Dunning Asylum in Chicago.

"Aunt Margaret, you need rest," Henrietta said gently and awkwardly tried to adjust her blankets for her.

"How can I rest when he sits there, waiting for me to die?" The old woman's voice trembled as she pointed toward the corner again.

Instinctively, Henrietta looked over her shoulder yet again and this time nearly screamed when she saw Mrs. Pennyworth standing in the doorway.

"Oh, Mrs. Pennyworth! You frightened me!" She clasped her chest.

"Excuse me, madam, but Mr. Howard is on the telephone for you. Mr. Stevens sent me to tell you."

"Oh!" Henrietta rose unsteadily. She had so much to tell him!

Mrs. Pennyworth, seeing her weakness, hurried over. "Perhaps I should tell him you are engaged?" she offered in a rare tone of generosity.

"No," Henrietta insisted. "If you'd just help me, would you, Mrs. Pennyworth?"

"Certainly, your ladyship—I mean, madam," the old servant said, sturdily taking her arm. "You needn't worry. I'll help you down to the study, and then I'll come back up and sit with her."

Chapter 29

Oldrich sat at the end of a long row of beds in a darkened ward. It was still daylight, but the shades had all been drawn so that the room was dim. Perhaps it was to encourage the patients to sleep, Oldrich considered. Or to keep them calm. Something he was decidedly not. Anxiously, he removed his watch from his vest pocket and again checked the time. He snapped it shut. It didn't matter what time it was; he was stuck here.

Oldrich had been trying to avert his eyes from the tiny girl in front of him, but it was hard to do. There was little else to look at besides his own wrinkled hands resting on the top of his walking stick, which brought him little comfort. He was getting old. He *was* old, and he needed to get things settled. He looked at the girl now. Her head and her right ear were bandaged in such a way that she looked almost as if she were a partially wrapped mummy, as if she already had one foot in the grave. Oldrich shuddered. Though he had no great love of children, this one, he observed, had very long lashes, tiny lips, and there was almost a fine down covering her skin, as if she were still a newborn. There was no denying that she was a beautiful child, but he willed himself not to be affected by it, not to give in to emotion.

Oldrich had accompanied Elsie back to the ward when they had called her and listened as the doctor reported that, while the surgery was successful in that they had been able to reattach the ear, they couldn't guarantee that her hearing would still be intact. At this news, Elsie had again begun to cry, which disturbed Oldrich more than the prognosis. He couldn't stand women crying. It would be the death of him, he suspected, as any time he had been a rare witness to it, it rendered him utterly helpless. It was a weakness he had not tolerated in his home.

Once the doctor had left the room and he was alone with the sobbing Elsie, he felt his irritation rising. "There, there," he had hissed. "Get hold of yourself, Elsie! Crying doesn't help anything."

Elsie had lowered her hands from her eyes and stared at him, her face flushed and blotchy. "I'm sorry, Grandfather. You're right, of course," she said blearily and reached into her pocket for her handkerchief. Blowing her nose, she stepped past him so that she could get closer to Anna. She brushed strands of her wispy blond hair back and kissed the girl's forehead a shocking number of times. "It's going to be okay, little bird." She stood up straight then and looked over her shoulder at him, still hovering close to the ward door.

"Grandfather, I must find Gunther. Will you sit with her while I try to telephone Mrs. Wilkins again?"

Oldrich's insides had squirmed. He did not want to sit at a sickbed, having never done so one day in his life, but what else could he do? The faster Gunther was located, the faster . . . what? The faster he could get on with his plan? Which was to commit Anna to some sort of facility, some sort of specialized colony? Oh, why was this becoming so complicated? "Fine, fine," he muttered wearily.

Elsie hesitated, looking as if she were about to say something—something dangerously emotional—but thankfully she did not and instead hurried past him and exited the ward.

Oldrich remained where he was for several minutes, but then, realizing that Elsie may be gone for some time, decided to sit upon the lone cane chair by the side of the bed. He pulled it back first, however, so that there were at least three feet between him and the bed.

With a sigh, he tried to think again about his plan. It seemed destined to fail. Even if he could somehow convince Elsie and Gunther to send the girl away, they wouldn't be able to do it any time soon. She would unfortunately have to heal first, which would waste time. He looked at the child again, her little chest barely rising and falling. Her little fingers began to tremble, and it oddly unnerved him. His instinct was to touch them, squash them, stop them from trembling, but he resisted.

He looked impatiently toward the ward door, still unmoving and silent, and then looked back at the girl. Her eyes were fluttering now, too, and for a moment he feared she might be on the verge of another fit. He half rose and was about to call for someone when the girl's eyes slowly opened. She stared at him for several moments, confused.

"Grandpapa?" It was the first time he had ever heard her speak, and he was amazed that her voice was so tiny and light, like he imagined a fairy's might be, if such things were real. He blinked, unable to move. Her voice was ethereal, like something otherworldly, and he could horrifyingly feel its tendrils wrap themselves around his heart, threatening to dislodge it, or maybe simply melt it. His breath quickened.

"Mama? Papa?" she said now, her eyes darting around in fear.

"Mama will be here in a moment," Oldrich tried to say calmly, though he was aware that his response had instead come out as sounding rather desperate. Immediately, he cursed himself for referring to Elsie as the girl's mother, which she was *not*. He eyed the girl nervously.

"Grandpapa, I'm scared," she said, her big blue eyes filling with tears. Oldrich felt his chest tighten.

"Now, now," he said brusquely. "Nothing to be scared of. You'll be home in no time," he said, pushing away the fact that, in actuality, he planned to rip her from her home, such as it was, as soon as he could.

"Promise?" Anna murmured and held out her tiny hand, obviously wanting Oldrich to take it. Oldrich hesitated. He did not want to hold this little girl's hand, and yet he couldn't bear the way she was looking at him, pleading. He hadn't touched another human being, besides a stern handshake, in probably twenty years, not since Charity had died. None of his children nor his grandchildren dared ever to embrace him, which is just how he wanted it. What need had he of any of that?

He glared at her, but it seemed to have no effect on the girl. She continued to hold out her little hand to him. He should rebuke her, he knew. Scold her. But instead he let out a loud sigh, as if he knew a part of him was going to his death, and reached out not his whole hand, but his index finger, which she wrapped her tiny hand around. Immediately, something inside of him painfully shifted. He wished he had his pills.

"You won't send me away will you, Grandpapa?"

Oldrich was taken aback. How could she know what his intention was? Goosebumps rippled down the back of his neck before he realized that she must have heard—and understood—what he had been saying to Elsie in the hut. "I—" he began, but then stopped. The lie would not come out. He stared again at her big blue eyes and thought for a moment that he was looking at Martha. They looked so similar. But how could that be? She obviously had no biological connection to Martha. He was getting confused. He pinched the bridge of his nose and tried to think, tried to use on himself all the arguments he had lined up for Elsie, but somehow all he could think of was Sr. Bernard's chastisement. Admittedly, he had been a little put out, a little ruffled by the nun's warning of damnation, but there was something else at play now. Something he couldn't explain. Something that had the peculiar flavor of mercy and compassion, something he hadn't felt since he had gone to Martha's shabby apartment on Armitage where she had taken up with the reprobate Von Harmon and had begged her to come back or to at least give him the child their union had produced, Henrietta. Not only had she refused, but she had scoffed at him as well. He had left a broken man. What had he ever done to deserve her hatred? Was it because he had sent her away to Switzerland? Granted, Charity had been hard on her, constantly chastising the girl, but hadn't it been for the girl's own good?

"Grandpapa," the girl whispered now. "Don't cry."

Oldrich blinked and lifted his free hand to his face. Shockingly, his cheeks were wet. He . . . he couldn't remember the last time he had cried. He had been a boy, more than likely. But how had he not felt these tears now? Were his cheeks as numb as his heart had grown? "Oh, Martha," he groaned, wiping them away. He gazed at the tiny girl, practically swimming in the big bed. She was smaller than his favorite dog.

Anna gripped his finger tighter, then, and he felt something give way in his chest.

He stared at the girl, ignoring the tears on his cheeks, as the full force of the realization that his whole life had been a mistake swept over him. How it had all gone horribly wrong! He suddenly wanted to weep. Maybe Elsie had been right. Maybe all these years he had simply been seeking revenge on Martha for breaking his heart and that, having apparently lost the ability to wound her, had sought to do so to Elsie instead. He felt utterly defeated and small and suddenly very, very old. He looked at the hand still encircling his finger. Her skin was new and velvety, while his was old and wrinkled. He moved to take her whole hand in his when Elsie rushed through the swinging door.

"Gunther will be here soon! Mrs. Wilkins has found him—" she broke off at the sight of Anna holding his hand, which he quickly withdrew. Her eyes shifted, then, and she saw that Anna was awake. Oldrich watched Elsie's face immediately light up as she hurried to the girl's side. "Oh, Anna!" she said, kissing her forehead, her cheeks, and her little hands. "We missed you, little bird."

Oldrich backed away from the bed. He could no longer bear it. Leaning heavily on his cane, he moved toward the shadows at the end of the bed. His chest was heavy and tight. He was having difficulty breathing, but he desperately fought to correct it. "Elsie," he finally said to the floor, his voice thick and raspy. "I'm . . . I'm sorry.

Sorry for everything." He looked up at them now, bathed in the light from the one bedside lamp. "I've been a fool."

Elsie stood up straight, still holding onto one of Anna's hands, and looked at him distrustfully. She did not speak.

"You needn't look so worried," he said with a deep sigh. "I . . . forget what I said earlier. I . . . I won't make you send Anna away." He tried to smile at Anna, but it failed, his face seemingly frozen in a permanent scowl. "I . . . I will find a specialist. See what can be done."

Elsie continued to stare at him.

"Well, say something, girl!" he said brusquely. "I mean . . . what do you think?"

"Oh, Grandfather, I . . . I don't know what to say. Do you really mean it?"

"Yes, I really mean it," he uttered quietly, silently despairing that she trusted him so little. But why should she? He had sought to make her life miserable from the first moment he had been reunited with her.

"Grandfather, you look ill," Elsie said, coming around from her place at the bedside. Gingerly, she took the crook of his arm and guided him toward the empty chair. "Here, sit here. Let me get you some water."

He waved her away. "I mean to help you. All of you," he said faintly. "If you will let me, that is." He grasped hold of his walking stick with both hands. "I mean to help Gunther get a professorship, and you can continue your studies, if that is your wish. I will find you a suitable house and a nurse for Anna." Words were pouring out of him now, and he was almost as amazed by them as Elsie seemed to be, staring at him as if he were a ghost or perhaps Ebenezer Scrooge come to his senses.

"Oh, Grandfather! That's very generous, but I don't think—"

"Papa!" Anna called weakly, and both Oldrich and Elsie turned to see Gunther striding into the ward, his eyes wild. Upon seeing Anna, he practically ran to her. Gingerly, as much as he was able, he scooped her up in his arms, holding her to him and kissing the side of her head through her bandages. "*Mein Mädchen, mein kleines Mädchen. Du wirst in Ordnung sein. Das verspreche ich*—My girl, my little girl. You're going to be all right. I promise."

He looked across to Elsie, and the look of love and worry that he gave her nearly crushed what remained of Oldrich's already melting heart. What was happening to him! He feared he was becoming unsettled in the mind, and yet, what could he do? Everything was out of his control, and all he could do was to let it proceed.

Gunther, still cooing softly to Anna in German, laid her back down on the bed. He turned, then, toward Oldrich, a look of wary challenge in his eyes.

"It is lucky that Grandfather was visiting," Elsie said, obviously sensing the tension in the room and moving closer to Gunther. "He was able to get us quickly to the hospital. Who knows what would have happened . . ." Her voice cracked. Gunther put his arm protectively around her.

"Yes, I thank you," Gunther said gruffly. He met the old man's eyes for a moment and then looked away disgustedly, as it pained him to look at him.

"Mr. Stockel," Oldrich began. "Might I call you Gunther?"

Gunther's brow furrowed, but he did not protest.

Oldrich went on hurriedly. "Gunther, I was . . . I was just saying to Elsie that I have been wrong. I am sorry for the distress I have caused you both. And Anna."

Elsie, Gunther's arm still around her, put her hand on Gunther's chest, as if cautioning him not to speak.

"I am an old man," Oldrich went on. "Forgive me. I've been blind and stupid and stubborn. I wish to make amends. Truly. Let me help you. Help the three of you," he nearly begged. His heart was pounding in his chest. He didn't know how much more he could take.

He saw Gunther stiffen.

"Grandfather was just telling me that he wants to help you get a professorship," she said tentatively, looking up into Gunther's face. "Wouldn't that be wonderful?"

"Yes," Oldrich agreed, grateful for her help. "And Elsie can continue her studies, if that is her wish. And I will hire a private nurse for Anna. Also, I will arrange for her to see a specialist. And a house must be found. I will—"

"No!" Gunther interrupted, releasing Elsie now. "No, this cannot be. I . . . I thank you, but no."

"Gunther," Elsie said pleadingly.

"No, Elsie, it is not right."

"You do not trust me, do you?" Oldrich asked plainly.

Gunther stared at him for several moments. Finally, he spoke. "No. I do not. This is a . . . a trick to get Elsie to return with you."

"I give you my word." Oldrich gave his cane a firm rap. "As a gentleman, if you can call me that."

Gunther continued to stare at him, only briefly glancing at Elsie.

"Can a man not change?" Oldrich begged. "I . . . I have been wrong. As I said. I . . . I wish to repent."

"Gunther," Elsie said eagerly, stepping in front of him now and drawing his angry gaze to herself. "Don't be stubborn," she pleaded softly. "Grandfather is . . . is admitting much. Think what this could mean."

Elsie looked tentatively over her shoulder at Oldrich, as if worried he might rescind the offer. "Gunther," she said, quickly turning back to him. "He is not offering us charity. He is offering you a way to earn a living. A better one. It is what you've always dreamed of. For once, don't be this way."

Gunther's frown deepened, and for a moment Oldrich feared he would outright refuse. "Elsie, the end does not justify the means," Gunther said quietly to her. "Of this we have spoken. Many times."

"In this case it does! The 'means' in this case are a man's restitution for past sins. Do you think yourself so superior that you can refuse such a gesture? Is that not in itself a sin?" she begged. "He has asked your forgiveness. Will you not give it?"

Gunther did not answer, nor did anyone else speak, the tension in the room thick and awkward. No one seemed even to breathe.

Finally, Gunther let out a deep sigh and turned away. "Yes, all right," he muttered. "I accept your apology and your gift of job," he said, looking briefly at Oldrich. "But I cannot accept house."

"Where will you live, then?" Oldrich asked cautiously.

"What about the Palmer Square house with Ma?" Elsie suggested. "Anna was already staying there with a nurse hired by Clive." Oldrich clenched his teeth a little that once again he had been bested by the Howards, but he squashed this thought, not wanting to break the tenuous link they were forging and trying to let go of his old ways. To be the bigger man. How he had once been, long ago, in his youth, before the world had soured him.

"Anna got on very well there," Elsie hurried on. "And she enjoyed playing with Doris and Donny. And Ma liked having her, too. And Nurse Flanagan was good with Ma, too. So, you see? It would be perfect . . ." Elsie's eyes darted between the two men.

Oldrich cleared his throat. "I see no reason why not, if it is conducive to all. If you're sure, that is. Sure that you don't want a place of your own."

"No," Gunther said obstinately. "No, we cannot accept from you *any* home. It is too much. A job is one thing. A doctor for Anna. But house? No. It is too much."

"Gunther!"

"You can pay me, then. You can pay me a small rent, or you can work it off in the form of caring for the gardens and the grounds." Oldrich paused, looking at Gunther for his initial reaction. He did not immediately object, so Oldrich quickly went on. "Karl is getting up in years, and it was my intention to hire a gardener. What if you took on that role yourself? Would that satisfy you?"

"Oh, Gunther, please say yes!" Elsie laid a hand on his arm. "I'll help you. It would be good for Anna to be there. And I would like to be with Ma for her final years. And I might be near my siblings. Please," she begged.

Gunther looked at her intently, as if they were the only two people in the room, and cupped her cheek with one hand. His angry scowl melted into a look of apprehension. "You would have this, *Liebling*?" He stared into her eyes so lovingly that Oldrich had to look away. "You ask me to consider what it would mean. But have *you*? Is this your wish? To put yourself in this man's hands?"

"I am not in anyone's hands but yours, Gunther," she said softly.

"Papa?" the ethereal voice tinkled.

Gunther lowered his hand from Elsie's cheek after rubbing it softly with his thumb. He looked down at Anna, a smile hovering about his lips. "What say you, *Kinder*? Do you wish to go back and live in the big house with Doris and Donny?"

Anna didn't answer but nodded her head vigorously, her finger in her mouth.

"You are sure, Elsie?" he asked, turning back to her.

"Yes, I'm sure." She kissed him on the cheek.

Gunther took a deep breath, then, and turned toward Oldrich. "We accept your offer," he said formally and stretched out his hand to Oldrich, who quickly shook it.

"You won't regret it," he said stiffly.

Gunther released his hand, and Elsie left her husband's side to wrap her arms around the old man, embracing him tightly.

"Thank you, Grandfather."

Oldrich's throat was tight, and he found he could not actually speak, so happy was he.

"Thank you, Grandfather," she said again as she released him, and Oldrich, for the first time in a long, long time, felt free and something marvelously akin to joy.

"Come, then," he said gruffly, "let's go home."

Chapter 30

"Darling, are you sure you can't come home?" Henrietta said into the telephone.

"Yes, I'm terribly sorry." Clive's voice sounded weary. "There's been some delay. The situation is a bit more complicated than I originally thought. I had to telephone Bennett yesterday about . . . about various matters from home."

"Such as?"

"I'll explain it all later. It would take too long to go into now, and I have to go soon. How are you holding up? Any more scares?"

"Not really," Henrietta fibbed, deciding not to tell him about her fall from the horse. It would only worry him. And, at least mentally, she felt fine today. In fact, better than fine. She felt astute and clear. She rubbed her belly. She longed to tell him about the baby, but she wanted to do it in person.

"How is Lady Linley?"

"The same. Still in bed. Very weak. The doctor's coming back today. She . . . she did say something very odd yesterday, though, Clive."

"Oh?"

Henrietta glanced at the open door. "Yes, but I don't think I should say it over the telephone . . ."

"Well, then don't. But, darling, I wouldn't put much stock in it, whatever it was. Very probably, she's delirious."

"Perhaps, but she seemed quite lucid. And, if it's true, I think it might explain a few things about the case," she said in a low voice, bending away from the door and cupping the receiver.

"Well, darling, don't do anything rash. Wait for me to come back. And, speaking of the case, I've managed to do that little bit of digging I'd hope to do, and I've unearthed a few interesting facts."

"Oh?"

"Well, for one thing, Miss Simms has not been entirely truthful."

"What do you mean?"

"Just that there is no Mrs. Christiansen's Ladies Association for the Promotion of Female Education Among the Heathen."

"What?"

"There *was* one, but it dissolved twelve years ago. Miss Simms, it seems, is a sham. Nothing more than a con artist, just as Wallace thought. I must give him more credit for his intuition."

"How very interesting," Henrietta said, twisting the cord thoughtfully, wondering how this fit into the bigger picture.

Just then, Edna scurried into the room without bothering to knock and looking very agitated.

"Listen, darling," she said into the receiver, her eyes widening as she observed Edna pull a lipstick from her pocket. "I must go. Edna needs me."

"Whatever for? Well, all right, but remember, be careful." "Yes, of course, darling. You needn't worry," she said as she balanced the receiver between her cheek and her shoulder so that she could take the lipstick offered now by Edna into her hands to examine it. It perfectly resembled Miss Simms's others, and, if her memory served, it matched the shade of the writing on Lady Linley's mirror.

"That doesn't sound in the least convincing."

"Well, I can't promise anything, Clive." She rolled her eyes for Edna's benefit. "But I really must ring off now."

"I'll try to be back tomorrow."

"Oh, I do hope so. Good-bye, Inspector."

"Good-bye, Minx."

Henrietta dropped the receiver back into its cradle, feeling a tiny bit guilty that she had not shared Edna's discovery with him, but she wanted to investigate it herself first. And, besides, it didn't, or probably didn't, have anything to do with the more dangerous parts of the case—the poisoning and the cut saddle. At least, she didn't think so.

"Oh, miss! You were right!" Edna exclaimed, not waiting for Henrietta to speak.

"Where was it?"

"In Mr. Beaufort's sock drawer. Not very well hidden, if you ask me."

"What about the letter? Did you search the colonel's room?"

Edna nodded. "I didn't find anything, though. I'm sorry, miss."

"It's not your fault, Edna. It was a long shot. But this is very important," she said, holding up the lipstick again. "Good work!"

Edna beamed. "Thank you, miss."

Henrietta examined the lipstick again. So. Phineas was the prankster after all. What else was he responsible for? And had Miss Simms known about it all along? In light of what Clive had unearthed, it was obvious that she had grossly misjudged Miss Simms's character from the beginning. What else had the woman lied about? "What can you tell me about Miss Simms?" Henrietta suddenly asked Edna.

Edna raised her eyebrows. "Miss Simms? Not much, miss. Nothing except what I hear below."

"Which is what?"

"That she likes her breakfast carried up to her most days. Likes a flower in a vase on the tray. Drives Mrs. Pennyworth crazy, it does. Calls her a spoilt tart."

"What about she and Mr. Beaufort? Do you think they are romantically attached?" she asked with pursed lips, deciding to test her theory despite the fact that Miss Simms had denied any such thing.

"Romantically attached?" Edna exclaimed with unusual enthusiasm. "Of course, they are. I thought you knew that."

Henrietta was rather taken aback. Yet another lie! "How do you know?" she asked, wondering if Edna could perhaps be mistaken.

"Why, miss, I . . . I've seen them, if you must know. Most nights I've seen them from my window. Down by the lake, kissing and all sorts. I . . . I didn't mean to look, but it was right there in front of me. Like something out of the films."

"Why didn't you tell me this before, Edna?"

Edna shot her a look of surprise. "It isn't my place to say what the betters is doing."

"We're not your betters, Edna!" she sighed, wondering if she would ever be able to reform the girl.

"Well, I suppose I didn't realize it was important," Edna said with a pout. "And anyway, it'd be my word against theirs, and who'd believe a servant? Excepting you, miss."

Henrietta sighed again, but something niggled. "Well, thank you, Edna. That's all for now."

"Are you sure, miss? Sure I can't get you something? You hardly ate any of the breakfast I brought up."

"No, I . . . I'm not hungry." She didn't want to tell Edna that she had been horribly sick this morning and vomited twice. "Thank you, though."

"Yes, miss." Edna gave her a wistful look and then silently exited the room.

The offending lipstick still in her hand, Henrietta turned toward the window and gazed out, trying to make sense of this case. If Edna had indeed seen Phineas prowling about the back lawns at night, did it not seem more than likely that he had been the mysterious intruder? But why would he have attempted to climb up the trellis if he and Miss Simms were already in the habit of meeting down by the lake? And how odd, then, that Miss Simms was apparently not in her room to receive her lover, but instead Lady Linley had been?

Henrietta gasped, a new realization suddenly occurring to her. Perhaps it *hadn't* been an accident that Lady Linley was in that room.

Perhaps she had been lured there on purpose by her music box, placed precariously on the sill. But why?

Henrietta began to pace. If Miss Simms and Phineas were indeed responsible, was it just their latest idea of a practical joke, or was there a deeper, more insidious reason? Given the fact that everyone was aware of Lady Linley's weakened heart, had they deliberately been trying to scare the old woman, possibly *to death*? The thought paralyzed her. The whole thing would require a level of cunning that Henrietta was not convinced Miss Simms possessed. And yet, she had lied several times now *and* had proven to be a bit of a con artist. Perhaps she really had succeeded in getting Lady Linley to change her will, and thus, knowing that she stood to inherit, sought to hasten Lady Linley's death before the fickle woman could change her mind, or before Wallace had a chance to sell it off, Henrietta guessed, her mind racing. She stopped abruptly in her pacing, suddenly wondering if it was also Miss Simms who had cut the saddle, seeking to do away with both Lady Linley and Wallace in order to get what she wanted? It seemed ridiculously farfetched, and yet . . .

Henrietta tried to think rationally. Who else would have benefitted from Lady Linley's death? Only Wallace and Amelie, she supposed, who, once Lady Linley was gone, would be able to unburden themselves from the estate and do as they wished, but matricide seemed out of the question, even for Wallace. And, even if he had wished to do his mother harm, why had he been the object of murder himself? No, it didn't make sense. She wondered, though, if Wallace knew of his illegitimacy despite Lady Linley's avowal that no one except the colonel and this Minerva, whoever she was, knew the truth. Perhaps Wallace had guessed it? Was this the reason he sought to sell the estate before the "rightful heir" could inherit it? No, she mused, rubbing her brow, that didn't make sense. Wallace wouldn't do such a thing. He wasn't the slightest bit interested in money, so why should he seek to sell the estate from under the feet of the heir, who would be . . . Henrietta reached for the velvet curtains, gripping them tightly . . . Clive, she realized suddenly with a crushing blow. Somehow, she had not made the connection before this moment.

It would mean that . . . that Clive was the real Lord Linley and she, by default, would become Lady Linley. She sat down in a small red velvet chair by the window. This is not at all what the two of them had in mind for their future together. Gone would be the possibility of operating a detective agency, or of having any sort of normal life at all. She looked around the room. All this would be theirs, but then again, perhaps not, seeing as the whole estate was bankrupt anyway. Clive could barely stand the weight of Highbury and Linley Standard, how would he ever cope with ascending to the aristocracy and all that it entailed? She shuddered and rubbed the flat of her stomach. What would it mean to their child, she wondered, thinking of how Wallace and Amelie were trying to raise the next little lord with no servants and no help. Panic began to well up in her chest, but before it could take root, she shook her head, attempting to dispel these thoughts. None of this was probably true, anyway, she scolded herself. Surely, Lady Linley was delirious, and her confession was simply the ravings of a mad old woman.

"I say, Mrs. Howard!"

Henrietta jumped and let out a little scream. She turned to look and saw that it was Phineas, of all people!

"Care for another game of croquet before it rains?" He gave his hair a flip. "Bloody nuisance. Miss Simms is leaving in the morning, so—"

"Leaving?" Henrietta stood up carefully, trying to calm her frazzled thoughts. She still held the lipstick and stared at it now, trying to bring her mind round to the questions she had earlier about him and Miss Simms.

"Yes, a friend in town is quite ill, apparently, and she must go. Very tiresome, if you ask me."

Henrietta wondered if that's all Miss Simms did—flit from one sickbed to another, although, Henrietta mused, the young woman wasn't particularly devoted to sitting at Lady Linley's bedside any longer. Perhaps she had somehow discovered she was not in the will after all . . .

"How 'bout it then, Mrs. Howard? Care for a game?"

"I'm afraid not," she said sternly. She held up the lipstick now. "Can you explain this?"

Phineas forced out what sounded like a nervous laugh. "Why, no, I can't, as a matter of fact."

Henrietta took off the cap and rolled up the stick to reveal the color. "I think you know very well what I mean, Mr. Beaufort. My maid found this in your room. Top drawer, under some socks. Now does it ring a bell?"

"I say. That's most irregular. Going through a man's things."

"She was putting away laundry, if you must know," Henrietta fibbed.

Phineas riffled a hand through his hair. "Well, I don't know why you're so concerned. I found it, as it happens. Meant to give it back to Miss Simms but must have forgot. You know how these things go."

"How did you know it belonged to Miss Simms?"

Phineas's face flushed, and he looked away. "Oh, all right. It was just a spot of fun. I didn't mean anything by it." He looked back at her now with a sly grin. "Everyone in this house is a stuffy old shirt. Take themselves much too seriously."

"It is a serious matter, Mr. Beaufort. A man was poisoned, and Lady Linley has suffered a potentially lethal shock. It was you, wasn't it, that scared her the other night? You climbed up the trellis, didn't you? You and Miss Simms had it all arranged."

"Now, hold on. That was not me!"

"You might as well admit it, Phineas. My maid has seen you and Miss Simms many nights by the lake."

Phineas blushed beet red. "Well, what is it to you? Contrary to what you might think, Mrs. Howard, I'm not the sort of man to discuss such matters when a lady's reputation is at stake."

"It's a little late to play the sanctimonious part, Phineas," she scoffed. "And your frightening of Lady Linley, who has a heart condition, might very well be the death of her, even still. So, I'd take this seriously if I were you."

"Now, look here. On my honor, I did *not* climb that trellis. I had nothing to do with scaring Lady Linley—"

"Besides writing a frightening message on her mirror."

Phineas angrily flipped back his lock of hair. "That's an entirely different thing altogether!"

"Is it?"

"Look, I admit that I'm in the habit of meeting Miss Simms by the lake, but I didn't climb the trellis. We . . . we can never be alone with Lady Linley herself right next door. So, Evie's taken to slipping down the stairs once everyone's in bed for the night and exiting out the back."

"Then why was the window left wide open with Lady Linley's music box playing? And how do you explain Lady Linley seeing a man? I saw someone, too!"

Phineas shrugged with irritating indifference. "Well, it wasn't me."

Henrietta eyed him carefully, folding her arms across her chest. "What else have you lied about, Phineas?"

"Nothing!"

"I've half a mind to report this to your father," she said, trying to scare him, though she suspected it wouldn't work.

"Well, go ahead," he snapped, proving her correct. "There's nothing he can do despite his bluster. I'm going to Oxford, and he can do what he likes. I'm not about to follow him around, mooching off annoyed relatives."

"What do you mean? He'll be posted somewhere soon, won't he?"

"God, no. He's been discharged. Doesn't want anyone to know."

Henrietta's scolding expression melted. "You mean retired, don't you? Not discharged."

"No, he's been *discharged*. Dishonorably at that. 'Mental instability' is what they termed it. Though I do think that was a bit out of order."

"Mental instability?"

"It sounds worse than it is." Phineas shoved his hands in his trouser pockets. "He got malaria a while back and went a bit barmy for a time. I daresay, he's fine now, but, well, you know. It's time he hung up his hat anyway."

"Well . . . what's to happen to him?"

Phineas shrugged. "I don't know. Perhaps he'll just hang on here. I can't worry about it."

Henrietta was stunned by his coldness. "Don't you care about what happens to your father?"

"Not particularly. He never cared for me or my poor mother all these years he dragged us around the world from station to station or left us alone in Bournemouth for years on end. Didn't give a thought to me. He forged his path; now I'm about to forge mine. Like father, like son." He gripped his lapels angrily. "So, you've nothing on me, Mrs. Howard. And if you've no more insults to hurl at me, I'll bid you good morning." He turned stiffly on his heels and marched out of the room.

Henrietta was stunned. He had, up until now, played the part of the spoiled boy very well, but this was an entirely different side of him. She wondered how this new information about the colonel affected the case. Essentially homeless, he had more than a passing interest in the sale of the estate, she realized. Henrietta braced herself against the desk and tried to clear her thoughts. She was suddenly feeling rather poorly. She needed something to eat, she decided.

She considered ringing for one of the servants but did not wish to draw attention to her weakened state lest someone guess the truth of her situation. She desperately wanted to keep it a secret until she could tell Clive herself. Woozily, then, she crossed the study and began the long trek to the kitchen, hoping that at this hour it might be relatively empty.

To her happy surprise, both Mrs. Pennyworth and Mrs. Godfrey were indeed absent. Only Addie was there, chopping an enormous pile of carrots, presumably for the evening meal.

"Oh, madam! Did you ring?" the girl asked hurriedly, setting down her knife.

"No, I didn't. I was hoping to make myself a cup of tea and maybe find a biscuit?" Henrietta asked, looking around for a tin.

"Oh, no, madam. I'll make it for you. Would you like me to bring it to you in your room?"

"No, I'll wait," Henrietta said, thinking that she probably wouldn't make it all the way back upstairs in her current state. Instead, she perched herself on the edge of a stool and watched Addie bustling to get a small tea tray ready. It reminded her of her days as a waitress in Chicago. She could never have imagined in those sad days that she would one day be the future mistress of a palatial estate in Winnetka and now maybe a lady of a castle! It was dizzying.

Addie disappeared into one of the vast stone pantries, and Henrietta turned her attention to the big casement windows on the north wall. She hadn't noticed that Amelie was without, playing on the lawn with little Linley, Alcott in her arms. She had the sudden urge to join her, desiring, perhaps, some encouragement after all that she had just learned, and walked carefully toward the little alcove by the back door. She paused when she reached it and held onto the wall, steadying herself. Perhaps she should wait until after her tea, she mused and looked back toward the kitchen, trying to decide. As she did so, her eyes fell upon a muddy set of boots that sat on a small rack by the door. Above them hung various jackets and a few aprons. Something seemed odd, but she couldn't figure out what.

"Whose are these?" she called to Addie when the girl reentered the room carrying a lovely large pound cake she had unearthed. Addie stepped closer, peering at the boots Henrietta was pointing to.

"Those would be Mr. Triggs's, madam," she said, setting the cake down now and reaching for a knife to slice it. "Or maybe they're Dick's. Neither of 'em is allowed to wear their boots in the house, but sometimes they do. If Mrs. Pennyworth catches 'em, she's fierce mad. Here now, I'll cut you a slice. And here's some tea, like."

Henrietta let go of the wall she was now leaning against and nearly fell. She gripped the aprons hanging above the boots to steady herself and shot a worried look at Addie, hoping she hadn't noticed. After a few moments, she found her balance and let go of the aprons, though one of them, she now noticed, had an embroidered name stitched into it. Henrietta's breath caught in her throat as she read the name.

Minerva.

Henrietta stood there, her mind racing as she stared at it, the last piece of the puzzle finally falling into place. Slowly, she turned and looked back out the window at Amelie, laughing and twirling with the children. Everything finally made sense. There was just one more person she needed to talk to, and that was Wallace.

Chapter 31

There was just one more person she needed to talk to, and that was Sidney. Julia still felt a chill run down her spine whenever she thought about the otherworldly experience she had had in her father's study. It had occurred over a week ago already, but it still felt as though it had just happened. She had been tempted to share the tale with her mother, but she was fairly sure Antonia wouldn't believe her. But more than that, Julia was worried that if she verbalized it, the experience would somehow evaporate, and she was desperate to hold onto it. It was the only thing that gave her hope, and it oddly strengthened her as well. She had come to a decision, one which she felt sure now that her father would have supported.

"Mother, I've made up my mind." Julia set down her still-full teacup. She wasn't sure she would ever be able to drink tea again. "I'm going to divorce Randolph." She and Antonia were seated across from each other, breakfasting in the morning room.

"What? Don't be ridiculous, Julia! Divorce is out of the question."

"It's not out of the question, and I am going to proceed. Advice, I might add, which I received from Sidney." Julia signaled the footman standing at attention at the end of the room. "Might I have some coffee, Albert?"

"Certainly, madam," he said with a bow and went to the sideboard to pour her a cup from the large silver urn that sat in the center of it.

"What's wrong with your tea?" Antonia's eyes narrowed.

"Nothing, Mother, I just fancy a cup of coffee this morning. Thank you, Albert," she said when the servant had set it before her. "Where *is* Mr. Bennett this morning?" she asked pertly, aware that he often spent the night in one of Highbury's guest rooms, though Julia suspected that he eventually found his way to her mother's room. But she didn't want to think about that. She felt deliciously invigorated today. On a mission. And nothing was going to get in the way of it.

"He left early." Antonia wiped the corner of her mouth with her napkin. "He had some business to attend in the city, I think is what he said, which is odd, since it's Saturday. He was really very mysterious about it."

"Well, I'll need to talk with him about drawing up the papers."

"Julia, dearest," Antonia continued in a pleading tone now. "Don't do anything rash. Why don't you take the rest of the summer to think about it. Go to Newport as I've suggested. The fall is beautiful there. I've already written to Aunt Lavinia, and she would love to have you. Please, Julia. Consider."

"Mother, I'm not a child to be packed off for the summer."

"Don't be flippant, dear. It isn't attractive."

"Mother, I'm going to divorce Randolph. I've made up my mind."

"Oh, darling, no. Don't do that. I understand that the situation with him is not . . . desirable," she said delicately, "but people live apart all the time. There's no scandal in it. In fact, it can be really rather freeing. At least say you'll go to Newport for a month and think about it."

"Mother, it's 1936. People divorce all the time. You're living in an outdated century."

"But not in our class, darling. It's very frowned upon, and many doors will be closed to you. You must think carefully about what you'd be giving up."

"Mother, why is it so hard for you to understand that I care nothing for that world anymore? I want to be free of it, and, anyway, this is the only way I can get the boys back. You've heard Sidney."

Antonia scowled. "It's not a guarantee."

"Well, even if it's not, I need to do this, Mother. It's what Father would have wanted. I know it," she said, feeling more and more confident the longer this conversation went on.

"Your father would certainly not have wanted you to get a divorce!"

"My father would not have wanted me to be beaten within an inch of my life by my husband. Don't you remember what he wrote in that letter that Clive found in the cottage? *I pray Julia may be happy always despite the unfortunate marriage she finds herself in. For my hand in that, I also bear much regret.*"

Antonia looked momentarily stunned before she quickly recovered, but her face was flushed. "Julia, everyone has regrets in life. You just have to get over it."

"Get over it?" Julia said, standing now. "Get over having my husband beat me and threatening me every other day with the loss of my children? No, I'm not going to just get over it."

"Where are you going?"

"I don't know! Out. I need some air." Julia marched out of the morning room and nearly collided with Billings.

"I'm very sorry, madam," he said, stepping back. Julia did not respond but hurried to the drawing room and let herself out through the French doors onto the terrace. She grasped the rough stones of the wall that encircled it and let herself breathe deeply as she stared out at Lake Michigan. She closed her eyes and lifted her face to the sun, feeling its warm rays. It would cause her freckles to emerge, she suspected, but she didn't care. She knew she shouldn't have argued with her mother, but it had felt good nonetheless. She was tired of being controlled, tired of being afraid.

The sound of the waves eventually soothed her, and the longer she remained, the more peaceful she began to feel, a gentle breeze slightly blowing her hair and her dress. She thought again about her episode in the study. The immediacy of the warmth and peace she had felt in that moment were sadly dissipating as time crept on, but she *remembered* them, even if she couldn't exactly feel them. She remembered that she had been given a gift, and for the first time in a long time, she allowed herself to believe that things were going to be okay.

She closed her eyes again, grateful for the tranquility, and considered whether she might walk down to the boathouse and put her feet in the water as she had done so often as a child. Her thoughts were interrupted, however, by a shout. Then another. It sounded like a child, and she wondered if the neighbors' children had somehow wandered onto Highbury's grounds. She tented her eyes with her hand and observed the lawn but saw no one. The shouts were louder now, and for a brief moment, her heart froze, thinking that it sounded like—

"Mama!" Howard shouted as he burst through the open French doors. He ran into her arms, and, astounded, she scooped him up. Randolph, Jr. followed, and she eagerly reached out to squeeze him, too, which was difficult with Howard already in her arms.

"Mama! We've missed you so much!" Howard squeaked.

Julia's mind was whirling as she gripped them, tears in her eyes. She couldn't believe they were here, really here in her arms, and for a brief moment she feared her sanity. She kissed each one on the head, breathing in the sweet scent of them.

"Oh, boys!" she finally murmured. "Oh, I've missed you, too! How did you get here?" she asked, setting Howard down now and guessing that perhaps this had been Sidney's mysterious business this morning.

"Oh, Mama! It took ever so long on the train," Howard exclaimed. "Didn't it, Randy?"

"Randy?" she asked, amused, as she took her eldest's cheek in her hand.

"That's what all the boys at school call him. And they call me Howie," he said, thrusting out his chest.

"Did you get my letters?" she asked Randolph, caressing his cheek. The boy nodded and she could tell he was trying to hold back tears.

"Well, never mind. We'll have loads of time to catch up," Julia tried to say gaily. "You'll have to tell me everything!"

"But won't Father be angry?" Randolph asked nervously. "He . . . he didn't even let us say good-bye to you. I'm sorry, Mother!" he said, burying his face in her dress, unable to check his emotion any longer.

"Randolph," she said. "Randy." She rather liked the sound of it. He stopped crying and looked up at her. "Do you like to be called that?"

He smiled through his tears and nodded.

"All right, then. Randy." She ran her fingers through his soft brown locks, and his eyes closed briefly at her comforting touch. "Let's not worry about Father at the moment. Mr. Bennett will sort things out for us. I'm sure of it."

"But it wasn't Mr. Bennett at all, Mother. It was Mr. Forbes. See? Here he is!" Howard exclaimed as Glenn Forbes himself stepped through the French doors.

At the sight of him, a small, strangled cry, like something from a trapped animal, escaped Julia's lips. She wanted to fly to him, throw her arms around him, but she held herself back, though her chest was heaving at the effort. She feared she might be sick, or worse, faint.

"Hello, Julia," he said quietly, holding his hat in his hands and smiling at her as if nothing had happened. As if they had just said good-bye to each other yesterday, not months ago. He was dressed smartly in a linen suit, his fine green cotton shirt matching the green of his eyes perfectly. He plopped his hat onto Howard's head. "Found these two boys. Said they belong to you. That true?"

Julia bit her lip.

"Go on, now, boys. Surprise your grandma. Reckon she'll rustle someone to bring up some cookies. Maybe even some cocoa."

Howard gave a whoop and ran into the house. Randolph looked up at Julia worriedly, as if afraid she might disappear, and she gave him a squeeze. "It's okay. I'll be in in a minute."

Randolph reluctantly released her and dutifully marched past Glenn, who playfully tousled his hair.

Julia watched Glenn watch Randolph and felt her stomach tighten when he then slowly turned his gaze to her.

"Hello, there." He smiled again.

"Oh, Glenn." Desperately, she fought to contain the tears that were causing her throat to ache. "I . . . I don't know how to thank you."

He grinned and stepped so close to her that she could smell his cologne. She trembled as he put a finger softly to her lips. "So don't."

Two rebellious tears spilled down her cheeks as she gazed into his eyes, only briefly, though, as she couldn't bear it. She turned her head away, ashamed.

"Julia," he said, putting a finger under her chin and drawing her eyes back to him. "Julia, my darling girl," he said, which sent a tidal wave of shock vibrating through her. *My darling girl* was her father's nickname for her.

She stared at him, stunned. So many thoughts were vying for attention in her mind that she couldn't actually get any of them out. Finally, she stammered, "Glenn, don't try to rescue me. I'm beyond saving."

His face remained unruffled. "You certain about that? 'Cause I'm pretty damn sure there's two little boys who sure as hell don't think so. And then there's me." His voice dropped as he said this last bit, and he caressed her cheek.

"Then there's you," she mumbled, his touch electrifying her. Every part of her being wanted to throw her arms around him, but still she hesitated. Could she really trust him? Trust that he meant what he said, that he wouldn't be a brute should she give him her hand? And even if she did decide to trust him, didn't he deserve someone better? Someone who was worthy, who was—

"Will you rescue *me*, then?" he asked abruptly. The sudden vulnerability in his voice nearly stopped her heart. "Julia," he said urgently, dropping his hand from her cheek and taking one of her hands instead. "I can't live without you. I haven't stopped thinking about you for one day. I sent you that letter hoping that you might answer, and when you didn't, I nearly despaired. Julia, I need you."

He paused and ran an agitated hand through his hair. "Julia, please," he whispered. "I'm in love with you. Can't you see that?"

Julia swallowed hard. She didn't know how much longer she could resist him.

"Julia, say something," he begged.

"Glenn, you . . . you don't want me. You just think you do. I'm . . . I'm too damaged." She looked away. "And when I divorce Randolph, I'll officially be anathema. You deserve someone so much better. You could have any woman, I'm sure. Don't saddle yourself with someone like me."

Glenn let out an explosive snort. "Anathema? Good God, Julia! I don't give a horse's ass about society. Don't you know that by now?" He dropped her hand and began to pace a little. "But you are correct in one department. I *could* have any woman, well, almost any woman." He laughed. "Hell, I've *had* many. But none have ever captured my heart the way you have, Julia," he said, stopping in front of her again, suddenly serious. "Make an honest man of me."

Julia stared at him, desperately sliding toward that which both terrified and thrilled her.

"Julia, you don't know your own worth. And how could you, you poor thing? But I mean to show you. Every day of my life. I'll woo you forever, Julia. If you'll let me."

"Glenn, I . . ." she finally muttered.

"Julia, my God, come back with me." He stared at her furtively for several moments, as if trying to search her eyes for her answer, and then, without waiting any longer, bent and kissed her. Tenderly, softly. "Come back with me," he whispered again, his lips still near hers. "You won't regret it. I promise."

Julia could no longer endure the torture. Something snapped inside her chest. She closed her eyes and simply let go. She was in love with him, body and soul, and there was nothing she could do about it. She returned his kiss, tentatively at first and then as a woman drowning. She felt his strong arms wrap around her as he continued to kiss her neck, her cheek, her ear.

She let out a little laugh. The first she had laughed in what felt like years.

"That a yes?" he asked, grinning at her.

She gazed up at him and slowly nodded, a smile still lingering. She felt light and free and unbearably happy.

"Good," he said, leaning his forehead against hers, "then let's go home."

Chapter 32

Henrietta perched herself on the chair nearest the fireplace, one which afforded the best view of everyone in the room. The assemblage, minus Lady Linley, of course, had just finished a rather quiet dinner and were now passing into the drawing room, Wallace suggesting as the servants cleared the dessert dishes that the men forgo their port and join the ladies immediately. Only Colonel Beaufort had seemed ruffled by this, but he nonetheless obediently rose and followed the company out.

Henrietta carefully studied each person as they listlessly wandered in, going over her theory one more time. She was convinced she had fathomed out the murderer.

Miss Simms threw herself down on a chair in a somewhat dim corner and picked up a novel lying on a side table and began flipping through it, taking on at least the appearance of reading. She wore a sullen frown. Henrietta accordingly looked across at Phineas, who sat at the game table, absently riffling through a deck of cards.

"I say, anyone up for bridge?" he called out, though he looked only at Miss Simms, who rolled her eyes at him before looking back at the book. Their romance, if there had been any real attachment to begin with, seemed to have decidedly cooled.

"I will," Amelie said tiredly from where she sat on one of the sofas.

"Mrs. Howard?" Phineas pleaded.

"Not right now, Phineas. Perhaps in a bit."

Phineas tossed the cards onto the table. "Well, it's no use asking Father," he said, looking across at the colonel, who had taken up the newspaper, "and I suppose we can't count on you, eh, Wallace?" he asked hopefully.

"Definitely not. In fact, I have a bit of an announcement."

Surprised, Henrietta turned her attention to him and wondered what he meant to say. Something about Lady Linley's health, perhaps? Or had he discovered something about the case, unbeknownst to her? Surely not. He seemed utterly uninterested in Mr. Arnold's death, believing, so he said, that between Clive and Yarwood, the culprit would eventually come to light. He had other things to worry about, he repeated often enough—mainly the sale of the estate and his mother's rapidly declining health, not to mention his wife's increasingly demanding pregnancy. Even when Henrietta had found him earlier this afternoon and asked to see a copy of the will, he had not seemed put out by her request, as she feared he might be, and had instead merely smiled, saying, "I say, playing the sleuth while hubby's away, eh? Or are you merely inspecting it to see if the two of you are in it?"

"That's not it at all, Wallace," Henrietta had mumbled as she examined the document. "Don't be droll. I just need to check something."

"Do tell." He seemed intrigued.

"I'll explain later," she said pertly and handed the will back to him. As it was, it had told her everything she needed to know. She fingered the beading of her peach Schiaparelli evening gown as she observed Wallace now, seeing him in a very different light than when she and Clive had arrived at Castle Linley. Everyone else had turned their attention to him as well, everyone except Stevens, who continued his task of pouring brandy and sherries at the sideboard.

"Inspector Yarwood has been in touch," Wallace began. "There have been some developments, apparently."

"Ah!" replied Colonel Beaufort, looking up from his paper. "Caught the blackguard, have they?"

"Apparently not." Wallace rubbed his forehead. "He telephoned to say that he's coming by tomorrow to interview us all again. No one is to leave. So, I'm afraid you're all stuck here for a bit longer. Not that all of you have been in a rush to leave," he snipped, turning his gaze fully on the colonel. Colonel Beaufort, however, seemed unaffected by the jab and continued perusing the paper.

"What do you mean, we can't leave?" Miss Simms demanded from the corner, lowering her book. "I've arranged to travel to Nottingham tomorrow. I'm meeting a friend. It's all been arranged!"

"Well, you'll have to delay it, Evie," Wallace said with what seemed little sympathy.

"And if I don't?" she asked coolly.

Wallace stared at her for a moment and then shrugged. "Then you'll have to answer to the police. I can't be responsible for what happens. If you insist on behaving like a child, then you'll have to take the consequences."

"Wallace!" Amelie muttered.

Colonel Beaufort cleared his throat. "I daresay, it does seem a bit of a nuisance. It's obvious that it was the Burmese. Nothing to do with us." Colonel Beaufort loudly folded the paper and, tossing it to the side, crossed his arms.

Henrietta bit her lip. She had been planning to wait for Clive to return to share her theory regarding whom she thought the murderer must be, but now she worried that if she delayed, it would be too late. Miss Simms seemed bent on leaving regardless of being commanded to stay, and she didn't see how Inspector Yarwood could possibly be on the right track. He was sure to muddy the waters further and very possibly arrest the wrong person, if it *was* his intention to arrest someone. Perhaps she should announce her theory now? She looked nervously around the room, wondering if she had the courage to do so without Clive at her side . . .

Miss Simms stood abruptly. "Well, you'll all excuse me. I've a bit of a headache, and I want to go to bed."

Henrietta shifted uneasily, trying to quickly weigh up her options.

This might be her only chance before Miss Simms disappeared from their grasp completely. She needed to act now!

"As a matter of fact, Colonel," Henrietta blurted. "The case has *everything* to do with us." Her pulse quickened as all eyes turned to her, even Miss Simms, who paused in her impending exit. Henrietta again bit her lip and tried to conjure up Mrs. Christie's elegant Hercule Poirot for inspiration, but his usual deft end-of-the-novel performance eluded her. Still, everyone was looking at her expectantly now, and she had no choice but to try. She gripped her hands tightly in her lap and took a deep breath.

"What do you mean?" Wallace prompted, clearly impatient.

Henrietta rose, albeit unsteadily, and cleared her throat. "I mean that I know who killed Mr. Arnold and why." She tried jutting out her chin. "And it was *not* Mr. Maung, as you keep suggesting, Colonel. It was, in fact, someone in this house." She looked quickly at each in turn, hoping to catch their initial reactions to her announcement. Almost everyone wore an expression of surprise or concern. Only Wallace and Colonel Beaufort seemed skeptical.

"By Jove, do you really know?" Wallace asked, intrigued, his hands on his hips now. "Does Clive?"

"No, he does not," Henrietta said tightly. "We haven't had a chance to discuss the case, but I believe I have it in hand."

"Well, by all means, enlighten us," Wallace said with a slight grin and plopped himself down on the sofa next to Amelie, seeming to relish the prospect of being at the very least entertained.

"Before I do, I'd like you to ask Mrs. Pennyworth to step in, Stevens," she said. The butler paused in his bent delivery of tiny glasses of port and stood up slowly.

"Mrs. Pennyworth, madam?" he asked, clearly confused. "Is there something amiss?"

"Not at all. I simply need her to corroborate a few things."

Stevens hesitated and then gave a slight bow. "Very good, madam."

While they waited for the servants to reappear, Henrietta decided to launch into a preamble of sorts and wished she had rehearsed one.

"I'm sure you are all aware that the estate, Castle Linley, that is," she began tentatively, "is in financial arrears following the death of Lord Linley. That certain death taxes, I think they're called, must be paid."

No one said anything.

"And I'm sure it's not a secret," she said, glancing at Wallace, "that Lord Linley left the estate in Lady Linley's name until her death, after which it would pass to . . . the rightful heir. Wallace, acting for Lady Linley, has been seeking a way to pay these back taxes and has proposed a number of solutions, none of which, from what I have gathered, is preferable to any of you in this room. One of you, however, was so distressed by Wallace's intentions that you resorted to murder, and, when that didn't go as planned, you attempted another murder, this time Wallace himself being the intended victim."

There was a surprised murmuring among them all as they quickly looked from one to the other.

"Surely this is not true, Henrietta, *oui*?" Amelie asked gently.

Before she could answer, Stevens and Mrs. Pennyworth silently entered the room.

"You wanted to see me, madam?" Mrs. Pennyworth asked stiffly. Despite her hard exterior, it was clear she was unsettled.

"Yes, Mrs. Pennyworth. A moment, please."

Mrs. Pennyworth accordingly stood back toward the wall, and Stevens moved to exit.

"You stay, too, please, Stevens."

Stevens hesitated and then acquiesced. "Very good, madam," he said and took up a spot beside Mrs. Pennyworth.

"As I was saying," Henrietta said, looking around at all of them again. Miss Simms had resumed her seat, but was now sitting ramrod straight, acutely attentive. "Wallace sought to pay the back taxes," Henrietta continued, "by either donating the whole Derbyshire estate to charity or by simply selling it in its entirety, or bits of it, or selling off the London house. None of you wanted any of those things to happen, especially given Wallace's threat of gifting the whole thing to the Fabians."

"Certainly not!" blustered the colonel, though it wasn't entirely clear to Henrietta what exactly he was opposing—the idea of donating the estate at all or the idea that the lucky recipient would be the Fabians.

"This proposal was very upsetting to you in particular, was it not, Miss Simms?" Henrietta stared directly at the young woman now. "You yourself hoped that your own charity would be in Lady Linley's gift."

"I told you that in confidence!" she blurted but then quickly regained her composure. "Anyway, what of it? It's not against the law."

"Preying on rich old women in hopes of extracting money from them? Perhaps not," Henrietta said with a slight tilt of her head, "but setting yourself up as a representative of a false charity probably is."

Henrietta enjoyed the collective murmur that was heard throughout the room. Miss Simms maintained an affronted look.

"I don't know what you're talking about!"

"I think you do. Clive decided to investigate Mrs. Christiansen's Ladies Association for the Promotion of Female Education Among the Heathen, to be exact, while he was in London. Turns out there is no such charity. Worse is the fact that this isn't the first time you've done this. That's where you were headed tomorrow, is it not? To the bedside of yet another sick old lady. Hedging your bets in case you weren't named in Lady Linley's will after all? Or with Wallace announcing yesterday that another buyer had presented himself, did you conclude that the jig was up here and so decided to cut your losses and go?"

"You're mad! The fall from the horse must have addled you, Mrs. Howard. Perhaps you should return to bed."

"You play the innocent very well, Miss Simms, but I wonder how far you were willing to go to get your hands on the estate."

"What on earth do you mean?" she demanded, prettily laying a hand on her chest.

"Just that perhaps it was you that killed Mr. Arnold."

"Me? Why would I do that? I had nothing to do with that horrible business!" Gone was her somewhat demure attitude.

"I wonder. Only you and Phineas were here when Mr. Arnold was poisoned."

"It wasn't *me*! I went nowhere near them. I had to be escorted up the stairs, remember?" she said triumphantly.

"Yes, with a sprained ankle that miraculously healed itself in hours. Maybe you were just the decoy while Phineas did the poisoning. Or maybe you didn't really have a sprained ankle at all . . ."

"I say!" Phineas exclaimed. "That's a bit out of order."

"Yes," blustered the colonel. "What exactly are you implying? Phineas would never do such a thing!"

"Perhaps not, but *you* might, Colonel," she said, looking at him now. "A man who has killed so many in battle wouldn't flinch to kill another."

"Yes, but this would have been murder," Wallace interjected. "That's another thing altogether."

Henrietta did not look at him but continued staring at the colonel. "Yes, but not something beyond you, was it, Colonel?"

"Nonsense!" the colonel flustered. "Why would you suspect *me*?"

"Because you came back to the house early, too, remember?"

"But I went to the library and fell asleep. I said as much on the day."

"Yes, that's what you *said*, but you could have easily dropped the poison, which you seem to have an excessive knowledge of, into the tea when it was sitting on the sideboard where Mrs. Pennyworth left it when she went to help Miss Simms. While everyone else, I should add, ran out to attend the mysterious fire in the stables."

"What do you mean by a 'mysterious' fire?" Amelie asked.

"Clive and I believe it wasn't an accident. We suspect that it was started by someone trying to get everyone, the servants in particular, out of the house." Henrietta looked pointedly at the colonel again.

"Balderdash! I had nothing to do with any fire! *Or* any poisoning, for that matter." He gestured widely. "What reason would *I* have to kill Mr. Arnold?"

"Perhaps you weren't *intending* to kill Mr. Arnold. Maybe your real target was Mr. Maung."

"What?" Wallace exclaimed.

"Yes, I got the idea after I was thrown from your horse," she said to him. "Clive's valet noticed that the saddle had been purpose-fully cut. At first, I was concerned about who would want to injure me, but when Pascal suggested that perhaps *you* were the intended victim, it dawned on me that perhaps the same thing had happened with the poison. Mr. Arnold was never the intended victim; it was Mr. Maung."

Colonel Beaufort's face turned a deep red. "Now look here—"

"Sit down, Colonel; let her finish," Wallace interjected, his face one of deep concern. "No, I will not sit and listen to this poppycock! Why would I want to kill Maung?"

"Because you hate foreigners," Henrietta explained matter-of-factly. "And more than once you stated very clear opinions on for-eigners coming in and buying up English estates. And, regardless of who the buyer was to be, you had a deep resistance to it being sold at all. Nor did you want Wallace to donate it. You placed all your hope on Wallace selling off the London house to at least perpetuate Castle Linley being in the Howard family for as long as possible."

"What's wrong with that?"

"Because you hoped to stay here indefinitely, as you've been dis-charged from the army, haven't you, Colonel?"

Wallace looked at him sternly. "You told me you were waiting for a new assignment."

"No, he's not. He's looking for a home. He was discharged with 'mental instability' after a bout with malaria. Is that not true, Colonel?"

Colonel Beaufort's face was now one of shock. "How the devil did you find that out?" He shot a fierce glance at Phineas, who did not meet his father's eye but looked at the floor instead. "Yes, all right," the colonel said bitterly. "I *have* been discharged. I was waiting for the right moment to announce it. As a matter of fact, I was about to begin inquiries about a set of rooms in Brighton I've recently heard have come open. But I didn't have anything to do with the poisoning or the cut saddle, I tell you!"

"You were seen in the stables the morning that Miss Simms and I went for our fateful ride," Henrietta persisted.

"That proves nothing!" The colonel looked wildly around the room as if searching for an ally. "Phineas! Vouch for me!" he shouted.

Phineas squirmed and looked about to say something, but Wallace cut him off. "Is any of this true, Uncle? Why wouldn't you have just come to me like a man and told me of your predicament? Did you really think me that heartless?"

"No, confound it! It wasn't me!"

Henrietta cleared her throat. "Despite appearances and possible motives," she continued, trying to keep her voice steady, "the colonel is telling the truth. It was *not* him. While he did arrive back early on the day of the picnic, Mr. Arnold and Mr. Maung would have long since finished their tea by that time."

"Then who was it?" Wallace asked mystified. "Phineas?"

"No," Henrietta said quietly, looking carefully around the room until her gaze rested on the housekeeper. "It was Mrs. Pennyworth."

All eyes darted to poor Mrs. Pennyworth, whose cheeks blanched.

"Henrietta," Amelie said in a sympathetic voice, as if she had really gone off the rails. "Are you sure?"

"Yes, very," Henrietta said simply and despaired that Hercule Poirot would not have announced the murderer so bluntly and with so little flourish, but she couldn't worry about that now.

"Everyone here had a reason to not want the estate to be sold or donated, but it was Mrs. Pennyworth who stood to lose the most should either of those happen. It was Addie who tipped me off, telling me that Mrs. Pennyworth has been on the estate since she was a girl and that it would be her who would suffer the most to find a new place, if any. With so many of the estates being torn down and with her advanced age, she worried she wouldn't ever find a new position."

"That seems hardly the cause for murder," Wallace said skeptically.

"Perhaps not, but it was more than that. It was the loss of the old way of life, as she has said many times, and her hatred of foreigners, including Amelie, that also roused my attention. She shared Colonel

Beaufort's views entirely, but she was even more zealous in their execution. When Wallace announced out of the blue that an estate agent was coming round with a foreigner intent on buying the place, she panicked and reached for the poison, not knowing what else to do. Am I right?" she asked Mrs. Pennyworth, who did not answer but merely continued to stare at her with a horrified expression.

"But that's ridiculous. He's just one man. Mr. Arnold could have brought a string of foreigners in after Mr. Maung. She couldn't possibly murder them all." Wallace gestured helplessly.

"No, she wasn't thinking that far ahead. She was just hoping that if they could hold onto the estate until Lady Linley passed, it would revert to the 'rightful heir.' "

"Poor Mr. Arnold," Amelie murmured.

"Yes, he was an innocent victim of murder, but, it turns out, not so very innocent. He was, in fact, a petty burglar."

"What?" Wallace exclaimed.

"My maid, Edna, saw him leave Lady Linley's room, and at first Clive and I suspected him of writing the cryptic message on Lady Linley's mirror, a theory we later discounted. But when the contents of Lady Linley's jewelry box were examined by Addie, at our request, it was discovered that one of Lady Linley's rings—a sapphire with two diamonds—was indeed missing. Clive and I went to see Mrs. Arnold, who told us that after her husband's death she went through his pockets and found a ring—a ring exactly matching the description of Lady Linley's—and assumed that he had bought it for her as a gift for their upcoming anniversary. A quick talk with the barkeep at the White Hart, where Mr. Arnold frequently drank, revealed that Arnold had a bit of a gambling problem, and so we assume he stole the ring to pay back some debts."

"Mother's sapphire is in this woman's possession? When were you planning on telling me this? We should call in the police!"

"We were waiting to see how the rest of the case unfolded, so we played our cards close."

"I'll say you did," Wallace said disgustedly.

"Oh, good show!" Phineas exclaimed, almost gleefully.

Henrietta ignored him and continued explaining her theory. "As far as I can guess, Mrs. Pennyworth, having decided on her murderous course of action to get rid of Mr. Maung, hurriedly called upon Mr. Triggs to create a diversion, a small fire in the stables. Once all the servants, including Stevens and Jeremiah, rushed outside to help extinguish it, Mrs. Pennyworth was left to her own devices. Cleverly, she laced one of the cups with the poison and then carried the tray herself toward the dining room, knowing, of course, which cup was which. She was unexpectedly thwarted, however, with the arrival of Phineas and Miss Simms and had no choice but to set the tea tray in the hall to assist them, seeing as how she had inconveniently sent everyone else outside to attend the fire. When she returned to the hall table, she was mortified, I'm sure, to discover the tea tray gone and that the two men had carried in the tray themselves and had already begun to eat and drink. Mr. Arnold, as we all know, chose the poisoned cup."

"Oh, jolly good!"

"Phineas, for once, be silent! This isn't a joke," Wallace scolded, standing up now. "I can hardly believe this!" He began to pace in front of the sofa. "Mrs. Pennyworth, is this true?" He turned suddenly upon her, but the woman did not respond, nor did she meet his eye. She remained statuesque, staring at the wall in front of her. "Was it you who cut my saddle?" he demanded, but still she remained silent. "Confound it, woman, answer me!"

"It was either her or Mr. Triggs," Henrietta answered, drawing Wallace's attention back to her.

"Mr. Triggs?"

"Yes, he was her accomplice. At first, I suspected Stevens might be, but I later dismissed it." Stevens shifted uncomfortably, but he remained silent.

"I do not understand," Amelie said.

"Yes," interjected the colonel, "even if Mrs. Pennyworth and Triggs *were* in league regarding Mr. Arnold, why would they want to harm Wallace?"

"Because," Henrietta answered coolly, "as I said before, Mrs. Pennyworth was hoping that if the estate could remain intact until Lady Linley passed, it would revert to the 'rightful heir.' She was worried that Wallace would sell it before that happened, so they arranged for his saddle to be cut, hoping to get rid of him. When that didn't work, they resorted to getting rid of Lady Linley herself."

A wave of surprise rippled through the room, but before anyone could speak, Henrietta quickly turned to face Mrs. Pennyworth. "Phineas's prank gave you an idea, didn't it? You used Lady Linley's nervous condition to further prey on her fears by arranging for Mr. Triggs to appear by her bedside from time to time, whispering to her and confusing her. In short, terrifying her. For a while that was enough, but then when talk of the sale again arose, you devised a more devious scheme, didn't you?"

Mrs. Pennyworth did not answer but stared at Henrietta now, her eyes full of venom and her chest heaving, apparently from either fear or anger or the pain of keeping silent.

"Knowing that Miss Simms was in the habit of meeting Phineas down by the lake each night," Henrietta continued, trying to ignore Mrs. Pennyworth's silent rage, "Mrs. Pennyworth took advantage of the fact that Miss Simms's room would be empty. She set the music box playing and arranged for Mr. Triggs to climb the trellis to frighten her, hopefully to death."

Wallace stared at Henrietta incredulously. "I can hardly believe this! First Pennyworth and now Triggs. Who's next? Has the whole house conspired against me?" He rubbed a hand agitatedly through his hair.

"Wallace, let us listen," Amelie appealed.

Wallace let out a deep breath. "All right, say that part of this is true," he said, glancing at Mrs. Pennyworth. "How can you be sure it was Mr. Triggs that climbed the trellis and not some stranger?"

Henrietta was surprised that this was the part of the theory that he was choosing to address, but she let it go, assuming he must partially be in shock. "Remember that I saw the intruder when I was in the study that night. He looked familiar, and at the time I assumed it was Phineas. But when Edna later confirmed that Phineas was indeed otherwise occupied with Miss Simms at that same time, I dismissed it and assumed I had been mistaken. But when I saw his muddy boots near the back door and recalled that Addie had to clear up bits of mud near Lady Linley's bedside, it dawned on me that Mr. Triggs had not only been the mysterious intruder, sloshing about on the waterlogged grounds that night, but that he was also in the habit of standing by Lady Linley's bedside whispering nonsense to her to aid her confusion and cause her to believe that she was being haunted by Lord Linley or some other . . ." she paused for only a moment, ". . . ghost."

"That seems a bit of a stretch," Wallace said, his eyebrows raised. "Wouldn't someone have noticed him wandering around upstairs?"

"You would think, but with the lack of staff and so few guests in this big of a place, it wouldn't have been difficult to move about undetected. It was only an odd coincidence that Edna happened to see him come down from the upper floors late one night while she and Addie sat in the kitchen. Not only was that strange, but she heard him and Mrs. Pennyworth arguing about 'timing' and 'getting it wrong.' I didn't think anything of it until later. And, anyway, Mr. Triggs was not the mastermind in this, remember; it was Minerva Pennyworth."

Wallace held his face in his hands for a moment as if trying to take in this fantastical story, and then slowly lowered them. His normally pale face was blotched with red patches. "Why?" he addressed Mrs. Pennyworth, his voice oddly calm now. "Why did you do this?"

Mrs. Pennyworth, true to form, continued to stare at the wall, as if she had actually lost the ability to move or to speak. "Answer me!" he commanded, but still the woman remained silent.

The eyes of everyone in the room were on Mrs. Pennyworth, the tension electric, when it was unexpectedly broken by the high-pitched voice of Miss Simms, still perched in the corner. "Why did you say the 'rightful heir' before?" she piped. "Why not just say 'Wallace'?"

All eyes turned to her now, and Henrietta took a deep breath. They had finally come to the crux of the matter. "Because when I looked at the will this morning," she said in a clear voice, "I read for myself the exact wording, and 'rightful heir' is the term used. And that was for a reason, wasn't it, Mrs. Pennyworth?"

Mrs. Pennyworth looked at her now, the wrinkles near the corner of her right eye twitching slightly.

"You see, Mrs. Pennyworth, being the oldest servant in the house, knew Lady Linley's secret, didn't you?" Henrietta asked her. "Likewise, as one of the witnesses to her will, she knew the terms."

"What secret?" Wallace asked.

"I'm sorry to tell you in this way, Wallace," Henrietta said gently, "but it seems you are not the heir to the Linley estate. Your real father was apparently one Simon Gaskell, a close friend of the colonel's, actually. Your mother told me herself. At first, I thought she was delirious, but now it unfortunately all makes sense. It was assumed that Lord Linley never knew, but I think perhaps he did, which is why he used such strange language in his will."

Wallace was silent. All the color had definitely drained from his face now. "But . . . but this is preposterous. Mother's delirious! There's no proof . . ."

Colonel Beaufort coughed. "It is true, my boy. Simon was my best friend. You were never to know he was your father. I fault myself for bringing him round after the war. I knew there had been an attraction between him and my sister once upon a time, but I thought all of that was long past. After all, Margaret was happily married to Montague, or so I thought, and had a child. I never dreamed that it would turn out . . . well, the way it did. Simon swore me to secrecy, and I was prepared to go to my grave with the secret, but there it is," he said tiredly.

Henrietta expected Wallace to explode in anger or fury or react in some violent way, but he did not. Instead, his eyes glistening slightly, he merely held out his hand to Amelie, who quickly took it. Wallace squeezed it and gave her a sad smile before releasing it. "I'm sorry, my love," he whispered. He released her hand and then turned to Mrs. Pennyworth. "If you knew this to be the truth, why not just say? Why resort to killing me?"

Mrs. Pennyworth looked at him now for the first time, her face full of spite. "Who'd believe a servant? Certainly not the likes of you," she spat out and quickly drew a small pistol from somewhere on her person and cocked it. Everyone in the room gasped.

"Mrs. Pennyworth! Hold on, now," Wallace pleaded. The gun was pointed directly at him.

"Minerva!" Stevens likewise exclaimed. He made a move toward her, but she responded by taking a step backward toward the door.

"Stop right there, Mr. Stevens," she said, her voice wavering slightly. "I wouldn't wish to harm you. I . . . I just want what's coming to me. I gave my whole life to this place, to this family. I wasn't about to let this interloper and his foreign whore wife sell it out from under the Linley name and then be out on the street."

"Mrs. Pennyworth!" Wallace shouted.

The old servant turned on him now. "You're so high and mighty, wanting to give it to the socialists or whoever they are, but not a thought to us who's worked for you our whole life!" she cried.

"Mrs. Pennyworth, I wouldn't have left you destitute. I would have arranged something for all the staff."

"Fine words. But why should we trust you? Never a kind word for any of us. I knew all along you weren't the rightful Lord Linley, and it killed me to have to scrape and bow to you." Her voice was tight with emotion, and Henrietta thought she saw rare tears in the woman's eyes. "I've had enough, I tell you."

The gun wavering in her hand, she took another step back. She gave a quick look over her shoulder as if contemplating making a run for it.

"Mrs. Pennyworth!" boomed Stevens. "You're disgracing yourself, for heaven's sake. And us!" He made another move toward her.

"Stop, Mr. Stevens!" she yelled. "Stop, I say!"

Mr. Stevens, however, ignored her command and made a dash for her. The gun discharged, then, and poor Stevens immediately dropped to the ground, which caused general pandemonium to break out. Miss Simms screamed, as did Phineas, and Wallace quickly jumped in front of Amelie. Colonel Beaufort, meanwhile, leapt to his feet and began inching toward Mrs. Pennyworth, but before he even reached her, Pascal suddenly appeared in the doorway and adroitly knocked the gun from her hand before she could fire another shot, if that indeed had been her intention. Pascal quickly grabbed the old servant by the arms and twisted them tightly behind her, immobilizing her. Both Wallace and Colonel Beaufort jumped to aid Pascal in his restraint of Mrs. Pennyworth, but Pascal tilted his head toward the interior of the house. "Triggs is in the stables." Both men took his meaning and dashed off.

"Edna, telephone the police," Pascal commanded when the young maid likewise appeared in the doorway. "And the doctor!" Pascal shouted. "Hurry!"

Henrietta, snapping out of what had been a momentary paralysis, rushed to poor Stevens now and knelt beside him, pressing her fingers to his neck. She felt nothing, and quickly moved her fingers to another spot on the man's neck. Still nothing. Her heart racing in panic, she looked up desperately at Pascal. "He's gone!"

Miss Simms screamed again. Amelie, who was the only one still seated at this point, rose and put her arms around the young woman in an apparent attempt to calm her.

"Cedric!" Mrs. Pennyworth shouted, straining against Pascal's hold on her. Tears rolled down her face. "Cedric, no! I didn't mean to harm you! I didn't mean to."

Pascal, apparently realizing that there was nowhere for the woman to go, released her, and she dropped to her knees by Stevens's dead body. Henrietta, kneeling on the other side of him, wrapped her arms around herself. She couldn't tear her eyes from the gaping hole in Stevens's chest, still oozing blood. She felt horribly responsible, a wave of nausea coming over her. She suddenly began to fear she was about to faint, but then felt two strong hands grip her upper arms from behind, miraculously raising her to her feet. It was Pascal.

"Come, *madame*, zis way," he said, putting an arm around her middle and holding her up as he led her out into the hallway. "Zis is *tres* distressing."

"How did you know, Pascal?" she asked faintly. "How did you know to come in when you did?"

Pascal deposited her in a green Chippendale chair in the hallway and gave her a rueful smile. "A good valet always anticipates his master's needs. Is zis not what Monsieur Howard has been saying to me so very often? And what better need does Monsieur Howard have in zis moment but for me to protect *you*?"

Chapter 33

"Honestly, Melody, what were you thinking? Dressing up as a nun? That's for sure a sin." Mrs. Merriweather's tone was crisp.

"I've explained all this already, Mums," Melody said defiantly as she picked up a piece of toast from the cherry-patterned platter in the center of the breakfast table. The fact that the patriarch of the family still lay abed in Mercy Hospital across town had not, apparently, affected the family's appetite, if the plentitude of the morning's breakfast table was anything to go by. It was indeed laden with all the usual favorites: sausages, eggs, bacon, potatoes, sliced tomatoes, toast, butter (real, not oleo), jam, juice, milk, coffee, and pancakes. Melody looked across the table at her mother and wondered, not for the first time since she had breathlessly arrived home, thanks to Douglas and his Ford V8, just how serious the familial situation really was.

Upon reaching Merriweather, she had barely said hello to her mother and Bunny before rushing to the hospital to see her father, expecting him, from the dire letter she had received from her mother, to be near death, so she was utterly surprised when she entered his private room to see him sitting upright in bed and reading the paper. She was likewise surprised to discover that he had *not* had a stroke, as her mother had indicated in her distressed letter, but had instead suffered what was essentially a heart attack, which, while certainly serious, had at least not resulted in any sort of paralysis, at least that they knew of.

Melody had been preparing herself for the worst during the long drive from Dubuque, so while she was certainly relieved to find that her father was not on death's door, as she had been led to believe, she could not help being slightly irritated. However, she considered, musing over it all, she *had* been looking for an escape from Mt. Carmel; it's just that this wasn't what she had in mind. But she should have known. Her mother was forever exaggerating.

"Melody," her father had rasped, dropping his paper and holding out his thick arms to her. He was massive. This plus the fact that he smoked at least ten cigars a day and drank bourbon every night for as long as Melody could remember probably explained his current position in a hospital bed. Melody felt hot tears in the corners of her eyes as she hugged him back.

"Oh, Pops," she said, squeezing him. "What happened?" She quickly wiped her tears and sat down on the bed beside him.

"I collapsed, Mel. I collapsed."

"Well, I'm not surprised. You work too hard, Pops. We've been telling you that."

"Nothing wrong with hard work, Mel."

Melody fought the urge to roll her eyes. "I know that, Pops, but you're getting older. You need to start slowing down. You and Mums should go on a trip or something."

Pops patted her hand and looked at her in a serious way, which, in truth, utterly terrified her. Normally there was always a hearty repartee between the two of them that had existed since she was a little girl. She knew that she was his favorite.

"What is it, Pops?"

"Didn't Mums tell you?" he wheezed.

"Tell me what?"

Pops let out a little sigh. "Well, all our money is gone, Mel. No use pretendin'. It's all gone."

"What do you mean?"

"Just what I'm sayin'. Uncle Joe invested it for me, and, well, it didn't do so good."

"But what about all your businesses?"

"Sold 'em. Just got the mercantile left." Melody groaned. It figured that it would be the only one left. She hated the mercantile. It was a big old lumbering building on High Street in downtown Merriweather, population 2,274, that was a hulking dinosaur from another century. Her grandfather had built it back in 1876 after he had made his fortune in the mines. In fact, being one of the founding members of the town, his fellows had chosen his name to grace the town, everyone agreeing that Merriweather, Wisconsin had a nice ring to it.

As a little girl, she had loved visiting her father at the store, especially as she was always allowed to choose a candy stick, tutti-frutti being her favorite. She had gone through all twenty-six flavors three times before deciding only to have tutti-frutti from then on, as she had determined it to be her official favorite. Her older brother, Freddy, had had to work at the mercantile on his summers off during high school, but her mother had put her foot down early on and declared that neither Melody nor her younger sister, Bunny, would ever work at the Merc, as the family called it. It was demeaning for her girls, Leola Merriweather had declared. She had bigger dreams for them, namely, to marry well and to have more choices than she had had. She had lucked out, she often said, having met and married Louis Merriweather, when she could have easily ended up on a dismal farm somewhere, which is where, coincidentally, she had grown up. It was the reason, she had confided to Melody, why she had insisted she attend Mundelein College in Chicago. It had nothing to do with getting an education and all to do with finding a rich Loyola boy to wed. "That way," she had more than once explained, "your father and I can visit Chicago more. You know how impossible it is to tear him away from the Merc." Melody *did* know. She and Freddy used to joke that there were three persons in their parents' relationship: Mums, Pops, and the Merc.

"Now, Mel, we've got to face reality, and you know as well as me that yer mom ain't no good at that."

Melody did know.

"These idiot doctors say I have to be off my feet for three, four months. Something like that. Give my heart a chance to rest."

"Good, Pops. You need to rest."

"But, Mel, yer not gettin' it. Who's gonna work the Merc?"

Melody began to feel a certain dread creep over her.

"I don't know, Pops. What about all your workers?"

"Had to let most of them go, Mel. Had to let most of them go. Can't pay workers with no money, now can you?"

"Well, don't look at me! I've got to go back to school at the end of the month."

Pops's brow furrowed slightly. "Didn't your mom explain about school?"

Melody felt almost panicked now. "What about it?"

"Now, Mel. Be sensible."

"Sensible?" She didn't like the sound of that. "What do you mean?"

"Well, Mel. That school of yours is mighty expensive. We can't afford that anymore. Yer gonna have to stay home and work at the Merc for me."

"Me?" Melody was incredulous. "Why can't Freddy come home from *his* expensive school and do it? He's the one that knows more about the Merc than me! He worked there every summer."

"Now, Mel. Think about it. Fred's nearly finished at Harvard, and then he's all set up to go to law school. He can't come home to work at the Merc!"

"Oh, but *I* can? That's not fair, Pops, and you know it!"

"Now, Mel, calm down. It might just be for a little bit. Till I'm stronger." He lay back against his pillows now, and Melody felt a wave of regret that she had blurted out something so selfish. She had arrived here thinking her father was close to death, and now, not twenty minutes later, she was arguing with him.

"I'm sorry, Pops," she said, taking his hand, "but can't Bunny do it?"

"Mel, Bunny's only sixteen. She can't run the Merc."

"Run the Merc? Pops, I can't either. I . . . I suppose I don't mind helping out, but I can't run the whole thing. I don't know the first thing. 'Specially the meat in the back." The back of the mercantile held a small butcher's counter.

"You don't have to worry about the meat counter. Cal's back there. He won't give you no trouble."

Cal? She didn't remember a Cal. "Who's Cal?"

"Don't you remember me sayin'?" In fact, Melody did not. She usually tuned her father out whenever he would drone on about the Merc on her vacations home. "Cal is Lyle's nephew."

"Well, what happened to Lyle?" *Why was she asking these questions?* She didn't actually care.

"Now, Mel. I told you all this at Christmas. Lyle got an infected toe. Had to have it cut off in the end. And now he has dropsy."

Melody sighed. None of this actually mattered. "Well, can't Mums do it?"

Pops actually laughed at this, which turned into coughing, which turned into a bit of a fit and caused two nurses to come scurrying in. By their disdainful looks in Melody's direction, she understood they thought her to blame, the proof of which was that they curtly suggested that perhaps her visit be over for the day. Melody, after giving her father another quick hug, had obeyed and gone home, thinking deeply about her situation and trying not to cry.

She finished the last of her coffee now and set her cup aside. Helenka was already clearing the table. That was another thing. It infuriated Melody that she had to give up her lovely Mundelein and all of her friends and parties and dates to work in the grubby Merc while her mother was apparently allowed to keep a housekeeper. She had suggested to Mums, once she understood the depth of their money problems, that perhaps they let Helenka go, but it had been met with fierce resistance. "We can't possibly let Helenka go," Mums had hissed. "Where would she go? She's been here for years!"

Even before she had suggested it, Melody had known the answer, as Helenka was probably Mums's best friend, though she would never admit that in public, of course. But Melody knew she told Helenka everything.

"Anyway," Mums had gone on. "She doesn't make much money. She's worked mostly for room and board all these years. Now the other servants. That was a different story. We had to let all of them go."

"Well, who's going to clean the house? It's not going to be me, not if I have to work at the horrible Merc every day. It'll have to be Bunny."

"Well, Bunny's still in school, Mel. You know that."

"Well, so was I until now!"

"Melody! Don't be so melodramatic. You couldn't have been all that serious about school—you were just masquerading as a nun in Dubuque, Iowa, of all things. I still don't understand what you were doing there, Mel. Young ladies didn't get themselves into those types of situations when I was young. Don't tell your father. He'll be very upset."

Privately, Melody thought that her father would think the whole thing very funny, just as she had, in the beginning, anyway, but now, she wasn't in a very joking mood. She was, in fact, in a very sour mood and more than once had flung herself down on her pink chenille bedspread and cried, thinking of everything she was going to miss—the Fall Frolic, Loyola's homecoming, the Delta Sigs' fall production! And, she had been elected president of the Student Activities Club this year and had been very excited at the prospect of hosting the annual New Student Tea. And then she would miss all the Christmas festivities, as well—Loyola's winter ball, Carols and Candlelight, holiday vespers. All of it. It was bad enough when she had thought that she was going to have to face Mundelein without Elsie, but now her woes were infinitely worse. Not only would she be deprived of Elsie's companionship but likewise that of the rest of her bosom circle, namely, Cynthia, Charlie, and, of course, Douglas.

Melody let out a little sigh. Douglas Novak was another problem altogether. Having escorted her back to Merriweather, Mums had declared that the least they could do was allow him to stay in one of the guest rooms, which he had accepted readily and now seemed somewhat reluctant to leave. Worse was when her mother discovered that his father was a surgeon at Rush, after which she insisted he stay indefinitely. It was embarrassing and not necessarily what Melody wanted at the moment. She needed to think.

She stood up from the breakfast table. "I'm going for a walk," she announced. Only Bunny and her mother were present. Douglas had thankfully not come down yet.

"Well, don't be gone for long," Mums said. "I told your father we'd come see him today."

"Yes, all right," Melody sighed and made her way to the kitchen and exited through the old screen door, letting it bang behind her. Though their rambling Queen Anne sat prominently on Ridge Street in the middle of town, it was accompanied by almost two full acres, most of which consisted of a rather charming backyard. It was not enclosed by any sort of fence but was differentiated from neighboring properties by tree lines on both sides and a small brook at the far end, near which sat a massive weeping willow.

Melody made a beeline for it, as it was her favorite spot, the place she often retreated to when she needed to think. She passed the various flower and vegetable gardens that dotted the lawn, thanks to the efforts of Pops, who listed gardening among his many weaknesses. He himself had designed the landscape of the property shortly after buying the house back in 1912, but he had little time for it now and had hired a man, Paddy O'Brien, to tend it for him, though now the upkeep would probably fall to her, Melody thought bitterly, like everything else.

Feeling immensely sorry for herself, she trudged past the white wrought-iron gazebo that sat in the middle of the lawn. Pops had bought it at an auction up north, somewhere near Chippewa Falls, and had dragged it home, much to her mother's dismay. She was forever scolding him for stopping at auctions and buying "useless junk"—apparently another of his weaknesses.

As Melody drew closer to the willow now, she groaned when she perceived none other than Douglas sitting in the metal two-seater swing perched somewhat precariously on a little slant that ran down to the brook. Partially hidden from view by the tree's drooping branches, Melody had early on in her childhood discovered the swing to be the perfect spot in which to exchange the most secret of whisperings with her little friends, and it irritated her that someone had breached this sanctum, even if it was Douglas. *What was he doing down here, anyway? Wasn't he supposedly still in bed?*

She quickly reversed course, having no desire to speak to him at the moment, but he unfortunately spotted her before she could disappear. "Melody!"

Reluctantly, she paused in her retreat and turned back around. He was clumsily climbing out of the swing. "Melody, wait!"

She let out a little sigh and walked back. "I thought you were still upstairs," she called and grabbed one of the drooping branches once she was near enough.

"No, I've been up for hours. Couldn't sleep."

Melody didn't respond and instead looked toward the brook. She could hear it, but she couldn't see it, so tall was the grass that grew alongside it. She knew she should probably say something to Douglas, but she didn't know what it would be. She hardly knew her own mind this morning. She had already tried to explain to him yesterday that she probably wasn't going to return to Mundelein in the fall, and he had taken it harder than she had expected.

"Oh, Mel, are you sure you can't come back to school?" Douglas begged now, as if he could read her mind. He pulled a leaf from one of the branches and began nervously shredding it.

Melody let out a deep breath. It was very disagreeable to try to have to defend the very thing she herself was fighting against. "No, I don't think so. At least not for a while. Maybe once Pops gets on his feet again," she said, not revealing the fact that even if her father *was* well enough to run the Merc, there was apparently not enough money left for her to go back. She was embarrassed by this new situation and hadn't fully figured out what it meant. Were they poor now?

But how could they be if they owned the Merc? Surely, it brought in *some* money, she reasoned, but probably just enough for the family to live off of. She pulled a leaf, too.

"But . . . but what about the Fall Frolic? And . . . and, well, everything?" he whined.

"Look, Dougie, I don't like it any more than you, but what am I supposed to do? I've got to stay and help. Pops needs me right now." She tossed the leaf.

"I can't possibly get through the year without you, Melody. You must know that."

"You'll have to amuse yourself with Charlie and Cynthia," she said with a sniff, a part of her momentarily enjoying his torment.

"That's not the same, and you know it."

"Well, unless you want to drop out of Loyola and come work at the dreadful Merc, I don't know what to suggest." She batted her eyelashes at him, not being able to resist a little flirting. It was so delightfully easy to tease him.

"Gosh dang it, Melody. Be serious!"

Melody looked at him in surprise and was further shocked when he abruptly grabbed her hands.

"Jeepers, Melody. You make a guy crazy. I . . . I can't live without you. Marry me."

She stared at him, her eyes wide.

"There. I said it. Marry me," he repeated, looking at her desperately.

Melody wasn't sure what to say to this. She was utterly stunned. She knew Douglas liked her. And she liked him, of course, maybe even loved him, as she had confessed to Elsie any number of times. But enough to marry him?

"Well, say something!"

"I don't know, Douglas." She pulled her hands from his and grabbed hold of one of the branches again, trying to think quickly. If she said yes, it would perhaps be a way to escape the Merc, she considered. But how could she abandon her family in their hour of need, and, anyway, she didn't necessarily *want* to be tied down. She wanted her old life back, not a new life at the Merc nor as Douglas Novak's wife, either. Maybe someday, but not now. "I can't just marry you!"

"Why not? My parents would love you, you know. I'll take you to meet them," he urged. When she did not immediately respond, he hurried on. "Think about it. You've had a shock, I realize, and of course I don't expect you to answer right away. But, Mel, think about it. Say you will."

Without any further preamble, he leaned down abruptly and kissed her. It was the first time he had ever done so, and she found, to her delight, that she rather liked it. He kissed her again. Stunned, she gazed up into his eyes. There was definitely something there.

"Okay," she said slowly, putting a hand on his chest. "I'll think about it."

Chapter 34

"It's a shame you couldn't have gotten here sooner," Henrietta said to Clive as she patted his chest and handed him a cognac.

"I beg to differ." Wallace shifted slightly on the wingback armchair where he sat near Amelie, his legs crossed casually. He turned his head to exhale a large cloud of smoke from his nostrils. "You were really rather marvelous, Henrietta. And if Clive had been here, he'd have stolen the show, as he always seems to."

Clive raised an eyebrow as he took a seat on the sofa. "That's utterly unfair."

"Perhaps, old boy, but there you have it."

"I wish I *had* been here, if only to see you in action, darling." Clive gave her a quick wink as he began fishing in his pocket for his pipe.

"You've seen me in action plenty of times and you haven't always been so approving," Henrietta reprimanded and took a seat next to him.

"Well, I'd loved to have seen the look on Yarwood's face when he turned up."

"Yes, it was rather amusing, poor git." Wallace let out a rare chuckle. "For a moment, I don't think he knew what to do, but then after it was all explained, he had the audacity to claim that he knew it all along and that he was about to arrest Mrs. Pennyworth and Mr. Triggs the very next day."

Clive leaned back. "I hate that sort of man. I really do."

"How did you know, Henrietta?" Amelie asked quietly. "How did you know it was Mrs. Pennyworth?"

"It was the aprons hanging by the back door. I saw the name *Minerva* embroidered on one of them, and it all made sense then. Lady Linley kept referring to a Minerva when I sat with her, telling me that she knew her secret. I thought she was referring to a friend or a companion; I never guessed it was a servant."

"Well done," Wallace said appreciatively. "Who would have thought?"

"Well, it is a popular mystery novel technique for the villain to be one of the servants."

"I wouldn't know," Wallace said, "as I'm not an aficionado of the genre."

"I'm not either, really. It's a new fascination for me."

"Well, perhaps you should try your hand at one," Wallace suggested. "I mean the writing of one, that is."

Henrietta laughed. "I hardly think I'm qualified, but I appreciate your vote of confidence."

"So, I guess there was nothing really to all of these stories of the place being haunted. Just a lot of trickery." Wallace snuffed out his cigarette. "Poor Mother."

Henrietta shot Clive a look, which he returned with merely a raised eyebrow. She had, of course, told him all about her supernatural experience in the study, but he had dismissed it, as usual, saying that it was more than likely a product of overexcited nerves. After all, he had explained rationally, she had been overwrought and distressed about the events of the day, so it made sense. Henrietta had countered this by pointing out how peculiar it was in that it very closely mirrored Julia's experience as a child in this house—getting locked in the attic and seeing a "white woman," but Clive had tut-tutted it. "It proves my point even more, darling. Your mind simply reached for a tale that was very near the surface and imitated it."

Henrietta groaned. "Must you be this way? There's more to reality than what we can hear and see, you know. Remember Madame Pavlovsky."

Clive looked momentarily uneasy. "Yes, I remember her all too well," he said bitterly.

Henrietta folded her arms across her chest.

"Listen, darling, don't be cross. Let's not quarrel about something so silly."

"It isn't silly."

"Okay, then, something we can't prove. I believe that you saw something, real or imagined, so let's leave it at that."

Henrietta was utterly unsatisfied with this answer, but she knew Clive well enough to know that this was as much as she was going to get from him.

She had instead found an unexpected ally in Amelie, to whom she had ventured to relate the whole of her story, and who corroborated her experience with several unnatural occurrences of her own, including one that involved little Linley when he was just a baby. He had been crying relentlessly one night, Amelie told Henrietta in whispered tones, so she had taken to pacing with him downstairs, hoping to bring him some comfort and to keep him from waking up Wallace. After only a short time, however, she felt a horrible chill enter the room, which she thought at first must simply be a draft, though it was odd because it was the middle of summer. Linley, she assumed, must have felt it, too, because he immediately stopped crying. He began staring at something across the room, then, which further chilled her. She strained to see what had caught his attention, but there was nothing. But it was obvious that *he* could see something, as his little head began slowly panning, tracking whatever it was as it apparently moved across the room. It must have eventually disappeared, however, as Linley stared at the far door for several moments, as if waiting for whatever or whomever it was to return, until he finally gave up and looked back at Amelie, his finger in his mouth, as calm as ever.

"Weren't you terrified?" Henrietta asked, remembering her own experience.

"*Mais, oui*, of course I was terrified!"

"Did you tell Wallace?"

"*Oui*, but he dismissed it." She gave a little shrug as she patted Alcott, who was propped on her shoulder, in an attempt to burp him. "But you know how men are."

Henrietta let out a little sigh. She *did* know.

"Listen, Wallace," Clive said seriously now. "We need to talk."

"Yes, old boy, I suppose we do. But before you go into some long, wrenching denial of the facts and misplaced sympathy, let me just say that I've never been more relieved in my life to not be Lord Linley. It is a title I all too willingly abdicate to you, thereby making you the most unfortunate of men, excepting of course, the fact that you have in your possession such a lovely, charming, and intelligent wife.

"Yes, except I'm not a possession," Henrietta put in, her brow slightly wrinkled. Amelie let out a little laugh.

"I do beg your pardon." Wallace tilted his head effusively.

"Wallace, are you sure?" Clive asked seriously.

"I've never been so sure of anything in my life, old boy."

"But it seems so horribly unfair," Henrietta said, glancing at each of them.

"It is not," Amelie said quietly. "It is the thing Wallace has always wanted. To be free of zis place."

"But what will you do?" Henrietta asked. "You can still stay here; don't you think, Clive? We have no need of it. Or you could move to London."

"No, we plan to return to France, just as we always dreamed," Wallace answered, taking Amelie's hand. "That way you can do what you like with this place. I don't envy you, Clive. Luckily, it seems that the sale of the London house might be a very real possibility, which will buy you a little bit of time. But it won't be long until fortune hunters descend upon you, hoping for charity."

"Speaking of, what happened to Miss Simms?" Clive asked, striking a match. He held it to the bowl of his pipe and puffed deeply.

"She left. As soon as Yarwood took Mrs. Pennyworth and Mr. Triggs away, she was gone. Didn't even say good-bye."

"I can't help but feel sorry for Mrs. Pennyworth. Don't you?" Henrietta asked.

"I suppose, but she did kill two people and tried to kill a third, namely me."

"Yes, I know. But it's sad. What will happen to her?"

"It will be up to the courts. Execution, most likely," Clive answered.

Amelie visibly shivered. "Let us not discuss it, *s'il vous plaît*."

"Quite right, Amelie. Forgive me."

"What about the colonel?" Henrietta asked.

Clive let out a deep sigh. "I don't know. Phineas is determined to go to Oxford. Perhaps the colonel can live with Aunt Margaret in the Dowager's House at the back of the estate. If she recovers, that is."

"What about that place in Brighton he mentioned?" Wallace downed the last of his cognac. "Or isn't there a place for old soldiers to go in London?"

"Yes, but he's hardly of an age for something like that," Henrietta mused.

"Well, we'll have to give it more thought." Clive blew out a ring of smoke. "Maybe that's the charity we could donate this place to. A home for old soldiers. Or young ones, if they can't get on in the world, just as you once suggested, Wallace."

"I think it should be a home for girls who find themselves in dire circumstances or in trouble and have nowhere else to go." Henrietta looked at each of them for their reaction. It was an idea she had been thinking about for a while, and she thought it a rather good one.

"Oh, *oui*!" agreed Amelie.

"Or maybe a school for troubled girls."

"*Oui*! Another good idea."

Wallace drained his glass. "Well, thankfully, it is not my decision to make any longer. Whatever you decide," he said, looking at both Clive and Henrietta in turn, "you will have my earnest support." He stood up and went to the sideboard and poured a splash more cognac in his glass. "There is just one other thing that hasn't been resolved." He raised the decanter in Clive's direction.

"Oh?" Clive asked, obliging him by holding out his glass for him to top off. "What is that?"

"Mother's ring. What are we going to do about it?" He set the decanter back on the sideboard. "I obviously didn't mention it to Yarwood."

"Ah, yes. I'd forgotten about that." Clive glanced at Henrietta.

"As Lord Linley, it's your decision," Wallace continued, sitting back down next to Amelie. "By rights, it should pass to Henrietta when Mother passes."

Clive did not respond, but took a deep puff of his pipe, as if trying to think.

"Oh, Clive," Henrietta finally said, breaking the uncomfortable silence. "Let Mrs. Arnold keep it. I have the one from your mother. I have no need of it. And it's the least we can do for poor Mrs. Arnold. Let her continue to believe it was a gift from her husband."

"Yes, but he wasn't really that noble of a character," Wallace put in. "Her image of him is a delusion."

"But we are all living in a sort of delusion, are we not, *mon chéri*?" Amelie said softly. "Let hers be."

Clive looked at Henrietta. "Are you sure?"

"Oh, yes, Clive. Please."

Clive let out a deep sigh. "Very well. It seems my first act as Lord Linley will be one of benevolence."

Wallace stood. "It suits you."

"Which? Being Lord Linley or benevolence?"

"Both." Wallace held out his hand to him. "Good night, Lord Linley," he said, a broad grin across his face. "Lady Linley." He gave a slight bow in Henrietta's direction.

Wallace now held out his hand to Amelie. "Coming, wife? Let us retire and leave our betters to discuss affairs far above our common heads. To bed we must go."

"No, Wallace," Amelie said, getting to her feet unsteadily. "Let's check on your mother. The nurse is with her, but I know she would welcome a visit."

"At this hour?" Wallace drew Amelie's arm through his.

"Just for a little bit," Amelie said wearily.

Wallace kissed her on the cheek. "No, my love. You're tired. You go on to bed. I will sit with Mother. There is much we should say to each other."

Amelie gave him a grateful look and patted his cheek softly. "*Oui*, but perhaps not tonight? It is late for such a discussion as the one you propose."

"True, but I don't know how much time I have, and I can't waste one more moment. Lord and Lady Linley," he said with a respectful nod of his head, "good night."

Amelie allowed herself to be led from the room, but before passing through the door, she turned and gave Henrietta a knowing smile. Only she, and the doctor, of course, knew her particular secret.

"Another?" Clive asked now, holding up the decanter of cognac.

"Perhaps just a small one," she said.

Clive poured out the amber liquid and then sat down heavily. He ran his hand through his hair. "Look, darling," he said with a sigh. "There's something I need to tell you. Well, several things, actually."

"There's something I need to tell you, too." She twisted her hands in her lap.

"It seems that Julia is divorcing Randolph," he said bluntly.

"What?" All thoughts of her own announcement left her.

"Yes, I could hardly believe it as well. Apparently, Randolph accosted her in the most severe way. Beat her to within an inch of her life, according to Bennett."

"Oh, my God." Henrietta put her fingers to her lips. "Poor, poor Julia. She must be devastated. I wish I could be there with her. Perhaps we should go home sooner than later, Clive."

"No, it's a good thing I'm not there right now, or I might actually kill him, Henrietta."

Henrietta was surprised by the quiet fury in his tone and wondered if he really might kill Randolph someday. "Couldn't Bennett do something?" she asked, though even as she said it, she couldn't imagine the slight, thin Bennett doing much in the way for rough-handling someone, nor was it his way.

Clive took a long drink. "He's helping her with the legalities."

"I can't believe Randolph is agreeing to a divorce."

"Bennett is being very persuasive; something he's good at. Apparently, Randolph, like our late Mr. Arnold, has a bit of a gambling problem, and he's deeply in debt. Bennett offered to arrange a loan for him if he agreed to the divorce. He put up his usual fuss, of course, but in the end, he consented."

"Poor Julia," Henrietta repeated. "What will she do?"

"Well, that's the rub. She's apparently leaving soon for Texas and taking the boys with her."

"Texas!"

"Yes. Bennett tells me that as soon as the marriage is annulled, she plans to marry Glenn Forbes."

"Glenn Forbes! The art collector?"

"Yes." Clive sighed. "Apparently, Julia is in love with him."

Henrietta remained silent, thinking about poor Julia and wondering if she was running to Texas because she really loved this man or because she saw it as her only choice. "Who is this Mr. Forbes? We don't really know anything about him."

Clive laughed. "Now you sound like Mother. Who's quite upset, apparently."

"Upset that Randolph beat her daughter or that she's running off to Texas?"

Clive shrugged. "Probably more the latter, knowing Mother."

"Clive!"

"Well, it's true."

"Goodness," Henrietta said with a sigh, "there will be no one left by the time we ever get home."

"Well, that brings me to my next subject."

"There's more?" She wasn't sure how much more "news" she could take. "Please don't say it's about Elsie. I—"

"I bought the London house."

Henrietta blinked several times, allowing this information to sink in. "What?"

"The London buyer? It's me. Or, I should say, us."

"Oh, Clive!" she faltered, her mind scrambling to try to understand what this meant.

"It was to help Wallace and the estate, of course, but it was for you, too, darling. I know how much you love it."

"But how? I . . . I thought Highbury's finances were 'not quite above board' after your father's extortion." She was secretly pleased, but surely this complicated everything.

Clive took another long drink. "I arranged to sell some of Father's cars. The Mercedes and the Isotta. And a couple of paintings."

"Oh, Clive! Your mother will be furious!"

"Well, she'll get over it."

Henrietta wasn't so sure about this, but she didn't say so. First Julia, now this. "But . . . but doesn't that mean that you've just bought what is essentially your own property?"

Clive laughed. "Yes. I have."

"Does Wallace know?"

"No, he doesn't. And I don't want him to. Not yet, anyway. That's why the buyer's identity has remained shrouded in mystery. I know Wallace. He's too proud to accept money from me, but I can't just let him and his wife and three children saunter off to France penniless."

Henrietta thought this through. "Well, what are you going to do?"

"You mean, what are *we* going to do."

Henrietta shot him a grateful smile.

"I've taken the liberty of speaking to Mr. Churchwood, Lady

Linley's solicitor, and have had him draw up a new will, which only needs Lady Linley's signature. I will explain to her that we are changing the will to dictate that upon her death, any assets in the bank go directly to Wallace, which will include, hopefully, the monies from the sale of the London house. In the meantime, we will donate the estate to some worthy charity, such as the one you suggested, minus the Dowager's House, which we will keep in the Linley name and allow Uncle Rufus to occupy for his lifetime."

"I don't think Wallace will agree to this, Clive."

"Well, he doesn't have a say in the matter. He can take the money or leave it. It's his choice."

Henrietta thought for a moment. "But what about the London house? What will we do with it, now that we own it?"

"Can you not guess?" Clive asked, tilting his head slightly in that way of his that she found so very attractive. He absently brushed something off his trousers and then looked up at her. "I had hoped *we* would live there." A small smile crept across his face. "If you'd like."

"Oh, Clive!" she murmured. "Do you really mean it?" Somehow, she had not imagined this possibility when he had announced the purchase of the property.

"It's not the cottage at the back of Highbury, but perhaps it will do," he said, resurrecting her old request to spend the early years of their marriage living in their own little home without servants' or anyone else's—namely Antonia and Alcott's—eyes upon them. It was a desire that at the time he had been helpless to accommodate, seeing as Antonia had already redecorated the whole east wing of Highbury for their private use upon their marriage.

Henrietta threw her arms around him. "Oh, Clive," she said, leaning against him. "It's . . . it's a wonderful idea. But what about your mother?" she asked, pulling away. "We can't just leave her alone to run Highbury."

Clive pursed his lips. "Well, that's the other thing I wanted to tell you." He let out another sigh. "Apparently, Mother and Bennett—Sidney, I guess I should start calling him—are also getting married."

"Married?" Henrietta was stunned. She had always sensed there was some hidden attraction between the two, but marriage? Antonia Howard, the daughter of Theodore Hewitt and the most eminent snob in Chicago, excepting perhaps Victoria Braithewaite, marry a lowly lawyer? And not only that, but her previous husband's best friend? It seemed incredible!

"Turns out you were right. Obviously, there is some history between them of which I was unaware. I guess I didn't want to see it." He shrugged.

Henrietta studied his face. "You seem remarkably subdued. After all, it's a bit sudden."

"Yes. I suppose I am. Bennett spoke to me about it on the telephone. Said he was waiting for me to come home to discuss his intentions, but seeing as he helped me arrange the financing of the London house, he knew I wasn't planning on returning any time soon. So, he asked my permission to marry my mother on the telephone." He let out an exasperated sigh. "What could I say? I was touched that he asked, but, I told him, mine is not the permission he need seek. I only want her happiness."

"Oh, Clive! That's wonderful! But . . . what does all of this mean? For us?"

"It means that Mother and Sidney can go on running Highbury, which leaves us free to live in London. If you want to, that is." He grinned.

Henrietta's mind raced. She would love to live in London, for a time, anyway, but she wasn't so sure Clive did. She searched his eyes. "Dearest, you must be honest. This isn't the life you wanted, admit it. Living in London and being a lord and all of that."

Clive let out a deep breath and took one of her hands in his. "Well, I can't escape being Lord Linley, no matter where I live. And as for London, I know it doesn't make sense, but I never felt like my place was Highbury. It was my father's realm, not mine. The same way that Castle Linley was Uncle Montague's. But I feel that I am suited—that *we* are suited—for the London house."

"And the title?" she asked nervously.

"Darling, I don't give two figs for the title."

She took his hand and placed it on her stomach, which had already begun to harden. "No," she said with a shy smile. "But your son might."

Epilogue

Montague Alcott Linley Theodore Howard, the future Lord Linley, was born on May 12, 1937 at 2:57 p.m. in St. James Place, London, England. The current lord looked on (some said there were rare tears in his eyes) as the baby was placed in Lady Linley's arms after a long and arduous birth. And while the bells of St. Paul's did not ring out as they would for the birth of a future monarch, they might as well have for the joy that filled Clive's heart that morning.

A steady stream of well-wishers and gifts began pouring in soon after, but it was with Pascal that Clive shared his first celebratory cigar. Both Pascal and Edna had been offered passage back to America upon the Howards' announcement some nine months ago, following the sad death of Lady Linley, that they planned to take up residency in London, but both servants had expressed their desire to stay with the happy couple and what was hoped to be their growing family. Pascal had thus been elevated to head butler and Edna to housekeeper, though it wasn't too long after the move to London that the pair also became husband and wife. Besides a parlor maid and a cook, they were the only two servants employed, though they could hardly be called merely servants, for they had also become friends, of a sort, to Lord and Lady Linley and were known to sometimes spend an evening with them in the drawing room, discussing the events of the day or playing cards.

Clive, previously uninterested in anything political, duly took his seat in the House of Lords and found that his duties kept him, if not passionately enthralled, then at least moderately interested. He also took up a more regular presence at the London branch of Linley Standard, and his continued close communication with Sidney strengthened the company's British holdings all the more. With all of this to contend with, his interest in detective work had significantly waned. Once in a while, he would read aloud a story from the paper of a murder or a robbery, and he and Henrietta would speculate as to who the perpetrator might be, but that was all. Perhaps, Henrietta frequently mused, he would take it up again in the future when he had fewer demands on his time, which now were many.

Besides his role in parliament and Linley Standard, there was also the running of the new school to be considered. Castle Linley had indeed been converted to the Linley School for Girls, which, despite its name, was not a repository for wealthy young ladies, but was, on the other hand, intended for destitute girls or girls of the working class who could come and learn a trade or a skill. Both Clive and Henrietta were quite involved in its administration, as were Amelie and Wallace, who had agreed to sit upon the governing board. It had been Henrietta's idea to ask them, if nothing more than to ensure that the two of them would then be forced to come to London more often. It was a scheme that seemed to be working, as Wallace and Amelie took their roles at the school very seriously and had already been to England twice this past year for various ceremonies regarding it. And it was on their last visit that Clive and Henrietta had had the joy of meeting their new little niece, Margaret Henrietta. Sadly, Lady Linley had died before getting to meet her namesake.

But it wasn't just Clive who was busy. Henrietta, too, had a very full calendar. She spent their first months in London setting up her new home, just as she had always wanted to do, though Clive annoyingly would not allow her to do anything too strenuous for fear that she might suffer another miscarriage. Still, he was frequently away, and then Henrietta and Edna would arrange curtains and portraits and direct Pascal to move the furniture around until it was absolutely perfect.

Likewise, much of her time was devoted to correspondence, especially at first, as it had taken an inordinate amount of time to explain to everyone back at home the strange twist of fate that required her to now live in London and to be addressed as not only Lady Linley, but also Mama, if everything went well, that is.

Elsie had been the first to write back, congratulating her in the warmest, sweetest possible way and elaborating her own bizarre change of fortune, which nearly eclipsed Henrietta's in its complete unexpectedness. Henrietta was thrilled to hear that Elsie was now comfortably situated back in Palmer Square, and that she had once again taken up studies with the goal of becoming a teacher. Gunther, meanwhile, with the help of Grandfather's connections, had likewise begun to teach German at Loyola.

Anna, too, Elsie wrote, *is improving almost daily, and seems to greatly benefit from her close association with Doris and Donny. She's getting ever so much better, Henrietta; I can hardly believe it. Her ear is healing nicely, and, as far as we can tell, she has not lost her hearing. She still has an occasional fit, I'm sorry to say, but we are working on finding some new treatment or medication that might help her. Grandfather has become like a guardian angel to her and seems not to be able to rest until he finds a way to cure her. I am not convinced what his true motivation is in this regard, but I have decided to simply accept his help and not attempt to explain it. But, Henrietta, he is quite a changed man. You will hardly recognize him when you see him next, should that day ever happily come.*

Henrietta paused in her reading of the letter and thought about this. Grandfather's transformation was something that continued to

baffle her, and she found it hard to completely trust it. His reform was
something she never thought possible. But if he really *had* changed,
it made perfect sense that the catalyst had been Elsie. Of all of the
strays she had brought and nursed back to health over the years, he
was probably the ultimate.

> *Ma has also changed so very much, Henrietta, Elsie con-*
> *tinued, though not always for the better. She is much more*
> *docile than she used to be, but her memory seems to grow worse*
> *every day. In fact, it seems that poor Nurse Flanagan, who*
> *remains with us, is increasingly in attendance of Ma rather*
> *than Anna, as the former declines and the latter improves.*
> *Only yesterday, for example, Ma called Anna 'Henrietta.' Do*
> *you not think that odd? She seems lost in the past, which is*
> *heartbreaking, and yet, she does not seem unhappy, except*
> *when she cannot think of certain words or phrases and then*
> *becomes most upset. She is almost childlike now, so much so*
> *that I find that I must act as the mistress of Palmer Square,*
> *and indeed, the servants now turn to me for direction.*
>
> *I must say, managing the Palmer Square house is quite*
> *a stark contrast to mine and Gunther's first meager home in*
> *Nebraska! I was nervous at first to return to Palmer Square,*
> *as it is not a place of happy memories for me, but seeing*
> *how happy Gunther is in his new role and how well Anna is*
> *doing, I have changed my mind and decided to embrace our*
> *new circumstances with grace and gratitude. I will strive to*
> *make Palmer Square a happy home, not only for us, but for*
> *the boys when they return home, which, hopefully, will be this*
> *summer. They are all doing well, especially Eugene, who will*
> *take a commission in the army as a second lieutenant when he*
> *graduates from Fishburne in the spring.*
>
> *Oh, Hen, I do hope you might visit sometime in the near*
> *future, as soon as you are able to travel with the baby. I pray*
> *every day that you will have a safe and easy birth. All the*

servants send their best wishes, and Mary, the cook, suggests you drink raspberry leaf tea each morning to help with the birth. Well, Hen, I suppose I should close this letter, as I should get back to my studies, and I promised Anna and the twins that I would take them to the park later.

Oh, but before I go—I nearly forgot one more piece of news that you will surely enjoy hearing. Stan and Rose have gotten married! Gunther and I were invited—if you can believe it! It was held at St. Sylvester's, back in our old neighborhood, and it was wonderful to see all the old neighbors. Many asked after you and could hardly believe that you've become a lady—a real one!—but they are worried about you living on foreign soil, as they call it, none more so, of course, than Mr. and Mrs. Hennessey, who send their very best love and good wishes. They are going on a trip of their own, they said to tell you, and are traveling to the East Coast to visit their daughter, the first time they've ever been invited, and so, as you can imagine, are most excited. Rose looked lovely on her special day and seemed happy, though a little quieter than perhaps a bride should be on her wedding day. Stan was beaming the whole time, of course, and seemed most intent on impressing upon us how much happier he was with the fried chicken and ham sandwiches the ladies of the church provided than with the dinner you and Clive served at your wedding at the yacht club. He seems fixated on your wedding day, does he not? So much so that a small part of me does wonder if he is perhaps still a little in love with you. But that is a wicked thought, especially now that he's a married man. Overall, they do seem quite happy and have found a little apartment on Dickens, where Rose's brother, Billy, will also live with them. Your friends Lucy and Gwen were also at the wedding and said to say hello to you and send their love.

Well, I really must go now. I can hear Doris and Anna running around downstairs causing havoc, so I must take

them out to give Nanny Kuntz a break. Consider coming for a
visit, perhaps at Christmastime. I love you so very much, Hen.
I am happier than I ever thought possible, and I pray you are,
too.

Your loving sister,
Elsie

Henrietta set the letter aside and could not but help feeling a
little conflicted. It was not the first time she felt like she was living
a double life, even stretching back to when she had taken the job as
a taxi dancer at the Promenade but had lied to Ma, telling her she
was working at the Electrics. Now, it seemed, things were no different. She was still torn. She *did* miss home and Chicago and everyone there, but, on the other hand, she relished her life here, too. She
loved her role as patroness at the Linley school, and to her surprise,
she likewise quite enjoyed being Lady Linley and receiving invita-
tions to the homes of the aristocracy for various luncheons, dinners,
galas, and balls, the descriptions of which delighted Antonia to no
end when Henrietta included them in her letters, which she now
addressed to Mrs. Antonia Bennett.

Antonia and Sidney had been married in a quiet ceremony almost
a year to the day after Alcott's death, and seemed, at least as far as
Henrietta could tell from Antonia's letters, quite happy. Clive, too,
who spoke to Sidney almost weekly via transatlantic call, reported
hearing a certain joy in Sidney's voice that he had never heard him
otherwise exhibit. And if Clive was pained by Sidney's new role in
his life, which was essentially that of stepfather, he did not show it
and seemed genuinely happy for his mother and likewise happy to
be shed of Highbury. What would happen when Antonia and Sidney
passed away was a quandary that neither Clive nor Henrietta wanted
to think about at present. It was a dilemma to be solved later.

But more than any official role or title or the privileges that came
with it, however, Henrietta appreciated simply being Clive's wife,

and now a mother, which she cherished more than she ever thought possible. She had been nervous in the weeks leading up to the birth, suddenly doubting her ability to be a mother, and had desperately wished she could talk to someone—anyone—about her fears. Julia came to mind, of course, but she was thousands of miles away, in Texas, happily living a new life, according to her letters, anyway, on a ranch of all places!

Before Henrietta could resolve her fears about the impending birth, however, the baby had made his way into the world, and Henrietta had found, with the help of a midwife and Edna, of course, that she knew what to do after all. Her heart instantly bonded with her little son, so much so that she could already not remember what life had been like before him. She loved dressing him and looking at his little body and his ten perfect fingers and toes, and, oh, how she had melted when he first smiled at her.

Clive had been eager to employ a nanny, but Henrietta had refused, saying that she herself would care for the baby. Clive's response was that this was surely naïve, as her duties as Lady Linley, not to mention those at the school, would certainly require her to leave him at home, sometimes for days at a time, and it was not fair on Edna, who had so many other duties, to mind him. In her heart, Henrietta knew he was right and that the day would come when they would need to employ someone, but for now she refused, happy to be the one to hold and cuddle and feed him, even if it meant shockingly less sleep.

Teddy, as they had begun to call him, stirred now in the cradle beside her, and she reached to pick him up. He was still partially asleep, and she studied him as she held him in her arms, which had fastly become one of her favorite pastimes. Already his strawberry-blond hair was curling and his chubby cheeks were a healthy pink. She kissed him, smelling his sweet baby smell, and felt a tug in her chest that she had never felt before. Gently, she adjusted his silk blue blanket and was surprised when she looked up to see that Clive had entered the room.

"Hello! I didn't hear you come in," she said softly, not wanting to wake Teddy.

"I've learned to be quiet." He gave her a slight wink and then kissed the top of her head before moving to the sideboard.

"How was your day?" she asked.

"Uneventful. I had lunch with Lord Farnsworth, but other than that, not too much." He poured out two sherries and offered her one. Gratefully, she took it with her free hand and took a sip. Clive sat down beside her.

"How is he?" He nodded at the bundle in her arms.

"Fine. He's had a good day." Gently, then, she stood and returned him carefully to the cradle. He let out a tiny sigh, his little legs flexing to his chest before they quickly relaxed. His eyes remained closed, thankfully, and Henrietta covered him with his blanket.

With her own little sigh, she sat back down beside Clive and took back the sherry he had taken from her to hold. She took another sip and was just about to ask him about his luncheon when he surprised her by taking her free hand in his. His look was serious, and for a moment, she was worried. "What is it?" she asked.

"Do you not remember what today is?"

She searched her mind but could think of nothing. She shook her head.

"It's the anniversary of me asking you to marry me. In Humboldt Park, remember?"

Henrietta thought back, her brow wrinkled. "I suppose it is," she said tentatively. "I forgot, darling. I'm sorry." She offered him a sheepish smile.

"Henrietta." He was still holding her hand, and he squeezed it now. "I love you."

"Well, I love you, too, darling," she answered casually, still a bit thrown off by his serious tone.

Clive cleared his throat and went on. "Thank you for being my wife." He continued gazing into her eyes. "For giving me a second chance at life." His eyes darted to the cradle now. "Thank you for him.

For making me a father. For giving me a son and an heir. An heir to two estates."

"Clive, sweetheart, there is no need to thank me."

He brought her hand to his lips and then released it. "I have something for you," he said, reaching into his inner jacket pocket and pulling out a shabby ring box.

Henrietta was intrigued. She felt she had seen this box before, but she couldn't quite remember where. "What's this? A present?"

"Of a sort. I've been meaning to give you this since Teddy was born. I was just waiting for the right moment, and given the day, this seems to be it." He opened the box to reveal a ring with a large pearl surrounded by tiny amethysts, and Henrietta suddenly recalled where she had indeed seen it. It was Helen's ring! . . . the old servant at Highbury whom Henrietta had tried to help and who had died during the Jack Fletcher affair, as that chapter of their life had subsequently been titled.

"Oh, Clive! I had forgotten about this."

Clive pulled the ring from the box and held it. "There is a British tradition that a man gives his wife an eternity ring upon the birth of their first child as a token of his love and devotion." He looked at her steadily, his eyes heavy with emotion. "I could have given you any number of rings from the family collection, but I thought this would be more meaningful to you. I've been saving it all this time, you see. Waiting for this day. So." He held the ring, hovering it over the tip of her finger. "Will you be mine? For eternity?"

"Oh, Clive," she whispered. "You needn't ask that of me. You have my heart completely. Forever."

Gently, he pushed the ring onto her finger and then kissed her tenderly.

Though he had kissed her probably a thousand times by now, his touch still excited her. She leaned her forehead against his. "I have something for you, too," she said with a small smile.

"Darling, I already have everything I could possibly want." His voice was hoarse.

She pulled away from him and put a finger to his lips. "Wait here." She stood and went to the desk at the far end of the room. Silently, she opened the top drawer and pulled out a small coin purse. "I've been saving something, too," she said softly, holding it up for him to see.

His brow was wrinkled in amused puzzlement as he watched her, one arm stretched along the sofa and his head perched on one fist. It suddenly reminded her of the time when they had sat in a similar fashion at her friend Polly's apartment in Chicago, back when she was just an usherette at a burlesque hall and he was just an inspector, employing her charms to try to catch a killer. Just like now, he had sat on a sofa opposite her, watching her intently as she mended her costume. She remembered looking up at him and naïvely wishing that the fragile moment they were sharing could . . . well, that it could go on forever.

Two little tears came to her eyes as she walked to him now, realizing that her wish, or a version of her wish, had come true. Granted, they weren't living in a small apartment in Lincoln Park, but they *had* ended up together.

Henrietta sat down beside him and snapped open the purse. "It's just a little thing." She drew out a small, rectangular, ordinary red paper ticket and handed it to him.

"What's this?" he asked with a grin, turning it over and inspecting it.

"You don't recognize it?" she couldn't help but tease.

He shook his head and looked at her ruefully.

"It's the ticket you bought to dance with me at the Promenade. Remember? It was ten cents."

Clive laughed. "You kept this? But why?"

"I just had a feeling." She put her hand on his stubbled cheek, and slowly he covered it with his own.

"I love you, Henrietta." His voice was tight.

"I love you, too, Inspector, forever and always."

Author's Note:

Well, gentle readers, we have finally come to the end—for now!—of Henrietta and Clive's adventures.

Thank you for coming along on this journey with me. It has been nothing short of extraordinary. I thank each and every one of you who might have sent an email, left a review, posted on social media about the books, called your library or local bookstore to request them, come to see me at an event, invited me to your book club, or simply told a friend about the series. You cannot imagine how I have felt your support and help and love. I can only hope that my humble scribblings in turn provided you with some entertainment and escape from reality, if only for a little while.

But do not fear! While I am closing the chapter on Henrietta and Clive for now, I have many future plans for them. First of all, **I plan to spin off Melody Merriweather into her own series**, as you might have guessed after reading her last chapter in this volume. She has many adventures ahead of her, and I hope you'll come along for the ride. And who knows, Henrietta or Clive or some of the other characters just might make an appearance in Melody's world, so please do stop by. I'm also planning on writing a Henrietta and Clive Christmas novella and maybe a series prequel. And maybe someday I will take up my pen and continue the series, perhaps in the 1940s.

Surely, much will have happened in Clive and Henrietta's world in the space of ten or so years. So please stay tuned!

The best way for you to keep abreast of Clive and Henrietta, Melody Merriweather, or any of the solo projects I have planned is to sign up for my newsletter, which will keep you up to date and also give you access to exciting giveaways and much more!

You can find out more here:

https://michellecoxauthor.com/newsletter-signup/

Thank you again for sharing your time with me. It has been an honor and a privilege.

Acknowledgments:

I'd like to use this space to thank all of the people who have helped me to bring not only this novel but the whole series into the world.

First, as always, I'd like to thank Brooke Warner for taking a chance on me and for creating a space in which to usher so many women's stories into the world. You are a force! Thanks, too, to Lauren Wise Wait for being my project manager throughout the whole of the series and who probably knows the series as well as I do. Thank you, Lauren, for your shepherding skills and for all that you do behind the scenes. Thanks to my editor, Susie Chinisci, for your talented ability to catch things I didn't and to make the books the best possible versions of themselves. I'm grateful for your advice and insights! Thanks to Yolanda Facio for your help with my website and newsletter, and to Bizzy Schorr who produces such beautiful graphics and designs for me. Also, I'd like to thank my audiobook narrator, Jayne Entwistle, for bringing all of my characters to life in such a professional and, might I say, charming way. And last but not least, thanks to my trusted beta readers: Marcy, Amy, Otto, Margaret, Ruth, and Susan for reading early drafts and providing your unique perspectives and advice.

A special thanks goes out to my family, who have had to share me these last ten years with Henrietta and Clive and all who inhabit the world of Highbury and beyond. Half of my brain lives in the 1930s with the Howards, and half of me lives in the present day with my own husband and kids. It's a strange reality to try to ride and not always easy, so, thank you, Phil, Nathaniel, Owen, and Ellie for letting me time travel back to the 1930s every morning, some evenings, and during almost every family vacation. Despite my side adventures, I hope you have never felt a lack in my love. I cherish each of you, but especially you, Phil. Thank you for your love and your support, for always being there, for not letting me quit. "You to me are everything, the sweetest song that I can sing."

About the Author

photo credit: Cliento photography

Michelle Cox is the author of the Henrietta and Inspector Howard series, a mystery/romance saga set in 1930s Chicago often described as "*Downton Abbey* meets Miss Fisher's Murder Mysteries." To date, the series has won over sixty international awards and has received positive reviews from *Library* Journal (starred), *Booklist* (starred), *Publishers Weekly*, *Kirkus*, and various media outlets, such as Popsugar, Buzzfeed, *Redbook*, *Elle*, Brit&Co., *Bustle*, Culturalist, *Working Mother*, and many others. Cox also pens the wildly popular *Novel Notes of Local Lore,* a weekly blog that chronicles the lives of Chicago's forgotten residents. She lives in the northern suburbs of Chicago with her husband and three children and is hard at work on her next novel.

SELECTED TITLES FROM SHE WRITES PRESS

She Writes Press is an independent publishing company founded to serve women writers everywhere. Visit us at www.shewritespress.com.

A Child Lost: A Henrietta and Inspector Howard Novel by Michelle Cox. $16.95, 978-1-63152-836-1

Clive and Henrietta are confronted with two cases: a spiritualist woman operating on the edge of town who's been accused of robbing people, and an German immigrant woman who's been lost in the halls of Dunning, the infamous Chicago insane asylum. When a little girl is also mistakenly taken there, the Howards rush to find her, suspecting something darker may be happening . . .

A Girl Like You: A Henrietta and Inspector Howard Novel by Michelle Cox. $16.95, 978-1-63152-016-7

When the floor matron at the dance hall where Henrietta works as a taxi dancer turns up dead, aloof Inspector Clive Howard appears on the scene—and convinces Henrietta to go undercover for him, plunging her into Chicago's gritty underworld.

A Ring of Truth: A Henrietta and Inspector Howard Novel by Michelle Cox. $16.95, 978-1-63152-196-6

The next exciting installment of the Henrietta and Inspector Clive series, in which Clive reveals that he is actually the heir of the Howard estate and fortune, Henrietta discovers she may not be who she thought she was—and both must decide if they are really meant for each other.

A Promise Given: A Henrietta and Inspector Howard Novel by Michelle Cox. $16.95, 978-1-63152-373-1

The third installment of the Henrietta and Inspector Howard series unveils the long-awaited wedding of Henrietta and Clive—but murder is never far from this sizzling couple, and when a man is killed on the night of a house party at Clive's ancestral English estate, they are both drawn into the case.

A Veil Removed: A Henrietta and Inspector Howard Novel by Michelle Cox. $16.95, 978-1-63152-503-2

In this fourth installment of the Henrietta and Inspector Howard series, Clive and Henrietta are once again pitted against their evil nemesis, Neptune, as they delve deeper into Alcott Howard's secret life and apparent murder.